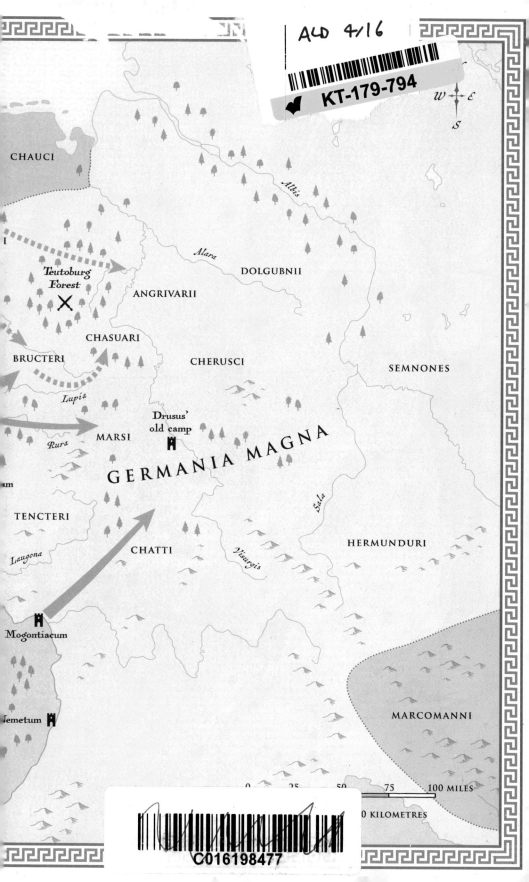

W ✦ E
S

CHAUCI

Albis

Alara

DOLGUBNII

Teutoburg
Forest
✕

ANGRIVARII

CHASUARI

CHERUSCI

SEMNONES

BRUCTERI

Lupia

Drusus'
old camp

MARSI

Rura

GERMANIA MAGNA

Sala

TENCTERI

Laugona

CHATTI

Visurgis

HERMUNDURI

Mogontiacum

MARCOMANNI

Nemetum

0   25   50   75   100 MILES

0 KILOMETRES

Hunting the Eagles

Also By Ben Kane

The Forgotten Legion
The Silver Eagle
The Road to Rome

Spartacus
Spartacus: The Gladiator
Spartacus: Rebellion

Hannibal
Hannibal: Enemy of Rome
Hannibal: Fields of Blood
Hannibal: Clouds of War

Eagles of Rome
Eagles at War

Hunting the Eagles

BEN KANE

preface

1 3 5 7 9 10 8 6 4 2

Preface
20 Vauxhall Bridge Road
London SW1V 2SA

Preface is part of the Penguin Random House group of companies
whose addresses can be found at global.penguinrandomhouse.com.

Penguin
Random House
UK

First published by Preface in 2016

www.randomhouse.co.uk

A CIP catalogue record for this book is available from the British Library.

ISBN 978 1 84809 406 2 (hardback)
ISBN 978 1 84809 407 9 (trade paperback)

Map illustration on endpapers by Darren Bennett, DKB Creative.

Typeset in 11.5/15 pt Fournier MT
Jouve (UK), Milton Keynes
Printed and bound by Clays Ltd, St Ives plc

For Selina Walker, one of the finest editors around.

Thank you!

List of characters

(Those marked * are recorded in history)

▣▣▣

Romans/Allies

Lucius Cominius Tullus, a veteran centurion, formerly of the Eighteenth
　Legion, now of the Fifth.
Marcus Crassus Fenestela, Tullus' optio, or second-in-command.*
Marcus Piso, one of Tullus' soldiers.
Vitellius, another of Tullus' soldiers, and Piso's friend.
Saxa, another of Tullus' soldiers, and Piso's friend.
Metilius, another of Tullus' soldiers, and Piso's friend.
Ambiorix, Gaul and servant to Tullus.
Degmar, Marsi tribesman and servant to Tullus.
Lucius Seius Tubero, a Roman noble, now a legionary legate and enemy of
　Tullus.*
Septimius, senior centurion of the Seventh Cohort, Fifth Legion, and
　Tullus' commander.*
Flavoleius Cordus, senior centurion, Second Cohort, Fifth Legion.
Castricius Victor, senior centurion, Third Cohort, Fifth Legion.
Proculinus, senior centurion, Sixth Cohort, Fifth Legion.
Germanicus Julius Caesar, step-grandson of Augustus, nephew of Tibe-
　rius, and imperial governor of Germania and Tres Galliae.*
Tiberius Claudius Nero, emperor and successor to Augustus.*
Augustus, formerly Gaius Octavius and other names, successor to Julius

Caesar, and the first Roman emperor. Died in late AD 14 after more than forty years in power.*

Aulus Caecina Severus, military governor of Germania Inferior.*

Lucius Stertinius, one of Germanicus' generals.*

Calusidius, ordinary soldier who confronted Germanicus.*

Bassius, *primus pilus* of the Fifth Legion.

Gaius and Marcus, mutinous soldiers.

Aemilius, Benignus, Gaius, soldiers with whom Piso gambles.

Publius Quinctilius Varus, the dead governor of Germany who was tricked into leading his army into a terrible ambush in AD 9.*

Germans/Others

Arminius, chieftain of the German Cherusci tribe, mastermind of the ambush on Varus' legions, and sworn enemy of Rome.*

Maelo, Arminius' trusted second-in-command.

Thusnelda, Arminius' wife.*

Osbert, one of Arminius' warriors.

Flavus, Arminius' brother.*

Inguiomerus, Arminius' uncle and recent ally, and chieftain of a large faction of the Cherusci tribe.*

Segestes, Thusnelda's father, ally of Rome and chieftain of a faction of the Cherusci tribe.*

Segimundus, Segestes' son and Thusnelda's brother.*

Artio, orphan girl rescued by Tullus in *Eagles at War*.

Sirona, Gaulish woman and carer for Artio.

Scylax, Artio's dog.

Prologue

Autumn AD 12

Rome

Centurion Lucius Cominius Tullus bit back a curse. Life had been different – more unforgiving – since the slaughter in the forest three years prior. The smallest thing flung him back into the searing chaos of those muddy, bloody days, when thousands of German tribesmen had struck from ambush, wiping three legions, his among them, from the face of the earth. In this case, it was a heavy rain shower over the city of Rome, and the resulting muck on the unpaved street that spattered his lower legs and caught at his sandals.

Tullus closed his eyes, hearing again the German warriors' sonorous, gut-churning *barritus*. *HUUUUMMMMMMMM! HUUUUMMMM-MMMM!* The battle cry, rising from men hidden deep among the trees, had soured his soldiers' courage the way milk curdles in the midday sun. If it had just been the chanting that Tullus relived, it might have been bearable, but his ears also rang with the sounds of men screaming in pain, calling for their mothers, and coughing out their last breaths. Showers of spears whistled overhead, punching into shields and flesh alike: disabling, maiming, killing. Slings cracked; their bullets clanged off helmets; mules brayed their fear. His own voice, hoarse with effort, roared orders.

Tullus blinked, not seeing the busy street before him, but a muddy track. On and on it led, for miles, through lines of never-ending trees and areas of limb-sucking bog. It was littered throughout with discarded equipment and the bodies of men. Legionaries. His legionaries. Before the surprise attack, Tullus would have argued with anyone who'd suggested that it was possible for his entire command – a cohort of over four hundred men – to be annihilated by an enemy armed mainly with spears. If they had proposed that three legions could be overwhelmed in the same fashion, he would have branded them insane.

He was a wiser, humbler man now.

The brutal experience – and its aftermath – had embittered Tullus too. Because his legion's eagle had been lost, the Eighteenth had been disbanded. So too had the Seventeenth and Nineteenth legions. He and the other survivors had been divided up among the other legions serving on the River Rhenus. The final humiliation had been his demotion, from senior centurion to ordinary centurion. With retirement beckoning, it had been a career-killing blow. The intervention of Lucius Seius Tubero, an enemy of his and a senatorial tribune at the time, had been the final blow that ensured an ignominious twilight to his army service. If it hadn't been for Tubero, Tullus brooded, he might still have commanded a cohort.

'TULLUS!'

He started, wondering who could have recognised him here, hundreds of miles from where he was supposed to be.

'TULLUS!' Even though the street was crowded, and the air was filled with everyday sounds – shopkeepers' competing voices, two mongrels fighting over a scrap of meat, banter between passers-by – the woman's shrill tone carried. 'TULLUS!'

It took all of his self-control not to react. Not a soul in Rome knows me, Tullus told himself for the hundredth time that day. At least, only a handful do, and the chances of meeting any of them are close to non-existent. I am nothing more than a citizen in a sea of others, going about my business. Imperial officials are ignorant of my identity, and don't care what I am doing in the city. Even if they stopped me, I can lie my way out of trouble. I am a veteran turned trader, here in Rome with an old comrade to see Tiberius' triumph, nothing more.

A solid man in late middle age, with a long, scarred jaw and army-cut short hair, Tullus was still handsome, in a weathered kind of way. He was dressed in an off-white tunic that had seen better days. His metalled belt marked him out as a soldier or, as he wanted to portray it, an ex-soldier. Marcus Crassus Fenestela, his red-haired companion, was uglier, thinner and wirier than he was, and his belt also marked him out as a man with military training.

'There you are, Tullus,' said the voice, a woman's. 'Where in Hades' name have you been?'

Casual as you like, Tullus turned his head, scanned the faces of those nearby. The Tullus who had been summoned, by his wife it seemed, was a squat slab of a thing, half his age, but shorter and with twice his girth. The wife was little better, a red-cheeked, bosom-heavy slattern standing by the counter of an open-fronted restaurant. Tullus relaxed, and as he did, Fenestela whispered in his ear, 'A shame that she *wasn't* calling you! You would have been fed, and got your leg over too, if you were lucky.'

'Piss off, you dog.' Tullus shoved his *optio* away, but he was smiling. Their differences in rank had been abraded by countless years of life together – and surviving horrors that few could imagine. Fenestela only called him 'sir' when there were other soldiers present, *or* when he was irritated with Tullus.

The two men continued tracing their way towards the centre of the city. Despite the early hour, the narrow streets were packed. Rome was busy day and night, they had found, but the prospect of a triumph today, in honour of the emperor's heir, had brought out everyone who could walk, limp and hobble. Young and old, rich and poor, hale and sick, lame and diseased, all were eager to witness the martial display, and to avail themselves of the free food and wine that would be on offer.

Past the Street of the Bakers they went, savouring the rich aroma of baking bread, and then Carpenters' Alley, which echoed to the sound of saws and hammers. Tullus paused at an armourer's on Forge Street to gaze with greedy eyes at the fine swords on display. Neither paid any attention to the offers of business from the tablet- and stylus-wielding men in Scribes' Court. Their gaze lingered on the fine-figured women in the better establishments along Whores' Lane, but they kept walking.

'It was mad to come here,' said Fenestela, shaking his head in wonderment at the imposing entrance to a massive public baths and the huge, painted statue of Augustus that stood outside it. 'I'm glad we did, though. The place is a bloody marvel.'

'To Hades with the official ban, I say,' replied Tullus with a wink. 'A man has to see the city of marble once in his life – *and* a triumph, if he can. After what you and I have been through, we've earned the right to see both.' He spoke in an undertone, the way they had talked since deviating from their official duty, which was to find recruits for their new legion, the Fifth Alaudae, in the province of Gallia Narbonensis, hundreds of miles to the north. After a fruitless few days of shouting themselves hoarse in various towns, it had been Tullus who had suggested travelling to Rome for Tiberius' triumph, the reward for his victories in Illyricum some years before.

To act as they had was not only a temporary abandonment of their mission, but a flouting of the imperial decree laid upon all survivors of the terrible defeat: a lifetime ban on entering Italy. As Tullus had said, however, who would ever know what they'd done? They could be back in Gallia Narbonensis within a month, and working night and day to find the recruits they needed. As long as they returned to their legion's base in Vetera, on the River Rhenus, with the required number of men, there would be no questions asked.

It had been easy to sway Fenestela: like Tullus, he had never visited the empire's capital, or seen a triumph.

'Taste the best-priced wines in Rome!' cried a voice to their left. 'Come and raise a toast to Tiberius, the conquering hero!' Tullus looked. The proprietor of an inn, or more likely one of his minions, was standing on a barrel to one side of the entrance, inviting passers-by inside with expansive waves.

'Fancy a quick drink?' asked Fenestela, stroking his red-and-grey-flecked beard.

'No.' Tullus' voice was firm. 'It'll be no better than vinegar, and you know it. We'd still end up having a skinful, and that would mean losing out on a good place to stand.'

Fenestela made a rueful face. 'Plus we'd need to piss all the time.'

The directions given to them by the landlord of their inn, a low-class, anonymous establishment at the base of the Aventine Hill, were good enough to get them to the Circus Maximus. From there, the man had said, it was a case of deciding where they wanted to watch the parade. On the plain of Mars, outside the city, they would get a good view of the triumphal procession as it assembled, but there was little of the atmosphere that prevailed inside the walls. The main livestock market had good numbers of temporary stands, but they'd have to get there at the crack of dawn to have any chance of a seat. Far more seating was available at the Circus Maximus, but it was a long way from where the crowning moment of the parade would be, and was prone to rioting. The Forum Romanum or the Capitoline Hill itself were the pre-eminent locations, but the density of the crowds at the former bordered on dangerous, and only invited guests were allowed up to the latter. 'Not to say that you're not fine fellows – or that you'd be put off by the risk of crushing or cutpurses,' the innkeeper had been swift to add.

Both Tullus and Fenestela wanted to see the procession from the best possible spot, so they had agreed to make for the Forum Romanum, which they had been impressed by during their sightseeing the previous day. Before long, however, it was clear that the crowds, and then the officials blocking off the streets along the parade's route, would prevent them getting anywhere near their destination before Tiberius had passed by. They needed a guide.

Tullus clicked his fingers at a sharp-eyed urchin who was idling on a street corner. 'You! Want to earn a coin?'

*   *   *

When he was younger, Tullus had been an optimist, someone who liked to see the best in others. No longer. The shocking revelation that Arminius was a traitor, his savage ambush on Varus' legions, and the shameful treatment heaped on Tullus and his comrades since – by their own kind – had given him a jaundiced view of the world. No one could be trusted, until they had proved themselves worthy. Tullus had dogged the urchin's footsteps, therefore, prepared to be attacked by lowlifes at any point during their journey.

In the event, their guide did not play them false, but led them, swift and true, through a maze of alleys and back lanes to emerge into a street that fed, he said, straight on to the eastern side of the Forum. The stupendous level of noise – cheering, fanfares of trumpets and, from some distance away, the creak of wagon wheels and the tramp of thousands of feet – was proof that the urchin *had* delivered them to the right place, and in time. He gave them a triumphant look, and stretched out his hand. 'My money.'

Tullus handed over the agreed price and muttered gruff thanks, but the urchin was already gone, vanished whence he'd come.

'He knows his way around,' said Fenestela.

'The *denarius* was well spent.' Tullus led the way. 'Let's see where the parade is before we decide where to stand.'

The press grew thick as they emerged on to the Forum. Used to close combat, Tullus and Fenestela eased their way through here, and used their shoulders to good effect there. Neither was above treading heavily on a foot if needs be. Few dared to object to their passage. Those who did soon backed down when faced by Tullus' unforgiving stare. Before long, the pair had moved far enough forward to have a decent view to the left – and the entrance to the Forum through which the front of the parade was just coming – and also to the right, along the Forum to the base of the Capitoline Hill. At the top towered the magnificent gold-roofed temple of Jupiter, Tiberius' final destination.

There were imperial officials everywhere. Ranks of them stood on both sides of the Forum as they had elsewhere, holding back the crowd with their staffs of office. Now and again, urchins similar to Tullus' and Fenestela's guide slipped between them and capered about in the street, chanting, 'Tiberius! Tiberius!' Laughter broke out among the spectators as the officials tried to catch the raggedly dressed interlopers. The urchins were rounded up in the end, and the sharp cracks they received from staffs ensured their good behaviour thereafter.

The procession drew nearer, drawing the crowd's attention, and that of Tullus and Fenestela. Amid the cheering and shouts, comments and screams of excitement filled the air. 'All my life, I've wanted to see a triumph!' 'You're blocking my view!' 'Shift then, you mouthy bastard. I was standing here well before you.' 'What's that in the first cart?' 'Weapons and armour.' 'Where's the gold and silver? That's what I want to see.' 'And the captives – where are they?' 'Tiberius. Show us Tiberius!'

Tullus was surprised and yet unsurprised by his own rising excitement. After a lifetime in the army, it would have been the crowning glory of his career to march in such a celebration. It wasn't inconceivable that he and Fenestela could have participated. For a brief period they had been commanded by Germanicus, Augustus' step-grandson, during the war in Illyricum. Tullus' old bitterness at his situation soon welled up. Demoted, serving in another legion, his chances of parading in a triumph were non-existent. How far he had fallen since the battle in Germania three years before. He quelled his self-pity with ruthless determination. Forget what happened, he ordered himself. Enjoy the spectacle.

For hundreds of years, triumphs had been the staple display to the Roman people by generals returning from war, but they had fallen out of favour during Augustus' rule. A full triumph had not been held for more than three decades, so even if Tullus had visited Rome before, he wouldn't have seen one. The reason, as everyone knew, was that the only star allowed to shine in the capital was the emperor's.

It was no coincidence that when Augustus had at last allowed a triumph to take place that it should be in honour of his heir, Tiberius. Not that Tullus had any quarrel with Augustus' choice of successor. He had served under

7

Tiberius in Germania almost a decade before, and the man had been a solid leader, who looked after his soldiers. You can't ask for more than that, reflected Tullus, thinking darkly of Augustus and the merciless order that banned him and Fenestela from ever entering Italy.

Loud metallic clattering announced the arrival of dozens of ox-drawn wagons, containing the weapons and armour of the Illyrian tribesmen vanquished by Tiberius. There were spears, axes, swords and knives by the thousand, and more hexagonal shields and helmets than could be counted. There was huge cheering at first, but it soon died down. One wagonload of arms looked much the same as the next. The applause revived with the next set of displays: carts with free-standing maps of the areas conquered by Tiberius, and three-dimensional reconstructions of the tribal hill forts he had taken, and paintings of the most dramatic scenes of the campaign.

Unsurprisingly, the vehicles full of silver coins and jewellery proved to be the most popular. The lines of sacrificial animals, cattle, sheep and pigs, being led by priests, were also well received. Benedictions rained down on them, asking the gods to bless Tiberius. Tullus was amused by the quieter comments, from the wittier spectators, about which cuts of meat they would like after the animals had been killed.

The crowd's excitement reached fever pitch as the first prisoners came into sight. Rotten vegetables, broken pieces of roof tile and pottery, even lumps of half-dried dog shit were produced from the folds of tunics. A barrage of the hoarded missiles began as soon as the captives came close. Tullus was disgusted. 'They're men, not animals,' he said to Fenestela. 'Brave too.'

'How could I forget?' Fenestela pulled down the neck of his tunic, exposing a red welt that ran across the base of his neck.

'Gods, I remember that day. A spear, wasn't it?'

'Aye.' Fenestela threw a sour look at the warriors in the nearest wagons. Despite the bombardment of objects, they remained proud-faced, straight-backed, even contemptuous. 'It's good enough for the whoresons, I say.'

The crowd's enthusiasm for abusing the tribesmen came to an end as carts loaded with women and crying children trundled by. People averted their eyes, asked for lenient treatment and muttered prayers. Tullus felt an overweening contempt for the citizens around him. These people are prisoners thanks to a war that was waged in your name, he thought. Face up to it.

He forgot his concerns as the highest-ranking captives came past, among them Bato of the Daesidiates, one of the leaders of the three-year rebellion. Broad-shouldered, tall, clad in full battle array, Bato received the crowd's acclaim by shaking his raised fists so that the chains linking them rang.

'Is he to be executed?' Tullus asked of the man beside him, a well-to-do-looking merchant.

'Tiberius has decreed that he should live because he allowed our troops to escape at Andretium, and he surrendered with honour.'

Tullus hid his surprise. 'He's a generous man, Tiberius.'

'The gods bless him and keep him safe. He has ruled that Bato is to live at Ravenna, with every comfort under the sun.'

'Do you hear that?' Tullus muttered to Fenestela when the merchant had looked away. 'A fucking barbarian gets better treatment than us.'

'Nothing surprises me any more,' said Fenestela with a grimace.

Despite the revelation, Tullus cheered with plenty of vigour as Tiberius appeared in a chariot drawn by four magnificent white stallions. His reaction was mirrored by everyone around him. The air resounded to the noise of cheers, screams and trumpets. Resplendent in the purple tunic and toga of a triumphant general, and with a crimson-painted face, Tiberius was holding a sceptre in one hand and a laurel branch in the other. Fleshy-chinned and long-nosed, he was no beauty, but he looked regal enough on this, his day of days. Behind him stood a slave, his job to hold a laurel wreath over Tiberius' head for the length of the procession.

'TI-BER-I-US! TI-BER-I-US! TI-BER-I-US!' chanted the crowd.

The chance of Tiberius recognising Tullus *and* placing him in context was infinitesimal – they had been introduced once – but Tullus still dropped his gaze as the emperor's heir came alongside his position. He hadn't expected Tiberius' nephew Germanicus, whom he had also met, to be riding right behind the chariot. Tall, big-framed and even-featured, Germanicus had a strong chin and thick brown hair. He was a striking man under normal circumstances, and in his dazzling gilded armour, he seemed close to a god.

As Tullus looked up, he found himself staring straight at Germanicus, who blinked and frowned. A heartbeat later, he mouthed, 'I know you!'

Tullus froze on the spot, like a new recruit shouted at by his centurion. To his horror, it was now that one of the occasional delays to the procession happened. Instead of riding on, Germanicus remained right where he was. Tullus wanted to duck down, to turn and run, but his strength failed him.

Fenestela had also noticed Germanicus; averting his face, he pulled at Tullus' arm. 'Let's get out of here!'

The physical touch brought Tullus to his senses. Even as it did, Germanicus called out: 'You! Centurion!'

Several thoughts flashed through Tullus' mind. The summons was for him, he was *sure* of it. He could pretend not to hear, look elsewhere and hope that the procession began to move before Germanicus had time to order him seized. He could flee, like a rat surprised by the opening of a sewer cover, and be pursued, or he could stand like a man and acknowledge Germanicus.

Ignoring Fenestela's hiss of dismay, he squared his shoulders and met Germanicus' stern gaze. 'D'you mean me, sir?'

'I do. You serve on the Rhenus, do you not?'

'You have a fine memory, sir,' answered Tullus, wishing that the ground would open up and swallow him. If Germanicus recalled what they had talked about – Arminius' ambush and the annihilation of Varus' army – he was a dead man. Breaking the imperial ban was a capital offence.

'Let's go,' urged Fenestela in a whisper.

'We met there last year,' said Germanicus.

'Yes, sir. I am honoured that you recall it.' From the corner of his eye, Tullus saw Tiberius' chariot start moving. Let me be, he prayed. I'm no one.

'Attend me once the sacrifices have been made. The front of the Curia.'

'Of course, sir.'

Any thought that he might have a chance to escape before the appointed time vanished from Tullus' mind as Germanicus jerked his head, and two Praetorian guardsmen pushed their way through the crowd towards him. Shit, he thought. He *does* know that I'm not supposed to be in Italy, or Rome. 'Go,' he ordered Fenestela. 'He hasn't seen you.'

'I'm not running from those peacocks,' retorted Fenestela, eyeing the Praetorians' burnished armour and helmets.

'Fenestela—'

Fenestela stuck out his jaw. 'I belong with you, *sir*.'

I'm a fool, thought Tullus. A proud, stupid fool. So is Fenestela. We survived everything Arminius and his mongrel followers could throw at us, only to be caught out by one of our own.

He could almost hear their death sentences being read aloud.

The wait outside the Curia – perhaps two hours – felt like an eternity to Tullus. The removal of the prisoners who were to be executed at the base of the Capitoline, the ascent of Tiberius to Jupiter's temple, the shouts from the crowd watching the ceremony there, and the distribution of bread and wine to the crowd passed by him in a daze. Even the arrival of the soldiers who'd marched behind Tiberius, the part of the procession that he'd most wanted to see, could not lift his mood. Miserable, blaming himself for Fenestela's fate, he strode about the Curia, watched by the stony-faced Praetorians.

At one stage, he began to consider killing their guards so that they could escape. It was fortunate that he confided in Fenestela, who was swift to disabuse him of the notion. 'You're not thinking straight. Even if we managed it, which is unlikely given our lack of weapons, we'd have the city's entire garrison after us. I wouldn't give much for our chances after that. Sit tight and pray. That's our best hope.'

Fenestela had never been much for praying, which said a lot about what he thought Germanicus would do to them. At a loss, Tullus did as Fenestela advised, and kept his peace. He felt like a murderer waiting for his capital sentence to be passed.

Germanicus' arrival, swift and silent, caught him off guard. He had just one cavalryman as escort, but his magnificent armour left no doubt as to his station. Close up, the commanding presence granted by his height and charisma was even more palpable. Tullus leaped to attention, his back as stiff, his shoulders as far back as he could manage. 'Sir!'

'Sir!' Fenestela was like his mirror image.

'Name?' demanded Germanicus.

'Centurion Lucius Cominius Tullus, sir, serving in the Seventh Cohort of the Fifth Legion.'

'Who's this?' Eyeing Fenestela, Germanicus slid from his horse's back with an easy grace. His escort took the mount's reins and led it to a nearby water trough.

'My optio, sir. Fenestela's his name.'

Germanicus gave Fenestela another casual look. 'He's an ugly whoreson.'

I can call him that, but not you, thought Tullus resentfully. 'He is, sir, but he's loyal and brave. I haven't met a better soldier.'

'High praise from an officer with . . . how many years' service?'

'Thirty, sir.' And all of it wasted because of today, thought Tullus.

One of Germanicus' eyebrows rose. 'Why haven't you taken your discharge?'

'You know how it is, sir. The army's my life.' Germanicus' easy tone was giving Tullus hope. It *was* possible that he didn't remember the details of their conversation, that he'd forgotten Tullus had been at the battle where Varus had lost his legions.

'Indeed.' Germanicus paced up and down without speaking.

Tullus' unease resurged.

'It was my understanding that soldiers who'd served in the Seventeenth, Eighteenth or Nineteenth Legions were banned from entering Italy.'

This was said in a low tone, but a chasm had opened before Tullus. Even though he'd said the Fifth was his legion, Germanicus *knew*. 'I, er, yes. They are, sir.'

'Yet here you both stand.' Germanicus' voice had gone ice-cold. He towered over Tullus.

'Yes, sir.' Hard as it was, Tullus kept his gaze fixed on Germanicus' face.

'Your lives are forfeit.'

'Aye, sir,' grated Tullus.

'Why are you in Rome?'

'We wanted to see the capital, sir, but we wanted to witness Tiberius' triumph even more. Both of us served in Illyricum, sir – it was only for a year, but we were there.'

'The glory of this triumph would wipe away the shame of what happened in Germania.'

'Something like that, sir,' muttered Tullus, who had not fully realised before that this *had* been part of his reasoning.

'Tell me again how the ambush went for you and your men.'

The memories that Tullus had relived not long before were still fresh in his mind. His grief for the soldiers he'd lost, buried as best he could since the disaster, was yet bleeding raw. As for the shame he felt over the loss of his legion's eagle, well, that cut like a knife – and now he would have to vocalise it all. There was little alternative other than to obey, though. Germanicus was one of the most powerful men in the empire.

And so Tullus laid out the suspicions he'd had about Arminius, first fuelled by a conversation that his servant Degmar had overheard. It was a grim litany: Varus' refusal to listen to him – twice; Arminius' lie about the Angrivarii tribe rising against Rome; Varus' decision to act against them, ordering the army off the road to Vetera and on to a narrow forest path; the initial attack, and the unrelenting horror that had unfolded over the subsequent days.

Tullus described the tribesmen's frequent, stinging assaults. The growing number of Roman casualties. The enemy's terrifying renditions of the barritus. The constant rain. The ever-present mud. The way the legionaries' morale had been chipped away bit by bit. The loss of first one eagle, and then a second – that of the Eighteenth, Tullus' old legion. The realisation that there might be no escape for anyone.

At this point, Tullus' throat closed with emotion. With an effort, he continued, relating how he had – somehow – dragged fifteen soldiers out the bloody quagmire that had been the end of the battle. With Degmar's help, they had made it to the safety of Aliso, a Roman fort. Together with its garrison, they had been pursued to Vetera, their legion's base, but had reached it at last. When Tullus was done, he let out a ragged breath. Those days, the worst of his entire life, were etched into his memory like a deep-carved eulogy on a nobleman's tomb.

Germanicus had said not a single word throughout. At length, he asked, 'How many men survived?'

Tullus scratched his head. 'Somewhat less than two hundred, I think, sir. That's not including those taken prisoner by the Germans.'

Germanicus glanced at Fenestela, whose expression had remained grim during the whole account. 'Well? Did it happen as your centurion says?'

'Aye, sir, except it were worse,' said Fenestela, bobbing his head. 'Far worse.'

Another silence fell, one neither Tullus nor Fenestela dared break.

Tullus threw a sidelong, grateful look at Fenestela, and wished again that his optio had obeyed his order to vanish. Deep down, though, he was glad to have Fenestela there. His optio was the truest of friends, who would stand by him no matter what. Facing the executioners would be their final battle.

But his interrogation wasn't over yet. 'If I recall, you were a senior centurion?' demanded Germanicus.

'Yes, sir. Second Cohort, of the Eighteenth.'

'That's not your rank now.'

'No, sir. I was demoted after the ambush.' Tullus didn't mention Tubero, who had orchestrated his reduction in rank. There was no point.

To his relief, Germanicus made no further comment. 'How many *phalerae* have you won?'

Mention of his awards for valour always made Tullus a little uncomfortable. 'Nine, ten, sir, something like that.'

'It's eleven, sir,' chipped in Fenestela, 'and he deserved every one of them.'

'Thank you, optio,' said Germanicus wryly.

Fenestela coloured and turned his head. Germanicus then studied Tullus' face for so long that *he* began to flush, and had to look away. Pronounce my sentence, and have done, Tullus wanted to say.

'It seems to me . . .' Germanicus paused.

Tullus' heart thudded. He kept his eyes fixed on the ground.

'It seems to me that you did what few others could have done.'

Confused, Tullus lifted his gaze to meet that of Germanicus. 'Sir?' he asked.

'I like to take men as I find them, centurion, and you seem to be a simple man. A brave one too, and a fine officer. I believe your story. To execute you would be a waste of a life. It would deprive the empire of a fine son.'

'I . . .' said Tullus, and words failed him.

Germanicus chuckled. 'You will not be executed or punished for flouting the ban, centurion, nor will your optio here. If I had been in your place, I might also have come to Rome to see a grand spectacle such as Tiberius' triumph, the first of its kind in thirty years.'

'Yes, sir. T-thank you, sir.' Tullus tripped over the words.

'My clemency is not altogether altruistic. The emperor, may the gods bless him, is soon to appoint me as governor of the province of Tres Galliae and Germania. I will have need of good soldiers. Solid officers, like you.' As Tullus struggled to contain his surprise and delight, Germanicus continued, 'The humiliations heaped upon us by Arminius have not been forgotten – no, indeed. I mean to lead my legions over the river, to retake *all* that was lost. I refer not just to territory and riches, but to the three eagles. Will you aid me in this? Will you see that Rome has its vengeance?'

'It would be my honour, sir.' Tullus could hear Fenestela growling in agreement.

'Good.' Germanicus clapped him on the shoulder. 'I will seek you out on my arrival at the frontier. Best return to your duties with the Fifth before too long, eh?'

'Of course, sir.' Tullus watched with astonishment as Germanicus called for his horse and rode away. The two Praetorians followed.

Tullus' knees were shaking. He sat down on a shop doorstep while Fenestela all but danced before him. 'Who'd have expected that, eh?'

'Aye,' said Tullus, wondering how one moment an ignominious death could beckon, and the next he could be praised by the emperor's step-grandson and *then* handed an opportunity to retrieve his honour.

Truly, the gods were smiling on him this day. Tullus had a good feeling that they would continue to do so during his quest for vengeance, and his hunt for his old legion's eagle.

PART ONE

Late Summer, AD 14

Near the town of Ara Ubiorum
The German Frontier

Chapter I

I
t was late summer on the German frontier, and four of the local legions – the First, the Fifth, the Twentieth and the Twenty-First – were gathered in a vast temporary camp near the town of Ara Ubiorum. After an afternoon spent with his men on the windswept parade ground outside the encampment, Tullus made his way to the Net and Trident, his favourite drinking hole in the village of tents that had sprung up nearby. Training manoeuvres and planning for the year ahead had brought half of the province's legions to the same place, not far from the border town of Ara Ubiorum. As was usual, a host of followers-on – tradesmen of every kind, innkeepers, food-sellers, whores, soothsayers and more – had descended soon after, keen for the business offered by upwards of sixteen thousand legionaries.

Tullus' preferred spot in the Net and Trident had been taken when he'd arrived, dry-throated and tired. Without making a fuss – the table at the back wasn't his property – he had taken a seat close by. He liked the 'inn' because its tent was small, hard to find, and close to a good brothel. Its land-lord was a retired soldier, an ex-optio; he took no nonsense from drunk customers yet retained a wicked sense of humour. The wine was of decent quality, and the food wasn't bad either.

Prices for both were higher than what was comfortable for ordinary soldiers, so most of its customers were officers. After a lifetime in the legions, that suited Tullus down to the ground. He loved his men, even the reprobates in the century he'd commanded for the last five years, but when his duties were done, he liked to be able to relax. To say things that he couldn't if ordinary legionaries were about.

Without company at first, he fell to brooding. Things weren't the same as they had been before, in the Eighteenth. How could they be? Tullus had served in it for a decade and a half, had become commander of the Second Cohort, one of the most senior centurions in the entire legion. Curse it, he'd known *every* centurion and most junior officers in the Eighteenth by name. I was a respected man, he thought, and now I'm just a rank-and-file centurion in the Seventh Cohort of a legion I barely know. The fucking Seventh! The majority of the legion's centurions were men ten years younger than he, or more. It was especially galling that these almost-youths were also of superior rank.

A good number of these centurions were courteous enough to Tullus, but there was a group of about a dozen who had taken against him from the start. He had come to recognise all too well their superior looks and snide comments. It went against the grain, but he tended to avoid confrontation with them where possible. There were only so many fights left in him, and Tullus wanted to keep them for those upon whom he wanted revenge – the *real* enemy – Arminius and the German tribes.

The future appeared promising in that regard. Germanicus was governor now, as he'd promised. His need to supervise a new census throughout the vast province meant that there had been no campaign into Germania this year, but in the spring, things would change. According to the camp gossip Tullus had heard, the force to cross the Rhenus would be large – up to eight legions – and there would be little quarter offered to the empire's foes.

Tullus drained his beaker in one swallow, taking comfort from the warm glow as the wine ran down to his stomach. The jug he'd bought was empty too, so he looked about for a waitress.

First to pass him was a skinny woman with awful teeth whose name he could never recall. 'More wine,' said Tullus.

'Yes, sir.' She took the vessel without even slowing.

Best take it easy, Tullus decided as she vanished in the direction of the bar. It could be a long night. 'Water it down, four parts to one,' he called out.

She turned, raised an eyebrow, but returned with a jug of dilute wine.

Time passed. Several centurions and *optiones* from the Sixth Cohort came in, and invited Tullus to their table. After an hour of pleasant conversation, his decision to moderate his intake of wine had been forgotten. He'd had at least another jug, and was thinking that it was time to order another. Fenestela's arrival was most opportune, therefore. 'My round,' he insisted.

Tullus raised his hands. 'Be my guest.'

Fenestela came back with three jugs. 'The place is getting crowded,' he explained. 'It saves having to queue up.' He slid one down the table, towards the other officers, and parked the others between him and Tullus.

They toasted one another, and drank. 'May Germanicus lead us to victory, and to recovering the lost eagles,' said Tullus, and clinked his cup off Fenestela's again. 'May we also kill or take Arminius.'

'Aye. To the spring campaign.'

They drank again.

'Happy with the men?' asked Tullus. He'd left Fenestela to march his soldiers back to the camp, and to oversee their last duties of the day.

'I am. They were complaining about the length of training, and how they wanted hot baths, not cold river water, to clean up in. The usual stuff. The conscripts were whingeing the most.'

'Nothing changes,' said Tullus with a chuckle.

'Piso volunteered for sentry duty again.'

'Thank the gods that we managed to keep him with us, and Vitellius.' The two were a little like him and Fenestela, thought Tullus, complete physical opposites. Where Piso was tall and good-humoured, Vitellius was short and acerbic. That didn't stop them being the best of friends, and excellent soldiers.

'They're both good men.'

'That's certain.' After the ambush, Tullus would have liked to have held on to every legionary from his original unit, but that wasn't the way the army worked. If it hadn't been for Caedicius, the former camp prefect of Aliso, now a good friend, Tullus would have retained none of his original command. Not even Fenestela. Tullus pushed away the thought. He *did* have Fenestela, and Piso and Vitellius. *That* counted more than his demotion.

The rest of his soldiers weren't a bad bunch, even if some of them – in particular the conscripts – weren't well suited to military life. The conscripts had been forced into the army during the widespread panic in the months after Arminius' ambush, when the emperor's initial request for volunteers to join the army had met with a poor response. Augustus' forcible draft had resulted in thousands of unwilling citizens joining the Rhenus legions. Every unit had a certain number of them, and some more than others. Tullus was grateful that his century had only twenty-five or so.

His bladder twinged. 'I'll be back,' he said to Fenestela. 'Keep my seat.'

Upon his return, Tullus was irritated by the sight, two tables over from his, of four centurions from the Second Cohort and a couple from the First, along with an assortment of junior officers from their units. It wasn't correct to call them his enemies. Relations between them weren't that bad. Adversaries perhaps, Tullus decided. He sat down opposite Fenestela, who had his back to them. 'Have you seen—' he began.

'Aye,' replied Fenestela, scowling. 'The cocksuckers didn't notice me, though.'

'Nor me.' That was the best way, thought Tullus, keeping his head down. He and Fenestela couldn't fight ten men, never mind the fact that such behaviour was considered unacceptable for centurions. He had no desire to end his career in a lower-ranking cohort, or even in the ranks.

'Listen to what they're saying.'

Tullus pricked his ears. As was natural, there was a lot of background noise: loud conversations, singing, an occasional shout, and bursts of laughter. It was fortunate that the two junior officers between their table and that of the group of centurions were talking in whispers. Like as not, they're gossiping about which whorehouse to visit, thought Tullus.

The centurions appeared to be discussing the next year's campaign. 'It'll be good to get out of camp, and teach the German savages a lesson. They've been let away with it for too long,' declared Flavoleius Cordus, a podgy-faced man with deep-set eyes. He was the senior centurion in the Second Cohort, which had been Tullus' position in the Eighteenth. That rankled enough, not least because Cordus was a good officer, and popular in the legion. He was also fond of reminding Tullus that – in his mind at least – it hadn't been right to allow some of Varus' disgraced soldiers into the Alaudae.

'We'll make a better fist of it than Varus,' said Castricius Victor, ranking centurion of the Third Cohort, and Cordus' main henchman. Built like an ox, with the temperament of a wild bull, he was feared in equal measure by his soldiers and junior officers. He was also an arrogant, loud-mouthed boor. In Tullus' opinion, his physical size and bravery had to be the reason he'd been promoted to the centurionate. 'Not that that would be hard,' Victor added with a snort.

There was a rumble of agreement, especially from the junior officers at the table: optiones, *signiferi* and *tesserarii*.

'I'd like to see the tribes try to surprise *us*,' said Cordus. 'The Seventeenth, Eighteenth and Nineteenth must have been sleepwalking to have been ambushed the way they were.'

Their comments revealed how little understanding men had of the massacre in the forest. Tullus battened down his fury. Making a scene would get him nowhere. 'As if the same wouldn't have happened to them,' he muttered.

'I know,' said Fenestela, glowering.

Tullus continued to eavesdrop on his adversaries' conversation. Before long, the topic had changed to the recent unrest among the legionaries. Some of the officers present felt that there was real cause for concern, but they were shouted down by Cordus and Victor.

Tullus had heard officers talking about it before, but wasn't aware of such feelings among his own men. 'You heard anything?' he asked Fenestela.

Fenestela's expression grew cagey.

A little alarmed, Tullus thumped a hand on the table. 'Speak!'

'Calm down.'

Those words would have made Tullus punch most men in the face. He had been through too much with Fenestela, however. 'Tell me,' he demanded.

'There have been meetings. Some of our men have attended. *I* haven't,' Fenestela added.

'What kind of meetings?'

'From what I understand, they're about demanding a rise in pay, and for the older soldiers, how to be granted their discharge. The vast majority of those present are ordinary legionaries. A lot of conscripts, as you'd imagine. The word is that men from the Twenty-First Rapax are involved too, but it may just be gossip.'

'Why in Hades haven't you told me about this before?'

'The meetings mean nothing. They're like the hot air rising off a pile of shit on a winter's morning: smelly but with no substance.'

'I'll be the judge of that. How many of our men are we talking about?'

'A few of the conscripts,' admitted Fenestela. 'Six, maybe ten.'

'By all the gods, Fenestela!' hissed Tullus.

Fenestela made an unhappy gesture. 'Maybe I should have mentioned it before.'

'You should have, curse you. I want to hear every snippet of information from now on, clear?'

'This from the man who didn't tell me of his suspicions about Arminius until the night before we set out for Vetera,' grumbled Fenestela. He raised a hand when Tullus let out another oath. 'All right, all right. I'll tell you everything I hear.'

'Good,' said Tullus, taking a drink and wondering if he was losing his touch. Five years earlier, something like this would not have escaped his notice. Like as not, he decided, it was because he now tended to avoid the company of his soldiers. His reasoning was simple: the conscripts were a pain in the arse, and his other duties – paperwork, meetings with quartermasters and so on – took up every hour of the day. Deep down, though, Tullus knew it was for another reason.

He was wary of becoming attached to the men under his command, plain and simple. The deaths in ambush of almost his entire cohort, and indeed his legion, had sliced a gaping wound in his soul, an injury that was slow to heal. Any time it showed signs of improvement, he only had to think of his butchered soldiers or the lost eagle for it to return to its original, agonising state.

Tullus' fists clenched around his wine cup. I will avenge my men and my legion one day, he swore to himself. All will be well when Arminius is dead, his warriors beaten and the Eighteenth's eagle recovered. Germanicus will lead us to victory – I know it.

'Well, well, if it isn't Tullus, the hero of the Saltus Teutoburgiensis.'

A red mist descended over Tullus. He looked up to find Cordus standing over him, a sneer twisting his chubby face. 'I'm no hero,' said Tullus, wanting nothing more than to smash Cordus' teeth down the back of his throat.

'I was being sarcastic.' Cordus called out to his companions: 'Tullus is here! The centurion who managed to save ten soldiers out of an entire cohort.'

Fenestela reached out a hand to stop Tullus launching himself to his feet, but it was too late.

'It was fifteen,' said Tullus, pushing his face so close to Cordus' that the man took an involuntary step away. '*Fifteen.*'

Cordus' complexion went puce. 'Move back, Tullus! You forget that I am your superior.'

'Forgive me, *sir.*' Tullus obeyed, his tone as insolent as he could make it.

'You impertinent dog!'

Tullus leaned in and placed his lips against Cordus' ear. 'You love to taunt me, but I'd wager a year's pay that *you* wouldn't have made it through the forest. You'd have shit yourself and run off into the bog, like I saw so many do, or committed suicide because you couldn't face death in battle.'

'How dare you?' hissed Cordus, furious.

Tullus glanced around the room. All eyes were on them. Good, he thought. 'I look forward to your leadership, sir, during the campaign next year, like every officer in the legion.' He saw heads nodding, and a few cups being raised. Apart from Fenestela, Victor and the rest at his table, the others present had no idea of the animosity between him and Cordus. Tullus lifted his own beaker. 'To our general, Germanicus, and to victory over the savages!'

With a great roar of approval most of the customers were on their feet, shouting, 'Ger-man-i-cus! Ger-man-i-cus!'

With poor grace, Cordus added his voice to the clamour. He gave Tullus a venomous look as he headed for the latrine, but Tullus didn't care. 'That round went to me, I think,' he muttered, retaking his seat. When Tullus revealed what he'd said, Fenestela let out a chuckle. 'He won't forgive you that one too quickly.'

'Maybe he won't,' replied Tullus, still angry enough not to care. 'But I won't take an insult like that lying down. Escaping that forest with you and the rest was the hardest thing I've done. It's also what I am proudest of, even if I should have saved more men.'

Fenestela gripped his arm. 'No one could have done more than you did, you hear me, Tullus? *No one.* Every single man who was with us would say the same.'

Fenestela's words could not convince Tullus that he had not failed, but he nodded.

As if sensing his anguish, Fenestela filled Tullus' cup to the brim and pushed it across the table. 'To fallen comrades. May we see them again one day.'

'One day.' Chest tight with grief, Tullus drank.

A horse galloped past the front of the tent with a thunder of hooves, moving in the direction of the road north. The rider's urgency was an unusual enough occurrence for heads to turn, and questions to be asked. An optio near the door flap went and poked his head outside. 'Looks like an official messenger,' he announced.

The clamour in the tent soon returned to its previous volume, although men were now debating the messenger's reasons for travelling with such speed. Later, Tullus would decide that no one could have predicted the calamitous news that he bore.

Not long after the rider had gone by, shouts and cries on the avenue outside became audible. This time, a centurion went to see what was going on. Not everyone spotted him come back, twenty heartbeats later, but Tullus did. The man's face was as white as a senator's new toga. Tullus shushed Fenestela and jerked his head at the centurion, who took a deep breath and said, 'Augustus is dead.'

Tullus felt a sudden lightheadedness. Fenestela's expression was so shocked it verged on the comical. Few others had heard, however.

'AUGUSTUS IS DEAD,' bellowed the centurion. 'THE EMPEROR, GODS REST HIS SOUL, HAS DIED.'

All conversation stopped. More than one cup of wine was dropped to the floor. The musician playing a double flute came to a stuttering, discordant halt.

'How can you know this?' called Tullus. His protest was echoed by a dozen voices.

'The news has just come in from Rome, they say,' replied the centurion. 'Messengers have ridden from the capital night and day since it happened, sent to every part of the empire.'

Pandemonium broke out, replicating the disturbances already happening outside the tent. Officers collapsed into their seats and placed their heads in their hands. Some wept openly. Others had begun to pray. More still were downing cups of wine, offering up extravagant toasts to the dead emperor.

'Fucking hell,' said Tullus, feeling as weary as if he'd just finished a twenty-mile march. Augustus had banned him from ever entering Italy, but he had been a good ruler overall. 'He was in power for forty-five years. Part of me thought he'd go on forever.'

'Most of us had the same idea,' said Fenestela.

Tullus glanced out of the tent. A group of legionaries stood just outside. No one had noticed, but the distress evident everywhere else was absent among them. Instead, the group had huddled together, with their heads almost touching.

Tendrils of unease snaked up Tullus' back. Years as a centurion had given him an uncanny ability to sniff out trouble. 'They're up to something,' he whispered to Fenestela.

It was worrying that instead of telling him that he was imagining it, Fenestela replied, 'I think so too.'

Tullus' enjoyment of what had been a pleasant evening vanished, like frost under a rising sun. There was trouble coming: he could feel it in his bones.

For the emperor was dead.

Chapter II

On the evening of the second day following the terrible news of Augustus' death, legionary Marcus Piso was taking a rest in the tent he shared with seven other men. He was tired – his centurion Tullus had seen to that with his endless marching – but he wasn't quite ready for sleep. That was what would take him, however, if he didn't soon stir from his bed. The warmth of his woollen blanket beneath him, the flickering of the oil lamps on the floor, and the quiet muttering of his comrades combined in a familiar, eyelid-closing mixture.

The snores reaching Piso's ears told him that at least one of the other soldiers was asleep. A quick glance confirmed that this was correct. The two nearest him were lying head to head, talking in quiet tones and sharing a skin of wine. He sat up a fraction, so that he could peer at the men in the far end of the tent. Vitellius, his closest friend, had his eyes closed. Two of the others were hunched over a *latrunculi* gaming board lying between them. The last soldier, another friend of Piso's, wasn't in his bed. He could be anywhere, thought Piso – the latrines, in another tent, or on the scrounge for wine or food. His best chance of recruiting other gamblers lay with Vitellius.

'Anyone for a game of dice?' asked Piso, ever the optimist.

There was no answer.

'Who wants to play dice?' he said, louder.

The snoring of the man opposite stopped. He grunted a couple of times and rolled over, presenting his back to Piso.

With a sigh, he eyed the drinking pair. 'Interested?'

'You know me. I've got no money,' answered one.

'Not a chance. You always win, maggot,' said the other.

Piso studied the two playing latrunculi. 'Either of you fancy it?'

'This game's just starting to get interesting,' came the reply. 'Maybe later.'

His frustration building, Piso stared at Vitellius. 'Pssst! 'Tellius!'

'Mmmmm . . .'

''Tellius, wake up!'

Vitellius' thin face twisted, and he rubbed a hand over his eyes. He gave Piso an irritable look. 'This better be good. I was in the middle of getting down to it with that redheaded whore in Bacchus' Grove.'

'You can't afford *her*,' said Piso with a snort. Bacchus' Grove was one of the better brothels in the tent village outside the camp, and the redhead was the one of the finest-looking whores in the place. Everyone in the legion wanted to lie with her, but few had the coin.

'I can in a dream, you fool,' retorted Vitellius. 'But you've woken me now. What do you want?'

'A game of dice.' Piso made a dismissive gesture. 'Not with this lot. With one of the other *contubernia*, or in another century's tent lines.'

'I remember a certain night when you started playing dice,' said Vitellius with a nasty chuckle. 'It didn't end well.'

'That was years ago,' Piso shot back, remembering how he'd stripped another soldier of his money, fair and square, not long before Arminius' ambush. The loser had been so angry that he and a gang of his friends had jumped Piso, Vitellius and another comrade soon after. If Tullus hadn't come along, they might all have been beaten to death, instead of black and blue. 'It's never happened since, has it, you dog?'

'I suppose not.'

'You'll come then?' asserted Piso. 'Imagine, you might do so well that you can afford the redhead. If your winnings aren't quite enough, I'll chip in with the difference – anything for a friend.' He winked.

'All right, all right.' With a grunt, Vitellius sat up.

Piso eased his tall frame upright, stooping under the low roof and avoiding the latrunculi players on his way out. Holding his breath, he delved into the ripe-smelling heap of sandals by the tent's entrance and found his pair. Once they were laced up, he checked his purse. His bone dice, made from the tailbones of a sheep and weighted *just so*, were in there, along with a handful of *asses* and smaller coins, and a few *sestertii*. Tiberius' fleshy profile gazed up at him from a solitary silver denarius. That's plenty, thought Piso, knowing it would have to be. The dice didn't always give him sixes – throwing them was an inexact art – and the next payday wouldn't come around for two months. 'Ready?'

'I have been since you woke me up,' replied Vitellius dourly, joining him outside. 'Where are we going?'

'Along our tent lines first.'

'Why not head straight to the Second Century's tents?' Vitellius lowered his voice. 'There was talk of a meeting there.'

Piso gave Vitellius a warning look, and got back a shrug. Both knew as well as the next man that Augustus' sudden death had brought the long-term simmering unrest about pay and conditions bubbling up to the surface. An illegal gathering wouldn't be the best place to seek out fellow gamblers, but previous experience – Piso had stung men in every *contubernium* of their century for money – meant that there was little point looking close to home, and he wanted company. 'We're not hanging around if they're talking about what I suspect they'll be talking about. I don't want the Second's centurion knocking my head off a wall, let alone Tullus when he hears what we were up to.'

'We'll be careful,' muttered Vitellius, jingling his own purse.

Piso decided to try the men of their own unit anyway, but a barrage of abuse met him from every tent as he poked his head in and asked if anyone was feeling lucky. Ignoring Vitellius' 'I told you so' comments, he led the way to the Second Century's tents, which lay a short distance from their own. There was plenty of light in the sky, and autumn's chill hadn't yet arrived to stay, so dozens of legionaries were still outside – gossiping, drinking, and repairing equipment. The scene was no different to any other night of the year, but Piso detected a certain tension in the air.

Faces were sour, and men were talking in hushed tones. Suspicious looks were hurled if his eyes lingered on anyone. Perhaps it wasn't the best night to gamble, he thought, before telling himself that things would be fine. They almost always were – Piso had a gift for making men laugh, helping them to feel at ease. It made beating them at dice easier. And safer. Nonetheless, a cautious approach was warranted – and he'd refrain from drinking wine.

Piso avoided the tents nearest those of the Second Century's officers. They were doing nothing wrong, but it was good policy to avoid the scrutiny of those in charge. Some centurions and optiones made it their business to find fault wherever possible.

Two soldiers were loitering close to the first pair of tents, which appeared to be packed. Piso didn't think anything of it at first, but as they drew nearer, the men's demeanour changed, the way doormen at an inn assess the troublemaking potential of new customers. He recognised them as brothers – they were like two peas in a pod. Raven-haired, sleek-skinned and with an athletic build, they were popular throughout the cohort.

There was nothing welcoming about their manner tonight.

'What do you want?' demanded one.

Piso glanced at Vitellius, who raised his hands, palm outward. 'There's a meeting on, or so we heard. Wondered if we could listen in.'

'I thought there might be some dice to be played too,' offered Piso.

The twin who'd asked the question looked a little less aggressive. 'Whose century are you in?'

'Tullus is our boss,' replied Piso, adding for good measure, 'and a bloody hard taskmaster he is too.'

'Like 'em all. Bastards,' snarled the first twin.

'Cocksuckers,' added his brother. 'In you go, if you can find space. Keep your lips stitched about what you hear, mind.'

'Aye, aye.' Muttering their thanks, Piso and Vitellius ducked down into the tent.

The press within was so great that they had to wriggle and use their shoulders just to get inside. Piso estimated that there were more than a dozen men present, in a tent made for eight. A tiny space had been left in the middle of the tent for some oil lamps, which lent an orange glow to the interior. As Piso sat down, cheek by jowl with Vitellius, he spied three soldiers from their century. He returned their greeting nods.

Someone was talking – a bony-faced, sunken-cheeked legionary whom Piso recognised – and pausing at regular intervals so that his words could be disseminated to those outside. Piso pricked up his ears, already worrying about what he'd hear.

'It can't be a coincidence, I say,' declared Bony Face. 'These things don't happen together unless there's a good reason. The last time I heard of standards turning to face the wrong way, against the wind, was before Drusus died, the gods rest his soul. That was a bad time, wasn't it?'

Rumbles of agreement and muttered prayers met his comment.

'Men in the First Cohort were on patrol yesterday, and got hammered by a shower of hailstones that were blood-red in colour,' said Bony Face. 'These are frightening times.'

'So it is. I heard some lads from the Rapax went swimming in the Rhenus and saw shadowy figures among the trees on the far bank,' said a soldier near the door. 'They wasn't tribesmen either.'

Piso didn't know if he believed such tall tales, but with so many others rubbing at their phallic amulets and asking for the gods' favour, it was hard not to feel rattled. Even Vitellius, the calmest of sorts, was frowning.

'I'm telling you, it's time to do something,' said Bony Face. 'Augustus was never going to give us what we deserve – what is *owed* to us. He was too busy penning his own biography and thinking about turning into a god.' The laughter that followed was a mixture of amused and nervous, but no one told Bony Face to stop. 'Tiberius needs to know that we soldiers can't be taken for granted. We have to be treated right, eh? We're entitled to proper pay, officers who aren't corrupt slave drivers, and discharge when our service is up. Is that too much to ask for? Is it?'

'No!' the legionaries muttered back at him.

Grinning, Bony Face gestured with his hands. 'Easy now, brothers. Keep it down. We don't want the centurion or any of those other bastard officers coming to investigate.'

'What can we do?' demanded a soldier with lank grey hair. 'I've been reminding my centurion for five years that my time is up. Because the records have been lost, I can't prove it, so he laughs in my face.'

'I was conscripted after the Saltus Teutoburgiensis,' said another. 'I shouldn't have to serve a day over the time I was signed up to, but, oddly, my documents can't be found either. If my centurion has his way, I'll be in uniform until I'm fifty.'

A wave of outrage and similar accusations rendered it impossible to be heard for some time. Bony Face watched and listened with evident satisfaction, and waited until it had died down. 'I will tell you what we'll do,' he said, lowering his voice to a confidential whisper.

Piso studied the faces around him – they were alive with anticipation. Bony Face was a natural orator, which made him a dangerous man.

'If we're to succeed, we will need not just every soldier in the Fifth, but those of the other legions too. Me and my comrades, we've been testing the water, so to speak, and the time is ripe. It's hard to find a happy man in the whole cursed camp! Each of you will know someone in another legion. Go and talk to them – as you have been already. Tell them that we *all* stand together on this.'

Heads nodded; men smiled. They liked the sound of this. Piso felt sick.

'Supposing the other legions do join us. What then?' asked the lank-haired legionary. 'The officers will only give us one answer, and it won't be pleasant.' Fear blossomed in many eyes, but before it could spread like the disease it was, Bony Face had begun to speak.

'This for the officers!' he hissed, miming a punch, and another. 'And this!' Now he rose, hunch-backed, and stamped on the ground with his hobnailed sandal. 'If they still won't listen, we'll give them *this*.' To Piso's complete surprise, Bony Face simulated the stabbing action of a *gladius*, driving his arm back and forth a number of times. A low, animal roar met his actions, and Bony Face smiled.

It wasn't a pleasant expression.

'Choose who you talk to with care,' he warned. 'If the officers get wind of it, you'll be whipped within a cunt hair of your life – and that's if you're lucky. It's important to spread the word fast, though. Something like this can't remain secret for long. Someone will blab, and our chance will be gone.' His eyes roved from face to face. 'Are you with me?'

'Aye,' answered every voice. Piso joined in as well, to avoid arousing suspicion. He noted Vitellius doing the same.

'On your way then,' ordered Bony Face. 'There's no time like the present. Meet me back here, tomorrow night at the same hour. Gods willing, we'll soon have four legions to call on.'

Piso's appetite for playing dice was gone, and Vitellius made no objection when he suggested returning to their tent. They filed out with the rest, taking care to avoid Bony Face's gaze, and those of the twins, who were still lingering by the door. The moment Piso judged it safe to speak without being overheard, he muttered, 'Do you think they're serious?'

'They sounded it to me.'

'I know our pay isn't as good as it should be – that's the way of things – but mutiny? It's fucking crazy.'

'Centurions like Tullus are rare creatures,' said Vitellius. 'He's one in ten thousand, Piso. Many are decent enough types, but there are plenty of rotten apples in the barrel. You know the types, like Septimius, the cohort commander, and the prick they call "Bring me another".'

The centurion with a habit of breaking vine sticks over his men's backs and calling for replacements was renowned throughout the camp. Piso gave thanks that the man wasn't his centurion. 'Lucilius, isn't that his name?'

'Aye. It's no surprise that men want to hammer seven shades of Hades out of whoresons like him, or to do even worse.'

'It's one thing to talk like that, though, and another to *do* it,' said Piso.

Vitellius slapped him on the back. 'You're a good man, Piso. Too good in some ways. If I had a centurion like "Bring me another", I'd slip a blade between his ribs given half a chance.'

Realising that Vitellius wasn't joking was almost as shocking as hearing Bony Face's proposal of all-out mutiny. 'D'you want to be part of this?' Piso whispered.

'That's *not* what I'm saying,' replied Vitellius. 'But if Tullus weren't my centurion, I probably would, yes. You aren't happy with the idea, I take it?'

'No chance! Tullus saved us in the forest. If it hadn't been for him—'

'Easy,' said Vitellius. 'I was there too, remember?'

'Aye.' Piso blinked away images of his friends and comrades – so many of them – dying.

'I would never raise a hand to Tullus. Never. Doesn't mean that a lot of officers don't need a good seeing-to.'

'But to murder them?'

'It can't end well, I know.' Vitellius sucked in his lip, thinking, before adding, 'Either way, Tullus needs to know.'

The tension pinching Piso's shoulders eased. He'd wanted to go to Tullus at once, but their last few moments of conversation had begun to make him doubt whether he could trust Vitellius. He could, which was an enormous relief, and not just because they were old friends.

What faced them next – revealing Bony Face's plan to Tullus – was even more terrifying.

Chapter III

After spending a day and a night in the oak-bound sacred grove close to his settlement, Arminius was walking back to his long-house. Dawn had broken a short while before. It was cool and crisp and a little damp, one of those mornings when the smell in a man's nostrils tells him that autumn is just around the corner. In the blue sky arcing over the woods, a handful of swifts still soared and dived, their melancholic cries a harbinger of their imminent departure.

Arminius was bone-weary from lack of sleep. The copious quantity of barley beer he'd drunk during the night had given him a thumping head-ache. Worse still, the thunder god Donar had given no sign of approval throughout his vigil — no sign of anything, if truth be told. Arminius tried to shrug off his disappointment. Why should a divine signal be given to him? Such a thing couldn't be manufactured, and it wasn't as if he was a devout follower of the deities. Compared to those — and there were many — who believed every thunderclap and winter storm to be sent by the gods, he was somewhat of a sceptic.

Despite his cynicism, Arminius could not forget the brutal ceremony he'd witnessed in the same grove as a boy, nor the wild weather that had so aided his warriors during the ambush five years before. His plans then had been meticulous, the Romans outnumbered, and his allies thirsty for Roman blood. Success had seemed probable, yet even the elements had come to their aid, to *ensure* it. The manner in which he had found the last Roman eagle had also been uncanny. His horse had been panicked by a corpse-feeding raven and had thrown Arminius, landing him arse-first in the bloody mire. Soon after, he'd discovered the golden eagle wrapped in the folds of a dead Roman's cloak. With the raven's disdainful croaks filling his ears – denoting its amusement at unhorsing him perhaps, or even a message from Donar? – Arminius had really felt as if the thunder god thought well of his actions.

Five long years had passed without a similar sign.

The Romans had not traversed the river they called the Rhenus much during that time, but that would change. Arminius had plenty of spies in the settlements outside the camps that dotted the western bank, and he'd heard the rumour on so many occasions that there had to be some truth to it. Come the spring, the tribes would have to be rallied for a second time, their chieftains persuaded to follow his lead once more. Arminius' standing among his people remained high. He could do it without a seal of divine approval, he decided, but Donar's backing would make his task far easier.

Give me a sign, Great One, he asked. Sometime soon.

The settlement was visible now, straight ahead through the thick-leaved beech and hornbeam trees. High-pitched cries and laughter from playing children mixed with the lower tones of cattle being herded to new grazing. The thud of a farmer's axe splitting logs came from his left, the chatter of women working their vegetable patches from his right. He would start to meet people any moment: it was important he looked like a leader. Arminius palmed his gritty eyes, wiped the worst specks of mud from his trousers and summoned what remained of his energy reserves.

He was a large-framed man in the prime of life, striking-looking rather than handsome, with a mane of black hair and a bushy beard of the same colour. His chin was square, his eyes grey and intense: the kind that made most men look away. Befitting his status as chieftain of the Cherusci tribe, Arminius' dark red tunic and patterned trousers had been woven from the finest wool, as had his tasselled green cloak. The long cavalry sword – a *spatha* to the Romans – that hung from his gilt-edged baldric was a work of art in its own right. Forged from the finest steel that money could buy, with a handle of rosewood and an ivory pommel, it was Arminius' pride and joy. Many Romans it had slain – and would do many more, when the time came, he thought.

Emerging from the trees as he had so many times over the years, Arminius picked up his pace, striding along as if he'd had the best night's sleep. He was soon noticed, for the trail led only to the sacred grove. Queries rained down from warriors standing at the doors to their longhouses, or talking together in small groups. Had Donar spoken to him? Was the death of Augustus, their emperor, a sign that the Romans' gods were weakening? When were the legions going to attack?

Arminius told them with a confident smile that Augustus' demise was a certain gift from their own gods, and that Rome's legions *would* cross the river, like as not, the following spring. 'The new emperor will want to make his mark, to punish us. What better way will he have to exact vengeance for what we did to that fool Varus? But we'll teach him a good lesson, won't we? Give the legions enough of a hiding and they won't *ever* come back!'

The warriors bellowed their approval, allowing Arminius to pass without further questioning, for which he was grateful. His weariness and hangover had shorn him of his usual eloquence. He wanted nothing more than to fall into his bed for a few hours, and forget the world. If his wife Thusnelda happened to be near, he might even persuade her to join him for a time. There was no quicker – and better – way to send a man to sleep, he thought, than to empty his seed into a woman.

His hopes of lying with Thusnelda rose when he heard her singing in their longhouse, which lay in the middle of the settlement. His pace quickened. Willow-slender, but with womanly curves, she had long, dark brown hair and gods-crafted features. She had been – still was, he corrected himself – the envy of every Cheruscan warrior. Arminius had desired her from the first moment he'd clapped eyes on her, at a massive tribal gathering some years before. The fact that she was the daughter of Segestes, leader of another Cherusci faction and bitter rival to Arminius, had only made the chase sweeter. By the time that Segestes had found out about their love affair, it was too late. Thusnelda had not cared if her father approved or not.

In the light of Segestes' opposition to their marriage, it wasn't surprising that he continued to rebuff Arminius' offers of alliance against the Romans. Entering the longhouse, Arminius shrugged. If Segestes' refusal was the price for Thusnelda's hand, *he* had won the better deal. Winning the allegiance of another grouping of the Cherusci people would have been useful, but there were other tribes who would join him in fighting the invaders, whereas there was only one Thusnelda.

He found her in the cooking area, which lay at the end of the longhouse closest to their sleeping area. Her eyes lit up at the sight of him, which made Arminius' groin stir. 'You're back,' she said, stepping away from the fire and the pot of stew bubbling over it. 'You look tired.'

'Not *too* tired,' he replied, pulling her into an embrace.

They kissed, long and hard. Arminius' hands began to roam over her dress, down to her buttocks, and up again, to her breasts. Thusnelda didn't pull away, and he decided his luck was in. 'Come to bed. Your chores can wait.'

'The slaves will hear,' she said, laughing and glancing towards the other end of the building. Two figures, one an old man, the other a stripling girl, were using pitchforks to heave hay from the doorway to its usual place by the animal stalls. 'They'll see.'

'What do we care?' retorted Arminius. 'They know enough not to look, or to stare.'

'It's not dark,' said Thusnelda, colouring.

'I didn't hear you complain the times we've lain together in daytime – in the woods, or by the river,' challenged Arminius gently.

'There was no one about then.'

'Come.' He trailed his fingertips along her jawline, and down the side of her neck the way he knew she loved. Her protest, more muted this time, died away before another kiss, and he edged her towards their low bed, which sat against the end wall.

Arminius was just about to ease Thusnelda down on to the blanket-covered hay mattress when someone with a purposeful footstep entered the longhouse. Arminius ignored the sound for as long as he could, but when

Thusnelda placed a gentle finger on his lips, he could disregard it no more. He half turned. Recognising Maelo, his trusted second-in-command, he swallowed his angry comment. 'What is it?'

'I called out at the door, but there was no answer,' said Maelo by way of apology. At a passing glance, he was unremarkable-looking – of medium build, with longish brown hair and a typical tribal beard. He was as solid as a slab of granite, however, and one of the most dangerous warriors in the tribe. The sword at his belt had ended more men's lives than Arminius' weapon.

'It's all right.' Arminius stepped away from Thusnelda, who brushed down her dress and returned to her pot of stew. Arminius motioned Maelo closer. 'You wouldn't come in without good reason.'

'Segestes is coming.'

Arminius had not been expecting *that*. 'To our village?'

'So it seems. A warrior from the next settlement ran all the way here so we'd know about it before he arrived. Segestes has an honour guard with him, but no more.'

The shock on Thusnelda's face told Arminius that she hadn't known either. 'What's the old goat playing at?' he demanded.

'Who knows?' replied Maelo.

'Maybe he's just paying me a visit,' said Thusnelda. 'I am his only daughter.'

'But to arrive unannounced? There's more to it than that.' Arminius eyed Maelo. 'Gather up fifty men and scout out the land between here and Segestes' position, in case he has anyone hidden in the woods. I want the rest of the warriors ready to fight.'

Thusnelda frowned. 'Is that necessary?'

'He cannot be trusted, my love, your father or no,' replied Arminius. 'He was the one who tried to warn Varus, remember?'

'That was only rumour,' said Thusnelda, with little conviction.

'Maybe so, but it wouldn't have been out of character for him to do so,' Arminius retorted. 'Rome has few allies more loyal.'

Thusnelda's sigh was answer enough.

While Maelo headed off to see his orders carried out, Arminius opted for a wash and a change of clothes. It would not do to be abed when Segestes appeared. Old he might be, yet his mind remained sharp – and devious.

It was mid-morning before Segestes and his party reached the settlement. Maelo's search of the surrounding area had found nothing, and Arminius had had ample time to prepare for the visitors' arrival. Six piglets had been slaughtered, and were already turning on spits over fires tended by a gaggle of high-spirited youths. Barrels of beer were being set up on trestles in the central meeting area. The tribe's high priest, a whitebeard in a dark green robe, was there too, attended by his acolytes. A hundred of Arminius' best warriors lounged about in their finest war gear, comparing weapons, swapping boastful stories, and wrestling. They were an overt demonstration of his power and protection against treachery rolled into one. Thusnelda was in their longhouse, clad in her finest raiment, and ready for Arminius' summons. He himself played dice with Maelo at a table by the door, appearing not to have a care in the world.

'Ha! I win again,' said Maelo. 'That's two silver coins you owe me.'

Arminius focused on the dice – Maelo had just rolled a five and a four. 'I scored ten, no?'

Maelo snorted. 'If you were anyone else, I'd call you a cheat. You got eight.'

'My mind's not on the game.'

'That's clear. I'd best make the most of it, eh?' Maelo handed over the dice. 'Your turn to roll.'

'Can it be as simple as coming to see his daughter? Surely not.'

'Perhaps he's coming to offer you his allegiance?' The outlandish idea made them both chuckle, before Maelo continued, 'The dog *will* have something up his sleeve. You'll see his intent before he has time to act it out, though.'

'Ah, Maelo, life would be a great deal harder without you,' said Arminius with real feeling. 'Here.' He laid a pair of Roman coins on the table top.

They and their type were the last vestiges of the empire's influence east of the river, he thought with considerable satisfaction. 'Your winnings. I'll take them back the next time we play, and more.'

'In your dreams!' said Maelo, grinning.

They fell to talking about the tribes. Which ones would answer Arminius' call to fight the Romans, and which would not? How easy would it be to win over those who lay in-between? What number of spears would each tribe send, and would they follow him for a whole campaigning season? It was frustrating how few of the questions they had answers to. Despite the promises of support he'd had from other chieftains, it wasn't uncommon for loyalties to shift. Like it or not, Arminius would have to visit each of his allies before the spring.

A new realisation sank in as Segestes and his party hove into sight. 'Could the prick be on his way to see Inguiomerus?' Arminius hissed.

'Perhaps,' said Maelo, his brows lowering. 'If he's heard the news about him.'

'He must have.' It had been a real battle to win the leader of the third Cheruscan faction over – Inguiomerus had not helped to ambush Varus five years before – but Arminius had succeeded in doing so not long before the harvest. 'Word of it will have travelled – you know how it is.'

'Aye, probably.' Maelo studied the approaching group, who numbered about twenty. Warriors all, with Segestes in the middle of them. 'Mayhap you're right. Segestes won't like it that Inguiomerus now stands with us.'

'Here he is.' Arminius got to his feet. 'Welcome, Segestes, defender of Rome!'

Arminius' men rumbled their disapproval of Segestes' allegiance.

Glowering at this veiled insult, Segestes' warriors parted, allowing him to walk towards Arminius. Segestes' smile stayed in place, but anger glinted in his eyes. Less brawny, more silver-haired and with fewer teeth than he'd had five years before, he still cut an imposing figure, in tunic and trousers of fine-woven wool, and wearing a sword as expensive as that of Arminius.

Ten steps from Arminius, he stopped. If the nod that followed was

43

perfunctory, his return greeting spoke even louder. 'I greet you, Arminius, oathbreaker.'

Arminius raised a hand to quell his men's rage. 'In my mind, an oath made to a hated overlord is never binding. A pledge made between equals – *that* is something to honour.'

The implication – that Segestes and others of his kind were nothing more than Rome's lapdogs – was lost on no one. His warriors shifted about, poor at concealing their fury, yet aware that a single false move would seal their doom.

Segestes was better at playing the game. 'Many would hold that a vow taken before the gods should be kept irrespective of whom it is made to. My conscience is clear! I have honoured my oath to Rome these fifteen years and more.'

'So you have.' Arminius' tone was contemptuous, and he made a dismissive gesture. 'We could bandy words until the sun falls from the sky, Segestes. Unless I am a fool, you are not here to win me over, nor am I callow enough to try and convert you to my cause. I bid you welcome, nonetheless. As father of my wife, you are an esteemed guest.'

'I thank you, Arminius.' Segestes inclined his head a fraction more than the first time. 'How is my daughter?'

'See for yourself.' Arminius turned his head. 'Wife! Come forth.'

As Thusnelda emerged from the longhouse, there was a general intake of breath. The sight of her filled Arminius with pride – and not a little lust. She was lustrous-haired, statuesque and more beautiful than any woman in the tribe. Her long green dress was of modest cut, yet its figure-hugging shape left nothing to the imagination. Gold winked at her ears and wrists, and a priceless necklace of polished amber graced her throat.

The smile she gave Arminius made his heart pound. Her father received a cool dip of her chin – there was respect there, just. 'You are welcome, Father.'

'Daughter.' Segestes' eyes were bright with happiness. 'It is good to see you.'

'And you, Father.' Thusnelda's tone was warm, but Arminius was relieved also to hear wariness in it. 'You will stay the night?' she asked. 'A feast is being prepared in your honour.'

'I am flattered. Thank you,' said Segestes, unbending a little more. 'Our journey this morning has been short enough, but I am no longer a young man. Sleeping in unfamiliar beds takes its toll.'

'Our home is your home,' said Thusnelda, as custom dictated. 'It is yours for as long as you wish.'

'You're a good daughter. We must depart tomorrow or the day after, however.'

'Are we your last port of call?' asked Arminius, fishing.

Thusnelda's smile disappeared, and Segestes' eyes narrowed. After a long moment, he said, 'No.'

'You will visit Inguiomerus after leaving here?'

'I will.'

'And your purpose?' demanded Arminius, no longer trying to sound friendly.

'My business with Inguiomerus is my own,' replied Segestes, his tone, like that of Arminius, granite hard.

'You will seek to break the alliance I have made with him.'

'Your words, not mine.' Segestes' smile resembled that of a wolf.

'Why else would you meet with him?'

'Can a man not call on an old friend and fellow chieftain?'

'Don't play games with me!' Despite himself, Arminius felt his temper rising.

'Stop it!' ordered Thusnelda. 'I will brook no arguments.'

'My apologies, dear wife. You will hear no more from me.' Arminius put on his most winning smile, the one that persuaded men to place their trust in him.

'Nor me.' Segestes' expression was as genial, and false, as Arminius'.

'Come, Father.' Thusnelda took his arm. 'Let us walk together. I want to hear the news from home. How is Mother? Are my sisters and brothers well?'

'It's as you thought,' muttered Maelo the instant the two were out of earshot.

'Aye,' said Arminius. 'Why else would the filth want to see Inguiomerus other than to pour weasel words in his ear?'

'There's not much to do about it either, other than kill him,' said Maelo. 'Cool as his relationship with Thusnelda is, I'd wager that to do so would see you unwelcome in her bed for a year.'

'Or more,' replied Arminius, snorting with black amusement. 'There is another option, just as effective, and nowhere near as like to turn her against me.'

'What's that?'

'Take the bastard hostage. Prevent him from seeing Inguiomerus *and* from returning to his own kind, there to foment further ill will against me.'

'You're suggesting we keep the loudmouth here for good?' Maelo rolled his eyes. 'He'll send us all mad.'

'It won't be forever. We can release him when next year's campaigning season is over. Men's heads then will be full of our victories over the Romans. They won't listen to him.'

'And his guards?' Maelo drew a sly finger across his throat.

'No. We must not create ill will in the minds of men such as Inguiomerus. He's our ally, but he is still a friend to Segestes. Just get the guards pissed at the feast tonight, so they can be disarmed. Once that's done, we'll explain to Segestes how it's going to be. He can keep two warriors as company. The rest we'll send home.'

Maelo gave him an approving look. 'A fine plan.'

'Segestes won't be feeling so clever this time tomorrow,' said Arminius, smiling. With his father-in-law out of the way, he would be able to concentrate on recruiting tribes to his cause.

Come the spring, his gut told him, he would again have twenty thousand spears to call on.

Germanicus and his legions would not know what had hit them.

Chapter IV

T ullus was walking back to his unit's position from a friend's tent, where he had consumed a decent quantity of wine, and put the world to rights. A fuzzy good mood encased him – the world always seemed a better place after an evening drinking in agreeable company. Despite the warm glow in his belly, it was impossible not to notice that the legionaries outside their tents seemed quieter than usual. Of an evening, it was the norm for men to sit and stand about, bantering with one another, telling filthy jokes and talking in loud voices. There was none of that tonight.

Tullus was accustomed to men avoiding his centurion's gaze. Now he felt the weight of many stares as he passed each little group. If he turned his head, however, the soldiers were quick to look away, or to study their camp-fires. Tullus didn't like it one bit, but he would prove nothing by challenging everyone in his path, so he marched on, affecting not to notice the unusual and unwanted attention.

The legionaries' mood was linked to the disquieting calm that had enveloped the camp as the news of Augustus' passing had spread – he was sure of it. Tullus had experienced something equally disconcerting once before, during the terrible time that had followed the ambush in the forest. The low morale and sad mood then had been because of a shattering defeat, not an emperor's death, but the feeling in the air now was angrier. More dangerous. Tullus worried that it was linked to the continuing rumours of unrest among the legionaries, and prayed with the same breath that it was not.

Matters weren't being helped by the inaction of Aulus Caecina Severus, the governor of Germania Inferior. Tullus couldn't work out Caecina's motive for doing nothing – in *his* book, decisiveness was *always* better than indecisiveness. Yet Caecina had delivered no impassioned speech praising Augustus' rule and looking forward to Tiberius' steady hand at the empire's helm. In fact, he had made no announcements at all. He hadn't even ordered a parade in honour of the dead emperor, which would have raised spirits and provided cause for drunken celebration. Germanicus might have done something, but *he* was far away in Gallia Belgica, supervising the collection of tax information.

The air of foreboding was added to by the soothsayers who had appeared in the camp, attracted like wolves to a fresh carcase. Patrolling the avenues, they offered their services without challenge, and proclaimed that tumultuous times awaited everyone in the empire. Tullus had heard one startling revelation from a soothsayer in the past, but it had not altered his opinion that the vast majority of them were complete charlatans. The day before, he had personally run off the first one spotted by his century's lines, beating the man with his *vitis*, or vine stick, until his arm grew tired. He had ordered the sentries to mete out similar treatment to any others they saw.

Spotting two figures engaged in quiet conversation by his tent, Tullus wondered if another soothsayer was looking for custom. His pace quickened, and he readied his vitis. 'If it's the same fool I saw yesterday,' he muttered to himself, 'I'll tear him a new arsehole.'

To Tullus' surprise, it was Piso and Vitellius. 'What are you up to?' he growled. 'Fancy yourselves some extra sentry duty?'

Piso let out an uneasy laugh. 'No, sir.'

'Clear off then. I'm tired.'

Piso shuffled his feet, but he didn't move. Surprised, Tullus was about to raise his voice when Piso whispered, 'Can we have a word with you, sir, in private?'

The request was unusual in itself, but the pair's nervousness was also odd. 'Very well.' Tullus glanced left and right, and was pleased that there were no soldiers close by. 'Sit.' He planted himself on the three-legged stool that had replaced the one he'd lost, with so much else, during the ambush. The two men sat cross-legged in the dirt, on either side of his still-glowing fire. 'Speak,' Tullus ordered.

Piso looked at Vitellius, who nodded. Encouraged, Piso began, 'I don't know how to say this, sir, other than straight out.' He lowered his voice even further. 'There's talk of mutiny.'

'Mutiny?' Tullus rolled his tongue around a suddenly dry mouth. Three decades he'd been in the army without witnessing such a thing. This might explain the camp's unhappy atmosphere, he thought. 'Tell me everything, from the start.'

He listened, grim-faced, as Piso spoke of the illegal gathering that he and Vitellius had witnessed. They had just been going to play dice, Piso repeated multiple times. In the end, Tullus told him to stop, that he knew they were both loyal – why else would they have come to him?

When Piso revealed that there had been men from his century there, Tullus held up a hand. It didn't surprise him that much – there were malcontents throughout the army – but it rankled. A lot. 'Give me their names.'

After a brief hesitation, Piso obeyed.

'Only three?' demanded Tullus, thinking: there are more conscripts and pissed-off veterans than that under my command. Fenestela spoke of six to ten.

'Those were the only ones I saw, sir, on my life.'

Commanding Piso to finish his story, Tullus stared into the orange-red embers of his fire, pondering what to do. A deeper gloom took him after Piso related how Bony Face had directed those present to recruit as many men as possible. Was it already too late to act? Tullus wondered, jabbing a stick at the burning logs until trails of sparks wandered up into the darkening sky. If it wasn't, what was the best action to take?

To arrest Bony Face and his cronies, as well as the three men seen by Piso, would be a start, he decided, and better than nothing. Unless the centurions of each cohort were blind, deaf and dumb, they would have a fair idea of the troublemakers within their units. A lightning-quick exercise carried out by loyal troops under the cover of darkness could see the ringleaders, or most of them, incarcerated before dawn. The potential mutiny would be nipped in the bud.

For that to happen, however, Tullus would need to persuade Septimius, his prick of a senior centurion, of the danger – and after him, a tribune. If Tullus managed to get that far, he had the mountain-sized problem that was his legate Tubero to contend with.

The man had been a pain in the arse since he first appeared, five years ago, thought Tullus. It was usual for noblemen to serve as legion tribunes from the age of twenty and upward, but Tubero's father's friendship with the emperor had seen him appointed at the tender age of seventeen. His subsequent rash behaviour and refusal to listen to Tullus' advice had helped to push one of the German tribes towards rebellion. The headstrong youth had escaped Arminius' ambush thanks only to a veteran who'd chanced upon him – so said a centurion friend of Tullus, who knew the soldier concerned. In the years since, Tubero had risen to the rank of legate. It was Tullus' ill fortune that he had been appointed to the Fifth Legion.

Even if Tullus could get past Tubero, above him, like Jupiter on his throne raised over the other gods, was Caecina. Success seemed so improbable that Tullus wanted to groan out loud. Conscious of Piso and Vitellius' eyes on him, he made no outward show of emotion. 'You did well to bring this news to me. Keep your ears to the ground. Report anything else you hear to me, double quick.' He jerked his head, dismissing them.

Rising, Vitellius saluted and made to leave, but Piso lingered. 'What are you going to do, sir?'

Tullus' instinct was to bite his head off, but Piso deserved better than that. 'I need evidence,' he said. '*I* believe you, but your word isn't enough to persuade someone like Legate Tubero that the sewer is about to burst. I'm going to do a little eavesdropping between now and the morning. Thanks to you, I know the right place to start.'

Piso looked as unhappy as Tullus felt about this far-from-certain tactic, but he was powerless to protest. 'Very good, sir. With your permission.' He strode off towards his tent.

Tullus went to find Fenestela. He needed someone to confide in. He also needed more wine.

A lot of it.

Some time before the sun had risen the following morning, Tullus was stealing down the narrow 'corridor' that ran between the back of his men's tents and those of another century. Experience had taught him that this was one of the best places to listen in on soldiers' conversations. This was not something he'd had to do much, but it was useful upon occasion, and necessary in this uncertain time. The trumpets to wake the camp had not yet been blown, but he and Fenestela had already roused the soldiers, so there was chatter to overhear. They were going on a twenty-mile march, Tullus had bawled, so they had to be up, breakfasted and ready to leave within the hour.

As he'd expected, most of the talk was complaining about the impending march. Tullus listened, smiling, to the bitching about him and Fenestela. Such talk was normal, and of no concern. What he didn't like were the comments by men who grumbled that the other centuries in the cohort weren't marching, so why should they? The sentiment wasn't serious enough to warrant intervening, though, so he kept picking his way over the tent ropes, hoping that nothing would come of his spying. Each step that took him nearer to the tent which held the three soldiers seen by Piso felt more and more ominous, however.

'Where d'you hear that?' demanded a voice in the fifth tent – the one he'd been aiming for.

The tone brought Tullus to a dead halt.

'At the meeting,' replied a second voice, one Tullus recognised as a conscript of five years' standing.

'It's a dangerous thing, gathering without permission,' said the first voice.

'Mebbe it is, but we didn't get caught. What's important is the way that legionary was talking. Most of the men in the four legions are going to take part, I'm telling you. We should too. As he said, any officers who try to stop us can have a good beating – or worse.'

'Not Tullus, surely?' protested the first voice. 'He's tough, but he is a good centurion.'

'If the man's got any sense, he will keep his head down,' replied the conscript. 'No harm will come to him then.'

'Tullus keep his head down? Ha!' The first soldier made an unhappy noise. 'I won't raise my hand to him. No way.'

'Nor will I,' chimed a third man, and a fourth, making Tullus' heart lift.

'You're fools,' swore the conscript. 'Forget about Tullus. Think about the miserable amount you're paid, and the way you're worked like slaves.'

'I'm with you,' said a fifth voice. There was silence from the rest, and Tullus wondered if he should act, or seek out the support of Fenestela. It might even be better to do nothing.

There was no time like the present, Tullus decided. He was unarmed, but the soldiers could well be too, and they wouldn't expect him to appear from nowhere. Surprise often made for success in battle. He padded on between the side of the tent and its neighbour. Halfway towards the front, he began to hit his vitis off the leather-panelled roof. *Thwack. Thwack.* 'Outside, you maggots!' he roared. *Thwack.* 'OUTSIDE, NOW!'

He was standing at the tent's front flap as its inhabitants emerged, one by one. Tullus was pleased that only two met his eye, and just one was armed, the conscript. He and the other man were the pair who had been urging the rest to join them. They hadn't succeeded, though, which meant that Tullus had the advantage. 'Form up!' he shouted. 'Here, in front of the tent. Move!'

The eight legionaries shuffled into a ragged line. The century's other soldiers watched, curious, as Tullus stalked along in front of them, delivering an icy stare to each. 'You've been talking about mutiny, eh?' He stopped before the conscript with the dagger. 'Eh?' Down by his right side, Tullus held his vitis at the ready. He was almost positive that he could drive it into the soldier's solar plexus if the fool thought about drawing his blade. 'Talk to me, if you're not to spend the next six months cleaning out the latrines!'

The man's courage wilted, as a plucked flower does without water. 'It's nothing but talk, sir.'

'Is that right?' Vitis still ready, Tullus shoved his face into the face of the second soldier who'd spoken, a salt-and-pepper bearded veteran. 'What's this about beating up centurions, or *worse?*'

To his credit, this man held his gaze. 'That's just anger talking, sir. Men are unhappy about their conditions. Me, I've served twenty-four years. I'm almost entitled to my discharge, but there are others in a worse boat.'

'If your words are true, there are wrongs that need to be righted,' said Tullus with a nod. 'But it doesn't entitle you, or any other legionary, to *mutiny. Mutiny.*' He glared at the veteran. This time, the man's eyes dropped away. So did the conscript's. 'If I hear so much as a fucking whisper about this again, you will all be running circuits of the parade ground until you fucking *drop*. There'll be no discharge or rise in pay because you will have all died of exhaustion! As it is, you two will receive ten lashes of the whip, and take care of the century's latrines until we break camp. Every three days for the same period, you will also make a twenty-mile march, under the supervision of Fenestela. Do I make myself clear?'

'Yes, sir,' the legionaries mumbled.

'Louder,' roared Tullus, bringing down his vitis on the veteran's shoulders, and then those of his companion, three, four, five times – and another for good measure.

'YES, SIR!' the eight soldiers yelled.

'Back into your tent, the lot of you.' Tullus walked away, exposing his back, sure that he had cowed them. His confidence was soured by the knowledge that his victory had been temporary. It sounded as if the men had reasonable grounds for their grievances, and the threat of mutiny remained high. Throughout the camp, the conversation he had just overheard would be taking place – without officers being aware. Bad feeling spread fast, and talk of mutiny would spread even faster. This was the proof he needed, he decided.

It was time to take the matter to his superior officer.

Chapter V

অ ন ন

After advising Fenestela and his other junior officers of what he'd heard, Tullus went to Septimius. He would have preferred to go over his senior centurion's head, but protocol had to be followed. A cynical individual with a sour face and spiky grey hair, Septimius had a privately held chip on his shoulder towards anyone more high-ranking. Unable to reveal this for obvious reasons, he took particular delight in lording it over Tullus, who had once outranked him by some margin. It was heartening, therefore, when he first took Tullus' concern at face value, and then announced that other centurions had come to him with similar worries. 'I've told them to come down hard on their men, as you did.' Septimius mimed using a whip. 'There are few things that ten or twenty lashes won't sort out.'

Tullus felt his relief slipping away. 'Wouldn't it be an idea to go to the senior tribune, sir? Or even the legate?'

Septimius fixed him with a stony look. '*I* am the cohort commander, not you. Understood?'

'Yes, sir,' said Tullus, swallowing his anger.

Septimius jerked his head. 'Dismissed.'

Remembering with bitterness how Varus had refused to heed his warning, Tullus obeyed, but his concerns continued to niggle at him as he made his way back to his tent. Perhaps he should sidestep Septimius anyway? He was weighing up his options when he spied the legate Tubero some distance down the avenue. The mere sight of him, self-assured and posturing, rammed home the truth to Tullus. If his chances of convincing Septimius were slim, they were non-existent when it came to Tubero.

On Tullus' current course, he and Tubero would meet within the next 150 paces. Tullus cursed. He didn't have the cushion, the distraction of his soldiers, with him, and Tubero had only a few of his staff officers as company. They were riding along, casual as you like, while ordinary soldiers scurried out of their way. He would notice Tullus, in his typical centurion's helmet, at once.

A barbed remark of some kind was inevitable. Tullus considered his options. If he ducked down between the tents to either side, Tubero wouldn't even notice that he'd gone. The alternative route would add moments to his journey, no more. The humiliation of it made Tullus seethe, however. *Must I spend the rest of my career tiptoeing around, avoiding contact with cocksuckers like Tubero?* he wondered. The internal question wasn't yet whole before Tullus had set his jaw and kept walking – towards Tubero.

Twenty steps before he had drawn level with the legate, a sudden impact from the side made Tullus stumble. He staggered to the side, and the broom-wielding legionary who had collided with him fell on to the flat of his back. 'What are you doing, fool?' barked Tullus.

'Your pardon,' said the soldier, picking himself up. His face paled as he realised Tullus' rank. 'A thousand apologies, sir! I didn't see you.'

'That's clear,' replied Tullus with a sardonic look. 'Sweeping?'

Looking even more embarrassed, the legionary raised his broom. 'I was walking sideways, brushing, sir, and—'

'You didn't see me, I know, I know.' Tullus considered disciplining the soldier, a man who looked to have only a few years' service under his belt. He seemed terrified, as well he might after colliding with a senior officer. It had been a genuine mistake, he decided, and there was no point in adding to the tension in the camp. 'Don't let it happen again.'

The legionary stared. 'Sir?'

'I said, piss off!'

'Yes, sir. T-thank you, sir.' The stunned legionary saluted. He took a few steps towards the gap between the tents.

'What's going on here?' Tubero demanded.

The legionary glanced over his shoulder. Fresh horror filled his eyes and he spun, coming to immediate attention. 'The centurion was telling me off, sir.'

Curse my pride. I should have avoided this, thought Tullus. He turned to find Tubero ten paces away. In expensive armour, with blue eyes, blond curls and chiselled chin, he was the epitome of a Roman nobleman. The arrogant curl of his full lips that Tullus despised was there; so too was the malicious look that came into his eyes each time they met. Tullus wished yet again that Tubero had died in Arminius' ambush, or that he had come across him during the savage battle. There was *no* doubt in his mind that Tubero had been terrified throughout the entire affair, pissing his underwear – and hiding, like as not, while his soldiers died all around him. If Tullus had possessed such information, Tubero would never have pressed for his demotion the way he had.

Yet Tullus hadn't found Tubero during the ambush, nor had he died. Somehow the shit had earned himself a reputation as one of the few heroes of the whole sorry affair, and now he was sticking his nose where it didn't belong. 'It's nothing, sir,' said Tullus.

'I'll be the judge of that.'

Tullus inhaled, long and slow, trying to stop the red mist from descending.

'Well? What was this imbecile doing?' Tubero stabbed a finger at the legionary, who squirmed as if he'd just been struck with a vitis.

'He was just sweeping, sir,' said Tullus. 'Wasn't looking where he was going, and walked into me. That's all.'

'*That's all?*' Tubero's eyebrows arched, and he glanced at his staff officers, who were swift to adopt shocked expressions. 'A common soldier knocks over a centurion, and you say, "That's all"?'

'He didn't knock me over, sir,' said Tullus, willing Tubero to let the matter drop. Frustration clawed at him. There were far more important issues to deal with, such as the brewing mutiny, which he couldn't even mention.

'I saw what happened, *centurion*, and I say that he did,' said Tubero with relish. 'What punishment is the idiot to have?'

Whatever I say, thought Tullus, will not be enough. If I lie, and the prick catches me out, I'm the one who will pay. He had had enough shit from Tubero over the years. 'I didn't punish him, sir. What he did was unintentional.'

'Do you hear this?' crowed Tubero. He fixed Tullus with a gimlet stare. 'What kind of example is it to let off a legionary after he's done something like this?'

I think it teaches a soldier to respect an officer, thought Tullus, but instead he said through gritted teeth, 'I didn't think it mattered, sir.'

'More and more I can see why it was a good idea to demote you, centurion. Unless you *want* to end your career in the ranks, I suggest you smarten up your act.'

'Yes, sir,' said Tullus in a monotone, fixing his gaze on the middle distance over Tubero's right shoulder.

'He's not under your command?'

'No, sir.'

'Tell his centurion I want him whipped. Twenty lashes minimum.' With a tug of the reins, Tubero pulled his mount's head around. 'See that it's done, centurion,' he called, riding off. 'I will find out if you disobey my order.'

Fall off your horse and break your stiff neck, thought Tullus. 'Yes, sir,' he replied. Giving the legionary a sympathetic look, he said, 'Who's your centurion?'

'Septimius, sir.'

'I see.' Tullus' frustration soared. With most centurions, it would have been easy to ask that the legionary's whipping be administered with a light hand. Not so with the disciplinarian Septimius. And it was over something so trifling. Tullus could think of no better way to create ill will, not just in this soldier's heart, but in those of his comrades, than to order the punishment carried out. He was bound to follow Tubero's order, however, for good or bad. This is what causes mutinies, Tullus thought, fighting a rising sense of frustration and impotence.

His chances of warning his superiors had now vanished. He would have to see what transpired in the coming hours and days, and pray that Bony Face and his kind failed in their attempt to win over the soldiers of the four legions. Tullus' cynicism bubbled up now, fierce and strong. What use was prayer? It hadn't got him far five years before, in the cauldron of blood that had been the Saltus Teutoburgiensis.

A tiny part of Tullus began to fight back. *He* had survived the ambush, and so had fifteen of his men, a child and a dog. Maybe Fortuna *had* been listening to him during those savage days of slaughter and mud. It wouldn't hurt to ask for her help again, he decided, muttering a heartfelt request to the goddess.

With the legionary delivered to Septimius, Tullus was free to lead his men out on patrol. The open road and monotony of the march made a welcome break from the claustrophobic atmosphere in the camp. Warm sunshine bathed the countryside, lending it a comforting orange glow. The bushes lining the road were heavy with blackberries, and in the fields beyond, the barley and wheat grown by local farmers was ready to harvest.

Tullus' apprehension eased as time passed. His men marched twenty-five miles in roughly six hours; like as not, they resented him for it, yet they were in good enough spirits to sing. Despite their fitness, which came from his continuous training, they were tired. Mutiny would be the last thing on their minds. Once they had unburdened themselves of their kit, had a wash and something to eat, they would be happy to sit by their fires before falling into their blankets.

Although Tullus had ridden – he didn't march much these days – he too was weary. His lower back ached, and there was a knot between his shoulder blades that needed the attention of someone practised at massage. His posture was still upright, however, and he continued to make regular checks on the marching column.

'You've done well, men,' he called out several times on his way back to the front of the patrol. 'You'll all have a cup of wine this evening.'

They cheered him then, even the legionaries he had caught out at dawn. They'll do, he decided with a sneaking pride. They won't mutiny.

Tullus was able to savour the feeling for perhaps half a mile, until the enormous training ground outside the camp drew near. Rather than being empty – a normal thing at this time of day – it was full. Thousands of legionaries stretched as far as the eye could see. His fears resurged with frightening speed. This was no parade. He could see no unit or cohort standards, let alone eagles. There were no neat divisions between cohorts, or indeed legions. What he saw was a mob, and an angry one at that, he thought, as the first shouts reached his ears.

'Halt!' Tullus barked. 'Optio, get up here! You too, Degmar.'

Fenestela let out a low whistle as he took the scene in. 'Vulcan's sweaty arse crack. They've done it. The mad bastards have risen up.'

Hearing it spoken out loud made it far worse. Tullus chewed on his cheek, and wondered what to do.

Degmar, a short, wiry warrior with black hair, looked mystified – and somewhat amused. He'd been Tullus' servant cum bodyguard since just before Arminius' ambush, and was like his shadow – ever present. 'What are your orders?'

There were two options, thought Tullus. The first, and easiest, was to march his men straight past the gathering, to their tents. He could then send Fenestela, or one of the other officers, to find out what was happening, while he assessed the state of affairs in the camp. His second choice was to lead his soldiers towards the mob, and see for himself. To do so would give him an immediate understanding of how serious the situation was, while running the genuine risk of losing control of his troops if this *was* a mutiny.

He studied his men, who seemed keen to know what was going on. Yet their ranks were steady, and Tullus' heart squeezed. Despite his best efforts, they *had* become dear to him. For the most part, they were good soldiers, and disciplined. He was almost certain – almost – that they would follow his orders here if things turned to shit. He didn't want to test them, though. The dressing-down he'd had to give the eight soldiers outside their tent was too recent, and the nearby gathering too large and unruly.

'We'll return to the camp,' he said.

Fenestela's eyes narrowed. 'Because of this morning?'

'In the main, yes.'

'A wise choice.'

Fenestela's opinion quashed any doubt that Tullus had had about choosing the more conservative path. He wondered about sending Degmar away for his own safety – when law broke down, men were prone to turn on those who weren't of their kind – but decided that that wasn't yet necessary. 'Ready yourselves, brothers!' he cried. 'Back to camp.'

A ripple passed through the ranks. Tullus wasn't sure if it was excitement, fear or anger at his command, and his guts twisted. Would they disobey him?

'Good news, sir. I'm fucking starving,' Piso called out.

There was a burst of laughter. 'Me too, sir!' cried Vitellius. 'I've got a skin of wine needs finishing as well.' In the blink of an eye, the soldiers' mood became jovial once more. A chorus of requests to return to their tents rang out. Tullus waited until it had died down before repeating that they would each have not one, but two cups of wine apiece.

His men cheered.

Tullus led them off at once, hoping that the thought of free wine would remain uppermost in their minds, rather than a desire to know what was going on.

'How many years has our pay been the same?' shouted a voice from the midst of the gathering.

'Twenty!' answered a voice. 'More than that!' roared another. 'Twenty-five, at the least!' said a third.

'There you are!' cried the first voice. 'How little the empire thinks of us to treat us so. We guard its frontier and keep the barbarians at bay. We suffer grievous wounds and lay down our lives in its name, and our reward is to be paid a pittance, and to serve until we die of old age. Why should we accept such injustice?'

The soldiers' reply, a swelling roar of anger, rose high into the sky.

Relief filled Tullus as his men – who were also listening to the exchanges – kept marching. He glanced at the mob. Fists were being waved, and so were swords. Already volatile, the situation was turning dangerous. He had to consult with Caecina, he thought.

Something had to be done, or blood would be shed.

Chapter VI

T ullus led his men straight to the camp's main entrance — worryingly, it was unmanned — and from there towards the *principia*, the headquarters.

The situation had deteriorated faster than he'd thought possible. Not all the soldiers were at the gathering. Gangs thirty to fifty men strong were roaming the avenues, singing and tearing down officers' tents. Some had been set on fire. Most of the legionaries appeared to be drunk, which suggested to Tullus that the quartermaster's stores had already been raided. His troops, disciplined and in formation, attracted nothing more than a barrage of abuse and an occasional stone. Others weren't so lucky, such as the optio who was set upon by a group of mutineers walking by his tent. A quick charge by Tullus and his men saw the rebellious legionaries flee, allowing the bruised and battered officer to pick himself up off the ground.

'What in Hades is going on?' demanded Tullus as the optio gabbled his thanks.

'It started not long after the morning meal, sir. Some say it began in the Twenty-First, others in the Fifth. The officers started getting it first. Insults, catcalls, you can imagine.' The optio wiped a string of bloody snot from his broken nose. 'Things got out of hand when some fool of a centurion — begging your pardon, sir — drew his sword. They turned on him like a pack of starving wolves, cut him limb from limb.'

Tullus absorbed this news with a rising sense of horror, and anger. It had been a mistake to go on the patrol — he should have ignored Septimius' orders and gone straight to Caecina. Yet he was unsure if it would have made any difference – Varus hadn't listened to him. Nor had Septimius. Would Caecina have been any different? It was too late to find out now in any case. It was also time for Degmar to go. 'Degmar,' he called.

The warrior appeared at his side like a ghost. 'I'm here.'

'You're to leave the camp.'

Degmar looked unhappy. 'I am here to protect you.'

'It will be safer if you don't stay, at least until things calm down.'

'If you order me to, I will obey,' said Degmar, scowling.

'I *am* ordering you to.' Tullus had no time to explain. He hoped that Degmar understood. 'Come back in a few days.'

'And if you're dead?'

Tullus ignored Fenestela's angry hiss, and the optio's startled reaction. His relationship with Degmar was a curious, deep-feeling one – in ways it was like that of two comrades, and in others like that of benevolent father and rebellious son. It was without question *not* that of master and servant. After Arminius' ambush, Tullus had used to wonder if Degmar's pregnant wife would lure him home. A chance meeting with Marsi who were trading on the Roman side of the river not long after their return had ended his concern. Degmar's wife had died with her baby during a prolonged labour. Tullus had offered to let Degmar go home to see their graves, but he had refused, saying, 'She's gone. I stay with you.'

Now, Tullus shrugged. 'If I'm dead, then you'll be free to go back to your people.'

Degmar's dark eyes regarded him, unblinking. 'I will try my luck at hunting.' He bent his head a fraction – for him a sign of respect – and loped off towards the camp's entrance.

Knowing that Degmar would be outside the fortifications and beyond harm lifted some of the weight from Tullus' shoulders. He eyed the optio. 'I'm heading for the principia. How do things stand there?'

'Caecina is barricaded inside, sir. By all accounts, the legates, the camp prefect and the tribunes have been placed under arrest in their tents.'

Tullus pinched the bridge of his nose. Should he attempt to rescue a few of the Fifth's senior officers first, or was it best to make straight for Caecina, and offer him his strength? Stick to the original plan, he decided. Caecina is the regional commander: he will know what to do.

The principia was being defended by the governor's guards and a mixture of legionaries from different centuries, some three hundred soldiers in total, when Tullus arrived. Some were digging a ditch and rampart, while the rest stood guard. The sentries' tense expressions and drawn weapons spoke volumes about the prevailing mood in the headquarters.

Caecina, the province's governor, was in the large command tent that served in place of the great hall that existed in every permanent camp. Perhaps ten score centurions were there too; a number bore the marks of beatings. Among them, Tullus saw most of his fellows from the Fifth, and Cordus and Victor, but not Septimius. He hoped that Septimius and the other missing centurions, about forty men, weren't dead. Not all were good officers, but that didn't warrant their being murdered out of hand.

'You're Tullus? The survivor of the Saltus Teutoburgiensis?' Caecina was a tall, stoop-shouldered man with a heavy brow and beaked nose, yet his voice was surprisingly high. 'I've heard of you.'

Tullus wasn't sure if that was a good or a bad thing. He came to attention, and saluted. 'I am he, sir. I'm now a centurion of the Seventh Cohort, Fifth Legion.'

'I'm told' – and here Caecina glanced at the centurion who had accompanied Tullus from the entrance – 'that your entire century is with you. That they have not rebelled.'

At once Tullus felt the weight of two hundred men's eyes upon him. 'That's correct, sir. They're a steady lot.'

'And you must be a fine leader. Your actions are to be applauded, centurion,' said Caecina in a warm voice. 'Few others have brought any legionaries with them.' He threw the gathered centurions a hard look. 'No one has come in with his whole command.'

'My soldiers are at your disposal, sir,' said Tullus, bowing his head and thinking with genuine pride: *my boys aren't so bad after all.*

'Several options remain open to us,' said Caecina to the room at large. 'We can stay here and wait for Germanicus to come, as surely he must when the news reaches him. I can attempt to deal with the mutineers, and listen to their demands. Rescue attempts could be made for the legates and tribunes. We could even attack the rebels, although I suspect that would not be wise.'

No one offered an immediate opinion, which didn't surprise Tullus. Caecina's position as governor was intimidating even to centurions, and the shock of their men's rebellion would still be fresh.

'Is there no one who will speak his mind?' asked Caecina with a frown.

'It would be best to remain here, sir,' said Cordus. 'There are too many of the whoresons for us to do anything else.'

A score of voices rumbled in agreement, and more heads nodded.

Caecina looked troubled. 'Maybe you're right,' he began.

'CAECINA!' The shout came from outside the principia.

Caecina gave an involuntary start and, like everyone else present, he stared towards the front of the enclosure.

'SHOW YOURSELF, CAECINA!'

'CAE-CINA! CAE-CINA! CAE-CINA!' roared a hundred, two hundred, innumerable voices.

'Don't go out there, sir,' cried a centurion. 'They'll kill you.'

Caecina's shoulders went back. 'What kind of man would I be not to respond?' He called out several names. 'Come with me. You too, Tullus.'

Stunned to have been chosen – the others were some of the most senior centurions of the four legions – Tullus did as he was told.

'CAE-CINA! CAE-CINA! CAE-CINA!' Outside the command tent, the noise made by the mob beyond the entrance was deafening. Terrifying.

Tullus saw Fenestela's questioning glance, and shrugged. Maybe his doom was to die here, at the hands of fellow Romans. He hoped not. It wasn't so much his death that concerned him, but that he'd lose any chance of avenging himself on Arminius and recovering his legion's eagle.

'CAE-CINA! CAE-CINA! CAE-CINA!'

The centurion in charge of the entrance to the principia gaped at Caecina's order to pull aside the wagon that straddled the opening.

'Do as I say!' commanded Caecina.

'Yes, sir.' The centurion rapped out an order. A dozen legionaries placed their shoulders against the back of the wagon and shifted it five, ten paces. 'That's enough!' called the centurion. He saluted Caecina. 'Want me to accompany you, sir, with some of my boys?'

'My soldiers can come too, sir,' volunteered Tullus.

'An honour guard will do,' said Caecina. 'A dozen of your men, Tullus.'

Tullus cursed inside. It was one thing for him to die at the hands of a baying mob, but he didn't want his soldiers to do so. He'd been given a direct order, however. 'Fenestela! Pick eleven men and get over here.'

'CAE-CINA! CAE-CINA! CAE-CINA!'

A moment later, Fenestela trotted over. The soldiers he'd picked were veterans, among them Piso and Vitellius.

'I'll go first, sir,' volunteered Tullus.

'Very well.' Caecina adjusted his red sash, and brushed an imaginary speck of dirt from his burnished cuirass. 'The gods be with us.'

'CAE-CINA! CAE-CINA! CAE-CINA!'

'No one should touch his sword, sir, or make any threatening move,' Tullus advised Caecina. 'I cannot emphasise that enough.'

'I understand. You're to do as Tullus says,' said Caecina to the other senior officers.

'Not a fucking twitch of a muscle unless I say so,' Tullus commanded his men. 'You hear me?'

'Aye, sir.' His soldiers looked scared, but steady.

'Follow me,' ordered Tullus. Despite what he'd just said to Caecina, it took all of his self-control not to unsheathe his own gladius. There was every chance that the mob might fall on them as they emerged, but to appear with a drawn weapon would only invite that response.

A wave of catcalls, derisive whistles and insults descended as they filed out. It was impossible not to find the waiting horde intimidating. At least five hundred legionaries, if not more, had assembled before the entrance. They were armoured, and many carried blades in their hands. More than one of those was bloody. To a man, their faces were hard. Expectant. Fierce.

These were the angriest, most determined of the mutineers, thought Tullus, ordering his soldiers to spread out in a line in front of Caecina and the other officers. To confront the governor in this manner took courage. Like as not, every troublemaker from the four legions was here – and they seemed prepared to shed blood.

A bony-faced, sunken-cheeked legionary was in a position of prominence, several steps in front of his fellows. This had to be the man mentioned by Piso. Three others were with him. Tullus recognised two, the twins described by Piso and Vitellius; with them was another man, a slight soldier with thinning hair and a bulbous, sausage-like nose. 'If things turn to shit,' he muttered to the nearest of his legionaries, 'we kill those four first. Pass it on.' It wouldn't save their lives, but it might stall the mutineers long enough to allow Caecina to get back inside the principia.

The noise made by the mob redoubled when they saw Caecina. Bony Face and his companions threw each other triumphant looks. It wasn't surprising, thought Tullus. Ordinary legionaries never spoke to the governor, let alone summoned him forth like a whipped dog from its kennel. This moment turned everything that was normal on its head.

Whatever else Caecina was, he wasn't short of backbone. Ignoring Tullus' restraining arm, he stepped forward until there were only a dozen paces between him and the mutineers' leaders. A hush fell. 'Here I am,' cried Caecina. 'What do you wish of me?'

'Our demands are simple,' said Bony Face. 'We want a raise in pay – a decent one, mind. The period of service is to be cut back to its original sixteen years, and all soldiers who have served twenty years will be allowed their discharge. That's it.' He gave his companions a satisfied nod, and folded his arms.

'Although I am governor, I do not have the authority to make such decisions,' said Caecina. He tried to continue, but so many insults were being hurled that it was impossible for him to be heard.

When the clamour had died down, Bony Face was first to speak. 'Is this your final answer?' he demanded, the contempt dripping from his voice.

'I am not trying to be difficult. Understand that I cannot implement such far-reaching changes without the emperor's authority,' said Caecina.

Again the legionaries roared their displeasure.

'Don't pretend that you're powerless, or without influence!' Bony Face stabbed a finger towards Caecina. 'You fucking senators and equestrians! You're so high and mighty, so superior. You take us for fools, who you can treat no better than slaves. Understand that those days are over! Bring forth the prisoner.'

Four legionaries emerged from the throng, dragging a centurion whose arms and legs were bound. The man raised his head, and Tullus took in a dismayed breath. It was Septimius. Beaten, dazed-looking and with two black eyes, but Septimius nonetheless.

Bony Face drew his sword and stepped to Septimius' side. 'Have you anything to say, filth?' he hissed.

'Let me go,' said Septimius. His eyes fixed on Caecina. 'Don't let them kill me, sir, please.'

Tullus clenched his fists. Prick though Septimius was, he didn't deserve to be treated like this.

'How pathetic,' said Bony Face with a sneer. 'What have you to say, governor? Will you meet our demands?'

Caecina's mouth worked. 'I told you. Without permission from the emperor, I cannot. I will do my best, however, to see that they are given the consideration that they merit.'

'Hear him!' Bony Face turned to the mob behind him and repeated in a mocking tone. '*The consideration they merit?* Is that good enough for us?'

'NOOOOOOO!' Purple-faced, neck veins bulging, and brandishing their swords, the mutineers screamed their disdain. Bony Face and his three cronies swaggered to and fro before them, egging the crowd on.

Tullus moved to Caecina's side, and spoke into his ear. 'If we move *right now*, sir, we might be able to cut down the legionaries holding Septimius and drag him to safety.'

Caecina's eyes flickered from left to right, over the mob.

'We have to do it *now*, sir,' whispered Tullus.

'They'll kill us,' replied Caecina.

Waves of impotent fury battered Tullus' mind. He wasn't sure that they could save Septimius, but they had to try. 'Sir—'

'Stay your hand!' ordered Caecina.

'Save me, sir! Save me!' Somehow Septimius had wrestled free of his captors' grasp. He took a step forward and tripped, landing on one knee. Half upright, his face twisted with terror, he called out to Caecina, 'Help me, I beg of you, sir!'

Caecina looked away.

Despite his best intention, Tullus laid a hand to the hilt of his sword.

Whether Bony Face's reaction was because he'd seen Tullus, or because he had already made up his mind, was never clear. With terrible swiftness, he strode in behind Septimius. Tullus watched in horror as Bony Face thrust with all his might. The blow was so savage that his sword travelled clean through Septimius' chest and emerged, crimson-tipped, from his chest. Spitted like a roast piglet, Septimius hung there, his eyes wide with agony and shock, and his lips twitching. Bony Face planted a studded sandal in the small of his back and shoved him forward, off the steel. Blood spurted from the wounds front and back as Septimius flopped on to his face, already a corpse.

'Our demands must be met!' shouted Bony Face, brandishing his bloodied weapon. 'If they are not, the same doom awaits you all!'

'KILL!' shouted a faceless legionary in the mob.

His cry was taken up at once, the way one stone starts a landslide. 'KILL! KILL! KILL!'

Decorum forgotten, Tullus had pushed Caecina halfway towards the entrance to the principia before the third 'KILL!' had been uttered. 'Inside, sir. Now!' Caecina didn't protest, and the other senior officers followed

Tullus with indecent haste. 'Orderly withdrawal, Fenestela,' he roared, praying that the mob didn't tear his men apart.

To his huge relief, the mutineers did not attack. Fenestela and the rest pounded in, and the wagon was rolled back across the entrance. Laughter and insults rolled in over the earthen rampart, buffeting their ears. 'Cowards!' 'Yellow-livered whoresons!' 'Arse-humping Greeks!' 'Come out and fight!'

'Fuck, that was close,' said Fenestela. 'If you'd moved a moment later, we'd be halfway to Hades.'

'Septimius was no good, but he deserved better than that,' said Tullus.

'You know that Bony Face is one of Septimius' soldiers?'

A ball of icy fury formed in Tullus' stomach. 'One of his own men murdered him?'

'Aye. I'm fairly sure that the twins and Fat Nose are in what was his century as well.'

Tullus swore, long and hard. Remember their faces, he thought.

'What do we do now?' asked Fenestela in an undertone as he eyed Caecina. His tone made clear what he thought of the governor's behaviour.

'Caecina was right to hold us back,' said Tullus, bringing his own fury under control. Fenestela looked surprised and Tullus added, 'We would have been massacred, and for nothing. We might be yet, if those defences aren't improved.'

Fenestela hawked and spat. 'It's a terrible thing to watch a man being butchered in front of you, even someone like Septimus.'

'It is,' growled Tullus, Septimius' terrified face vivid in his mind. Yet another man to avenge, he thought.

'What now?'

'We send messengers to Rome, if that hasn't been done already, and to Germanicus. We finish the ditch and rampart, and hold this position. In the middle of the night, we can go to the well and raid the stores, and take enough water and food to last us a while. Then we wait. That's what we fucking do.'

'Germanicus better get here soon.'

Fenestela was right, thought Tullus, listening to the mutineers' bloodcurdling roars. If Germanicus came too late, he would find nothing but corpses.

Chapter VII

᥏᥏᥏

Three days went by in the great summer camp. Piso and his comrades were often on sentry duty, watching the groups of mutineers who surrounded the principia. To Piso's relief, they made no attempt to attack the position. Much of the time, it seemed that the rebellious legionaries' only purpose was to drink every drop of wine they could find. Once it became clear that there was to be no assault, morale within the headquarters rallied a good deal. Because of the mutineers' drunken state, Piso and Vitellius didn't object when Tullus sent them out at night to collect water and steal much-needed supplies.

Each day, Caecina sent messengers on horseback to find Germanicus. As he said repeatedly, 'One might fail to get through, or two, but not all of them. Germanicus will soon hear of our plight.'

His words did little to reassure Vitellius. 'How will Germanicus bring the mutineers around?' he asked Piso over and over. 'Other than by granting their demands of course, which isn't likely.'

Piso had no answer, but he'd heard Tullus saying that Germanicus would know what to do, and that was good enough for him. All they had to do was hold out until the general arrived. He was less than impressed, therefore, when Tullus sought him and Vitellius out early on the fourth morning with orders to go out into the camp to see what they could discover about the mutineers' intentions.

'It won't be that dangerous,' Tullus declared. 'The stupid bastards have only placed a couple of sentries around the sides and rear. It'll be easy to slip out.'

'It's not that, sir,' said Piso, his fear giving him the courage to answer back. 'What if we get recognised?'

'Wear a hooded cloak. Avoid the Fifth's tent lines – go and see what's happening where the other legions are camped. If you do happen to spy anyone you know, just walk the other way. It can't be hard to avoid attention in a camp of seventeen thousand men.'

Tullus was right, Piso told himself. 'All right, sir.'

'Good lad. You'll be fine.' Tullus gripped his shoulder. 'I'd come with you, but Caecina has forbidden it. Says he needs me here.'

'Is anyone else to go, sir?' asked Vitellius.

'Six others from the century. You will operate in pairs, though. You'd attract more attention in larger numbers. It's tunics, belts, swords and a cloak each – nothing more. I'll be back soon.' With an approving nod, Tullus left them to it.

Piso and Vitellius exchanged a meaningful glance.

'It can't be worse than the forest was,' muttered Vitellius.

That was small consolation, thought Piso. If they were denounced by a single legionary, they'd be beaten to death in the blink of an eye, as traitors.

'Ready?' hissed Piso. They had both just clambered over the rampart and ditch that now ran around the principia. There was no one in sight, but that would change fast, even at this early hour. Not every mutinous legionary lay abed until midday.

'Aye.'

Piso was already walking north. He wanted to put a good distance between them and the Fifth's lines, which lay near the camp's southern gate. Apart from a handful of former comrades from the Eighteenth, he didn't know a soul in any of the other three legions, and was glad of it at this moment.

'Hood up or not?' asked Vitellius, pacing alongside.

'Heart says up, head says down,' answered Piso. 'It's not cold, though, is it?'

Vitellius' hand fell to his side. 'Aye, I suppose you're right. Makes it a shitload more frightening, though, eh?'

'Gods, aye.' Piso was fighting a continual battle to keep his fingers from straying to his sword hilt. He gave the phallus amulet at his neck a surreptitious rub. 'What should we talk about? We can't walk in silence – that might draw attention too.'

'That's easy,' replied Vitellius, chuckling. 'Stories about hunting, drinking and whores will keep us busy for hours. Longer, if *you* talk about gambling.'

'You start.'

'All right.' Vitellius launched into the tale of a three-day drinking spree that he'd been on once, with Afer and two others of their old contubernium in the Eighteenth.

Piso's heart twinged at the mention of Afer, who had been his first friend when he joined the army. Now his bones mouldered in the forest, like so many thousand others. Afer had died saving Piso's life, and Piso remembered him every day for that. However, Vitellius' tale was riotous, all men falling into latrine trenches and being sick in other men's drinking cups, and its gutter humour helped Piso to stop brooding about the danger they were in – for a time at least.

Emerging on to a larger avenue, they aimed towards the northwest corner of the camp. Neat rows of tan-coloured goatskin tents ran off in every direction. Dozens, scores, hundreds of them, each home to a contubernium of legionaries. There was nothing unusual about the tents – the complete opposite in fact. Their presence and layout was something Piso was accustomed to, but it drove home more than he'd anticipated how *alone* he and Vitellius were.

The men standing about, talking, cooking, and farting inside their tents, were all mutineers. Vitellius' voice faded into the background as Piso studied the nearest soldiers sidelong. That man there, stretching as he came out of his tent, and that one, striking flints together to light a fire, and another, scratching his stubble and giving them a friendly nod, they were no longer comrades. They were rebels, men who would gut him and Vitellius for staying loyal. They were the *enemy*.

'You hungry?' asked Piso as the familiar smell of cooking porridge filled his nostrils.

Vitellius looked irritated at being interrupted. 'I had a bite before we left. Reckoned we mightn't get a chance to eat until tonight. You?'

'Not even a crumb, worse luck. If the truth be told, I was feeling sick,' said Piso. 'Funny thing is, I'm fucking starving now.'

'You're getting used to being out here,' whispered Vitellius, giving him an evil smile. 'I don't want to hear how hungry you are for the rest of the day, mind. It's your own fault.'

'Screw you,' retorted Piso, giving Vitellius a shove.

They both laughed.

'Want something to eat?' called a voice.

Terror closed Piso's throat. How could they have been so stupid, he wondered, talking loud enough to be overheard? Casually, he turned his head. Fifteen paces away, a squat barrel of a man in a stained tunic stood over a fire. A ladle dangled from his hand, and at his feet, wisps of steam rose from a battered pot perched amid the burning logs. Somehow Piso found his voice. 'What are you cooking?'

'Porridge, same as every other whoreson in the place,' came the reply, with a dirty chuckle. 'You two have been on sentry duty at the front gate, eh? Your tent mates will have shovelled down all the porridge at your tent by the time you get back. I know what the bastards are like. My *friends'* – and he jerked a dismissive thumb at the tent behind him – 'did the same to me two nights ago, so you're welcome to share mine.'

'You're a generous man,' said Vitellius. 'But you will leave yourself with none. We'll find a morsel somewhere.'

'We have plenty.' Barrel nudged a nearby sack with the toe of his sandal. 'Yesterday I broke into part of the quartermaster's stores that by some miracle hadn't yet been ransacked. I came away with this and half a ham. You're not having any of the meat, but I can manage a bowl of porridge.'

Piso glanced at Vitellius, who gave him a look. Piso wasn't sure if it meant 'Why not?' or 'Walking away will look suspicious', but he couldn't prevaricate either, because that *too* might cause suspicion, so he smiled at Barrel. 'Gratitude, brother. I'm famished.'

'The hours seem to double in length when you're pacing up and down a fucking rampart, with only the corpses of centurions in the ditch to look at. Come on over,' said Barrel. He shoved out a meaty hand. 'Gaius.'

'Piso. My friend's called Vitellius.' The situation in the camp was *really* bad, Piso thought, if there were dead centurions in the defensive ditch beyond the rampart. He wondered how many had been murdered.

Gaius gave them both an amiable grin. 'No sign of Germanicus, was there?'

Fresh alarm bathed Piso. He had to pretend that they had been on watch all night. 'No, not a thing.'

'I didn't think so. The way I've heard it, whoever is on sentry duty has to alert the whole cursed camp when that happens. The leaders want everyone there to greet him.'

'That'd be right,' agreed Piso, his palms prickling, hoping not to get caught out.

'I'd love to see Germanicus' face when he realises how many of us there are,' said Gaius, filling a cracked red Samian bowl and handing it to Vitellius. 'Four entire legions, bar the few miserable cocksuckers who remained "loyal".'

'The prick will shit his perfumed undergarment,' said Vitellius, with a grateful nod for the porridge.

Chuckling, Gaius passed a bowl to Piso, whose heart was still pounding at the mention of 'loyal' men. 'Got your own spoon?'

'Aye.' Piso fumbled in his purse, grateful that he hadn't removed his spoon before leaving the principia. He blew on the steaming oats, and took a mouthful. 'It's good.'

'There's no need to lie,' said Gaius with a snort. 'The shit tastes the same as always. Plain but filling.'

'It's more than we had a moment ago, and we're grateful,' said Piso.

Gaius looked pleased. 'You going for a kip after this?'

'Might as well, eh?' replied Vitellius. 'It's not as if any cursed centurion or optio will stop us.'

'It's like being in Elysium not to have fucking trumpets wake me before sparrow's fart every morning,' said Gaius, chuckling. His face grew serious. 'What did you do to your centurion?'

'Gave him a good hiding,' lied Piso. 'I'd say we cracked most of his ribs before we'd finished.' Gaius stared at him, and Piso felt his pulse flutter. 'And yours?' he asked.

'He's dead. Happened on the first day.'

Gods above, thought Piso. He was glad when Vitellius stepped in. 'A bad 'un, was he?'

'One of the worst. The type who'd beat a man because one of his belt buckles wasn't shiny, you know. The funny thing is, the fool could have got away. We hadn't decided to kill him when it all started. I don't think he really believed us when we told him that we were taking control of the camp and that he should clear off. He laughed in our faces. That riled us, but when he reached for his vine stick, well . . .' Gaius' eyes went out of focus for a moment, then he spat into the fire, making it hiss. 'When we were done, he had more holes in him than a wine strainer. Good fucking riddance to him, that's what I say.'

'He's no loss,' said Piso, surprised to mean what he said. Life under such a centurion would be miserable beyond belief. Tullus wasn't just a good leader, he decided – the man was fair too.

'There were a few centurions like that in our legion,' growled Vitellius. 'They got short shrift.'

'They say that at least twenty centurions have been killed, and one tribune. You heard that?' asked Gaius.

'Aye,' Piso answered, adding for authenticity, 'The figure varies a little, depending on who you're talking to.'

'And on how much wine the fucker has had,' interjected Vitellius with a wink. 'Some would have it that there isn't an officer left alive for twenty miles, apart from those who made it into the principia.'

They all laughed.

'Did you hear about the centurion from the Rapax?' asked Gaius.

'There have been so many stories,' said Piso. 'Which one are you talking about?'

'The sewer rat who used to put lead in his men's kit before a march so that their yokes weighed half as much again as normal.'

'Men talk about him,' said Vitellius with a realistic scowl. 'A nasty piece of work.'

'Not any more,' revealed Gaius in triumph. 'He went for a swim in the Rhenus on the first day – after his soldiers had tied a lead weight to each of his feet. It turned out that the bastard was a strong swimmer – he managed to stay afloat for an age. In the end, his men used him as target practice for their javelins.'

'That's a bad way to die,' said Piso without thinking.

'Sounds as if he deserved it, though,' Vitellius put in.

'He did. Him and the others.'

Piso was quick to mutter his agreement, but he wondered if he'd seen a flicker of distrust in Gaius' eyes. He swallowed a last spoonful of porridge, and said in a regretful tone, 'I don't know about you, 'Tellius, but I need my bed. Gratitude once again, Gaius.'

Accepting their bowls with a nod, Gaius looked Piso up and down. 'What legion are you in?'

'The Twentieth,' lied Piso, not knowing which legion was best to say.

'Which cohort?'

The casual question fell with the speed and lethality of an incoming sling bullet. Gaius knew men in one cohort or another, Piso decided, perhaps several. He was trying to catch them out. If Piso named a cohort in which Gaius had friends, he and Vitellius would be denounced before the scrapings of porridge in their bowls had gone cold. 'The Tenth,' he answered, his tongue rasping off the dry roof of his mouth.

Gaius' calculating expression eased into one of dissatisfaction. 'I've got mates in the third and fourth.'

'I might know them to see, but not to talk to,' said Piso. 'You know how it is.'

'Aye,' said Gaius sourly. He cast a look at his tent. 'Marcus! Didn't you say once that you knew some men in the Tenth Cohort of the Twentieth?'

'One or two,' came the reply.

Piso wanted to rage at the heavens. Why me? Why now? He cast a quick look at Vitellius. What should we do? he mouthed. If they ran, Gaius and his comrades would be on them like a pack of hounds on a lame hare. By staying, they ran the risk of being exposed as frauds, which would result in the same thing. They were caught between Hannibal and his army, and the deep blue sea, as Piso's grandfather had been fond of saying. Screwed, in other words, he thought with supreme bitterness.

'Get out here,' called Gaius.

'I'm having a nap,' came the irritated reply.

'It won't take a moment,' said Gaius, smiling at Piso, who was reminded of the jagged-edged teeth he'd seen once in the mouth of a shark, hauled up in a fisherman's net.

'All right, all right,' grumbled Marcus.

'You're bound to know Marcus' friends,' said Gaius, putting down the bowls.

Piso nodded in what he hoped was an enthusiastic manner. I'm not fool enough to stand here and die, he decided. Vitellius' stiff-legged posture, like a male dog facing up to another, seemed to say the same thing. Cut down Gaius and they could be thirty paces away before Marcus emerged, or any of Gaius' other tent mates reacted. Duck down *that* avenue and they stood a decent chance of losing themselves among the tent lines, from where they could trace a path back to the principia.

The option was fraught with risk. Failure to kill Gaius would result in a sword fight here, against overwhelming odds. The guy ropes holding up the tents were difficult to wend past at a walk, never mind a sprint. One trip, and either he or Vitellius would have a snapped ankle – the prelude to a far nastier fate. The legionaries they'd meet during their flight – of which there would be many – might obstruct their path, or even attack them. Scaling the rampart at the principia would render them as helpless as babes.

Hannibal or the sea? Piso wondered, pulse hammering, mouth bone dry. The sea or Hannibal?

'Stop him!'

Every head turned towards the cry, which had originated further up the avenue. The distinctive sound of hobnails pounding off the earth came next.

'Halt that officer! He's making for the principia!'

Like every man within earshot, Gaius' attention had moved, in his case away from Piso and Vitellius. Piso was about to suggest, sotto voce, that they make a run for it, but the sight of scores of legionaries charging towards them put paid to that idea. If Gaius denounced them, as he would, half the mob could easily split away from their prey – a lone officer – to pursue him and Vitellius.

They had to remain where they were, and as Vitellius tugged out his sword, Piso realised with horror that he had to copy the move. Not to do so would reveal his loyalty more truly than a wrong answer to any of Gaius' probing questions.

'With me, brothers,' roared Gaius, moving to the middle of the avenue. 'We can't let the cocksucker escape!'

Piso took up a position to Gaius' right – which brought him closer to the tent lines opposite. Vitellius did likewise. Gaius' comrades, with Marcus among them presumably, soon joined them, swords and shields in hand. So too did a dozen other legionaries from their unit. It took no time to form a solid line across the avenue. Piso's palms grew sweaty as he saw that the officer – a centurion, from the look of his phalerae and other decorations – was aimed straight for *him*. Was he going to have to murder a man to save his own skin? Piso didn't know if he could, but the bloodlust-filled faces swarming behind the terrified centurion were a strong persuader.

In twenty paces, he would have to decide.

Eighteen.

'Come on, you maggot,' shouted Gaius, neck veins bulging. 'There's no way through for you here.'

Sixteen.

Bile stung the back of Piso's throat. He swallowed it down, gripped his sword until his fist hurt.

Fourteen.

'Gut him!' screamed one of the centurion's pursuers. 'He murdered the sentry outside his tent!'

An animal roar went up from Gaius and the rest. Vitellius' voice joined in, and Piso was ashamed to hear his own too. The centurion was so close now that he could make out the scars left on the man's cheeks by the pox, the sweat beading his brow and even the colour of his eyes – slate grey.

Eight steps, and Piso tensed. He *would* stab the centurion if he had to. The man's death was certain – why add his own, and possibly that of Vitellius, to the ugly mixture?

The centurion had conquered his fear – or at least made peace with it. Slowing his pace, he dropped a shoulder towards Piso and readied his right arm, which held a bloodied gladius.

Crushing panic suffused Piso's every pore. Chances were he was going to die in the next few heartbeats. Like the centurion, he had no shield, which made sliding a blade into him that much easier.

'Die, you filth!' bawled Gaius, darting forward.

Too late, the centurion's gaze moved from Piso. Too slow, he tried to twist and face the new threat. His eyes widened with shock, then fear, then pain as Gaius' sword rammed deep into his groin. A cracked wail left his lips and there was a *thump* as, carried forward by their momentum, the two men collided, chest to chest. Gaius delivered a savage head-butt, and blood spurted from the centurion's smashed nose.

Gaius gripped the centurion's shoulder with his left hand, steadying him so that he could drive his blade even deeper. 'How d'you like that, you mongrel?'

The answer was a low, awful moan. The sound of a man in mortal agony. It had the same effect as a trussed-up criminal revealed in the arena to a pride of starving lions. Legionaries drove in from every side, their sword points searching for a home in the centurion's flesh. Eight, ten, twelve wounds blossomed on his neck, arms and legs.

Struck rigid, Piso watched in horror.

'Let's go!' Vitellius' breath was hot in his ear.

Like a drunk waking, sore-headed, in an alley, Piso came back to life. He stared at Vitellius. 'Eh?'

'They'll kill us next. *Come on.*' Vitellius took his right wrist in a grip of iron.

With shame scourging every part of him, Piso turned and ran.

Chapter VIII

⊡⊡⊡

Fortune had favoured Piso and Vitellius, thought Tullus when they reported to him that evening. Fortune, and the bloodlust that had swept over Gaius and the rest. No one had pursued them into the tent lines. After a hundred paces, and three sharp turns – left, right, right – which had taken them out of the line of sight of the avenue, Piso explained how he'd thought to slow to a walk. Everyone looks at the man who is running, he told Tullus, but the man who walks draws no more than passing attention. So it had proved. Emboldened by their success – and intimidated by the reception Tullus would have given them if they returned early – the pair had continued with their mission. Because Gaius' friend Marcus had acquaintances in the Twentieth Legion, they had visited the First's tent lines.

All had gone well there, and the pair had spent the morning watching a set of wrestling matches organised by the bored legionaries. A large crowd had gathered to watch the contests, and food- and wine-sellers had come in from outside the camp. It had been perfect ground for wandering about and eavesdropping on conversations.

For the most part, Tullus brooded, what they'd heard was bad. It seemed that Gaius' information had been accurate. Almost every soldier in the four legions – the First, the Fifth, the Twentieth and the Twenty-First – had rebelled. Perhaps fifty legionaries appeared to be in charge; their number included Bony Face, Fat Nose and the twins. More than a score of centurions *had* been murdered. More senior officers were being held captive in their tents, with the obvious exception of the tribune who had been slain.

There was talk of violence beyond the camp's walls. Some civilians had been killed, and women raped. There were even rumours of attacking the nearest town, Ara Ubiorum. About the only cheering news was the fact that, as far as Piso and Vitellius could tell, none of Caecina's messengers had been apprehended.

That meant, thought Tullus, that Germanicus *would* know by now what had happened. He would arrive soon. What would happen then was anyone's guess – the mutineers weren't going to lie down and present their throats like submissive dogs. Too much blood had been shed for that.

How many more lives would be lost?

Tullus continued to send out his men each day, with Caecina's blessing. On the fifth day, Piso returned earlier than normal, bearing the news that Germanicus had been seen nearing the camp. A delighted Tullus took him straight to Caecina, who was incarcerated in his office with the *primi pili*, the most senior centurions of the four legions.

Caecina's delight at Piso's news didn't last. 'Imagine if the mutineers fall upon him,' he declared. 'The governor must not enter the camp until it is safe! Word must be sent to him at once.'

'I'll go, sir,' offered Tullus. 'I can pass myself off as a veteran.'

Caecina studied Tullus for a moment. 'The mutineers have a point about men serving for too long, eh?' His frankness made the primi pili give each other surprised looks, but Tullus nodded.

It wasn't unusual for a centurion to be almost fifty years old, but ordinary legionaries, who joined the army at eighteen or nineteen, were eligible for discharge at forty-three or -four. Poor record-keeping and insufficient numbers of recruits meant that this deadline was often 'overlooked' by the more unscrupulous centurions. No wonder men had grievances, thought Tullus, and shame on Caecina for not doing something about it before. 'With your permission, sir, I will take my optio and twenty men.'

'Do as you see fit. Just make sure that you reach the governor outside the camp. He will have an escort, but because he'll be riding like a demon, it's bound to be small. Things could easily go wrong, and I don't want to be held accountable for the death of the emperor's heir as well as the cursed mutiny.'

Tullus winced inwardly. If Germanicus was slain, and *he* was also blamed, the death penalty would beckon. His dead soldiers would never be avenged, and he would lose any chance of recovering the Eighteenth's eagle. He threw back his shoulders. 'I'll see the governor into your presence, sir. I swear it, on my life.'

Wandering the camp out of uniform, pretending that he was an ordinary legionary, was a bizarre experience for Tullus. His secret visit to Rome with Fenestela had been one of the only times that he had acted in such a way. That had taken some getting used to, but it had not been as risk-laden. Here, among so many soldiers, Tullus expected to be recognised as an officer at every turn. To this end, he had pulled the hood of his cloak up, and walked along with his head down, letting Piso and the others guide his path. They all wore swords under their cloaks, but none were in armour. So few of the mutinous soldiers were in full kit that to do so would have drawn immediate attention to themselves.

Tullus was able to gain an impression of the situation as they made their way towards the camp's northernmost gate, the entrance at which Germanicus would arrive. At first glance, things appeared normal enough. The legionaries' tents were still in position. So too were some of the unit standards. Yet there were gaps in the tent lines that shouldn't have been present; Tullus saw that most of the centurions' large tents had been torn down. A closer look revealed that they had been slashed to pieces, or burned. Near more than one tent, tell-tale bloodstains bore witness to darker deeds. Rubbish lay underfoot everywhere — discarded amphorae of wine, broken plates, rinds of cheese, and a sandal with a broken strap. There were items that had to have been pilfered from officers' quarters and then discarded: an iron-bound chest lying on its side, a half-unrolled fine carpet, a massive cast-iron stand with hooks for two dozen oil lamps. The stink of urine, and worse, was proof that reaching the latrines had not been a priority for many.

If the camp looked vaguely normal from a distance, its inhabitants did not. The mutinous legionaries lounged about before their tents, or roamed the avenues in large, unruly groups. A significant number were drunk. Crowds of them were heading in the same direction as Tullus and his men, and from their conversations, it seemed that they too wanted to see Germanicus, and lay before him their demands.

No one gave Tullus' party a second glance, and they soon reached the northern gate, where a queue had formed to exit the camp. Word was spreading that everyone was to assemble on the parade ground as soon as possible, so that Germanicus would appreciate their overwhelming numbers. Tullus had Piso scale the ladder that led up to one of the entrance's watchtowers. He was back within the space of thirty heartbeats. 'A party of riders is approaching, sir. They're perhaps a mile away.'

'That's got to be Germanicus,' said Tullus, his heart beating faster. Instinct told him that the governor might tackle the problem head on, and Tullus wondered if he could reach him before the parade ground. Whether Germanicus, renowned for his determination, would heed Tullus' advice was another thing altogether. Furthermore, to do so would reveal themselves to the mutineers.

'We'll head to the speaking platform,' he said to Piso and the rest. 'Fast as we can. Avoid meeting anyone's eye.'

Men with purpose always moved quicker than those without, and the effect was exaggerated when wine had been consumed. Tullus' party slipped between and around the rowdy mutineers, breaking into smaller groups when needed, coming at last to the low platform from which officers addressed troops on parade. The only people to protest their passage were a number of aggressive, pissed soldiers, who were easy to bypass. Tullus kept his men away from the front, because Bony Face was close to the dais with Fat Nose and the twins. The legionaries around them *were* sober, and seemed to be spoiling for trouble.

Time dragged as they waited for Germanicus to arrive. Tullus kept his head down, and spoke little, but he kept his ears pricked. It was heartening to hear that the mutineers' strong feelings about their grievances were mitigated by a clear devotion to Germanicus, and notable that, despite their mutiny, the ringleaders hadn't positioned themselves on the platform.

'He'll give us what we want,' opined a beefy-jawed legionary to Tullus' right.

'Aye,' said his companion, whose face was as narrow as the other's was wide. 'Germanicus is a fair man and a fine general – everyone knows that.'

'He will offer us what is ours,' snarled Fat Nose, who had heard the comment. 'Else he'll get what's coming to him.'

'There's no need for that,' said Beefy Chops, but a sizeable number of legionaries seemed to agree with Fat Nose.

Tullus gave Fenestela, who was a few paces to his left, a meaningful glance. This could be bad, he mouthed. I'm ready, Fenestela mouthed back. So are the men. Tullus inclined his head, and dropped a discreet hand to his sword, making sure the hilt was sitting just so. There wasn't much else to do but pray. Tullus wasn't one for asking favours of the gods, but at dangerous times like this it helped him to feel a little better. Fortuna, he asked, great goddess, keep these soldiers calm and my men safe. Let Germanicus say his piece and go in peace.

'He's coming!' shouted a voice from the direction of the road north.

A ripple of excitement passed over the gathering. Men twisted and stretched to get a view of the newcomer, Tullus among them. The first indication of Germanicus' arrival was a thinning of the crowd. It was noteworthy that they didn't form up in even ranks, or offer an honour guard.

Imposing, tall, Germanicus strode into sight. He was bareheaded and stern-faced; his armour gleamed like sunlight. A collective *Ahhhhh* went up. Three companions followed in his wake, two cavalrymen and a staff officer. He's got balls of steel to come here, and with such a small escort, thought Tullus, his admiration for the man growing. What was far from clear was whether Germanicus' move had been wise. The situation oozed with danger.

Tullus hoped that the governor's famed courage and oratory skills would be enough to keep him alive. If things went wrong, Tullus' men would not be enough.

'Where are your standards, soldiers of Rome?' cried Germanicus, his height setting him a handspan and more over every man present. He clambered on to the platform, which made him as tall as a giant. His companions stayed at the base. 'I want to see them, so I may recognise your units as I speak with you,' said Germanicus.

'We can hear you well enough without standards,' retorted Bony Face, his voice throbbing with anger.

Germanicus made no acknowledgement. 'Raise your standards,' he shouted. 'You are proud of your units, are you not?'

'We are!' answered a score or more of voices.

'Ignore him,' ordered Bony Face.

'If you are proud, show me your standards!' urged Germanicus.

Bony Face and his fellows glared as first one, then two, then a dozen century and cohort standards were lifted up from men's sides. Before long, they were everywhere, and Germanicus nodded in satisfaction. 'It is good knowing to whom one speaks,' he said, pitching his voice to carry. 'You all know me. I am Germanicus, imperial governor of the province of Germania and Tres Galliae, and heir to the emperor, Tiberius, praise his name! I am also your commander.'

The rumblings of discontent and comments about Germanicus' pedigree that followed were muted, pleasing Tullus and angering Bony Face and his cronies in equal measure.

'I stand before you this day to speak of many things,' said Germanicus. 'First among those must be Augustus, our blessed father who is no more.' He smiled a little as a few shouts acclaiming the dead emperor went up. 'From humble origins, he forged an empire that is the envy of all. For the last half-century, his legions – *you brave soldiers* – have won countless victories and conquered vast territories in his name. Of recent years, you have followed his heir Tiberius to glory in Germania and in Illyricum. Your courage, your sacrifices, your blood achieved these glories! This province – no, the empire – is at peace today because of you.'

Heads shook in agreement, men muttered 'Aye', but there was none of the usual cheering that would meet such lavish praise.

'I rode here in haste when the news of this disturbance reached me,' said Germanicus, pacing about on the platform. 'Rome relies on you. You are the force that guards its northern borders. What has happened to your discipline, your obedience? Where are your officers?'

Tullus was prepared for the total uproar that descended, but Germanicus was not. He seemed shocked by the host of legionaries who stripped off their tunics to reveal their scars, and the marks left by punishment whippings. Encouraged by Bony Face, Fat Nose and the twins, they pressed forward, raining down a litany of complaints: 'Our centurion beat us black and blue every day!' 'Look here! This was made by a red-hot poker. *That* was the penalty for not digging a latrine trench deep enough.' 'My centurion took bribes to let men off sentry duty and the like. If we couldn't pay, he'd have us whipped!'

'These are grievous accusations, and they *will* be investigated,' said Germanicus, regaining his composure. 'I cannot believe, however, that every centurion was guilty of such crimes.'

'That's why we only slew the worst of them,' cried Bony Face, and many of legionaries cheered.

A deluge of grievances followed, about the backbreaking jobs that the legionaries were supposed to do – ditch-digging, transporting fodder and timber, cutting down trees, the construction of latrines and ovens. These had to be done, complained the soldiers, even when there was no real need. The centurions used the hard labour just to stop their men being 'idle', and if they didn't obey, the most fearful punishments were administered. 'All this,' roared Bony Face, 'and we receive a pittance for it! That's if we are even *paid*. Over the last few years, our money's come late, sometimes by months. And that's not mentioning the men who should have received their discharge.'

'Look here, at this soldier, Germanicus,' shouted the first twin. 'He hasn't got a tooth left in his head. Thirty-five years he's been a legionary, and he is not alone.'

'Are he and his fellows to die in their armour?' chimed in the second twin.

Fresh cheering erupted, and the toothless soldier beamed at his moment of notoriety.

'These issues must also be addressed,' Germanicus declared in an even tone. 'I give you my word that every one of them will be recorded, and looked into. What say you to that?'

Some in the crowd appeared pleased, but more did not. 'Promises mean little,' Tullus heard Bony Face say. 'We want our objections answered *now*.'

'Seize the purple, Germanicus,' yelled the first twin. 'Take it from that fat fool Tiberius!'

'Tiberius is an old man, with cabbage for brains. It is *you* who should be emperor, Germanicus. March on Rome – we'll help you!' cried the second twin.

Tullus stared at Germanicus, who seemed disgusted, but that didn't stop the legionaries' acclaim. 'GER-MAN-I-CUS!' they yelled, over and over.

Germanicus jumped down from the platform, but some of the mutinous soldiers moved to block his passage. Germanicus' guards reached for their swords, but he barked an order for them to stay their hands. The air prickled with tension.

'Gather the men,' Tullus ordered Fenestela. 'Follow me.' He shoved forward through the throng, using his elbows and shoulders. The confusion was such – legionaries were shouting for Germanicus, against him, that they should raid the nearest town, or march on Rome – that within twenty heartbeats Tullus could almost touch Germanicus. There he halted, however. Two mutineers stood in Germanicus' path, drawn swords in their hands. If Tullus made a wrong move, the emperor's heir might be slain. Germanicus' escort of three were at his back, powerless thanks to the press on either side.

'You're going back on that platform, sir,' growled one of the mutineers. 'Accept the honour that's being shown you.'

'I will do no such thing! I would rather take my own life than be disloyal to the emperor.' With a grand gesture, Germanicus drew his own blade.

This isn't the place to be theatrical, thought Tullus, even as a pair of soldiers grabbed Germanicus' right arm and held it tight.

'Calusidius is my name, sir,' said another man, shoving his face into Germanicus'. 'I think you'll find *this* a little sharper than your toy.' To loud applause, he proffered a standard issue gladius, its wooden handle shiny with use, and its steel blade well oiled. 'You're welcome to use it.'

'I will choose the time of my death, legionary. Not you,' snarled Germanicus.

Cowed by Germanicus' contempt, Calusidius lowed his weapon.

Bony Face was harder to dominate. 'Don't be fickle, governor. If you're so loyal, kill yourself,' he jibed. 'Go on!'

'Do it!' roared a hundred voices.

'You'll be no loss,' added Fat Nose. 'The more patricians who go into the mud, the better.'

Tullus was watching the men around him like a hanging hawk focuses on a mouse far below. He had noted their expressions changing throughout the unfolding drama, from impatient to awed, uncertain to angry to fearful and back again. Now he saw bloodlust creeping in. It would take but a word from Bony Face or his cronies to have the mob descend on Germanicus in a flurry of fists and blades.

He was moving at once. 'Fenestela! After me!'

Two, three, six steps and he was in beside the soldiers who were holding Germanicus. Despite the press, Tullus was able to draw his sword underarm. Pushing its tip against the nearest man's lower back, he hissed, 'Release the governor. Don't protest, or I'll split your right kidney in two.'

'You heard him,' said Fenestela, using his blade to encourage the other soldier.

The shocked legionaries did as they were told. As those in the immediate vicinity struggled to realise what had happened, Tullus was speaking in Germanicus' ear, motioning to his escort, and retreating away from Bony Face, Fat Nose and the twins. Pre-warned by Fenestela, Tullus' twenty men formed a narrow, V-shaped wedge in front of Tullus and his valuable companion. Germanicus' escort of three were quick to take their places in the formation. The party was twenty paces away before Bony Face and the rest began to hurl abuse after them, and fifty before the lead mutineers were calling for Germanicus to be apprehended.

At this point, Tullus slipped his hooded cloak over a protesting Germanicus, and pulled the cowl low over the governor's face. 'I'm sorry, sir, but you'll have to bear with me,' he muttered. 'MOVE!' he barked at his soldiers.

They were two hundred paces from the platform, and the gathering was thinning, before Bony Face had organised enough men to pursue them. Loud cries trailed over the crowd's heads. 'Catch him!' 'With Germanicus as a prisoner, our demands will be met!'

The legionaries further away weren't listening, were too pissed, or had no interest in apprehending Germanicus. There were curious stares aplenty, but few even remarked at the group's passage. Nonetheless, Tullus did not let Germanicus lower his hood until they had reached the principia.

'By all the gods,' said Germanicus, recognising Tullus. 'It's you.'

'Yes, sir,' said Tullus, concerned at once that there be no mention of their meeting in Rome. Despite Germanicus' leniency, the fewer people who knew about it, the better. 'I'm sorry for manhandling you back there.'

'No apology is necessary, centurion.' Germanicus dipped his chin. 'It was fortunate indeed that I acted as I did when last we met.' Tullus breathed a sigh of relief at the way their encounter had been mentioned, and Germanicus continued, 'I appear to owe you and your men my life, perhaps. If not that, my freedom.'

'I was just doing my job, sir.'

'You risked much, and when things seemed as if they might get out of hand, you acted with real initiative. Take the praise, centurion.'

'Thank you, sir,' said Tullus.

'It's good to know that I have men like you behind me. Things are likely to get worse here before they get better.'

'Blood will flow, sir?' It was dispiriting to hear his worries given voice by another.

'I'm sure of it, centurion. Even when the mutineers have been brought to heel, some of their leaders will have to die. The best way to remove canker is with the first cut of the knife, my father used to say.' Germanicus' eyes now looked like two chips of flint. 'If you don't do that, the rot soon spreads.'

'As you say, sir,' agreed Tullus. Inside, he was horrified by the idea of killing his fellow soldiers.

What choice had he, though, other than to obey?

Chapter IX

〔〕〔〕〔〕

While Germanicus closeted himself in the largest tent with Caecina and the senior centurions, news reached Tullus of Tubero's arrival while he had been outside the camp. It threw him into a foul humour. Tubero had escaped through the back of his tent, it seemed. Disguised as an ordinary legionary, he had made his way unhindered to the headquarters. 'Somehow the maggot always comes up as a winner,' Tullus grumbled to Fenestela.

'You never spoke a truer word,' observed Fenestela, spitting.

'One law for them, and one for us, eh?'

Fenestela grinned. They both spoke the same lines every time. 'As it has always been, and always will be.'

'I heard it was bad out there,' said a voice.

Tullus found Senior Centurion Cordus standing ten paces away, his podgy face pale and strained. I don't need this now, Tullus thought, remembering their angry exchange in the Net and Trident. 'Bad enough.'

'They're saying that you rescued the governor.'

'Aye.' Tullus rolled his eyes at Fenestela, and waited for the sarcastic response.

'You went into the midst of thousands of unhappy legionaries, men who have murdered centurions, and somehow extricated Germanicus,' said Cordus. 'That was well done.'

Tullus gave Cordus a startled glance. What in hell's name was he playing at?

'It would have been a terrible thing if the governor had been killed,' Cordus went on. 'We are all in your debt.'

'Anyone would have done the same,' demurred Tullus.

'Except they wouldn't.' With a friendly nod, Cordus walked away.

'Prick,' muttered Fenestela. 'I'd trust him as much as a sewer rat. What was he up to?'

'No idea,' replied Tullus. 'Maybe he's changed his mind about me.'

Fenestela made a *phhhh* noise of contempt.

'I need wine,' said Tullus. Cordus' comment had driven home the magnitude of the danger that they had been in. 'See if you can scrounge some from the quartermaster. Enough for the men who came with us too.'

'The words "blood from a stone" spring to mind.'

'Tell him it's for the man who "saved" the governor,' said Tullus with a wink. He pulled an *aureus* from his purse and handed it over. '*That* should move his fingers towards his keys. I want a decent vintage, mind, and lots of it.'

Fenestela winked back. 'I'll drive a hard bargain.'

Tullus busied himself for a time by congratulating the twenty legionaries who had come with him and Fenestela. They were good boys, he told them. He was proud of what they had done, and so was Germanicus. 'It's quite a thing to have saved the life of the emperor's heir,' Tullus said. 'You'll only get one chance to do that in this lifetime.'

They gave him the fierce, relieved grins of those who have survived the storm of iron and steel. There had been no combat, but the risk of dying had been as high as it was in the fiercest battle, and every one of them knew it.

'All centurions, gather round!'

Flanked by Germanicus and Tubero, Caecina stood in the doorway of the main command tent.

Tullus made his way over, and was pleased by the recognition he received from other centurions: nods, muttered congratulations, even a few claps on the back. It was heartening that some of the acknowledgements came from men who had shunned him before. Perhaps the stain on his character – for having survived Arminius' ambush – wasn't impossible to wash away. Not everyone was pleased for him: Victor, Cordus' ox-like henchman, was among those who said not a word. He glowered as Tullus was allowed to take a place at the front.

'We are honoured by the presence among us of Germanicus Julius Caesar, our governor,' announced Caecina.

The centurions were well schooled – and relieved that their supreme commander had arrived. A loud cheer went up.

'I give you the imperial governor,' said Caecina, half bowing to Germanicus and stepping back.

More cheering erupted.

Tall, imposing, Germanicus stood forward, and raised his hands for calm. 'The time for celebration is not here yet, I am afraid. Having seen the gravity of the situation with my own eyes' – and he gave Tullus a nod of appreciation – 'the only way to placate the legionaries is to agree to their demands, in principle at least. I can see that you like that as little as I do, but there are few options open to me. I propose sending a letter to the mutineers' leaders.'

Germanicus threw a look at Tubero, who all but preened himself. 'Legate Tubero came up with the idea: a letter purporting to have Tiberius' authority. It will grant discharge to legionaries who have served for twenty years and longer. Soldiers with sixteen or more years of service will receive a conditional discharge; their only obligation will be to fight – if there is need – in the four years following their release from the legions. Their official donative will be doubled. Legionaries' pay will also be increased, by a half.'

Tullus saw his own disbelief mirrored in almost every centurion's face. The mutineers weren't stupid, he thought. Tiberius was known for his steady, cautious nature. He wasn't the type to offer such generous terms, without any fight whatsoever. Was anyone prepared to say so, though?

Germanicus was an observant man. He sensed their unhappiness. 'What is it? Speak up,' he ordered, his gaze roaming from face to face. They settled on Tullus. 'Well?'

Tullus took a deep breath. 'They won't fall for it, sir. I have no idea how the emperor thinks, the gods bless him forever, but I doubt that he would capitulate to such demands in the first instance. The mutineers will think the same.' Tullus could hear no voices agreeing with him, and his guts churned.

Germanicus' lips tightened, but he uttered no rebuke. Beside him, Caecina was scowling and Tubero's cheeks were marked by red pinpricks of fury. Germanicus eyed the centurions again. 'Are any of you of the same opinion?'

'I am, sir.' Surprising Tullus yet again, it was Cordus who had spoken. 'They'll be expecting to haggle over their demands, not just have them agreed to straight away.'

There were some rumbles of agreement, but few centurions would meet Germanicus' eyes. It wasn't surprising, thought Tullus, hoping that he hadn't done the wrong thing. Only fools disagreed with high-ranking officials, let alone the emperor's heir.

'Can you offer me any other immediate choices?' asked Germanicus.

A resounding silence followed, broken only by the drunken shouts of legionaries outside the principia.

We could sit and wait, thought Tullus. Send for the legions upriver, in Germania Superior. The local auxiliaries could even be used to put down the rebellion. He had had enough, however, of speaking up, of offering himself as the sacrificial sheep. While Germanicus held Tullus in some regard, Tubero still had it in for him, and was more than capable of turning Caecina, and perhaps even Germanicus himself, against him. Tullus had spent too long in the wilderness to risk losing the regard of his newfound, powerful benefactor, so he stitched his lip.

'In that case, we shall proceed with the letter,' declared Germanicus. 'May the gods ensure that it puts an end to this madness.'

The divine help that Germanicus had wished for did not materialise. Some hours after the letter had been delivered to the mutineers' leaders under a flag of truce, a vast crowd of legionaries assembled outside the principia. Many were drunk, and all were irate. Shouting that Germanicus should come forth – he did, with Tullus and his full century as protection – they destroyed his letter, calling it a forgery. Their demands were repeated, and this time, the legionaries threatened, they were 'to be looked at with the respect they deserve'. In other words, Bony Face shouted, a settlement had better be forthcoming within a day, or Germanicus could expect to have the principia burned down around his noble ears. With him inside, the twins added, to a swelling roar of approval.

The furious mutineers didn't wait for a reply. Their intimidating threats hung in the air as they marched off.

'Curse them to Hades! Their insolence is unforgivable,' snarled Germanicus. He glanced at Tullus, who was quick to keep his expression blank. There could be no 'I told you so' attitude with someone so high-ranking.

'You were right,' admitted Germanicus after a long moment. 'They're no fools.'

'As you say, sir,' replied Tullus in a neutral tone. 'We'll make them pay in the end.'

'Indeed, but other matters are more pressing,' muttered Germanicus. 'What to do now?'

Tullus wasn't sure if the question was rhetorical, and discretion was the more prudent choice. He said nothing.

'I could promise them an increase in pay, to be given on their return to barracks,' said Germanicus. He shot a look at Tullus. 'Would that work?'

Caught by Germanicus' penetrating stare, Tullus *had* to answer. Hating the fact that he was a poor liar, he answered, 'Men like to feel coin in their hands, sir, not listen to the promise of it days into the future.'

'I am the imperial governor,' said Germanicus, his jaw hardening. 'I'll not roll over to them, d'you hear?'

'I understand, sir,' said Tullus, thinking: you *have* to give them something tangible, or more blood will be spilled.

'Take me inside,' ordered Germanicus. 'I must reflect on the best course of action.'

'Sir.' Tullus led the way, hoping that inspiration of a better kind would strike Germanicus before the mutineers' patience ran out.

Tullus' hopes were in vain. Whether through pride or inability to come up with a better option, Germanicus went ahead with his suggestion to the soldiers that an increase in pay would be paid when they marched back to their camps. Tullus was ordered to deliver the offer to the mutineers the following morning. He wasn't surprised when Bony Face and his fellows rejected it out of hand. Red-faced with fury, Bony Face whipped his followers into a frenzy. Insults and then stones were thrown. In a calm voice, Tullus had his men close up and draw their swords. A stand-off developed, with both sides nervous and ready to fight, but neither quite prepared to begin the bloodletting. Tullus wanted to pull his soldiers back into the safety of the headquarters, but he had to get an answer for Germanicus first. 'Will you accept the terms?' he called out.

Bony Face stalked from the protection of his fellows, closing to within a dozen paces of Tullus' men's shields. 'Tell your *governor*,' he hissed, uncaring of the sword tips pointing at his heart, 'that he had best come up with an offer that we actually *believe*. He's got until sunset.'

'Or what?' demanded Tullus in a bullish tone.

'Or I lead four legions against the principia,' Bony Face retorted. 'See how long you can hold out then.'

Germanicus was incandescent with rage when Tullus relayed the mutineers' response. 'The dog said *what*?' Germanicus' bellow was as loud as a centurion's best parade roar.

Tullus repeated what he'd been told and, difficult though it was, continued to meet Germanicus' gaze. 'You have until sunset to give them your answer.'

'Until sunset? I, the imperial governor, have to reply to *that* rabble? I, the emperor's *nephew*, have to bandy words with scum who aren't fit to polish my boots?' Germanicus emitted a short, high-pitched laugh of disbelief. His eyes, sparking with anger, moved from Tullus to the other officers present. Most, Tubero included, were quick to drop their gaze.

'It's a terrible state of affairs, sir,' ventured Caecina.

'Jupiter on high, it's insufferable!' shouted Germanicus, pacing up and down. 'Intolerable!'

No one dared answer him.

If only they had until the following morning, thought Tullus. Under the cover of darkness, he could have led a select group of men to assassinate Bony Face and the other ringleaders. While dangerous, the mission wouldn't have been impossible. In daylight, however, it would border on suicidal. Valuing his soldiers' lives more than anything, Tullus decided not to say a word. Germanicus was no fool; he *had* to realise that his back was to the wall.

'What can we do?' demanded Germanicus, his eyes still roving around the tent.

There was a sudden interest in belt buckles and the toes of men's boots. Uneasy coughs vied with throats that were being cleared. Tullus' pride wouldn't let him bend his head, and he cursed inwardly as Germanicus honed in on him.

'Do we lead an attack on the ringleaders, and cut off all the Hydra's heads?' Close up, Germanicus' great height was even more pronounced. He glared down at Tullus.

'I will if you order me to, sir,' said Tullus in a monotone.

Germanicus scowled. 'You don't think it's a good idea?'

'We're too few, sir. Even if we made it to wherever the ringleaders are, they would tear us apart. Like as not, the mob would then turn on the head-quarters.' Tullus wasn't sure about the last part, but he was *not* going to offer his men up as sacrificial sheep on the altar of Germanicus' pride.

Germanicus considered his words, and then he let out a long breath. 'In darkness, we might have succeeded, but not during daylight.'

'That would be my thought, sir,' said Tullus, hiding his relief.

Germanicus stalked off, coming to a halt before Tubero. 'It's rare for you to be silent, legate. What have you to offer?'

Tubero puffed out his chest. 'I'd be happy to lead an attack on the ringleaders, sir, but, as you say, it would be too dangerous.'

Germanicus made a little sound of derision and walked on. 'Anyone else?'

Tullus' frustration rose as no one said anything for several moments. Why should it be down to him to speak? Officers far more senior than he were present. Nephew of the emperor or no, imperial governor or no, Germanicus *had* to be told.

In the end, Caecina had the balls. 'The way I see it, sir, we only have one option.'

Germanicus whirled around, his face taut with emotion. 'What is that?'

'The mutineers must be paid their money, sir,' said Caecina. 'In my opinion, that is the only thing they'll accept.'

'The *only* thing? The *only thing*?' Germanicus' face was purple with rage; the veins stood out on his neck.

'Yes, sir,' said Caecina, looking nervous.

Germanicus raised his bunched fists to the heavens and a drawn-out *Ahhhhh* of anger and frustration left his lips.

Everyone watched; no one dared speak.

'If we are all slain, the mutiny will continue.' Germanicus' tone was flat. 'Restoring order is imperative, even if it means giving into the mutineers.'

Heads nodded; voices muttered, 'Yes, sir,' and, 'Agreed, sir.' Tullus gave silent thanks to the gods.

'I doubt that I have enough funds to pay every soldier in four legions what he's "owed",' said Germanicus with a bitter laugh. His eyes moved to Caecina, and on to the legates present. 'I shall have to ask for a loan.'

Tullus watched sidelong as the senior officers fell over themselves to offer their assistance. Germanicus won't forget this, he thought. For an imperial governor and royal family member to have to beg financial aid of his subordinates was a humiliation of the first order.

'Good,' said Germanicus, a slight inclination of his head the only sign of gratitude. 'From the sounds of it, we shall have enough coin to pacify the rapacious dogs.' His gaze stopped on Tullus. 'Will the legions return to their bases now?'

'I'd wager so, sir.'

'That's all we need for now.' There was a short pause, and then Germanicus added in an icy voice, 'Justice can be served later.'

Chapter X

◫◫◫

'Gods, how I hate this shithole!' Segestes' voice carried, as it was meant to, some distance from the longhouse he'd been confined to since his arrival. 'Donar take Arminius, the flea-ridden mongrel!'

Arminius, standing on the grass close by, laughed. So did Maelo and the score of his warriors who were there, stretching their muscles. It was their habit each morning to exercise and train with their spears and swords – not something most men did, but they were the cream of Arminius' followers.

'Do you want me to shut him up?' called one of the men standing watch by Segestes' door.

'Leave him be. I like hearing his complaints,' Arminius replied, causing more amusement. 'They're a constant reminder that I did the right thing. If I'd let him go to Inguiomerus, we would have four thousand fewer spears to call on in the spring.'

'I'm sick of the sound of him.' Thusnelda came bustling from the direction of the woods, a basket of fresh-picked mushrooms balanced on her hip. 'You can hear his voice half a mile away.'

'How can you say such things about your father?' asked Arminius with mock seriousness. He dodged away from the clout she swung at him.

'I respect my father, but I cannot abide him whingeing from dawn till dusk. Couldn't you keep him further away?'

Arminius had been keen from the outset to have Segestes close to hand, the better to monitor the guards he'd set upon his prisoner. Despite his jokes, several days of Segestes' unrelenting, high-volume complaints meant that he too was growing weary of his prisoner. 'I suppose we could put him in one of the houses near the edge of the settlement. Just for you,' he said, trying to slip an arm around Thusnelda's waist.

She dodged away from him with surprising agility. 'Get off! Don't expect to lay a hand on me until it's done.'

Arminius scowled after her, as Maelo chortled. The others were amused too, but they hid it a little better. Arminius pretended not to hear any of them. Allowing himself to be the butt of an occasional joke – thereby proving he was as human as the next man – was no bad thing. 'How about a plate of fried mushrooms instead?' he called out.

'Move him first,' came the sharp retort. A moment later, the door of their longhouse slammed.

Fresh laughter erupted from Maelo and his men, and Arminius said, 'You heard the woman. I'm going to starve *and* suffer from a constant erection if we don't move Segestes.'

'Best get it done soon then,' declared Maelo. 'I can see the bulge in your trousers from here.'

As his men's mirth increased further, Arminius let himself chuckle. 'We'll move him after we've trained.'

They had been exercising for some time – running circuits of the settlement, lifting great sections of tree trunk, sparring with swords – when Arminius' attention was drawn to the path that led westward, towards the Rhenus. Small boys and girls, and the pups that followed them, were dancing about what had to be a party of visitors. How was it, he wondered, that children were always drawn to the newcomer?

It was beneath his station to go and see who had arrived. There was no need anyway, for people tended to converge on the open central area where he and his warriors were gathered. Nonetheless, Arminius' attention strayed from the task at hand, allowing Maelo to land a couple of painful blows on him with the flat of his blade. 'Enough!' Arminius cried.

'Take your eye off an enemy, and he'll have you,' warned Maelo with a leer.

'Piss off,' retorted Arminius, grimacing back. 'I can take you any time.'

Wiping his brow with the arm of his tunic, he waited for the party to reach them. Instead of sheathing his sword, he let it dangle by his side. Innocent enough, given the training men around him, but also a veiled threat if needs be. Fifty paces off, Arminius recognised an unruly mop of blond hair that could only belong to one man he knew. Cupping a hand to his mouth, he yelled, 'Segimundus!'

A hand was raised in acknowledgement, and Arminius grinned. 'I haven't seen him in years, maybe since the ambush even.'

'A little odd that he appears so soon after we've imprisoned his father, don't you think?' muttered Maelo.

'Don't be so suspicious,' chided Arminius. 'Segimundus stands with *us*. Rallying the tribes would have been much harder without his support. Remember too what he did to Varus.' Arminius wasn't sure if that last detail was true – no one had seen who had mutilated the Roman general's body – but rumour then and since had Segimundus as the perpetrator.

'Blood runs thicker than water,' rumbled Maelo with a frown.

'Yet my brother Flavus and I cannot abide each other. I'd save your life before his a thousand times,' retorted Arminius, challenge in his tone. 'And Segimundus was with us in the forest when Segestes was nowhere to be seen, wasn't he?'

'Aye.'

'Well, then. Set aside your distrust. He'll want to visit his father, I wager, but I'm the person he's come to speak with.' Sliding his sword into the scabbard, Arminius took a few steps towards the approaching party. 'Welcome, Segimundus! It has been too long.'

'The years pass swiftly, do they not?' Segimundus, an imposing figure in a priest's dark green hooded robe, dismounted and came to meet Arminius, arms outstretched. They embraced.

'It's good to see you,' said Arminius, pulling back to stare at Segimundus.

'And you. Are those grey hairs I see in your beard?'

Arminius gave his chin a rueful stroke. 'There are a few, perhaps. You've got the same, I see.'

'None of us can stop the march of time.' Segimundus made a solemn face. 'They add to my authority, don't you think?'

'As if you ever needed that. Men always listen to a priest.'

'Not so. It takes more than a green robe or, for that matter, a chieftainship to win men's hearts and minds. You know that as well as I do.'

'Aye, perhaps.' Arminius smiled. 'The timing of your visit couldn't be better. I will need your help again in the coming months.'

'I thought it would be useful for us to take counsel together. Is it true what they say – that Germanicus is going to wage a new campaign against us?'

'It's all that the legionaries talk about in the taverns and whorehouses of Vetera. Eight legions and a similar number of auxiliaries he'll lead over the river, or so they say. What's heartening is that there's been a mutiny in two of the camps of recent days. Germanicus will have sorted it out before the spring, but he might not be able to rely on some of his soldiers – and that will help us.'

Segimundus' expression remained dark. 'Even if some of his troops are untrustworthy, he'll have upwards of fifty thousand soldiers.'

'I know,' said Arminius with a grim nod. 'If they are not to lay waste to the entire land, every tribe between here and the river will be needed for the fight. Will you help?'

'Of course! Anything to keep Rome's hobnailed boot from our necks.'

Arminius noticed for the first time the lines of weariness streaking Segimundus' face. 'Forgive me – you must be weary from your journey. Come. You will lodge with me and Thusnelda. Maelo will see to accommodation for your followers.'

'Gratitude.' Segimundus' eyes cast about the settlement before returning to Arminius. 'Word reached me that my father is also here.'

Arminius remembered Maelo's suspicions, but could spy no trace of guile in Segimundus' face. 'That is true. He came a few days since, pretending he had come to see Thusnelda. In fact his purpose was to visit Inguiomerus, and to turn him against me.'

'I'd heard that Inguiomerus had joined your cause – fine work on your part. What makes you so certain that my father planned to bring him back into Rome's fold?'

'He told me as much,' Arminius replied with a snort. 'As you know, Inguiomerus is a tricky customer. It's taken years for him to shift allegiances. I am not about to let my hard work be undone by your father. Segestes has been my captive since, but every comfort has been provided for him, never fear.'

A faint line marked Segimundus' brow. 'How long do you plan to hold him prisoner?'

'Until the end of next year's campaigning season.'

'By which time his counsel to Inguiomerus will be useless.'

'Aye.' Arminius searched Segimundus' face again for an indication of his feelings, but could detect nothing that indicated his visitor was angry with him.

After a long moment, Segimundus said, 'What you've done is for the best.'

Despite himself, Arminius' breath came out long and slow. 'I'm glad you see it that way.'

'How else could I take it?' Segimundus' grip on his arm was solid. He added, 'You won't hold it against me if I visit him?'

'Please – you don't have to ask. Spend as long with your father as you wish,' said Arminius with an expansive gesture. It might keep the old dog quiet for a time, he thought, which would be a gods-sent blessing for everyone.

Segimundus' visit to his father was brief, pleasing Arminius. He turned out to be a pleasant house guest as well, charming Thusnelda with his compliments by day, and content by night to listen to, and comment on, Arminius' plans. The warriors also took to Segimundus, relishing the unusual company of a priest who wrestled *and* drank.

On the second night, Arminius took Segimundus to the sacred grove. Barley beer and blankets kept the worst of the chill away during the long, unnerving hours of darkness. Arminius saw nothing, and dreamed less during the fitful periods of sleep that came to him. Creaking branches, wind rustling the last leaves on the trees, the hooting of an owl, mice skittering about in the undergrowth – these and Segimundus' pacing were the only sounds he heard, and could not be assigned to Donar. Hugely frustrated by the time dawn had come, Arminius had given up hope that a sign would be revealed to them. Red-eyed, belly rumbling and muscles stiff from inaction, he motioned to Segimundus that they should go.

Segimundus shook his head – no.

Arminius was about to ask why, but Segimundus motioned for him to remain silent.

Krrruk.

The hair on the back of Arminius' neck prickled. Only one bird made that sound.

Krrruk. Krrruk.

He turned his head to see not one but two ravens alighting in the largest of the oak trees that ringed the sacred space. The birds were common enough in the area, but he had never seen one in *this* place. When first one and then the other raven flew down to the rough-hewn stone altars that sat in the centre of the circle, Arminius thought his heart would stop.

The birds began tapping to and fro on the stone with their powerful beaks. Of course, thought Arminius. The sacrifices practised here meant that there would be congealed blood, and perhaps more, on the altars – appealing food. Nonetheless, it felt god-sent for the ravens to arrive when he and Segimundus were present. It seemed that Segimundus had drawn the same conclusion, for his lips were moving in fervent prayer.

Arminius squeezed his eyes shut and did the same. Great Donar, I thank you for this sign of your favour. I will have a fine ram killed here in your honour before the sun sets. In return, I ask for your help in uniting the tribes. If the Romans are to be defeated once and for all, they *must* follow me to battle. Let my words, and those of Segimundus, fall on the chieftains' ears as spring rain on young barley, and when the time comes, let us reap Roman legionaries as we did for you in the forest.

Krrruk. Krrruk.

Startled, Arminius looked up. The nearest raven had cocked its head to the side; a red string of ichor trailed from its beak on to the altar. One beady black eye regarded him, as if to say, 'This is my price.' With a flick of its neck, the blood clot was thrown up in the air. It flashed, crimson red, for a heartbeat, before disappearing down the raven's throat.

Krrruk. The satisfied note in the bird's voice was distinct. *Krrruk.*

Krrruk. Its partner replied in kind from the other altar.

Donar *did* regard his mission as worthy, thought Arminius. Surely he could take that meaning from what had just transpired? He glanced at Segimundus, whose eyes were still closed, whose lips yet moved in reverential prayer. Eager that he should be seen in the same light by the god, Arminius bent his head and did likewise. He remained in this humble position for some time. Even when his knees began to ache, and his lower back to complain, he did not stir.

The dull flap of wing beats signalled the ravens' departure.

'They have gone,' said Segimundus a moment later.

Arminius studied the priest's face. 'Were they sent by Donar?'

'Aye.' Conviction throbbed in Segimundus' voice.

'And the meaning of their presence?'

'I cannot yet be certain.'

'They must have been a good omen.'

'Perhaps. I will have to think on it.'

To show his disappointment would appear weak. Although he wanted to shake Segimundus and demand an immediate interpretation, Arminius did nothing more than nod solemnly. 'I understand.'

'It's time to return. I would rest, and afterwards visit my father.'

'Of course.' Irritated as well now, Arminius made a show of collecting up the vessels that had contained their beer, and folding his blanket. In his eyes, Donar had shown approval for his plans, and so, during their silent walk back to the settlement, Segimundus' refusal to comment niggled away at him, like an itch that cannot be scratched.

Did the priest have another motive?

Chapter XI

⌐⌐⌐

Germanicus did not deign to show his face as the money was presented by Tullus and his men to the cheering mutineers. Fighting broke out the instant the mule-drawn wagon had left Tullus' control; legionaries scrambled aboard, seizing money bags or slitting them with their daggers. Showers of *denarii* and sestertii rained down on the frenzied crowd as men hurled handfuls of them at their fellows.

Tullus looked on in disgust. 'They're a disgrace to the uniform,' he muttered to Fenestela.

'If they'd been paid what was due, this whole situation mightn't have happened,' said Fenestela.

It was an uncomfortable truth, thought Tullus, but rebelling against their commanders, not to mention murdering centurions, went too far against the grain. Military discipline had to be maintained, or the world would descend into bloody chaos.

Retribution would also have to be taken for what had happened.

Tullus wasn't looking forward to that.

The day after the legionaries had been paid, Germanicus ordered the Fifth and Twenty-First back to Vetera. Bony Face and the rest agreed, bringing the mutiny to an end, and in theory allowing normal life to resume. It didn't for Tullus. The brutal and unexpected events had tainted his love of the legions, for so many years his main reason for existence. He wasn't alone – the mutiny had had a profound impact on everyone. The abiding sense of order, a reassuring and solid part of army life, had been destroyed.

Its absence was palpable everywhere, from the surly looks cast at officers by the legionaries, to the units lacking centurions and the waste that still littered the avenues. The rubbish could be cleaned up, and the camp abandoned, but it would take far more than that to restore the sense of trust that had been lost between officers and men. Tullus wasn't sure if it could be done at all.

To his relief, Degmar had returned from over the river to lurk in one of the rough 'boarding house' tents outside the camp. His reappearance was an enormous relief to Tullus. Degmar brought with him a rumour – heard from an itinerant trader – that one of the three eagles taken during Arminius' ambush had been given to the Marsi tribe, his people. This intrigued Tullus, and he resolved to tell Caecina or even Germanicus about it when the opportunity arose.

During the sixty-plus-mile journey to Vetera, which took place with little of the usual singing and banter among the legionaries, Tullus had plenty of time to brood. There was no doubt that most of the slain officers had been unpopular taskmasters. A number *had* been corrupt. A few had perhaps deserved to die for what they had done, but no more, and *not* at the hands of common soldiers. So many men had been complicit in the killings that it would have been impossible to punish them all, but if life were to return to normal, action had to be taken against some. That meant the ringleaders: men such as Bony Face, Fat Nose and the twins.

Germanicus had been right, Tullus concluded. Mouldy apples had to be removed from the barrel before the decay spread. That way, the other fruit would last for months. The rotten items in this case were men, not fruit, but the harsh principle was the same. Bony Face and his cronies would have to die. Life, as Tullus said to Fenestela, was often like that. Brutal.

Back in Vetera, it was even more apparent that the canker's excision needed to be sooner rather than later. The men of Tullus' century, whom he bound to him with a mixture of regular training and supplies of wine, remained solid. Things were different in the other centuries in his cohort, however. Bony Face and his cronies continued to foment unrest. Other mutineers did the same in other cohorts in the Fifth, and among the ranks of the Twenty-First. The discontent and ill discipline could have been overlooked in a few units perhaps, but spread over two entire legions they were a huge cause for concern.

The dawn trumpets, which were supposed to send every man tumbling from his blankets, were ignored. Routine tasks such as the felling of trees and transporting of firewood were not completed, or took twice as long as normal. Instead of patrolling the camp's battlements as they were supposed to, sentries stayed in the watchtowers – dozing, according to some. Junior officers were disobeyed; even centurions found it hard to see their orders followed through. Tullus didn't like to admit it, but he wasn't in full control of his new command, the cohort previously led by Septimius. This didn't weaken Tullus' determination to establish control, though. Restoring him to his former rank was a mark of considerable favour from Germanicus, and such chances didn't often come a man's way.

Rumours abounded, of uprisings by legions elsewhere in the empire, of legates murdered in their beds, and of Germanicus' auxiliaries being sent to Vetera, their mission to exact vengeance upon the mutinous legionaries. Gossip gleaned from the traders in the settlement outside the camp spoke of unrest among the German tribes on the far side of the river. Even the gods seemed to be unhappy. Winds and heavy rain flattened the last of the summer's crops before they could be harvested, and on a local farm, a grotesque pair of calves, joined at the chest, were cut out of the mother that had died trying to birth them.

Under normal circumstances, such apparent divine intervention would have cowed the soldiers, most of whom were as superstitious as the ordinary man in the street. Now, though, it fuelled their resentment. The final proof that action had to be taken – as if Tullus needed evidence of that – came when news arrived from Ara Ubiorum, the camp that was still home to the First and Twentieth Legions, who had mutinied alongside the Fifth and Twenty-First.

Tullus was at the quartermaster's office, demanding equipment needed by his unit, when word reached him. One of the quartermaster's staff, a veteran with fewer teeth in his lower jaw than a newborn lamb, came barging through the door. 'Jupiter's cock, have you heard the news?' He took in Tullus' presence, and looked discomfited. A hasty salute followed. 'Sorry, sir, I didn't see you there.'

'No matter.' Tullus was pleased; the soldier had shown him the respect that he was due, which was more than could currently be said of many others. He indicated the quartermaster and the rest of his staff. 'We all want to know what's happened. Speak.'

'A ship's just come downriver from Ara Ubiorum, sir. Things have gone to hell there over the last ten days and more. Germanicus was away, placating the legions of Germania Superior, when a senatorial embassy arrived from Rome. By the time Germanicus had returned, the soldiers had panicked. They assumed that the embassy was there to order the deaths of their leaders, so they stormed the principia and seized their legions' eagles. Germanicus' wife and baby son were taken captive for a time.'

Stupid fools, thought Tullus, closing his eyes. 'Were they harmed?'

'No, sir, thank the gods,' replied Toothless. 'The soldiers love Agrippina and Little Boots too much to do them any injury. When they were released, Germanicus sent them away for their own safety to Augusta Treverorum, with auxiliaries as an escort. It seems that the legionaries were shocked to the core that he should entrust his family to the care of non-citizens, loyal though they are. When Germanicus addressed the troops the next day, and harangued them about their duty to Rome, they capitulated at once. The mutiny's ringleaders were rounded up and handed over to the legions' legates.'

'They were executed, I assume?' asked Tullus, dreading how many would have to die here, in Vetera.

A shadow passed over Toothless' face. 'About a hundred, they say, sir. It seems the prisoners were forced up on to platforms in front of their entire legion. A tribune called out to the troops, asking if each man was guilty or not. If the answer was yes, he was pushed off the platform into their midst, to be slain by his comrades.'

The savage scene was easy to picture. Tullus could almost hear the men's pleas for mercy, and the animal roars of their fellows as they called for blood. 'Is the same to happen here?' he demanded. 'Did the messenger say?'

Hobs clacked off the floor as Toothless shuffled his feet. 'I don't know, sir.'

I do, thought Tullus, with a sinking feeling. Germanicus couldn't – wouldn't – punish two of the once-mutinous legions while letting the other two off. Ordering the quartermaster to deliver his supplies by the next day or face his wrath, he took his leave. It was time to speak with the cohort's other officers, and his men.

The news was spreading faster than a fire started in a hay barn. Everywhere Tullus could see, knots of legionaries were talking in lowered voices. Men were moving between barrack blocks, calling out to their comrades. Resentful looks from soldiers had become common of recent times, but it concerned Tullus to note more than a dozen during the short walk to his quarters. He even heard one insult – 'Cocksucking centurion!' – but by the time he'd wheeled, the culprit had vanished inside his barracks. Tullus considered storming in to find him, but judged it wasn't worth the risk. There was no way of knowing if he would succeed in apprehending the right man, and his intervention might aggravate the situation. He didn't want to be the one who relit the fire of mutiny, which was an outcome that felt all too possible.

Tullus could sense more ill will in the faces that stared at him from the barrack blocks' tiny windows, and in the insolent way that legionaries moved out of his path, or saluted just a moment too late. Trouble was brewing. Violence was inevitable. Whether the blood that flowed would be that of officers or ordinary soldiers – or both – Tullus had no idea. It was clear, however, that the thorny issue of dealing with those who had mutinied could no longer be avoided.

*   *   *

Somehow ten days dragged by in this uneasy fashion. Each morning, Caecina called together the senior officers under his command, including the centurions and standard-bearers, and ordered them to report. Everyone, including Tullus, had the same thing to say. An odd status quo had developed in the camp, whereby the officers of the Fifth and Twenty-First did not demand much of their men. In return, it seemed, the legionaries' behaviour did not worsen further. The uncomfortable situation was akin, Tullus decided, to having an unpredictable, large dog living in the house. Things were fine while the dog didn't feel threatened – but when it did, it was liable to bite. Living with it meant walking around on tiptoes, always looking over one's shoulder. In his mind, there was but one way to deal with such an animal, and that wasn't by talking in a sweet voice and patting the brute on the head.

Caecina was prepared to let the uneasy state of affairs continue, however. Without authority from Germanicus, he said, he had no mandate to take action, drastic or no. 'I have sent messengers asking for guidance,' he told his officers. 'Until word comes back from the governor, we will do nothing.'

There were grumbling comments about being murdered in their beds, but Caecina's word was law, so the centurions kept their heads down and prayed to whatever gods they held dear.

Tullus didn't pray. He worked on the soldiers of his new century – Septimius' former one – keeping them busy with training manoeuvres and long marches. When they complained that other men in the cohort weren't having to do the same, Tullus said that that was because he was turning *them* into the best soldiers in the whole cursed legion. Using a mixture of flattery, fresh meat and wine, Tullus jollied them along the way an experienced salesman softens up a potential customer. It worked – just – but he knew that his men wouldn't listen to him forever. All he could do about those in the cohort who'd been prominent in the mutiny was to order Fenestela, Piso, Vitellius and more than a dozen others to keep an eye on them. Keen to keep the soldiers who'd been in the Eighteenth with him, Tullus had managed to have them moved from his former century to his new one.

It was an exhausting, stressful existence. Every few days, Tullus allowed himself an outlet for his tensions, heading into the settlement late at night, after his soldiers had retired. His destination was the Ox and Plough, his favourite watering hole, and where Artio, the girl he'd rescued during Arminius' ambush, lived. With no possibility of looking after her himself, Tullus had entrusted Artio to the care of the tavern's owner, Sirona, a feisty Gaulish woman with a heart of gold.

Tullus had no children, and over the previous five years Artio had become as dear to him as a daughter. It was apt that she'd been called after a goddess whose favourite animal was a bear, he often thought, because she was fond of sweet things, in particular honey. She was more spirited than was perhaps wise for a girl, something he was secretly proud of. Her temper was ferocious too – gods help the man who weds her, Sirona was fond of saying.

Under normal circumstances, Tullus visited Artio often when he was off duty, but of course it hadn't been possible during the uncertain time since his return from the summer camp. A peek into her bedroom, a tiny chamber over the inn, was the best he could manage each time he visited late.

Eleven nights after the arrival of the news from Ara Ubiorum of the mutineers' executions, he was doing just this. Artio was fast asleep, her long brown hair trailing behind her on the pillow, her dog Scylax dozing on the floor by the bed. Tullus studied her for a time, his heart swelling. Where does time go? he thought, feeling old. She was a tiny little thing when I found her. He glanced at Sirona, who had crept up with him, and whispered, 'She's growing fast.'

'Cherish the time when she's young,' replied Sirona with a wistful look in her eyes. 'One moment they're babes, and the next, they are adults.'

It was hard to believe that Sirona had three full-grown sons, Tullus reflected, admiring her still-comely features and generous curves. He had made several advances to her over the years, each of which she had rebuffed. 'I've been made a widow once,' she had said every time, her smile taking the sting from her words. 'I'm not about to be one to the army as well.'

Tullus was distracted at this point by a head butting against his leg, and a tail swooshing the air. Grinning, he reached down to pat Scylax, who had padded out of her room. 'Good boy.' When he'd saved Artio during the ambush, he had also rescued a mongrel pup, whom she had named Scylax. Girl and dog had been constant companions ever since.

At that moment, Artio's eyes opened. She took in Tullus' shape at her door, and hurled herself from her blankets into his arms. 'Tullus!' she squealed.

Tullus gave her a fierce hug, then set her back on her feet and gave her a mock stern look. 'It's well past your bedtime.'

'You shouldn't stand outside my room gossiping with Sirona then,' came the tart reply.

'True enough. We might as well have a talk now that you're awake,' said Tullus, ignoring Sirona's disapproving look. 'You have to get back into bed, though.' He perched on a stool, drinking in her chatter of new sandals, the wild birds that Scylax had caught, and what she had got up to with her friends. After the camp's toxic atmosphere, this was a breath of fresh air. At length, however, Artio began to yawn. Kissing her farewell, and promising to return soon, he gave Scylax a final pat and left them both to sleep.

Placing his feet with care, so that his hobs didn't clash off the floorboards, Tullus made his way to the head of the precipitous stairs that led back to the inn. The noise of the tavern's customers, which he'd been aware of in the background, returned to the fore. He was halfway down the staircase when the front door opened and shut with a bang. 'Tullus! Are you here?' Despite the clamour, he recognised Fenestela's voice.

Sudden dread gripped Tullus. Had the troops mutinied again?

He hurried down into the main room, catching Fenestela's eye with a casual wave of his arm. Plenty of the patrons were ordinary legionaries; whatever the reason for Fenestela's arrival, there was no point in drawing attention.

Fenestela reached his side in ten paces. 'It's good you're here.'

'Where else would I be?' replied Tullus, adding for the sake of those who were nearby, 'Need some wine?'

'My thanks.' Fenestela leaned in close, and muttered, 'Caecina has called a meeting. Every centurion, every optio, *tesserarius* and *signifer* in the two legions is to meet him at the principia.'

'In the morning?'

'Now.'

If Fenestela's face hadn't been so grim, Tullus would have thought he was joking. He wondered if it had been wise to come out in his tunic, with only a dagger for protection. 'At this time of night?'

Fenestela placed his lips against Tullus' ear. 'A messenger arrived from Germanicus not an hour ago.'

Despite the two cups of wine he'd had, Tullus suddenly felt stone cold sober.

Tullus was well used to wandering the straight, wide avenues of the camp in the dark, using a torch to guide his way. He wasn't accustomed to creeping along them in the pitch black, trying not to be heard by a soul. However, Caecina's orders had been unequivocal – his officers were to arrive at the principia without being seen. As he and Fenestela neared their destination, they had several false alarms, and laid hands to their daggers. To their relief, those they encountered were other officers making their way to the meeting. Apart from the sentries at the camp gates – who had assumed Tullus and Fenestela were returning from a night out – the ordinary soldiers appeared to be asleep.

At the principia's entrance, members of Caecina's bodyguard demanded their names, ranks and units. A second officer had to vouch for each man before he was admitted. This additional security measure was something that Tullus had never encountered before. 'Whatever Caecina says is going to be bad,' he said to Fenestela.

After the blackness outside, the light in the headquarters' main hall was dazzling. Hundreds of oil lamps – on stands, hanging from chains, placed in the wall niches – lit up the room almost as bright as day. Light glittered off the eagles and standards of the two legions which had been carried from the shrine and placed against the back wall. Caecina had engineered this because the emblems would stir his officers' emotions, thought Tullus, his heart swelling at the memory of his last visit here, some months before Arminius' ambush. The standards represented the courage, pride and status of each unit, each cohort, each legion. Men would do almost anything to keep them safe. Losing an arm or a leg, even dying, was preferable to seeing one's standard taken by the enemy. Gods, but Tullus knew that; he lived with the shame of it every day. Eyeing the Fifth's eagle, he tried to relish the small amount of pride he took from serving in its legion.

Hundreds of men were already present, and more were entering with each moment. Each legion contained sixty centuries, every one of which had a centurion, optio, tesserarius and signifer. When the musicians were also taken into account – Tullus saw them gathering too – there would be more than five hundred soldiers present. He spied Cordus and Victor, and their cronies, most of whom acknowledged him. Victor didn't, of course.

Caecina emerged from the shrine with his legates and tribunes, and as they moved to stand by the eagles, silence fell. Despite the hour, the governor and his companions wore the full regalia of their office. Winks and flashes of light bounced off Caecina's armour, which had been burnished to a mirror-like sheen. He looked magnificent, from head to toe the important man he was, and radiating the authority to issue the harshest of orders.

'Is everyone here?' Caecina's voice carried across the hall to the entrance, where a dozen of his bodyguards stood. Receiving a nod, he ordered the doors shut. His eyes raked the gathering. 'In these sad and uncertain times, you are the only soldiers I can trust in all of the Fifth and Twenty-First. I have called you together to advise you of Germanicus' letter, which arrived not long since. He will be travelling here soon with a strong escort.' Men began to exchange relieved looks, but Caecina's expression grew sombre.

'There's more. Before his arrival, Germanicus expects me to have executed anyone disloyal, else he will do it himself.'

'I knew it,' said Tullus to Fenestela. Part of him was relieved. Getting the brutal deed out of the way would restore order, and allow life to continue. Part of him felt like the worst sort of criminal, however, left with no alternative but to murder a comrade.

'Two grim choices lie before me – and you,' Caecina announced. 'We can complete the task, or wait until Germanicus comes to do it for us. I don't have to tell you which is the better option. We deal with this tomorrow. By "deal with", I mean, we kill the foremost mutineers.'

His words sank in for three, six, ten uneasy heartbeats.

Tullus cleared his throat. 'Who is to die, sir?'

Men stepped aside, both to see who he was, and to allow Caecina a view of him. It felt uncomfortable, and Tullus thought: we're all in this together, you dogs.

'A pertinent question, Tullus,' said Caecina. 'The simple answer is that each of you, from senior centurion down to musician, has to decide on the guiltiest soldiers in your unit. Talk about it now, come to an agreement and compile a list. Some centuries will have more disloyal men than others – that cannot be helped. What's vital is that we cut every dead branch from the tree with one pass of our blades.'

Our blades? thought Tullus, bitterness pouring through him. You won't be bloodying your noble hands, oh no – that's for us poor fools.

'When is it to be done, sir?' asked Cordus.

'At midday, while the men are preparing their meal. You will have time beforehand to instruct those of your soldiers who are to aid you in this.' Caecina's smile was brittle, cold. 'Questions?'

There were none.

'When I return in one hour, you will have your lists ready,' ordered Caecina. 'There are writing tablets and styluses by the entrance.'

An air of foreboding, of doom, sank over the assembly as the senior officers made their way to one of the offices at the side of the hall.

Men were avoiding each other's eyes, but Tullus and Fenestela shared a bleak look.

'I never thought I'd see a moment like this,' Fenestela said, muttering an oath that would whiten a man's hair. 'This ain't what I signed up for.'

'Nor I, but the situation's like an abscess that won't come to a head. Besides, Caecina's given us the order,' retorted Tullus, feeling angry, sad *and* resentful. 'I can tell you the first four names to write down.'

'Bony Face. Fat Nose and the twins.' Fenestela swore again. 'I'll get the tablet and stylus,' he said, and joined the queue.

Tullus had a sour, unpleasant taste in his mouth. He and Fenestela were about to draw up a list of men they intended to murder.

How had it come to this?

Chapter XII

◫◫◫

The third watch had sounded by the time Caecina's emergency meeting was over. Urging the officers to ready the best of their soldiers, and to fall on those who'd been selected when the signal came, Caecina had dismissed them. 'The gods are with us,' he'd called as the hall's doors were opened. 'Right always prevails.'

Caecina's talk was hot air, thought Tullus, as he tossed and turned in his bed. None of the men in his old century had been chosen, a small thing to be thankful for, but thirty-eight names had been handed to him by the centurions of his cohort. Naturally, Bony Face and his associates featured high on the lists. There weren't as many men mentioned as some of the other units, perhaps – Tullus had heard figures of fifty, and even sixty soldiers per cohort being bandied about – but that didn't mean what faced them the next day wasn't horrific. He had taken it upon himself to rid his century – Septimius' former one – of its condemned men.

He didn't sleep a wink.

If the night had been hard to endure, the day was no better. Red-eyed, weary, Tullus had decided on the unorthodox method of leading the soldiers of his old century, including Piso and the ones he'd moved into his new unit. The men who'd served under Septimius couldn't be relied on to do exactly as he ordered. Tullus had to bring his trusted legionaries in on Caecina's plan, override their shocked reactions and tell them that *this* was what had to happen. Upwards of ten seemed so reluctant that Tullus decided to leave them out of it, or at least to keep them away from the actual killing.

Then he had to get through the hours until midday. Tullus had no appetite — if he'd eaten, the food would have come straight back up again. Many of his old soldiers seemed to feel the same way. Tullus ordered them to their usual routine duties — a training session on the parade ground with their new centurion and optio. He spent an hour walking the cohort's barrack blocks, scrutinising the legionaries as was his habit, and chatting in private with the officers. They reported that every loyal man had been told of Caecina's plan.

As with Tullus' soldiers, most had accepted their gruesome task. Some seemed nervous, to Tullus' eye at least, but the men who'd mutinied didn't appear to have noticed. Whether they would in the time before the trumpets sounded Caecina's signal — the charge — was a risk they would all have to live with.

Tullus didn't check on any of the rest of the Fifth's cohorts, or the Twenty-First's. He had his job, and the centurions of the other units had theirs. It was a shitty enough detail without worrying about men and things beyond his control. Once he'd satisfied himself that his co-conspirators were ready, he went to join his old century.

Time on the training ground helped. There was nothing like the dull monotony of marching to and fro, forming battle lines and engaging in simulated combat to make the hours go by. Tullus usually supervised these tasks, but *this* morning, he took part. He wanted not to have to think. Sweating, feeling his muscles work, having to bellow orders at the same time, kept his mind from the bloody job at hand. Up and down, over and back, marching as he had in his youth. It was good to realise that he was still fit enough to keep up with his men. *I'm not done yet*, Tullus realised with pride. He became so engrossed that it was somewhat of a surprise when Fenestela came from the barracks to find him. 'It's nearly midday.'

Tullus glanced at the sun, which had emerged from behind a bank of cloud. Fenestela was right. 'We'd best get back.' He ordered his soldiers to halt. Their perspiring, expectant faces regarded him as he stalked down the column. 'This is it, you maggots. Things have been bad since the mutiny, haven't they?' There was a rumble of agreement. 'I don't like what we've been ordered to do any more than you do, but it has to be done. Let's get it over with.'

No one replied – Tullus didn't really expect them to – but there were no protests either. His men stood there, looking tense but ready. He wanted more than that. 'Are you with me?' he cried.

'Aye, sir,' Piso called out.

'Me too,' said Vitellius.

Ten voices joined in, then a few more. In the end, Tullus wasn't sure that all of his men had answered, but most had. This wasn't the time to make them shout back, as he did before a battle. They'd followed him through the mutiny. They were here, combat ready, and prepared to follow his orders. That was enough.

'Form up, usual files. Follow me, and wait for my command. I'll tell you which men are to die. Go in fast and sure. Gods willing, the dogs won't know it's going to happen until they're already dead.'

The march back to the camp, usually a reason for good humour, was made in complete silence. Their iron hobnails crunched off the gravelled surface of the road. Leather straps creaked. Metal glanced off metal. Voices, both human and animal, carried to them from over the ramparts. Men called out to comrades, officers issued orders and mules protested – as they always did. Tullus listened, his mouth dry with tension, but could discern only normal, everyday sounds.

Under the arches of the main entrance, and into the main camp they went. Tullus headed straight for his cohort's barracks. The avenues weren't busy, but there were still plenty of legionaries about. The general indiscipline meant that no one had been able to come up with a plan to ensure that all the men, let alone those designated to die, would be in their quarters when the signal rang out. Most would, because midday was a traditional time to eat, but others might not.

If any of the whoresons aren't there, we'll just hunt them down, thought Tullus, trying not to think about how the mutineers could band together if they realised their intended fate.

At the barracks belonging to Septimius' old unit – Tullus' new one – Fenestela readied half the soldiers to move towards the other end of the long building. Tullus' design was to wait with the rest by the nearest entrance, close by the centurion's quarters. The narrow corridor between his unit's barracks and the next was a natural space for men to gather in good weather, and today was the same. Indifferent glances met their arrival, but that would soon change if they didn't disperse as normal. Troops didn't ever linger about outside their barracks in full armour.

Tullus felt his heart beat twenty, then thirty nervous beats. His soldiers shifted from foot to foot. Fenestela's gaze bored into the side of his face. Two men nearby stopped their game of dice to glance at the assembled legionaries; both frowned. Screw it all. We look far too obvious, thought Tullus. His mouth opened, ready to order his men into their quarters, but the resounding call of numerous trumpets silenced him. Over and over they sounded, not one of the usual daily summons, but the charge, something never heard except on the training ground or battlefield.

Confusion registered on the faces of the legionaries outside the barracks. Confusion, and then fear.

'Spread out to fill the gap. Draw swords, shields at the ready!' shouted Tullus. He heard Fenestela leading his half of the century around the adjacent building, saw Septimius' old signifer appear in the doorway of his quarters. He came trotting over, and then the tesserarius appeared at the far end of the barracks, clearly waiting for Fenestela.

All conversation ceased in the 'corridor'. Dice and bone playing pieces lay untouched. Men stopped wrestling, laid down the greasy rags with which they'd been polishing their kit. 'What's going on?' cried a soldier, backing away from Tullus.

Tullus ignored him, and gave the signifer a terse nod. They had spoken the previous night, and at dawn. 'Nine names on your list, eh?'

'That's right, sir.' The signifer's face was pale, but set. 'Four of them aren't here.'

Tullus knew who they were. He wanted to scream. 'And the other five?'

'Three are behind me, sir. The brawny one, and the red-haired man he's been grappling with, and the soldier who's leaning against the barracks, swigging from a jug. The others are in their rooms, down the other end of the building. They're in bed, I think.'

'Fenestela can take care of those two. We'll tackle the three out here. You deal with the fool who's drinking.' Tullus turned his head. 'Eight men, follow me. Eight, go with the signifer. The rest of you, make sure no one leaves. No one. Follow!'

Tullus made a beeline for the big legionary and his redheaded companion. Piso, Vitellius and six others dogged his heels. Soldiers melted away before them, their questions and demands dying on their lips. They were twenty steps away when their quarry realised what was happening. The pair, who were unarmed, made a run for the door to their quarters – where their weapons lay.

Tullus had chased down fleeing men countless times before, on battle-fields when the enemy had broken. It was an easy way to kill, and the red-haired legionary fell before he'd reached the door; in the same time, Piso and Vitellius had slain the brawny one. Standing over the bodies of their victims, the three gave each other bleak looks. Tullus struggled for something to say, then gave up. Nothing could make this better.

The signifer had done his job too. A scarlet trail was smeared down the barrack wall, the bloody track left by his chosen legionary as he slid to the ground. Soon after, Fenestela emerged from the barracks, his blade stained. He gave Tullus a grim nod.

'The other four are the bony-faced prick, the one with a fat nose and the twins, I take it?' Tullus demanded of the optio.

'Yes, sir. They're as thick as thieves.'

'Where are they?'

'The gods only know, sir,' said the signifer with an apologetic look. 'They've been spending time with some of the troublemakers in the Eighth Cohort, I know, but they could be anywhere in the camp.'

'What in Hades' name have you done?' 'Who gave the orders for this?'

As the remainder of the legionaries realised that they weren't to be attacked, the questions and accusations came raining down. 'Murderers!'

Tullus wheeled with blazing eyes, and the soldiers quietened. 'These men were central to the recent mutiny. They were traitors,' he cried, stabbing his blade towards each of the corpses. 'You know it. I know it. Caecina knows it, and so does Germanicus. Understand that with their deaths, the unrest ends. Remain loyal, and there will be no further retribution.' He prayed that the last part was true.

Some of the legionaries met his eye, but most would not. Their dampened mood and slumped shoulders told Tullus that these ones at least would pose no further problem. 'Into your quarters,' he ordered. 'Stay put until things quieten down. Fenestela, gather the men.' To the signifer, he said grimly, 'We'd best start our search.'

Nothing could have prepared Tullus for the carnage that met them in the rest of the camp. It was clear at once that not every mission to hunt down the leading mutineers had gone according to plan. Tullus was used to battlefields, habituated to bodies and bloodshed. Terrible as the screams of wounded men were, he was accustomed to blocking them out. Never before, however, had he seen and heard these things *inside* the walls of a camp.

Corpses lay everywhere: on the avenues, in between the barrack buildings, across thresholds. Blood spatters marked the spots where men had died, or been wounded. Crimson smears and scuff marks traced the path taken by the injured as they tried to get away from their assailants, or dragged themselves into a quiet spot to die. The wounded calling for help competed with those men who were crying for their friends, or their mothers.

Freed somehow from their stable, a trio of riderless horses cantered past, their hooves clattering off the paving stones. Soldiers ran hither and thither, in ones and twos, and in larger groups. They were unarmed, part-dressed in armour and fully equipped for battle. Some were being pursued; others appeared to be fleeing in blind panic. Yet more were being directed by officers – but to what purpose, it was hard to tell.

No one seemed to know what was going on.

The unmistakeable smell of burning wood reached Tullus' nostrils. Searching for its source, he saw threads of smoke rising from the area of the principia. Had some fool actually set fire to the headquarters? he wondered. He warred with himself for a moment, before deciding to stick to his plan. There were enough soldiers on hand to bring the conflagration under control, but if Bony Face and the rest weren't tracked down, they might escape.

How they would find the four legionaries in the mayhem, Tullus wasn't sure, but he couldn't forget the glee with which Bony Face had executed Septimius. The whoreson needed to pay for his actions, and if Tullus could be the one who dispensed justice, so much the better.

They didn't find their quarry at the Eighth Cohort's barracks, where the situation was also under control. Numerous bodies lay outside the buildings, and there were plenty of wounded too. A weary-looking centurion told Tullus how the mutineers had armed themselves and fought back. A small group had broken through his men's lines. 'My boys had slain most of those on the list. They weren't up to chasing the rest,' he said, unable to hold Tullus' eyes.

With little chance of finding Bony Face, who could have been anywhere in the vast camp, Tullus decided to head for the principia, to help extinguish the fire. An abrupt change to his plans was forced upon him as he entered the *via praetoria*. He glanced towards the main gate, some hundred paces away. There a desperate fight was taking place: men strived against each other, weapons rang, shrieks of pain and war cries combined in a familiar cadence.

The sentries were trying to prevent a mob of soldiers from leaving the camp, Tullus decided – and losing. 'To the gate!' he roared. 'They're killing our brothers at the gate!'

By the time they made it to the entrance, only two of the sentries were left. They went down just as Tullus and his men struck their attackers from behind. Some of the mutinous legionaries heard them coming and turned, but the rest were concentrating on getting out of the camp. Tullus' legionaries hit them with a great crash, thumping their shield bosses into men's backs, using their swords with short, efficient thrusts, trampling the fallen. Enraged by the innocent sentries' fate, they needed no encouragement to kill.

Tullus' temper was up too. He met the shield thrust at him by a swarthy-faced legionary with a savage thwack from the iron boss of his own. The shock of the impact rippled through wood and metal into his arm, and Tullus struggled to keep the shield high, but his opponent, surprised by the move, had fared worse. His top shield rim had bashed backwards into his face, smashing a couple of teeth. He was still moaning and dribbling blood through split lips when Tullus' blade sank deep into his throat.

Tullus closed his eyes as his sword slid free. Crimson droplets showered the top of his shield and his cheeks, and then the legionary had dropped out of sight. Just like that, Tullus was in the mutineers' midst.

'With me!' he roared.

Tullus sensed someone shoving in behind him, but he was too busy stabbing, barging and creating panic to see who it was. One of the twins died beneath his blade, and another legionary he recognised. Tullus wounded two more men, and then he found himself on the far side of the melee. He twisted his head to left and right, searching for Bony Face. There was no sign of him or Fat Nose, and Tullus spat an oath. The hammer of hobnails on the road dragged his attention back to the road out of the camp. Two armed figures were sprinting away from the fight.

Tullus *knew* that one of them was Bony Face. Like as not, the other was Fat Nose or the second twin. 'Fenestela! Piso! Grab a *pilum*!' Sheathing his bloodied sword, he lifted a discarded javelin from the detritus on the ground and ran after the fleeing pair. Tullus didn't trust his legs to catch them, but he had an outside chance with a javelin if he could just close the distance – already some seventy paces.

Within two dozen fevered heartbeats, he was being outpaced by his quarry. It was now or never. Tullus came to a screaming halt, steadied himself by planting his left leg in front, and cocked back his right arm. With one eye closed, he took aim, heaved his arm back a little further, and threw. Up, up, up went the javelin. His prayers that it found a target rose alongside.

I don't have the range any more, thought Tullus. Curse it all.

But to his astonishment, the javelin struck one of the legionaries in the lower leg as it plummeted to earth. Mortal wound it was not, but that didn't matter. With an agonised cry, the man collapsed. His comrade threw a look over his shoulder, and Tullus recognised Fat Nose. He prayed that he had hit Bony Face.

Some words passed between the two – but Fat Nose didn't slow down, or even stop.

What kind of cocksucking coward leaves a friend to die? wondered Tullus.

Metal scraped off stone as someone ran past him and skidded to a halt some twenty paces distant. With a heave and a grunt, Piso lobbed his javelin up in a steep arc. Fenestela appeared next, running further down the road before he too released his pilum.

Piso's effort was so Herculean that his shaft smacked into the ground in front of Fat Nose, who let out a terrified squeal. He jinked to the side, put off his pace by the shock, and then Fenestela's javelin came down like a bolt of lightning and skewered him between the shoulder blades. Fat Nose went down in a sprawl of limbs.

'You might have missed, Piso, but that throw was worthy of an Olympian athlete,' said Tullus. 'You only succeeded by chance, Fenestela!'

Fenestela jutted out his beard, his habit when annoyed. 'Who's to say that I didn't take Piso's effort into account?'

'Ha! It was well cast, though.' Tullus stared at the gate with relief – the fighting there was all but done. 'Follow me,' he ordered. He, Fenestela and Piso tramped after the wounded legionary, who had managed to pull the javelin from his flesh and was hobbling as fast as he could towards the settlement. Spatters of blood marked his trail, and his face was desperate as he looked back. To Tullus' delight, it was Bony Face. They caught up in no time, Tullus outpacing him to block his path while Fenestela and Piso stood at his back.

Bony Face threw down his sword with a clang, and raised his hands. 'I surrender. Don't kill me, please, sir!' His voice was taut with fear.

Tullus felt a deep loathing for the man. His actions had wiped out any justification for his grievances. 'You murdered Septimius in cold blood, filth, yet you expect mercy for yourself?'

Bony Face quailed before Tullus' rage. 'I'm sorry, sir. Septimius was a good man – he deserved better.'

'You're wrong there. Septimius was a prick of the first order.'

Bony Face blinked in surprise.

'But you are also right. He deserved better. Most men do, because being slain in cold blood is a shitty way to die.' With a smooth motion, Tullus unsheathed his sword and placed its tip under Bony Face's chin.

'I—' began Bony Face, and stopped as Tullus' blade slid through skin, muscle, blood vessels, cartilage, parting all with ease. Bony Face's spinal column brought it to a shuddering halt.

Tullus stared into Bony Face's wide, horrified eyes, listened to the odd, choking sound issuing from his bloody lips. With other enemies, he might have felt some regret, but not with this one. He was glad the man was suffering – if it hadn't been for men like him, Septimius and so many others, mutineers included, would still be alive. 'Die, you scum.' Tullus let Bony Face hang on the sharp steel until the life left him, and then he kicked the corpse off, on to the ground. 'The second twin?' he demanded. 'Has anyone seen him?'

'He's dead, sir,' said Fenestela. 'I saw him fall.'

Tullus' anger drained away as fast as the blood pouring from Bony Face's gaping throat. A pathetic figure now, he lay at Tullus' feet like an outsized children's puppet. Yet he wasn't a plaything, thought Tullus, regret sweeping in. Bony Face had been a man who had lost his way, and paid the ultimate price for his mistake. 'On another day, on a battlefield, he might have saved my life,' he muttered. 'And I killed him.'

'You did what you had to,' said Fenestela.

Tullus gave him a bleak look. 'Gods, but it had better end here. Today.'

If it doesn't, he thought, we will all become monsters.

Chapter XIII

◫◫◫

D usk was falling as Arminius traced his way along one of the myriad of paths that led from the woods back towards the settlement. A bow hung from one shoulder, a hide quiver from the other, and he carried a broad-bladed hunting spear. He stamped the worst of the mud from his ankle boots as he walked, making the pair of rabbits hanging from his belt twitch as if still alive. They weren't much to show for a day spent freezing his balls off, he thought, tugging the hood of his cloak tighter around his numb ears. It wasn't as if he'd brought his catch down with his arrows either: they had been in two of the snares he had set several days before.

The rabbits weren't the only creatures hiding from his bow. Arminius had had few sightings of other local wildlife – deer, boar and game birds – all day. Footprints, yes. Fresh-voided dung, yes. Traces of their passage and plants that had been eaten, or ground dug up, yes. But clapping his eyes on the quarry? Hardly ever. Twice, he'd come close to creeping up on something large – a boar, maybe – only to have it flee before he drew near enough to nock a shaft. A red deer on a ridge had been silhouetted against the sky, but it had heard or smelled him as soon as he'd started to try and work his way towards it, and vanished. Shooting birds with arrows was difficult even for a practised archer, and Arminius was no better than competent. No less than seven of his arrows had hissed off into the canopy without result before he'd given up trying.

His lack of success didn't mean that Donar or Tamfana, the goddess of the trees, were angry with him, Arminius reasoned. He had two rabbits, did he not, and hunting was one of the hardest skills for a man to acquire. During his youth, when he might have learned it, he had been in Rome, a boy hostage sent by his father to learn the empire's ways. After that, he'd joined the legions, to learn the art of war. I am a master at that, he thought with cold satisfaction, and I have a way with men. When I speak, they listen.

The notion of winning new allies made him think of his recent visit to the Angrivarii tribe, which had gone well. They would send their warriors to join with his in the late spring. So too would the ever-reliable Marsi. It had been likely from the outset that these two tribes – both haters of Rome – would ally themselves to him again, but it warmed Arminius' heart to have heard their chieftains' sworn promises before the first snow had fallen. If the mild weather returned before winter, he would range westward, to the Bructeri, and south, to the Chatti. Among these peoples, too, he hoped to find more allies. With luck, Segimundus would already have laid the groundwork for him.

And yet. And yet . . .

The memory of the two ravens in the sacred grove still shone bright in his mind, as did Segimundus' inability – refusal? – to interpret the meaning of their appearance. The most Arminius had been able to glean from him was a dissatisfying 'Ravens are Donar's messengers. They go hither and thither, doing his bidding. Often it is impossible to discern the god's purpose for their presence.'

Was it coincidence that Segimundus' replies to Arminius' questions had grown even more ambiguous after his last visit to his father? Or that Segestes, who had been *so* angry about his detention, should have become for no apparent reason the model prisoner? The only word for Segestes' recent behaviour was smug, thought Arminius, ducking under a spindly length of bramble that hung over the track.

An unseen, jutting piece of deadwood made him stumble a moment later. Pain radiated from his left shin, unbalancing him. A sharp cry leaving his lips, Arminius toppled forward over the log, dropping his spear and trying not to land face first in the mud.

Ssshhhewww. The unmistakeable sound of an arrow shot over his head.

His desire to get up vanished as he pressed himself flat to the cold ground. He heard no questioning cry, no apologetic shout from a hunter who had released in error. The continuing silence revealed that the shaft *had* been meant for him. If he hadn't tripped, it might well have done its work. His mind raced. Who in Donar's name was trying to kill him – and so close to the settlement?

Low voices off to his left, the direction from which the arrow had come, told him that his assailant wasn't alone. Were there two men, three, more? Fresh sweat beaded Arminius' brow. Maelo and the rest of his warriors – hundreds strong – could have been in Rome for all the good they were to him now. If he stood, the archer would loose again. So too would his companions, if they were similarly armed. By the time Arminius had restrung his own bow, he'd have at least one shaft in him – and his attackers would have closed in. They would have spears too.

Voices conferred. Twigs crackled. Footsteps drew nearer.

I'm not leaving this life cowering in the mud like a spineless worm, thought Arminius with rising fury. Go out fighting, and he had some chance of being welcomed into the warriors' paradise. Quick as he could, he slipped off his bow and quiver and unslung the rabbits from his belt – they would hinder use of his spear. Praying that his enemies weren't on top of him, he gripped his spear shaft and threw himself up on to his knees. A quick glance to his left, to his right, and behind revealed six approaching figures, none of whom he recognised. They were no more than twenty paces away, and Arminius' stomach clenched. Unless this was some kind of dreadful mistake, someone really wanted him dead.

Ssshhhewww.

An arrow ripped through his tunic, opening a shallow, stinging cut in his left side, and sped off into the undergrowth. Arminius ducked down out of reflex but, two heartbeats later, he had to risk another look at his attackers.

A second man was armed with a bow, but the rest appeared to be wielding spears. If he ran for the settlement, the archers could take him down with ease, and the same would happen if he charged the spearmen. Mind made up, Arminius sprinted towards the bowman who'd just shot at him. With bared teeth and levelled weapon, he screamed a mad, desperate war cry.

A shaft from the second archer winged past, embedding itself in the gnarled trunk of an old beech, but the first bowman flinched before Arminius' wild dash, his nerves making him fumble with his next arrow. Arminius had closed to within ten paces before he had managed to nock it, and to six by the time he had pulled the string to half draw. With no option but to release, he let the string go with a pathetic-sounding *twang*.

Arminius ducked, and the arrow flew over his head. Using his momentum, he drove his spear deep into the archer's belly. The man's *oomph* of shock was followed by a prolonged shriek of pain. Arminius jerked to a halt and ripped his blade free. Ignoring the archer, who sank whimpering to the mud, he cast about for the others.

The spearmen were running forward, and the second bowman was about to loose. Spear discarded, Arminius wrenched his victim up by his shoulders, protecting himself from further arrows. A meaty thump, and a fresh howl of agony from his captive signalled the arrival of another arrow. He had acted in the nick of time. Flinging the doubly wounded warrior towards the spearmen, he turned and fled.

He had a good pair of legs, and therefore a decent chance of outstripping his attackers, yet his skin crawled with every pounding step. Unless the archer was a hopeless shot, he also had every likelihood of taking an arrow in the back before reaching the tree line. Twenty paces hurtled by. The man had to be ready to release again, thought Arminius, terror gnawing his belly. He made a sudden jink to the right, and hurdled a fallen tree. Immense satisfaction filled him as an arrow flew off to his left.

Another thirty-something paces, and still the archer had not loosed again, although loud curses and hammering footsteps told Arminius that the spearmen were on his trail yet. The thick undergrowth and profusion of fallen wood made the risk of tripping too great to look back. Ten more steps, and he began to wonder if he'd run beyond the archer's effective range. If he could reach the edge of the trees, and there bellow for help, any warriors within earshot would come running. His pursuers might be put off. He might survive.

Ssshhhewww-tthhuunnkk.

A ball of blinding agony – such as Arminius had never felt – burst from the back of his right thigh. He stumbled, hearing at the same time a triumphant cry from behind. Hissing with discomfort, and balancing on his left foot, he looked down. The barbed head of an arrow was jutting clear of the front of his right trouser leg, and a quick feel behind revealed its shaft protruding from his thigh. There was no time to snap it off, still less pull it out. If he even tried, the pain would make him faint.

A hobble was all he could manage – walking was out of the question. Arminius glanced back, and his hopes plummeted. The spearmen were less than fifty paces away, and the archer was but a little further off. All five were running straight at him.

His only weapon now was a short-bladed dagger – useless against men with spears and a bow. He tugged it free nonetheless, and hopped around to face his enemies. What a pointless way to die, he thought with supreme bitterness. After all that he'd done, after the crushing defeat he had inflicted on Rome, he would end his life like a wounded deer, powerless to stop those who had hunted him down.

Foliage rustled behind him. Guts lurching, Arminius tried to turn to face the attacker who had somehow got between him and the village. Before he fell, he had a brief impression of a slight figure leaning forward into the arch of a full-drawn bow, and then: *ssshhhewww.* An arrow flew past him, coming to rest a heartbeat later in the throat of the lead spearman, who dropped without a sound.

HUUUUMMMMMMMM! HUUUUMMMMMMMM!

The tone was reedy, surely made by a child, but there was no mistaking the barritus, the war chant used by most tribes. A second voice took it up, somewhere close to the first, and through the dizzying waves of agony that enveloped him, Arminius heard two more arrows scudding overhead. A third volley resulted in another casualty. All the while, Arminius' saviours kept up the barritus, interspersing their chant with aspersions on his attackers' parentage and relationship to swine, rats and other animals.

'Let us at him,' a man demanded. 'This ain't your quarrel.'

'How is it not?' The boy was standing over Arminius. 'He's *my* chieftain, and *you're* trying to kill him. Clear off to whatever shithole you call home, before we put a shaft in you, as we did with your friends.'

Despite the boy's bravado, there was a tremor in his voice.

Stars flashed across Arminius' vision, and nausea clawed the back of his throat, but a desperate sense of urgency helped him to half sit up. His rescuers were two boys, one tousle-headed, the other short and stocky, both close to manhood and brandishing full-drawn bows. They were ranged against four warriors, one of whom was wounded in the arm. Worse luck, one of the uninjured was the archer, who had a shaft ready to loose.

Seeing Arminius, he swept his bow round and down. The barbed iron head of his arrow pointed straight at Arminius' face, and he thought, I'm done.

Ssshhhewww-tthhuunnkk.

The archer was punched backward by a shaft that took him through the chest.

'Here.' With a kick of his foot, the boy who'd shot pushed a hunting spear towards Arminius. Using it as a crutch, he struggled to his feet, trying to ignore the stabbing blades of pain from his thigh, and the sticky feeling of blood pouring down the inside of his leg. Upright, he was able to balance on his good foot and hold the spear ready to use.

There were three spearmen left, but one was hurt. Their hesitation when the boy who'd killed the archer was nocking a fresh arrow had been fatal, and they knew it. Now they faced a pair of ready bows, and Arminius' spear. They glanced at one another, uncertain.

'Come on, you filth,' snarled Arminius. 'At least one of you is going to die – if not all of you.'

His insult might have spurred the trio into action, but the sound of men approaching from the village put paid to any notion of finishing what they'd come to do. With a few choice curses, the warriors turned and ran.

Ssshhhewww! The second boy loosed, and missed.

'Let the cowards go,' said Arminius, slurring his words. His world spun, and his eyes could no longer focus. He would have fallen if the first boy hadn't gripped his left arm and steadied him. Arminius' head seemed too large and heavy for his shoulders, but he managed to look at his rescuer, whom he dimly recognised as the grandson of Tudrus, one of his father's most trusted men. 'My thanks . . .'

After that, he was falling, falling, down a bottomless, pitch-black well.

The first face Arminius saw when his eyes opened was Thusnelda's. Red-eyed, cheeks drawn, it was clear that she'd been crying. Her gaze was fixed over him, towards someone on his other side. He was flat on his back. Above him, he recognised the roof of his longhouse.

Thusnelda let out a happy gasp, and caressed his face. 'You've woken up!'

Arminius ran his tongue around a dry mouth. 'It appears so,' he said wryly. 'A drink, please.' After a mouthful of water, he asked, 'How long was I unconscious?'

'Perhaps an hour.' She mopped his forehead with a damp cloth. 'Long enough for the priest to remove the arrow.'

Hazy memories of an agony even worse than when the shaft struck floated around Arminius' mind. His right hand roamed down, finding heavy bandaging on his thigh. A throbbing pain radiated from the area, not as sharp than before, but no less uncomfortable. 'Did it come out easily?'

'Easy enough,' said Maelo.

Arminius rolled his head and grinned at his second-in-command, who was sitting on the other side of the bed. 'Where were you when I needed you?'

Maelo made a guilty face. 'I came the instant I heard the racket.'

'Did you catch any of them?' Maelo shook his head, and Arminius added, 'Who were they – have you any idea?'

'They were Cherusci, like us; I know that much.' Maelo's eyes glittered. 'Who else could they have been but Segestes' men?'

'Killing me wouldn't free Segestes,' said Arminius, confused.

'Maybe they were here to try and rescue him, but the dogs chanced upon you while scouting out the village. Seeing who you were, a hothead loosed an arrow. The rest had to follow suit.'

Maelo's reasoning made sense, thought Arminius, feeling a swelling anger. He heaved himself upright, clenching his jaw against the stabbing needles this elicited from his thigh.

Thusnelda laid a restraining hand on his chest. 'You have to stay abed.'

'I must talk to your father,' Arminius snapped. 'Did you know about his men?' Hurt filled her eyes, and her hand dropped away. He felt an instant remorse. 'I shouldn't have said that.'

'No, you shouldn't!' She rose and stepped away from the bed. 'Do as you wish. Start the bleeding again. I don't care.'

Arminius watched her go.

'Maybe you'd best stay here and rest. Segestes can wait,' advised Maelo.

'Help me stand,' ordered Arminius. 'Nothing's going to stop me giving the old bastard a going-over.' He chuckled. 'I should say, watching while *you* give him a going-over.'

The discomfort from his wound was so great that he had to ask Maelo for help before they'd reached the door. Even with his arm around Maelo's broad shoulders, it took three times as long as normal to hobble to the longhouse where Segestes was being held. The eight warriors on guard leaped up, their faces concerned.

He made a shushing gesture. 'I've had worse wounds from sharpening a sword,' he added, low enough for Segestes not to hear.

The warriors responded with unconvinced looks.

'Any news?' asked Arminius.

'Not a thing,' replied the first warrior. 'He has eaten, and had his walk. Like as not, he's having a nap. That's what he tends to do much of the time.'

'We'll wake him up,' declared Arminius with an evil smile. 'Fetch a bucket of water.' One man hurried off, and he eased down on to the low bench used by the sentries and closed his eyes. He would rest out here, so he didn't look like complete shit before Segestes.

His strength had rallied somewhat by the time the warrior returned with a slopping wooden pail. The locking bar was lifted from its hooks with gentle hands and placed on the ground. A few creaks were unavoidable when the door was opened, but there was no cry of alarm. One of the sentries eased within, soon returning with the news that Segestes was still asleep. His two men were awake, however. 'They'll keep quiet if they know what's good for them,' muttered Arminius. 'Tie them up as soon as we're inside. Silence them if needs be.'

In they went, on tiptoe, all ten of them. Segestes' followers looked startled, and one asked what in Donar's name they wanted, but Arminius' warriors had swarmed forward and overpowered the pair, and gagged them, before too much noise had been made. It gave Arminius huge satisfaction that Segestes' slumber continued through the scuffle. He lay on his straw-filled mattress, a blanket half-covering him. Loud snores echoed from his open mouth, and a trickle of saliva ran from one corner of his lips.

They drew near enough to stand right over him. The man with the bucket stood ready. Arminius paused, taking deep breaths to control the waves of pain radiating from his thigh. Thinking of the warriors who'd ambushed him helped. Ready at last, he nodded.

The contents of the pail landed on Segestes with a mighty splash. He jerked up, roaring with fright and shock. Arminius' warriors hooted with amusement, but he kept his expression stony hard.

Spluttering, wiping his face, Segestes focused at last on Arminius. 'What was that for, you bastard?'

'I was going to ask you the same thing,' retorted Arminius, jabbing a thumb at his bandaged thigh.

Segestes looked down, and back up again, confused. 'I don't know what you're talking about.'

'I was attacked not long since, just outside the village. Six warriors, all Cherusci.' Something flickered in Segestes' eyes, and Arminius cried, 'Ha! They *were* your men. Were they here to liberate you – was that it?'

'You're raving. The wound has given you a fever.'

'Not yet it hasn't.' Arminius gave the largest of his warriors a nod. The man lunged forward and grabbed the front of Segestes' tunic, heaving him to the floor. Segestes let out a cry of pain, and tried to move backwards, on his hands. A mighty kick to his belly drove the air from his lungs, however, and he collapsed on to his side, sobbing for breath.

Arminius motioned the warrior to stand back. He waited until Segestes had managed to sit up. 'Did you ask Segimundus to send a party of men to rescue you?'

'Aye.'

'I *knew* it,' cried Maelo.

'I wouldn't have cared if they had slain you, but they had no orders to do so,' said Segestes.

Segestes seemed to be telling the truth, but Arminius was still furious. If Segimundus' followers hadn't been in the forest, he would not have been attacked. 'Bring his followers over here.'

'Those men have done nothing,' Segestes croaked as the pair were dragged forward.

'They would slay me given half a chance, just as the others tried to do,' snapped Arminius. He glanced at Maelo. 'Kill them.'

For several heartbeats, Segestes' shouted objections mingled with the gagged men's muffled protests. Then blood gouted from one warrior's throat, reducing the noise by some degree. His corpse flopped down, slack-limbed. Maelo moved on to his next victim without pause, slitting his throat with expert precision. Fresh torrents of blood spattered, darkening patches of the earthen floor. When the second body had been heaped on top of the first, right in front of Segestes, Arminius hobbled forward to glare down at the old man.

Fire flashed in Segestes' eyes, and Arminius felt a tiny thrill of fear.

Confrontation was the best tactic, he decided. 'Go on, try! Wounded or not, I'll take you.'

Segestes sagged, like a wine skin pricked with a blade. 'Do what you must. May Thusnelda never give you a child, let alone a son.'

If Arminius had had a weapon in his hands at that moment, he would have slain Segestes, so great was his rage. In, out, he breathed, several times, until he was calm again.

He reached for the support of Maelo's arm. 'Beat the shit out of him. Nice and slow. Break a few bones, but don't kill him, or leave him so hurt he'll die.' Arminius spoke in a voice quiet enough for Segestes not to hear. The attack in the forest had been unplanned, Arminius decided, and Thusnelda would never forgive him if he had her father murdered. He could live with the disapproval she'd shower him with because of the beating, however. Had he not a grievous wound, caused by Segestes' men?

'Donar take you, Arminius!' shouted Segestes.

Arminius didn't reply, or stay to watch the old man's punishment. His strength was waning fast. From the comfort of his bed, he could consider what to do about Segimundus.

Enemies within could be as dangerous as those without.

Chapter XIV

Tullus watched as Germanicus arrived at Vetera two days later. Straight-backed, cold-faced, he rode in at the head of a mixed force of more than two thousand auxiliaries. His use of non-Roman soldiery – an intentional move – was a stinging rebuke to Caecina and every legionary in the camp. It was a relief, however, that they weren't needed – the day of slaughter that had begun with the trumpets' call had brought the unrest to a gruesome close. Almost six hundred soldiers had been slain between the two legions. The majority were mutineers, but more than five score loyal men had also died in the bitter fighting. These were grievous losses, a sorrowful Germanicus declared on his tour of the battered camp, in which the signs of destruction and death were still widespread. 'This has been damage rather than remedy,' he chided Caecina – and then cast a reproving look at the other senior officers present. 'It should have been carried out in a more controlled manner.'

Flushing, Caecina muttered an apology. The others, Tubero among them, took great interest in their belt buckles, or sword hilts.

Tullus wanted to say to Germanicus that it was *his* orders which had brought about the carnage, but he held his tongue. In truth, there was nothing to say that the killings – a necessary evil – would have gone more smoothly if an alternative method had been used.

'At least the matter has been dealt with,' said Germanicus, echoing Tullus' thoughts. He led the way up one of the sets of stairs that provided access to the walkway that ran along the battlements. Everyone clattered up behind him.

Tullus leaned against the top of the wall and looked east, as Germanicus was doing. It was a familiar view. Beyond the deep defensive ditch, a gentle, grass-covered slope led down the hill upon which Vetera was built. At its bottom lay an irregular pattern of farmers' fields. Small houses and barns were dotted here and there, but what caught the eye most was the wide silver band of the River Rhenus.

Once the far side had been familiar tramping grounds, but since the massacre in the forest, Roman troops seldom crossed the river. Tullus had last done so more than twelve months before, and that had only been a probing patrol that stopped a few miles from the bridge. Some soldiers were content with this, although many others felt the need to reassert the empire's dominance, even men like Cordus and Victor. To campaign on the far bank was a burning desire for Tullus. The following spring and Germanicus' proposed campaign couldn't come soon enough.

'The weather is fine for the time of year, is it not?' asked Germanicus, looking up at the clear sky.

'It is a deal milder than normal, sir, yes,' replied Caecina.

'I am unused to the change in seasons in these parts. Have you seen conditions like this before?'

'On occasion, sir. There is no way of knowing if it will continue,' Caecina added, as if he and Germanicus had already discussed something.

'Yet it has been settled for – what? A month now?' Germanicus addressed not just Caecina, but the gathering at large.

'That would be right, sir,' replied Caecina, with similar answers echoing from others present.

Germanicus paced to and fro, which emphasised how much taller he was than everyone else. He tapped a fingernail against his teeth. 'The mutiny and its aftermath must be put behind us, and a winter spent in barracks will not achieve that. If anything, it will do the opposite.'

This was true, thought Tullus. With fewer duties during the cold months, the legionaries would have time to brood – and gossip. He pricked up his ears.

'I propose a swift raid over the river,' said Germanicus, his keen eyes roving from officer to officer. 'Cross, march hard, find a nearby hostile tribe, and attack. There's nothing like a common enemy to bring men together. The Marsi are one of the closest, are they not?'

'Yes, sir,' said Caecina. 'You would lead men from the mutinous legions, I assume?'

'You are a mind reader, Caecina. Not every soldier of the four legions, but most. Ten, twelve thousand legionaries, plus a similar number of auxiliaries, should be sufficient.'

Tullus' spirits soared at Germanicus' words. The Marsi had been an integral part of Arminius' forces. They deserved to be punished – and this was not his only reason to feel excited. 'Sir?' he asked.

'Speak, Tullus,' ordered Germanicus, with an expansive gesture.

'I have a servant who is Marsi, sir. He's heard a rumour of recent days that one of the three lost eagles is with his tribe.'

Germanicus' eyes lit up. 'Is that so?'

'Yes, sir. He wasn't sure which legion it had come from, though.'

'No matter,' cried Germanicus, glancing from face to face. 'Let us hope the story is true, and that we recover the eagle even as we wipe out the Marsi.'

Tullus' conscience began to twinge. The penalty paid by Degmar's people was always going to be severe but he hadn't anticipated the *entire* tribe being sentenced to death. Part of him didn't care, but he couldn't help picturing Degmar's parents and sisters, whom the warrior had sometimes mentioned, being butchered. Innocents died all the time, Tullus told himself. It's not as if his family are friends to Rome.

Tubero had read his mind. 'Keep your dog of a servant on a tight leash. Better still, silence him,' he said with a nasty smile. 'The last thing we need is for the Marsi to be warned of our approach.'

The gaze of every man present bore down on Tullus. He felt that of Germanicus the most. 'There's no need for concern, sir. My servant is faithful. If it hadn't been for him, we would not have made it to Aliso.'

'You will take responsibility for his actions?' demanded Tubero.

'I will, sir,' replied Tullus. 'I'll have him watched.'

It seemed as if Tubero might press Tullus further, but Germanicus raised a hand. 'The centurion's word is sufficient.'

Tubero subsided, while Tullus raged inside. He had just placed his reputation, perhaps his life, on the line when he wasn't sure if Degmar would remain true, in particular if the lives of his family were at stake. The best solution, Tullus concluded, was to do as he'd promised, and prevent Degmar acting until it was too late.

'When do we leave, sir?' he asked Germanicus.

'The legions from Ara Ubiorum will be here in three to four days. The combined force can leave the day after that.'

Once the assault on the Marsi was over, Tullus decided, Degmar could be released from his oath. What man would wish to serve another who had helped to massacre his people?

Tullus summoned Degmar the moment he got back to his barracks. His rooms weren't the ones he'd lived in while serving in the Eighteenth – a move had been inevitable after his demotion – but he had salvaged many of the fixtures and fittings, and his personal possessions. In the dark months after the ambush, he had been surprised how these old, familiar objects had made his life easier to bear. The effect had been most noticeable in his bedroom, a more private chamber than the rest of his quarters, which were so often filled with visitors of one kind or another.

There were woollen rugs that he'd bought in the local market. A wooden stand he used to hold his armour, its arms worn shiny from the rubbing of mail. A waist-high stone shrine, decorated with a few tiny figures – among them those of his father and grandfather – standing in the opposite corner to his bed. The threadbare military blanket that he preferred more than any fine bedcover. A pair of simple stools that faced each other across a low table, upon which sat a jug, two cups and a set of ivory gaming pieces.

Moving from this to the sparsely decorated room that doubled as both living room and office, Tullus paced about, trying to come up with the best way of breaking the news to Degmar. He was still struggling for an answer when there was a sharp rap at the door, and the Marsi warrior entered.

Tullus smiled. Even Fenestela would have called out his name before presuming to come in, but not proud Degmar. He never called Tullus 'sir' either. While other Romans found this behaviour impertinent, Tullus didn't. The relationship between German chieftains and their followers was more equal than the Roman equivalent. Degmar deferred to him out of respect, not because of his rank.

'You wanted me?'

'Yes.' Tullus searched Degmar's face for signs that he was aware of their mission, and was relieved to see none.

'Do you need your sandals cleaned, or your armour polished?'

'No.'

Degmar's eyes cast around the room. 'Where's your sword? You said something about it needing an edge.'

'It's not that either. I have to talk to you, to tell you something.'

Degmar's dark eyes came to rest on Tullus' face. 'That sounds serious.'

'It is.' Tullus tried again to think how the blow might be eased, and failed. 'Germanicus has ordered an immediate expedition over the Rhenus. Twenty-five thousand men. Half of them are to come from the Fifth and Twenty-First, and the legions at Ara Ubiorum, and the rest will be auxiliaries. It's an exercise, to give the men a common purpose after the mutiny.'

If Degmar was surprised, he concealed it well. 'Am I to accompany you?'

'Yes, but that's not why you're here. Curse it, there's only one way to say this. Germanicus has ordered us to attack the Marsi settlements.'

Alarm flared in Degmar's eyes. 'Which ones?'

'Those that are nearest.'

'And are the people to be enslaved, or to . . . ?' Degmar's voice died away.

Tullus shook his head. 'I'm sorry.'

There was silence as Degmar stared at the floor, his jaw working. 'I have to go,' he said at length. 'They must be warned.'

'You know I can't let you do that.'

Degmar took a step towards him. 'Why should my parents and my sisters die? They have done nothing to Rome!'

'I know,' said Tullus, torn between his desire for revenge and his sympathy for Degmar.

'And the womenfolk and children, the old – what have they done?' Degmar's voice throbbed with anger.

'The Marsi rose against Rome. The warriors took part in Arminius' ambush.'

'Of course they did!' spat Degmar. 'Why wouldn't they? You and your kind were the invaders, the ones who didn't belong east of the Rhenus – not us. Among the tribes, we live our lives as free men, not as the subjects of some fucking *emperor*. What does that word mean anyway? Subjugation. The Roman boot on our necks. Laws. Tax. Not much else, as far as I can see.'

Tullus had long known of Degmar's antipathy towards Romans and Rome, and chosen to ignore it. The warrior served him, not his senior officers or the emperor. Hearing his feelings laid out in such a plain manner was still shocking, but Tullus couldn't help thinking that his response to such a threat might have been similar. 'Rome is what it is,' he began.

'This for Rome!' Degmar made an obscene gesture, and for a moment it seemed as if he might strike Tullus, or flee the room. Then his shoulders slumped. 'Am I to be held captive until after the raid?'

'Can you give me your word that you will not run?'

'Why should I?' demanded Degmar, rage still simmering in his eyes. 'Everyone I love who remains living is soon to die, thanks to Germanicus.' He spat the last word.

Degmar's anguish brought Tullus to an instant and unexpected decision. 'I am bound to follow the governor's orders – you know that. The Marsi settlements *will* be destroyed, and thousands of people *will* die. That's not to say that a few individuals might not escape.'

Degmar threw him a look loaded with suspicion. 'I don't understand.'

'Your loyalty these past years places a responsibility on me.' Even though they were alone, Tullus lowered his voice. 'I will help you smuggle your family to safety before the attack. Once it's done, you can stay with them.'

There was wonder in Degmar's eyes now, and a trace of disbelief. 'Why do this for me?'

'I would never have reached Aliso after the ambush, nor would my men.'

'Pah! I was your guide, nothing more.'

'No,' said Tullus. 'I've told you before. You didn't have to try and find us after the slaughter began, but you did. You then saved my life – all of our lives. That was more than enough to repay my freeing you from the Usipetes.'

'Leading you along some forest paths for a few days is nothing. The only way I can erase *that* debt is by saving your life in combat,' refuted Degmar with the same stubbornness that emerged each time the issue came up.

'Look on my helping you with this as recompense for your services as a guide then,' said Tullus with a smile. 'As for your obligation to save me in battle, well, you will have to set that aside when we part company. I will not have it any other way.'

'If you are caught, if someone like Tubero found out . . .' Degmar began.

'We had best ensure that no one realises what we're up to, eh?' Despite his tone, Tullus was far from confident. To locate Degmar's family while the legions massed nearby, to keep them from telling their friends or neighbours, and then spirit them to safety without being spotted by either side, verged on the impossible, and the insane. He was still going to try, though.

For Degmar.

Chapter XV

॥॥॥

P iso was at the bar of the Ox and Plough, which had become his second home since the recent bloodbath in which the mutineers had been killed. The place was jammed with legionaries and officers, and a smattering of civilians. All the tables were occupied, and the standing customers were pressed together like the unfortunates in the bowels of a slave ship. A trio of musicians in one corner made valiant but vain attempts to be heard over the drunken singing and shouted conversations. The innkeeper Sirona patrolled the length of the bar, smiling, serving wine and food, and keeping an eye on her patrons.

'More wine,' said Piso, banging his cup on the counter. 'MORE WINE!'

Vitellius gave him a sour look. He was being more abstemious than Piso, as usual. It was no surprise, therefore, when he grabbed Piso's arm before it struck the wooden top again. 'Haven't you had enough?'

'No,' snapped Piso. 'I fucking haven't.'

Vitellius glanced at Sirona, who was approaching with a sour face and a fresh jug. 'Water it down, will you?'

'I have,' came the tart reply. 'Five to one.'

'Excellent,' said Vitellius, slapping down coins worth twice the wine's normal price. 'Keep the change.'

'Five to one?' slurred Piso. This was degrees more dilution than legionaries – than he – liked. Sirona's expression had turned thunderous, however. Drunk or not, Piso realised that further objection would result in the wine being poured over his head. He swallowed his pride and said no more.

Sirona placed the jug in front of Vitellius – not Piso – and swept the coins into her hand. 'This is your last drink. You're both pissed. You' – here she gave Piso an unfriendly look – 'in particular.'

Stung, Piso began to protest, but a sharp jab of Vitellius' elbow made him turn on his friend instead. 'What was *that* for?'

Vitellius ignored him. 'As you say, Sirona – we'll go after this. Won't we, Piso?'

'Aye, I suppose,' Piso muttered darkly.

Pursing her lips, Sirona stalked off.

'What's wrong with you?' demanded Vitellius. 'Do you want to end up barred?'

'She wouldn't dare,' said Piso with a sneer.

'Why ever not? She has more than enough customers, and her sons are fucking enormous. If she tells them you're not welcome, you won't get in again.' Vitellius indicated the two strapping men by the door, both of whom had clubs. When Piso made a *phhhh* of contempt, he added, 'She's friendly with Tullus too, you fool. This is Artio's home, remember? One word from Sirona to Tullus, and you'll find yourself with punishment duty as well as being barred from here.'

'All right,' grumbled Piso. Wine slopped on to the bartop as he filled their cups with an unsteady hand. He toasted Vitellius and downed the lot in one gulp. The warm feeling as it hit his stomach was pleasant, but it couldn't erase Piso's graphic memories of how close he'd come to stabbing the fleeing centurion, still less how he had helped Tullus to kill some of the mutineers. The frank terror in their faces, the disbelief that their comrades could turn on them, was as fresh in his mind, and as jarringly painful, as if it had just happened. He hung his head, stared down at the sawdust-covered floor and wondered about vomiting.

After a moment, his stomach settled. 'I thought nothing could be worse than the fucking forest.'

Vitellius looked more sympathetic. 'I felt the same way, but those men had to die. Left alone, they would have been a weeping sore in the legion's side – always painful, always causing trouble. I know that. You know that. Everyone knows it.'

'But to make *us* the executioners?'

'That was pure genius on Germanicus' part, don't you see? If he'd sent in auxiliaries, every legionary on the frontier would distrust allied troops for the rest of his life, and rightly so. Making us complicit means that we have to forget the whole sick affair. Moving on, leaving it in the past, is our only option.'

Vitellius' explanation made sense, thought Piso, but it didn't diminish his shame, which he often saw mirrored in Vitellius' eyes, as well as those of their comrades. He refilled their cups again, emptying the jug. 'How long will that take, eh? To forget it?'

'I don't know.' Vitellius' voice was weary. 'But it will happen. Think of it as you would a broken heart. In the end, it heals. Time is all that's needed.'

Piso had never had a broken heart, but he didn't want to admit that, so he grunted in agreement and finished the dregs of his wine. He planted his cup on the counter with a thump. 'If we're no longer going to get served, let's find somewhere else. I don't want to go back to barracks.'

Vitellius sighed. 'You can't go on drowning your sorrows like this. It's only a matter of time before Tullus or Fenestela catches you.'

'I can't sleep if I don't drink.' Piso heard his whining tone, and hated himself for it.

'You'll have to find another way then,' replied Vitellius with a scowl. 'I don't want to go to Hades because you were too hung over to protect me.'

The accusation stung. In battle, every legionary was supposed to defend the man to his left. Piso guarded Vitellius, just as another of their tent mates did for him, and so on. 'That would never happen!'

'A cripple with a crutch would have bested you for the last few mornings,' replied Vitellius with a knowing look.

Piso's cheeks reddened. Vitellius was right. If they'd been forced to fight in recent days, he would have struggled to keep himself alive beyond the first clash with the enemy, never mind protect Vitellius. Pride smarting now, he cried, 'Gods above, leave me alone!'

'Why should I?' Vitellius' eyes were understanding but hard. 'You're my friend. My comrade. It's my job to look after you, wherever we are. Which means you should climb on the wagon for a while.'

Piso absorbed this with the ponderousness of the blind drunk. At length, he nodded. Being responsible for the death of a friend like Vitellius would be worse, far worse than his current troubles. And so the nightmares that plagued him every night would have to be faced in the company of someone other than Bacchus, who, if truth be told, had not done a good job of preventing them anyway. 'Very well. I'll do it.'

'That's the spirit.' Vitellius threw a brotherly arm around his shoulders. 'Let's head home, eh?'

Watched by a sour-faced Sirona, they weaved their way between the packed tables to the door. They were half a dozen steps away when it burst open, framing a legionary on the threshold. Spying his comrades – a party of soldiers in the middle of the room – he roared, 'We're heading over the Rhenus, brothers!'

Conversations ground to a halt. Men stared. A little abashed, the legionary repeated his words. An expectant silence fell. Inspired by the opportunity hitherto denied them, the musicians struck up a merry tune, but they were soon cowed by a barrage of abuse.

'Tell us all!' Piso demanded of the new arrival. 'What news do you bring?'

'The clement weather is too good an opportunity to miss, Germanicus says. We are to attack the enemy at once.' Surprised reactions erupted throughout the room – it was unheard of to wage war after the harvest. 'Most units from the four . . .' Here the soldier hesitated, unwilling to say the word 'rebellious', eventually opting for: '. . . *local* legions are to take part, as well as a similar number of auxiliaries. We march out when the troops from Ara Ubiorum get here, in three to four days.'

'Kill the German filth! KILL!'

Piso didn't see who began the cry, which was taken up with the fervour of men who need a cause to support. In the blink of an eye, every customer in the place was chanting. 'KILL! KILL! KILL!'

The sound followed them outside. It was still audible at the end of the alleyway, and for some distance along the *vicus*' main street. Similar sounds echoed from other drinking holes. A gang of soldiers staggering along in front of them were singing, 'Ger-man-i-cus! Ger-man-i-cus!'

Piso felt his foul humour slipping away with each step. After a time, he said, 'D'you feel it?'

Vitellius cast him a questioning look.

'I don't know how to say it, but the air – it feels lighter.'

Vitellius glanced up and down the street. All the legionaries within sight were cheering, or belting out endless repetitions of 'Ger-man-i-cus', 'KILL!' and 'Revenge for Varus!' Some were even praying out loud, thanking the gods for sending Germanicus to be their leader. 'Aye,' said Vitellius, a smile sneaking on to his face. 'I see what you mean.'

'A common enemy is exactly what we need,' said Piso, thumping his friend on the back.

Life had just regained some of its purpose.

Chapter XVI

◻◻◻

Ten days had passed since Germanicus' announcement, and night had fallen over the temporary camp that housed his vast force, thirty miles east of the Rhenus. Tullus was in his tent, Degmar and Fenestela by his side. Facing him were Piso, Vitellius and two other old soldiers of his from the Eighteenth, Saxa and Metilius.

Both Piso and Vitellius had expectant looks on their faces. Saxa and Metilius seemed more bemused. Since their move from Tullus' command, they had seen him and their other former comrades on but a few occasions. Army life didn't lend itself to reunions. Saxa was a bear of a man with shaggy brown hair. Metilius' slight build, dimpled cheeks and cheerful expression gave the impression that he would be a poor fighter. In fact, the truth was quite the opposite.

Tullus' promotion and newfound regard among his fellow officers had allowed him of recent days to secure the transfer of Saxa and Metilius into his own century once more. He hoped that the bond they had shared in the Eighteenth was still strong, because what he was about to ask them ran contrary to everything they stood for. Fenestela, who knew already, was in, and Tullus had little doubt that Piso and Vitellius would volunteer, but the other two were still an unknown quantity.

'You must be wondering why I asked you here,' he said to the legionaries. All four nodded their heads in agreement. 'I will tell you, but you must swear never to speak of this meeting, except to one another. I mean it. If you won't make such a pledge, leave now.'

The legionaries exchanged perplexed looks, but none protested. It took a few moments to make their oaths.

Feeling a little less worried, Tullus began. 'You remember Degmar?' This was more aimed at Saxa and Metilius – Piso and Vitellius saw him every day.

'Aye, sir,' replied Saxa, giving Degmar a civil nod. 'He's the one as got us to Aliso.'

'Correct. If it hadn't been for Degmar, our bones would be strewn across the forest floor, like those of so many former comrades.'

'Marsi, aren't you?' Metilius directed this at Degmar.

'I am,' came the proud reply.

'That'd be part of the reason we're here, sir, I'd wager,' said Metilius with a knowing look.

'I'd forgotten how shrewd you are, Metilius,' said Tullus, chuckling. 'We all know what's going to happen tomorrow.' Degmar's face twitched, and Tullus felt grateful that he had ordered two men to guard the warrior since they had left Vetera.

Their target, a cluster of Marsi villages scattered over a five-mile radius on the other side of an expanse of forest, lay within easy striking distance. Caecina's scouts, two cohorts of light-armed auxiliaries, had been sent into the woods at sunset, their task to find a path through. The entire force would mobilise at dawn, and make straight for the settlements. No quarter was to be given, not to man, woman or child. When the slaughter was over, fire and sword was to be taken to the entire area. If possible, Germanicus had ordered, the entire Marsi tribe was to be slain.

'Our debt to Degmar can never be repaid in full,' said Tullus. 'Tonight, however, I will redress the balance somewhat. The three of us' – and he indicated the Marsi warrior and Fenestela – 'are going to find Degmar's family. We'll help them to escape, and return to our allotted positions before dawn.'

The four legionaries' expressions varied from incredulous to aghast.

Piso was first to regain control. 'How will you get out of camp, sir?'

Tullus winked. 'You can't always trust the auxiliaries, I told one of the tribunes. He gave me permission to check the lie of the land.' His eyes moved from face to face. 'For once, I cannot order you to follow me. I ask instead that you remember what Degmar did for each of us five years ago, and make your decision based on that.'

'Degmar has helped me since too, sir. I'll come,' said Piso at once, giving the warrior a friendly glance.

'And I,' added Vitellius.

Tullus gave them both a nod of appreciation, before looking at Saxa and Metilius. 'Well?'

'Your pardon, sir, but you're mad,' exclaimed Saxa. He paused, making Tullus' heart skip a beat, and then he added, 'I'm not fond of tribal types, not after what happened with Varus, but Degmar saved us, and a debt's a debt. I'll help.'

Metilius snorted. 'I'm not going to miss the fun, sir. I'll string along too.'

Just like that, they were all part of it. Tullus couldn't quite believe his luck.

His zeal soon cooled. They were seven men against an entire tribe. Seven men who somehow had to keep their mission secret from their own kind, or face the most severe consequences.

In reality, their chances of success were slim to none.

It was a cold, bright night, and the Marsi settlements lay directly ahead, to the east of the forest. That didn't mean it was easy to keep a straight line under the trees' shadowy canopy, and Tullus was content to give Degmar the lead. If Tullus had taken it, they would have gone wrong within a few hundred paces. With the Marsi warrior in charge, however, they picked their way past vast patches of brambles, around towering beeches and sessile oaks, and through streams. They travelled in single file, Degmar first, followed by Tullus and the legionaries, with Fenestela taking his customary place at the rear. In the larger glades, moonlight turned their shadows into great black figures, ghosts going about their silent business.

On several occasions, they encountered groups of auxiliaries, but each time the hissed challenge to identify themselves came, Tullus was at Degmar's shoulder, ready with the password. Although they received a few odd looks, their presence in the forest wasn't challenged. Step by step, quarter-mile by quarter-mile, they made their way along the narrow paths found by Degmar. Checking the moon's passage across the starlit expanse above was the only way of judging time. By Tullus' reckoning, they had been travelling for perhaps two hours when Degmar came to an abrupt halt.

Tullus peered into the gloom ahead, but could see nothing. 'What is it?'

'The village is near. You had best shed your armour here.'

'How will we find it again?' asked Tullus, concern gnawing his guts. If there was pursuit from the settlement, it could be the least of their worries that night, but having to explain why he and his men were without their kit the next morning would also be his undoing.

Degmar pointed to a sessile oak a short distance off the track. Halfway up its height gaped a great split in its trunk. 'That was struck by lightning when I was a boy. It's where my friends and I used to meet. I can find it with my eyes closed, in the dark, the fog or the snow.'

Tullus was already directing his men to the base of the tree. 'Off with your armour, quiet as you can.' There had been no sign of any auxiliaries for some time, but this was one of the riskiest parts of their mission. To be found divesting themselves of their kit by their own kind would rouse the suspicions of an idiot.

To his relief, they stripped down to their tunics without interruption. The only equipment left to each man was his belt, sword and dagger. Degmar took them to a nearby boggy patch, where everyone applied a generous covering of mud to a comrade's arms, legs and face. That done, they dogged his footsteps once more. He walked a great deal slower now, stopping often to listen and stare into the darkness.

A pleasant smell of wood smoke hung in the still air, an indication that they were drawing nearer to the village. Tullus had just made out the outline of a building when Degmar halted again. He whispered into Tullus' ear,

'I've guided us to the closest point to my parents' house, but we will have to enter the settlement now. Everyone has a dog. One is sure to bark when it hears us, and that could rouse the rest.'

'And if the villagers wake?' Tullus was picturing the scores of warriors they would face if the place came to life.

The gloom couldn't conceal Degmar's smile. 'I have a trick up my sleeve. Games will have been held here yesterday to honour a local goddess, and there was a feast last night. Everyone will have been pissed out of their heads by the time it finished. Donar willing, they're all unconscious. If they do wake, they're more likely to give their dog a kick than to look around.'

Tullus' tension eased a fraction, and he twisted around to pass the information on to Piso, who was next in line. He gave the order for each man to unsheathe his dagger. 'Ready,' he said to Degmar, who also had a knife in his fist. What an ugly reality that was, thought Tullus. He's prepared to kill his own kind to save his family.

Taking a parallel course to the length of the first longhouse, Degmar led off. They had gone halfway when a surprised *ruffff* went up. Another followed, and soon the dog was barking fit to burst. A dog in the next house joined in. Degmar froze; so did everyone. Fixing his gaze on the house's door, Tullus waited, dry-mouthed. Ten heartbeats thumped by, then twenty. A muffled voice growled something; the dog's barking lessened a little, but continued. Heavy footsteps echoed within; there was a thud and a curse as a person's shin collided with something solid. Another, meatier thud was followed at once by a chorus of yelps. Muttering to himself, the dog's owner tramped back to bed, farted loudly and fell silent.

Relieved and amused, Tullus waited until the second dog calmed down before signalling Degmar to continue. They padded onward, their hobs picking up clods of mud in the frequent vegetable patches. The group skirted around two more houses without disturbing their inhabitants, animal or human. Degmar revealed to Tullus that the next longhouse belonged to his parents, and the one after that to his older sister. He had just finished speaking when a dog inside his parents' home began to yap. 'Wait here,' Degmar hissed. 'I won't be long.'

You'd better not be, thought Tullus, his stomach knotting. He ordered Piso and the rest up against the wall – the better not to be seen – and to keep a sharp eye out. He did the same. The darkness didn't stop him from feeling as exposed as a naked bather who walks through the wrong door to find himself on the street outside the bathhouse.

His alarm grew at the sight, fifty paces away in an open space, of tables and benches with the figures of sleeping men sprawled everywhere between them. Hoping that Degmar had been right about the amount of drinking that would have gone on, Tullus watched the slumbering men with bated breath. No one stirred, and after a few moments, the dog quietened inside the house. It knew Degmar, Tullus presumed, but he didn't let down his guard even a little. Eyes roving from side to side, his dagger ready, Tullus watched the feasting area, and the two nearby longhouses. He waited. Counted his heartbeat so that he knew how long Degmar had been gone.

Twenty beats went by. Tullus had almost reached fifty when a stifled exclamation came from within. He tensed, but instead of an outcry, muted voices began a conversation. Degmar had found his parents, it seemed. Fresh worry consumed Tullus. What if Degmar's mother or father decided to warn the entire village? A few cries for help would rouse their neighbours, drunk or not. 'Be ready to retreat on my order,' he hissed to Piso.

At a hundred heartbeats, Tullus began to wonder whether Degmar had any chance of persuading his parents to leave. Tullus' men's nerves were jangling too: they were shifting about, and jumping at the slightest sound. The longer they stood here, the more chance there was of being seen.

Off to Tullus' right, a door banged open. He spun, knife at the ready. A tall figure staggered out from the longhouse opposite – not the one belonging to Degmar's sister. A loud belch broke the silence, and the figure – a man – weaved a few steps towards Tullus and the rest. Muttering to himself the way only the drunk can, the man tugged at his garments. A moment later, a stream of urine arched into the air; there was a simultaneous sigh of relief.

The man pissed for so long – sixty heartbeats at least – that Tullus wondered if he'd ever stop. In the end his bladder had been emptied, however, and he shrugged himself back into his trousers.

Degmar, unknowing, chose that moment to walk outside, leading several others.

Inebriated or not, the man saw them at once. He called out in German. Degmar tensed and hissed something back. His answer wasn't satisfactory, because the man asked another question, and took several steps towards Degmar, who told him – Tullus thought – to piss off. The man ignored this advice, and repeated what he'd said. Degmar flicked his hand in a clear gesture for the man to leave. The only response he got was another, louder demand.

Tullus' mind raced. If he did nothing, the man would raise the alarm. That was, if others hadn't been woken already. Or he could kill him, and hope that *that* didn't set Degmar's parents to screaming. The second option was best, he decided, indicating that Piso should follow him.

In ten steps Tullus was close enough to see that the man was much younger than he, and more heavyset. The man was more plastered than a drunkard on the feast of Bacchus, however, and he did nothing but gape as Tullus swept towards him like a vengeful spirit. His last words – another question of some kind – were muffled as Tullus' fingers wrapped around his mouth and his throat was sliced open. Trying to avoid the gouts of blood, Piso stabbed him twice in the chest for good measure.

Even as he lowered the man's corpse to the ground, Tullus' eyes were sweeping over the house he'd come out of, and across the sleeping revellers. There was no sign of anyone else emerging, and no one stirred by the tables and benches. How long could their luck hold? Tullus wondered. He hurried to Degmar, who had one man and two women with him – his parents and one of his sisters, Tullus presumed.

'He's no loss,' revealed Degmar before Tullus had to explain himself. 'The prick was forever trying to steal my mother's hens. If he wasn't at that, he was propositioning my youngest sister.'

The filthy looks that Degmar's family were giving Tullus showed they didn't feel the same way about what he'd done.

'My father,' whispered Degmar, pointing at a shorter, older version of himself, who glowered even more, and muttered a curse. 'My mother.' A fine-boned woman with long hair met Tullus' glance with icy disdain. 'My youngest sister.' The last of the three, an attractive woman in a dark cloak, sniffed and turned away.

'I am glad to meet you,' Tullus said in careful German. 'We must hurry from here.'

Degmar's father spat on the ground.

'I would be the same,' Tullus said as Degmar's mouth opened. 'Fetch your other sister.'

Degmar sped off, leaving Tullus and his men to guard his resentful family. To everyone's relief, he returned soon after with a man and a woman, both of whom looked surprised, angry and resentful. A sleeping baby strapped to the woman's chest remained oblivious to its parents' unhappiness.

Degmar's father chose this moment to begin arguing with his son. The older sister's husband leaped in too. Degmar's demands for them to be quiet were in vain. Tullus watched with increasing anxiousness. Every heartbeat that thudded by, every angry exclamation, increased the danger they were in. Two horrifying thoughts soon struck him. Had the argument been staged by Degmar, to make fleeing Tullus' only option? Perhaps the Marsi warrior even intended that he and his men should die here?

A solid smack rang out, and Tullus' eyes shot to Degmar's father, who was reeling back, clutching his cheek. Degmar bristled before him, his hand raised to strike again. 'We leave *now*,' he hissed. 'All of us.'

Tullus felt instant remorse for having doubted Degmar.

Degmar's father gave a meek nod; his brother-in-law glowered, but did not argue further. Quiet sobs racked his mother; she was being comforted by her younger daughter, while the other one rocked to and fro, caressing her baby as if this were an everyday situation.

'Who's there?' called a voice from the direction of the feasting area.

Curse it all to Hades, thought Tullus, signing his men to group together.

'None of your business, you sot. Go back to sleep,' called Degmar.

'Screw you!'

'Move! Now!' whispered Degmar, pushing his parents and sisters forward. 'To the split oak.'

'Piso, Vitellius, Saxa, Metilius, go with Degmar. We'll follow when you've got a head start,' whispered Tullus. 'See you at the tree.'

With relieved looks, the legionaries did as he ordered. Fenestela stood by Tullus' side, watching the man who'd challenged them. He was some fifty paces away, and was rousing his companions, but he was also casting frequent looks in their direction.

'There are *many* places I'd rather be at this moment,' muttered Fenestela. 'And I'd give a year's pay for my armour.'

'You'll be able to run faster without it,' advised Tullus, eliciting a snort by way of reply.

Humour aside, there was a grim reality to Fenestela's words. The warrior who'd confronted them had woken four others. They were struggling to their feet, while their comrade kicked at other men to stir them too. Tullus had no illusions about taking on so many enemies. Drunk or not, they would overwhelm him and Fenestela. 'Best go,' he said, ignoring the sweat slicking down his back. 'Otherwise, we'll never leave. You first.'

It was reassuring that there was no immediate pursuit. Tullus moved as fast as he could without losing the trail. He glanced back often, but they reached the safety of the trees challenged only by a few dogs inside the nearby longhouses. Tullus had taken a dislike to forests since Arminius' ambush, but he was right glad to be in the midst of one now, to have the trunks close around him and the canopy lowering overheard.

They found Degmar and his family in an odd stand-off with the four legionaries. The two little groups were glaring at each other over the piles of armour and equipment. Tullus eased into the gap. 'We made it,' he said. 'Well done, all.'

'I don't trust this lot, sir,' said Saxa, his eyes gleaming. 'Especially the father.'

'They don't trust *you*,' Degmar retorted. 'Truth be told, I don't either.'

Tullus didn't see who moved first, but more than one hand went to a sword hilt. 'Stop it!' he ordered. 'You lot, get your armour on, double quick, and quieter than you've ever done in your miserable lives. I don't want a sound to be audible more than fifty paces away.' To his relief, the legionaries obeyed, and there was an instant drop in tension. Tullus shot a look at Degmar. 'You had best leave.'

They locked eyes. Emotions flickered back and forth like bolts of lightning between them. Like, dislike. Trust, mistrust. Friendship, enmity. There was even love – and a trace of hate.

'So this is what it has come to,' said Tullus, sighing. 'I wish that things could have been different.'

'And I,' answered Degmar.

'I thought you were going to set the whole village upon us back there.'

Degmar chuckled. 'I was thinking about it.'

I *did* read him correctly, thought Tullus with a thrill of dread. 'What stopped you?'

'My oath, and the knowledge that even if I'd helped my people to escape, the Romans would still hunt them down.'

Again Tullus was grateful for Degmar's sense of honour. He wondered if Degmar would warn the village's inhabitants once he and his men had left. If the village was empty at sunrise *and* there was no sign of Degmar, Tullus was the one who would be blamed.

The *crack* as someone stood on a piece of fallen wood somewhere to their left, followed by another and another, were therefore a welcome relief. 'That'll be some of the auxiliaries,' he whispered. 'Go, before they catch you.'

Disappointment flared in Degmar's eyes, and Tullus knew that the Marsi warrior *had* been intending to alert his people. He wouldn't risk it now, with his family in danger – whatever he was, he was no fool.

'I don't think we will meet again,' said Tullus, feeling a rush of sadness. 'My thanks for your service.'

'I am still in your debt,' growled Degmar. 'I *will* find you again one day.'

'Gods grant that you do so,' said Tullus, offering his hand. 'In happier times.'

They shook, hard, and then Degmar urged his family away, towards the south.

Despite the fact that their mission had succeeded, Tullus felt a deep melancholy. He didn't know which was worse: the loss of a loyal friend or the fact that, come the dawn, he would have to take part in a massacre.

Chapter XVII

T he rest of Tullus' night passed in a chilly daze of sentry duty, liaising with units of auxiliaries as they appeared, and trying to get a little sleep. By the time tinges of pink and red were visible in the eastern sky, he was tired, hungry and short-tempered. His cohort had found him, however, and the 'net' that was Germanicus' army had been tightened around the village without any indication that the Marsi had realised what was happening.

As the sun rose, Tullus convened a meeting of his centurions, repeating Germanicus' command that there were to be no survivors. No one questioned his orders, but he noticed his own distaste, mirrored and quickly concealed, in a few faces. It was one thing to act so in a war, thought Tullus, and another to destroy a village that had been feasting the day before. What choice had they, however, but to follow orders? He hardened his heart, remembering the hordes of warriors descending on his soldiers in the forest, the crimson-spattered, spear-decorated bodies decorating the mud and the piercing screams of the wounded.

The Marsi were not a peace-loving people – they were proud and warlike, and had been willing participants in Arminius' uprising. The elderly among them had been young once and, like as not, they had slain legionaries aplenty then. Their women had birthed the warriors who'd taken part in the ambush. The children would be old enough one day to fight Rome's legions, or to bring new members of the tribe – more enemies – into this world. They all had to die.

After a time, his conscience had been silenced. The fate of the Marsi would send the starkest of messages to every German tribe, and in particular to the ones that had been allied to Arminius five years before.

Defy Rome, and this will be your destiny, thought Tullus.

He said the same thing to his men. They were avenging their comrades, who had been so foully betrayed and murdered. Blood had to be shed – oceans of it – before the tormented ghosts of the dead could rest in peace.

He was glad when the trumpets sounded the advance. Glad that their waiting was over. Glad, after so long, to be in a position to begin avenging his slaughtered men.

His pleasure soured fast as they approached the now familiar Marsi settlement. Degmar had been correct, Tullus thought. Vast amounts of beer must have been consumed the night before, as the only figures visible as they neared the buildings were those of children. They clustered together as the lines of armoured legionaries closed in, crying out in fear, abandoning their play and forgetting their animal charges – sheep, goats and cattle. Alerted by the commotion, women rushed screaming from their doorways. Late – too late – warriors began to emerge from longhouses, or pick themselves up from where they'd been sleeping, staring in disbelief at the advancing Romans and grabbing whatever weapons were to hand. In twos and threes, they charged forward. Voices hoarse from drinking sang the barritus, but the rendition was thin, reedy. The last time Tullus and his men had heard it, his legionaries had quailed in fear, and even wept. Now they laughed. Jeered. Spat.

In unison, the centurions halted their troops. When the charging warriors were fifty paces away, a volley of javelins went up. Against so few enemies, its effect was devastating, and corpses and wounded men soon littered the ground. Only a few warriors remained unharmed, but, desperate to defend their families, they ran on, straight into the shield wall. They fell without killing a single legionary. They're dying like men, thought Tullus, but to what purpose? If he had been in their place, with Sirona, say, he would have run. You're getting soft, he told himself. Stop it.

The efficiency with which their fellows had been slain snapped the remaining Marsi warriors' courage the way a child breaks a twig in two. Gathering their womenfolk and children, they fled from the advancing Romans. Hoots of derision rose from the legionaries. 'Ah, don't go!' 'You won't get far!' 'There's a nice surprise waiting for you on the other side of the village!'

'Hold your lines,' roared Tullus. Like cats with captured mice, his men's instinctive reaction was to chase after their prey. The grim truth was that there was no need to run. 'Shields ready. Draw swords. Forward, at the walk.'

When they reached the first longhouses, their lines had to break up. Parties of legionaries were sent in to search for anyone who hadn't yet run. Tullus and the rest continued on into the settlement, cutting down a warrior here and there. It wasn't long before the first screams reached Tullus' ears – the voice was that of a woman, or perhaps even a girl. His stomach did a nauseating roll, but he didn't intervene.

Rape was the norm during brutal situations like this. What was happening in the longhouse behind him was about to be repeated scores of times, all over the settlement. Tullus could no more prevent it than he could stop the tide. Stay focused, he thought. Keep control of your men as best you can. Make sure there are no casualties. Endure. It *will* end.

Despite his resolve, their time in the village seemed to last an eternity. Tullus grew weary of the sight of bodies, the piteous cries of the wounded, and the acrid stench of burning flesh wafting from burning houses. Men and women, children, greybeards and crones: they lay everywhere. On their backs, their fronts, sprawled on their sides, or heaped on top of one another in death's emotionless embrace. Flies swarmed over the pools of clotting blood. Overhead, crows and ravens gathered, black-winged messengers of doom.

The animals weren't immune from the savagery either. Dogs were slain out of hand. Hens had their necks wrung or were tossed, squawking, into the blazing houses. Shrieking pigs writhed on the javelins spitting them through and through. A horse that had been disembowelled walked in ever-decreasing circles, winding tight the sinuous loops of bowels around its lower legs. Laughing soldiers chased sheep around pens, stabbing them so many times that their wool turned crimson before they collapsed.

By midday or thereabouts, the slaughter was over. Faces blackened with soot and caked with blood, wild-eyed legionaries sat around, swilling the beer they'd found and arguing over who had killed the most tribesmen, and other, uglier things. Tullus issued orders to his officers, and then, calm and methodical, they re-established control over their troops, the way a rider of a bolted horse coaxes it back to his hand. According to a messenger, Germanicus had ordered the army to move on to the next village, which was some five miles distant. There was enough daylight left to reach it and put its inhabitants to the sword, the messenger said, before riding on.

At last the contubernia and centuries began to re-form under the direction of Tullus' officers. He watched in silence, standing with his back towards a longhouse that was a little smaller than most. It was positioned at the edge of the settlement, almost as if the person living in it hadn't really wanted to live close to anyone else. It hadn't been burned down, but the smashed-in door and a couple of nearby dead sheep were evidence that it had been ransacked.

Or so Tullus thought.

Amidst the uproar of bellowed orders, tramping feet and the soldiers' resentful comments, he heard a low cry, as a child might make in fear. It was stifled by something – or someone – which drew Tullus' attention at once. He might have done nothing, but other men had heard it too. One of his centurions asked permission to send men into the longhouse. 'I'll do it,' said Tullus. 'Piso! Vitellius!' he shouted. 'Over here.'

The two legionaries were with him in a few strides, their faces as sweat-covered and dirty as anyone's. Vitellius had scratches running down one cheek, as might have been made by a woman's fingernails. Tullus put that image from his mind. 'Come with me.'

Tullus led the way. He stepped inside the longhouse with care, sword ready by his side, shield high enough that anyone hurling a spear would have to hit him in the face. Nothing was thrown, and he paused to let his eyes adjust to the gloom. It was a typical farmer's dwelling, with a packed-earth floor. Livestock pens – empty – filled the space to his right, and living quarters – low beds, a stone ring fireplace, blackened pots and pans – the area to his left. Dried herbs and meats dangled from the beams above. Tools and implements – rakes, hammers, a twig broom, a saw, two axes – leaned against or hung from the walls to either side.

Tullus shuffled a few steps further inside, allowing Piso and Vitellius to enter. 'Search the pens,' he whispered. 'Be careful.'

Ignoring their curious stares, Tullus moved towards the living area, treading light, eyes darting from side to side. There was no sign of life. Every few steps, he stopped to listen. The only audible sounds were Piso and Vitellius murmuring, and the creaking of wicker hurdles as they were moved aside. Closer to the fireplace, he could see that it had been used that morning – the embers at its heart were yet glowing. Some kind of broth steamed in a pot that hung from an iron tripod over the fire, and Tullus' belly rumbled. He hadn't eaten in many hours.

Whoever had been cooking appeared to have fled. So too did whoever, or whatever, had alerted him. Tullus propped his shield against a wooden pillar and picked up a ladle. Scooping up a measure, he blew on it until it was cool enough to swallow. The broth was delicious – root vegetables with herbs, he thought, bending over the pot for a second time.

A tiny sound behind him – a sandal scraping off the floor, perhaps – rang an alarm in his head. He wheeled around, ladle in one hand, sword in the other, feeling like a complete fool. To die because his hunger had got the better of him would be a stupid way to go. To his huge relief, he saw no hulking warrior with a ready spear, no woman brandishing a carving knife. He wasn't alone, however. Tullus was *sure* of that. Laying down the ladle, he moved, cat-soft, towards the beds. There were six of them, three facing three, with narrow gaps between the head of one and the foot of the next.

Bad places to hide, thought Tullus, spying a shape covered by an old blanket in one gap, and opposite it, a second. Only a simpleton could think they wouldn't be found here. That, or the legionaries who'd been in here had already been pissed out of their minds. He poked the first shape with the tip of his sword. 'Get up,' he ordered in German. 'Now.'

With a resentful shrug, the blanket slid to the floor, revealing a freckle-faced girl of about ten years. Clad in a shapeless dress, she was barefoot. Rags or no, she was proud, glaring at Tullus despite the fear in her eyes. She stood, calling out in a soft voice to whoever was hidden opposite her.

The toe of a worn shoe was poking from under the second blanket. This had been the person Tullus had heard. 'On your feet,' he ordered.

There was a sigh, such as the old make when their joints hurt, and the covering fell away. An ancient woman, her face lined with deep wrinkles, stared at Tullus with calm resignation. 'Kill us and be done.'

Tullus extended a hand and helped her up. The crone gasped with pain as she came fully upright. To Tullus' surprise, she chuckled. 'At least my hip won't trouble me when I'm dead.'

It all made sense now, thought Tullus. Only a fool would stay behind in such a poor hiding place – or a child who wouldn't leave her lame grandmother.

'There's no one in the pens, sir,' said Piso, arriving with Vitellius. He eyed Tullus' captives. A flicker of distaste passed across his friendly face. 'D'you want me to finish them?'

If the two didn't speak Latin, they understood his tone. The girl rushed to her grandmother's side and clung to her. The old woman muttered something Tullus didn't catch, but which might have been, 'We won't suffer.'

'Shall I kill them, sir?' repeated Piso. Vitellius stood ready beside him, his face a mask.

Is this what I am now? Tullus asked himself. What we are? Murderers of the helpless and infirm? He looked at the girl again, who was similar in size to Artio, and the old woman, who would have found it difficult to swat a fly, let alone harm his men. 'No,' he grated. 'Vitellius, watch them. Piso, come with me.'

Like other longhouses, the walls had been built by fixing a lattice of small branches between wooden posts driven into the ground. The meshwork of branches had then been slathered with a generous covering of mixed clay, earth, dung and straw. Tullus found a spot in the back wall and slammed his heel against it. Brown clods broke away, and he stamped again, snapping a few branches. Using his sword to enlarge the gap, he soon created a hole large enough for the girl to get out. He peered outside, and was pleased to see the tree line no more than twenty steps away.

'Make it large enough for the old woman,' he ordered Piso. 'Do it fast.' Tullus could have sworn that Piso looked pleased – he certainly set to with a will.

'You must go now,' Tullus said to the pair. 'Through the hole at the back. The forest is close. Our soldiers are no longer encircling the village, so you will be able to escape.'

They stared at him with disbelief.

Tullus repeated what he'd said. As the trumpets ordered the advance outside, he added, 'Move! Someone might still come in. They won't be so merciful.'

'Merciful?' the girl hissed, her eyes now wild with hate. 'You call butchering the inhabitants of a village merciful?'

'Move,' Tullus ordered, pointing with his sword.

The girl's grandmother whispered in her ear, and she quietened. Together they walked to the hole in the back wall. As Piso stood aside, he proffered a lump of bread. 'You need this more than me,' he said in broken German.

Again the girl seemed about to express her anger, but the old woman took the bread with gratitude. She urged her granddaughter outside. Then, easing herself into the hole, she glanced back at Tullus and gave him a nod, before also disappearing.

Tullus felt a little less soiled. He eyed Piso and Vitellius, who were waiting for him to speak. 'Not a word about this to anyone, you understand? Not a fucking word. If I hear as much as a whisper, you'll wish you had never been whelped, so help me.'

'Aye, sir,' they both muttered.

'Outside,' ordered Tullus.

He was emerging from the longhouse's doorway when Tubero came riding up, his usual retinue behind him. As usual, the sight of Tullus made his lip curl. 'I come to inspect your cohort, centurion, and instead find you ransacking a hovel for scraps like some common soldier. So much for the pride of the legions!'

A dutiful laugh rose from his staff officers, and Tullus' temper, so often his bane, flared. 'I wasn't looking for food, sir. I heard something inside, and went to investigate.'

'That's more commendable. How many more did you kill?'

'None, sir,' replied Tullus, forcing a regretful expression on to his face. 'It must have been a scavenging dog. There's a hole in the back wall, you see.'

'A dog?' The disbelief was clear in Tubero's voice. His gaze fell on Piso and Vitellius. 'Did either of you set eyes on this *dog*?'

'No, sir,' said Vitellius, 'but I heard it.'

'Me too, sir,' lied Piso with relish.

Tubero's lips thinned, but his interest moved on. 'Time to leave this shit-hole, centurion. Are your men ready?'

'Yes, sir.'

'I understand that the next village is larger than this. We'll have to work hard to ensure that all of the Marsi filth are laid in the mud before dark. I expect your cohort to play its part.'

'It will, sir, as ever,' replied Tullus, wishing that a battle awaited, not another massacre.

With another contemptuous look, Tubero rode on to the next unit.

Tullus tried to find solace in the fact that he had saved two lives, but in the face of what they had done, and what awaited them a few miles away, it was impossible. The coming days would prove no better, he knew. The only choice left open to him was to wall off what happened — even to pretend it wasn't happening — and carry on.

Perhaps there was one benefit to the mass slaughter, he decided. Germanicus' campaign of death and destruction would attract Arminius' attention in the same way as the screams of a wounded rabbit drew in a hunting fox.

To Tullus' frustration, Arminius and his Cherusci warriors did not materialise during the following days. Unhindered, the legions and auxiliaries laid waste to every Marsi settlement that they found. News of their presence spread fast, and a good number of the villages were deserted by the time the army arrived. It was a secret relief to Tullus, although he admitted that to no one.

They found no sign of the eagle mentioned by Degmar. Numerous chieftains and tribal priests died under torture ordered by Germanicus, protesting that they knew nothing. The prisoners were either telling the truth, Tullus concluded, or regarded the eagle as a prize worth dying for. Either way, the Romans' failure to locate even one golden standard – most particularly for Tullus, that of the Eighteenth – boded ill for their recovery.

He drank a lot of wine during the month-long campaign.

The Romans' brutal tactics soon provoked the local tribes – the Bructeri, Usipetes and Tubantes – to take up arms. Wary of confronting Germanicus' heavily armed legionaries in open battle, they began to harass the force as it marched back to the Rhenus, the job of restoring morale complete. They attacked the Romans inside forested areas, as Arminius had done, where the legions could not deploy in their usual battle formations. Over a two-day period, more than half a dozen assaults were made on the miles-long column. Scores of soldiers were killed and injured, but discipline remained good, limiting the tribesmen's success. On the third day, knowing that Germanicus' host would soon reach the relative safety of open ground, they attacked in greater force, striking hardest at the rear.

That day, it was the turn of the Twentieth Legion to form the end of the column, so Tullus only heard the dramatic tale of what happened afterwards. Confused by the strong enemy attack, the Twentieth's lines had wavered. Heavy casualties were being sustained, and things were looking bleak until Germanicus, who had heard what was going on, rode back to seize control of the situation. His exhortations to the Twentieth's legionaries to turn their 'guilt into glory' had dramatic results. The tribesmen were driven back, allowing the army to stop and construct a fortified camp for the night.

Resistance melted away as the Rhenus drew near, allowing the army a safe passage to the western bank, and their camps. Spirits were high and the camaraderie of old had returned as the expedition came to an end. Wiser to his soldiers' needs since the rebellion, Germanicus discharged scores of veterans who had served their time. He also laid on several days of games. Food and wine was provided in great quantity for the festivities' duration. These unexpected bounties fell like spring rain on young seedlings. So too did the usual four-monthly payday, which was boosted by the addition of a special bonus paid for by Germanicus himself. Soon after, the governor departed for Rome – his mission there to report to Tiberius – content in the knowledge that normal life had resumed in Vetera.

He left instructions with Caecina, which were soon relayed to Tullus and the other centurions. The legions were to prepare for a major campaign the following spring. To keep the officers' minds focused on the task in hand, Germanicus' final words were repeated verbatim at the end of every meeting in the months that followed. 'Varus and his men *will* be avenged. Arminius and the tribes who massacred the three legions *will* pay. The lost eagles *will* be found, and our honour restored.'

They became Tullus' refrain as he knelt nightly before the shrine in his quarters.

'My soldiers will be avenged. Arminius and the tribes who massacred them will pay. The Eighteenth's eagle will be found, and my honour restored. Grant me these things, great Mars, and you can have anything.'

Each and every time, Tullus paused before adding, 'including my life'.

PART TWO

Spring, AD 15

Cherusci territory, deep in Germania

Chapter XVIII

॥॥॥

Arminius had been woken by the dawn chorus yet again. Although used to sleeping until later, he didn't mind. Each winter, the dark, the cold, the lack of sunlight and the drab brown of the countryside ground him down, month by dragging month. Spring's arrival – and with it, the birds' sounding of joy – was to be welcomed. He had slipped from under the bearskin and blankets, taking care not to wake Thusnelda. After a fond look down at her sleeping, pregnant form, he had dressed and gone alone to the sacred grove.

Some hours later, belly rumbling with hunger, right thigh aching, he came striding back into the settlement. A word with the guards outside Segestes' quarters – a daily habit – told him that the old man was up and about, and as irritable as ever. During Segestes' prolonged recovery from his beating, he had complained little, but things had changed of recent days. Arminius took a sour pleasure from hearing how pissed off he was.

Arminius' own wound from the arrow had healed well – the priest had seen to that. It had taken months to return to full health and, truth be told, his right leg wasn't as strong as before. It might never be, the priest had said. Keen to do all he could, Arminius was careful to do the exercises he'd been shown, and to have frequent massages. His efforts had paid off in part – training sessions with Maelo and other warriors were easier now. No one said it, but he knew he was no longer as dangerous a fighter.

I will be, one day, he told himself. Shoving away the bad mood that threatened, he returned the numerous greetings thrown his way, stopped to talk to an old friend of his father, and praised two boys driving a flock of sheep to pasture. By the time Arminius had reached his own longhouse, he was in good spirits again, and the rich smell of frying pork and mushrooms emanating from within made him smile. Thusnelda was preparing his breakfast.

He stole inside, putting a finger to his lips to silence the slaves working at the animals' end of the building, and stroking his dog's head to quieten it. Thusnelda had her back to him. She was busy, alternately stirring a pan on the fire and kneading dough on the large stone slab that served as a work surface. Arminius padded to within half a dozen paces of her before she realised. She let out a little gasp.

'I've told you not to do that! It's bad for the baby,' she scolded. Her happy expression contradicted her words, however, and she didn't resist as he wrapped his arms around her middle, caressing her belly.

'My son is a warrior! He won't be so easily scared,' Arminius said.

'You know it's a boy?' Her hands reached up to stroke his hair.

'Of course,' he replied, nuzzling her neck. 'He's my first-born. What else could he be?'

'Ha! The midwife says it will be a girl.'

'How can she know?' With gentle hands, Arminius turned her around. They locked eyes, and kissed. Thusnelda pulled away after a moment and Arminius cried, 'Hey!'

'The pork is about to burn,' she retorted, laughing and flipping the meat in the pan. 'Are you hungry?'

'Starving.'

'I thought you would be. You went to the grove?'

'Aye.'

She studied his face, searching for a clue.

'I saw nothing,' he said with a dismissive flick of his wrist. 'It doesn't matter. The god isn't going to offer me something every time I'm there, is he?'

'I suppose not.'

'Inguiomerus is with us, and his people. After the Roman attacks last autumn, so are the Marsi. The Angrivarii won't take much persuading, nor will the rest. I'll have to visit the chieftains, but by spring's end, I will have an army large enough to tackle Germanicus.'

She frowned. 'You'll have to leave soon.'

'There's no way around it, my love. But I shall return inside a month.'

'Not for long, though, and then you will be away all summer, fighting.'

'You knew the type of man I was when you married me,' he said, his voice hardening. 'Rome has to be taught another lesson if we are to free ourselves from its yoke – and its taxes.'

'And if you succeed, will that be the end of it? What's to say the legions won't cross the river again? Will you have to go to war every summer, until one year you do not return? I'll be left a widow, and your children fatherless.' She was crying now, and smoke was rising unnoticed from the frying meat.

He took a step towards her, but she motioned him away. 'Don't!'

His own anger rising, Arminius turned.

'Wait. Your pork is ready.'

Arminius hesitated. Leaving without a word, letting her cooking go to waste, would be satisfying. To do so, however, would deepen the rift that had just opened between them. The resulting argument might last for days, or even longer. Their fiery relationship had seen that happen before. Better to stay, he decided. 'Thank you,' he said in a conciliatory tone. 'It smells delicious.'

'I've gone and burned it,' she replied, scowling.

'You haven't, my love. Come, have some with me. You're eating for two now.'

She shook her head: no.

'Feeling sick?'

'It will pass.' She motioned him to the table. 'Sit. I'll join you.'

'I'm a lucky man,' said Arminius as she piled his plate high and placed it before him. 'Not only are you a skilled cook, and beautiful – you're bearing my son.'

His flattery worked, and she took the stool beside his. 'You're not the only fortunate one. My husband is a fine, honourable man, and the greatest chieftain in the land. The man who united the tribes.'

They kissed again. Thusnelda pulled away at length. 'Eat. It will go cold.'

'You've put in some wild garlic,' Arminius said halfway through the first mouthful. 'It's delicious.'

Thusnelda smiled. 'I do my best.'

'You do far more than that.' He squeezed her hand.

An easy conversation, the kind held between two people who know each other inside and out, followed. Arminius had just cleared his plate when excited shouting broke out some distance from the longhouse.

Using his tunic to wipe his lips, and ignoring the disapproving look that Thusnelda gave him for it, he kissed the top of her head and made for the door. 'My thanks for the food.'

Osbert, one of Arminius' best warriors, hove into sight as he emerged. Squat, barrel-chested and a lover of drinking and fighting, Osbert had seized one of the Roman eagles during their ambush on Varus' legions. His thunderous expression revealed much, and Arminius cursed. Life had a way of souring things just when they were going well, yet it didn't pay to let on that he could be so easily upset. He raised a hand. 'Ho, Osbert! Looking for me?'

'Aye. Two Chatti warriors have just ridden in.'

The Chatti lands lay some distance to the south and southwest. Dealings with them weren't uncommon. Nor were they everyday, thought Arminius with a trace of unease. 'Their tidings?'

'Not good. Germanicus has taken advantage of the lack of rain, and crossed the river early, in strength.'

'I'll see them at once.' Ignoring his twinging thigh, Arminius strode the way Osbert had come.

A large crowd – men, women and children – had gathered in the central meeting area, but they made way for Arminius and Osbert. Pressing through the throng, Arminius found Maelo sitting with two warriors, one of whom was wounded. Both men were spattered with mud and had haggard, grey expressions. Arminius had never seen either before, but wasn't surprised that they seemed to recognise him. He was well known among the tribes.

'Arminius,' croaked the uninjured warrior, a yellow-bearded, short man in the prime of life.

'Well met,' said Yellow Beard's companion, who had a wide face and drooping moustache. His clothes were so crusty and red-stained that Arminius judged some of the blood had to be Roman.

'And the same to you. You are welcome in my village,' said Arminius, inclining his head. 'Has the priest been called for, to see to this man?'

'Aye,' replied Maelo.

'I've ridden day and night to get here,' said Drooping Moustache. 'The priest can look at me after we've told you our news.'

'Germanicus has attacked your people,' said Arminius.

Yellow Beard grimaced. 'Aye. He divided his forces so that they could attack us from two directions. There were five legions, or the equivalent, in each "prong".' Arminius exchanged a dismayed look with Maelo as Yellow Beard continued, 'We had no scouts out. The first warning we had of their arrival was a few hours before their host began surrounding our settlements.'

'No one expects to go to war this early in the year,' said Arminius, grateful that his people's territory lay so much further from the Rhenus. 'Scheming Roman bastards.'

'Every warrior who could fight marched out to face them.' A deep sadness filled Yellow Beard's eyes. 'We left our homes undefended.'

'In the face of an overwhelming attack, that is sometimes the best tactic,' said Arminius.

'Except we were driven back, over the Adrana River,' came the bitter reply. 'The Romans fell upon our villages like wolves on a flock abandoned by the shepherd. Thousands of our women and children were slaughtered or enslaved.' Yellow Beard's voice caught, and he had to compose himself. 'Our counter-attack made some ground at first, but we were forced to retreat a second time when they brought their archers and bolt-throwers into action.'

A silence fell, and Arminius waited. Tragedies of this magnitude hit a man hard.

After a time, Yellow Beard began again. 'Some warriors thought Germanicus might negotiate. We argued for hours, but in the end an embassy was sent to the Roman camp.' A heavy sigh. 'It was foolish even to think he might deal with us. The dog rejected our offer out of hand. Germanicus said that he had not come to make peace, but war. The news made many give up hope. Perhaps half the tribe surrendered without conditions, while the rest fled into the forests and hid.'

'This is terrible,' Arminius said. 'May the gods succour your people in their time of need.'

'There wasn't any sign of the gods when the Romans attacked, I can tell you,' said Yellow Beard, his face twisting with anger. 'When the killing was done, they destroyed what grain supplies remained, and burned every settlement to the ground, including our capital, Mattium. My people are destitute.'

'The Cherusci will send as much aid as we can spare: food, blankets, weapons, medicines,' said Arminius at once. 'A hundred of my warriors will accompany you back to your lands, and stay until shelters have been built for all.'

'You are generous indeed. We thank you.' Yellow Beard bent his head. So did Drooping Moustache.

'Let me guess Germanicus' next move,' Arminius continued. 'He is going to strike north at us, the Cherusci.'

'That would be my guess,' replied Yellow Beard. 'You know the old camp built by Drusus' legions?'

'I do.' Built a generation before on one of the sources of the River Visurgis, the fortress had been deserted for many years. A strong hill position made it almost impregnable, thought Arminius, but of far greater concern was its proximity to his tribe's territory.

'Roman scouts occupy it already.'

Arminius absorbed this news with real alarm. If the rest of the Roman host was heading to Drusus' old camp, which now seemed possible, Germanicus *was* intent on attacking his people next. 'This is what you rode here to tell me?'

'Aye,' said Yellow Beard. 'No man would wish what befell the Chatti on his worst enemy.'

'Then it is my turn to thank *you*,' said Arminius. He turned to Maelo. 'Send a summons to all the settlements. Every whole-bodied warrior must be ready to fight within two days. I want every senior chieftain here by tomorrow.'

Maelo was up and moving before he'd finished talking. Arminius eyed the Chatti warriors again. 'You are exhausted, and grieving for your loved ones. Take rest now. We can talk again later.'

Yellow Beard and Drooping Moustache gave him grateful nods as they were ushered away. Arminius raised his hands, silencing the unhappy muttering that had broken out among those listening. 'Do not let fear enter your hearts!' he shouted. 'Remember what I did to the Romans the last time they were in our lands!'

Faces lit up. 'Those were blessed days.' 'The gods were smiling on us.'

'It seems the bastards weren't taught enough of a lesson five and a half years ago. They will learn it anew! The ground will be soaked in their blood, and the forest carpeted with their dead. Our warriors will return laden with booty. Victory will be ours!' Arminius raised a fist and they cheered him – not as loud as he would have liked, but enough to show their courage hadn't been destroyed by the Chatti warriors' bloodcurdling tale.

Arminius felt little of his proclaimed confidence. With the Romans so close, there wouldn't be time to rally more than the warriors of his Cherusci faction, as well as those of Inguiomerus. Their total strength would be perhaps nine thousand spears, nowhere near what was needed to defeat Germanicus' entire host – or even half of it.

Fear, real fear such as Arminius had not felt in many a year, raked at his guts.

Chapter XIX

Tullus' mount tossed its head, and gave its neighbour to the left a playful nip on the ear. Its target was unappreciative, whickering and biting back. Tullus and the other rider – no less than Flavus, Arminius' brother – had to spend a few moments reassuring their horses before calm had been restored. The pair, along with three *turmae* of auxiliary cavalry, were concealed in the forest some distance to the south of Arminius' settlement. Sunrise wasn't far off, and four days had passed since the Roman army had marched west, leaving them behind as the last Roman forces in the area.

Wary of the potential for disaster so deep in the tribal hinterland, Germanicus had opted not to strike at the Cherusci settlements and Arminius' jugular. Instead, he had led his high-spirited soldiers back to their camps. Germanicus hadn't taken all his troops, however. Frustrated by his own cautious decision to withdraw, he had ordered a daring raid to free Segestes. Speed would be of the essence during the mission, and so a cavalry force had been the obvious choice.

Flavus, a trusted ally still, had stayed behind with two turmae of his men and a *turma* of Chauci. He had been picked by virtue of his origins and relationship to Arminius; the Chauci because, unlike Flavus' warriors, they would arouse no suspicion when they rode in twos and threes as spies into the local settlements. Tullus was there because he was one of the few senior Roman soldiers left who would recognise Arminius. At first, Tullus had not been happy that Flavus was in command – he was Arminius' brother after all. Tullus had buried his misgivings after Flavus had explained the reason he had stayed loyal to Rome when his brother had not.

'Arminius and I never got on, even as boys,' he had said. 'A promise meant nothing to him then, and it still doesn't. Taking an oath is different for me. I'd rather die than go back on my word.' Flavus had stared at Tullus, meeting his gaze for long moments. In the end, Tullus had decided that Flavus telling the truth, and he respected him for it.

Hiding nearly ninety men and horses was impossible for long, and the force had ridden – under the cover of darkness, two nights running – from Germanicus' last camp straight towards Arminius' settlement. Their luck had been in, and no one had found their daytime hiding places in the forests. On the third morning, groups of the Chauci had gone to scout the area, and to see how many warriors they might face. They had returned with good news. Segestes was still a captive, and most of Arminius' best men were absent. The bad news was that so too was he, visiting the nearby tribes. Germanicus' other order, to kill Arminius if they could, had become an impossibility. Tullus couldn't help but feel disappointed.

Dawn had yet to break, on this, the fourth day, but it wouldn't be long coming. Birds were calling from every tree. An orange-red colour was seeping up the sky from the east, and the night chill was receding. Tullus bent his neck to one side, then the other, stretching taut muscles. They would move soon. Arminius' absence now meant that Tullus was not needed, yet he was glad to be here. Success would be akin to giving Arminius a hefty kick in the balls, and a real blow to his pride. Better that than nothing. And failure? Tullus didn't dwell on that, beyond asking Mars not to let him be taken by the enemy. Death would be preferable.

'Ready?' asked Flavus. A blocky man, he had the blond hair that had given him his Roman name, but his scarred face was similar to that of Arminius. Despite having only one eye, he had the same intense stare, the type that won fights before they had started.

'Run through the plan one more time,' replied Tullus.

'It's two miles to the settlement. We travel there at the trot. On the outskirts, we split up. The Chauci will ride among the houses on the left, and one of my turmae those to the right. I'll take my second turma and surround the building where Segestes is being held – one of the Chauci will be there to point it out. You'll be with me.'

'We kill Segestes' guards, and free him,' added Tullus. 'Any horses present are to be driven off, and then the longhouses are to be sacked.' Germanicus had given orders to search for standards and other valuables lost during the ambush. Rumour was that the Cheruscan leader had given the three eagles as rewards to his allies, but Tullus still dared to hope that this was not the case.

'Aye. The warriors mustn't lose control of themselves, or the whole thing might come undone. If Arminius' second-in-command Maelo is about, he could rally the warriors.'

'Will your men do as they're told?' asked Tullus. Once the bloodlust took hold, soldiers became hard to rein in, and auxiliaries' discipline was nothing like that in the legions.

'They will, or they'll face this,' replied Flavus with a grim tap on his sword hilt. 'The chieftain leading the Chauci has sworn his riders will obey him. If it goes to plan, we'll be riding away within the hour.'

Tullus nodded. All *I* have to do is not fall off my horse, or get hit by a spear, he thought. He fixed his mind on the outside chance that they might find an eagle, maybe even *his* eagle. Such cheering thoughts were hard to maintain, however, and he was relieved when Flavus gave the order to ride out.

Tullus had travelled to this region once before, under Tiberius, but never with so few companions. As the farmers' fields and scattered houses passed by, Tullus brooded on the fact that ninety riders was a puny force compared to the number of warriors a large settlement could put out. He hoped the scouts' information was accurate, and that most of Arminius' men were away. Tullus couldn't say this, but it was unsettling to have German auxiliaries around him rather than Roman legionaries. Yet the dice had been thrown, so he shoved away his concern as best he could.

Thanks to the early hour, few souls registered their passing, although many must have wondered from their beds what the pounding hooves signified. An occasional figure, herding cattle or sheep to pasture, or fetching water from a well, watched in awed silence as the group trotted by. A farmer called out a greeting, but no one replied.

Tullus was riding at the front, with Flavus. He'd been given a calm chestnut from among the horses on offer – 'I want a battle-steady mount that will go all day, and obey my commands,' he'd told the lead groom – and thus far it had served him well. 'Good boy,' he muttered, rubbing its sweating neck. 'Not long now.'

At first, their approach did not cause any alarm. Indeed, those tending livestock shouted greetings. Even the startled old man squatting on his haunches by a dungheap lifted a hand. Tullus felt little sympathy for those who were about to die. These were Arminius' people – Cherusci. Men, women and children, their hands were stained with Roman blood. With the blood of Tullus' men.

Astute, Flavus maximised the shock of their arrival by giving the order to ready weapons only when they had ridden up to the first longhouses. 'To your positions,' he cried, pointing to left and right. 'With me,' he yelled to his chosen warriors, and headed towards the central meeting area.

Tullus was without a spear, and he left his sword in its scabbard as they pounded along – he was no cavalryman. What fighting there was to be done, he'd do on foot. His decision left him vulnerable, and he kept close behind Flavus. Happily, the path to Segestes' longhouse lay bare of warriors. A vacant-looking youth who didn't get out of the way was cut down, and a woman standing in her doorway took a well-hurled spear through the belly, but there was no one to confront them. Four guards stood outside Segestes' prison, but they stood no chance against thirty fast-riding, combat-ready warriors. A volley of spears scythed in with lethal force before the sentries had had a chance to do anything. They fell to the ground, dead or dying.

The party dismounted, handing their reins to the three men delegated to hold the horses. In the lead, Flavus was already throwing open the door, his sword ready. He exchanged a look with Tullus – 'Ready?' – and they ducked inside. The place reeked of damp, mouldy thatch and sweat. There was little furniture, apart from a bed near one end, a table and one chair. This last was being brandished by a wild-eyed Segestes who had heard the commotion outside.

'Come on, you cowards!' he roared.

'Peace,' said Flavus, lowering his sword and motioning Tullus to do the same. 'We have come to free you.'

'Eh?' Hope mixed with the suspicion in Segestes' rheumy eyes as he lowered the chair. 'Flavus? Can it be you?'

'It is, and I am Senior Centurion Tullus,' said Tullus in Latin, stepping into the light entering from the chimney hole in the roof and pulling back his cloak so that the phalerae on his chest winked and glittered. All of a moment, Segestes' bravado vanished, and a smile worked its way on to his lined face. 'Segimundus' message got through.'

'It did. Your captivity is over. Come.' Flavus beckoned.

'We've been told that Arminius is away,' said Tullus, his heart pounding. 'Is that true?'

'Aye. The whoreson is off recruiting more chieftains to his cause.' Segestes spat on the floor.

The news wasn't unexpected, yet fresh bitterness scourged Tullus.

'But my daughter – Arminius' wife – is here,' said Segestes. 'And she's carrying his child.'

New options presented themselves to Tullus. 'Are they happily wed?'

'They've been like two moonstruck calves since they met. My disapproval meant nothing to either of them.' Segestes spat again. 'To you Romans, Arminius is the violator of a treaty, but to me, he's the abductor of a daughter.'

They had to seize her, Tullus decided. If Artio, the person he cherished most, were taken hostage, it would drive him close to madness. Flavus seemed to have come to the same conclusion. 'Is she in their longhouse?' he demanded.

'I expect so,' replied Segestes.

'Take us there. Now,' ordered Flavus.

'It will be my pleasure,' replied Segestes, looking smug.

Outside, Tullus was happy to surrender his mount in order that the weakened Segestes could ride. Holding the reins, he was able to talk with the old man as he guided them between the longhouses, with Flavus and his warriors as protection. Around them, chaos reigned as some buildings were ransacked and others set on fire. The reek of smoke and burning flesh was thick in the air. Women screamed, men called for their comrades and babies wailed. Distinguishable as auxiliaries only because they were on horseback, Flavus' followers trotted hither and thither, killing at will.

Tullus took no joy from the indiscriminate carnage, yet he derived satisfaction from each dead warrior and retrieved Roman standard. There were plenty of both, but no legion eagles. Segestes appeared discomfited by the bloodshed, and when Tullus noticed, he said, 'Know that I became Rome's ally not because I hated my own kind, but because peace is better than war. If Arminius had not acted as he had, this would not be happening. The land would be at peace—'

'And upwards of fourteen thousand legionaries would still be alive,' interjected Tullus bitterly.

Understanding bloomed in Segestes' eyes. 'You served in one of the three legions! You were *there*?'

'I did, and I was. Like you, I tried to warn Varus before the ambush.' Segestes looked surprised, and Tullus went on, 'I'd had suspicions about Arminius for some time, but I had no proof, nothing solid to give Varus. Perhaps if I'd managed to speak with him just after you had, things might have been different, but he had gone hunting by the time I got to his tent. I didn't manage to approach him for days afterwards. Even then he wouldn't heed a word that I said.'

'Arminius' silver tongue has ever been able to win people over,' said Segestes with a scowl. 'Man or woman.

'She's in that one.' Segestes pointed at a longhouse to their left. 'How will Arminius react to the news of his pregnant wife being in the custody of Rome, I wonder?'

'My brother loves Thusnelda, and he has always wanted an heir. Their loss will drive him frantic,' said Flavus, his eye glittering. He shouted a command, and a dozen of his men barged their way into the house. An indignant scream went up, and then another. It wasn't long, however, before they emerged with Thusnelda, who kicked and struggled like a wild cat, needing four warriors to restrain her. One of her captors had a bleeding scratch on his face and a second was limping. 'She's spirited,' said Flavus.

'Aye.' Tullus felt little sympathy for Thusnelda — she was his hated enemy's wife. As long as they reached the nearest Roman forces before the inevitable pursuit caught up, they would have delivered a more humiliating blow to Arminius' pride than the freeing of his father-in-law. His fury would know no bounds. The next time there was an opportunity to face Germanicus' forces in battle, Arminius would not hold back.

But there would be no repeat of the bloody ambush in the forest and bog, thought Tullus with relish. Germanicus' eight legions guaranteed defeat for Arminius and his allies.

Chapter XX

A rminius was riding hard. He was, he thought, less than three miles from his settlement, and individual twists and turns of the woodland path were becoming familiar. A little way to his left, there, was a good spot for fishing the nearby stream. In the distance, he could see the low hill favoured by the local priests.

He'd been riding at breakneck speed for some time, and his mount was floundering. Strings of saliva ran from its open mouth and down its neck, and its sides were dark-streaked with sweat, but Arminius didn't give a shit. Infuriated by its gradual loss of pace, and without a whip, he had taken to slapping its haunches with the flat of his sword. If the beast died beneath him, so be it. Getting back was all that mattered.

Over the course of the previous two days, he'd crippled one horse and exhausted several others in his efforts to return. The warriors in his party had long since been left behind, but he didn't care about that either. 'On, curse you!' he cried, bringing down his blade on the horse's rear again, eliciting a deep grunt of pain. There was only a fractional increase in speed, which soon fell away. Arminius was about to strike the horse again, but it staggered, and he lowered his arm. There were no farmhouses in sight. If his mount collapsed, he would lose valuable time searching for a fresh one, or running to the settlement. Better, then, to ride on slower than he wished.

The news of Thusnelda's abduction and the freeing of Segestes could have reached him in few worse places. He had been on the far side of the River Albis, visiting the Semnones tribe, who lived to the east of the

Cherusci lands. At the time, it hadn't mattered that the chieftain he wanted to talk to was on a hunting trip a day's ride further east. That was until a warrior sent by Maelo had come looking for Arminius with the calamitous tidings. He could still see the fear – of his reaction – in the warrior's eyes, and his ears yet rang with Maelo's gut-wrenching words. 'Your brother Flavus has raided the settlement. Your wife has been taken, and Segestes freed. Our horses are gone too, but I have given chase.' A throbbing fury pulsed behind Arminius' eyes, causing a momentary darkening of his vision. *Thusnelda!* he wanted to scream.

Maelo got it wrong, he told himself. *The fool has addled his brain with too much barley beer, and dreamed the whole thing.* The tactic didn't work for even two heartbeats. He knew that his second-in-command was more loyal, more dependable than anyone. The stars would fall from the sky before Maelo sent such a message in error. Arminius ground his teeth. *I'll find you, Flavus, brother,* he thought, *and cut your beating heart from your chest – but not before I've fed you your own balls.*

He could see the first longhouses now. The chances of Maelo having rescued Thusnelda were slender, but Arminius' heart quickened anyway. 'Come on, you useless creature,' he shouted, hitting the horse again. This time, it didn't speed up at all, and despite his frustration, Arminius had to accept that its energy was spent. He threw himself from its back and began to run. 'Maelo? Where is Maelo?' he shouted, haring past a surprised-looking woman carrying two pails of water. He was past her so fast that her reply was lost. Arminius broke into a sprint, making for *his* longhouse.

He found a smouldering ruin. The walls remained, and the great oaken truss at each end that had held up the roof, but that was it. Even the doors had been burned away. The smell of charred flesh, whether animal or human, lingered in the air. The shock brought him to his knees, slumped his shoulders and bowed his head. Tears, such as Arminius never cried, welled in his eyes and poured unchecked down his cheeks. 'Thusnelda,' he whispered.

The attack was beyond anything he could have imagined from the Romans. It was so fucking clever. They must have known my warriors weren't here, Arminius decided, and that I was away. The realisation crashed in at once. Flavus had sent spies to the settlement beforehand. Finding its defences weakened, he had gone ahead with the raid, taking not just Segestes but the extra prize of Thusnelda.

'You're here,' croaked a familiar voice.

Arminius twisted around. Shock filled him. His left arm wrapped in a grubby bandage, his face spattered with mud and sweat, and with hair sticking out at every angle and purple craters under his eyes, Maelo was almost unrecognisable. Filthy-clothed, limping, he looked like a bog-buried corpse brought to life. Arminius rose. 'What news?'

Maelo shook his head, and the motion sent knives stabbing through every part of Arminius.

'I'm sorry,' said Maelo. 'I sent warriors after Segestes and Thusnelda on foot the moment I got back from my uncle's village, while we tried to round up the horses. Doing that took more than half a day. We then rode after them day and night, but the Romans' lead was too great, and Germanicus had five cohorts lying in wait thirty miles away to meet them. I led one attack anyway, and lost more than half the men with me. I thought about going at the whoresons again, but it would have been suicide.'

Arminius bunched his fists, and breathed deep, and unclenched them again. 'Tell me everything. Do not leave out a single detail.' He listened in grim silence as Maelo laid out the sorry tale from beginning to end.

'I should have been in the settlement. If I had, maybe I could have got her away to safety,' said Maelo, his eyes tortured. 'Forgive me.'

'Why shouldn't you have been visiting your uncle?' The words almost choked in Arminius' throat, so great was his own feeling of guilt. Why hadn't *he* been here? 'Gods,' he said. 'She'll be on the Roman side of the river by now. With her father.'

'Aye.' Again Maelo's gaze met Arminius'. 'Do you want me to raise a war party and see if we can free her?'

Arminius sighed. 'You're a good man, Maelo. There's nothing I would like more, but think of the strength of the Roman forces on the west bank of the Rhenus. We would be throwing away our own lives, and those of the warriors with us, for nothing. Thusnelda will be taken to Italy at once, as a trophy. The Romans want to ensure I never see her again, and that my son grows up without a father.' A wall of grief hit him, and he closed his eyes.

Maelo's hand on his shoulder, unasked for, gave him strength and focused his mind. The situation could have been far worse. The casualties suffered during the raid had been light. If Germanicus had attacked with greater force, they would have been cataclysmic. Not to do that, Arminius decided, had been a grave mistake by the Roman general. He let his rage swell again, letting its power fill every corner of his being.

'I will renew my war against Rome, not by treasonous means, nor against pregnant women, nor in darkness, but with honour, attacking its soldiers in daylight. If our fellow tribesmen love their lands and forefathers and their ancient ways more than life under the emperor's heel, then they *will* follow me. I will lead them to glory and to freedom rather than *Segestes*' – Arminius spat the word – 'who would give them nothing but shame and slavery.

'Give me the chance, great Donar, and I will slay not just Segestes and my motherless get of a brother, but Germanicus too,' he vowed, his voice throbbing with fury. 'And every legionary and auxiliary that follows in their wake.'

Vengeance had become the sole reason for Arminius' existence.

Chapter XXI

◰◰◰

His stomach churning, Piso studied the mainsail with jaundiced eyes. It had been hanging limp for some time, but now it fluttered and fell back against the mast. A heartbeat later, it did the same. And again. Air moved against Piso's cheek. A wind had come up at last. Standing close to the mast amongst his comrades, he watched as the great hemp rectangle billowed forward and sagged back by turns. Before long, it had swelled to its maximum, aiding the sweating oarsmen and driving the long, shallow-bottomed craft out into the Mare Germanicum. Less than a month had passed since the morale-boosting capture of Arminius' wife and freeing of his father-in-law, and Germanicus had been swift to act, launching a three-pronged attack into the enemy hinterland.

It was Piso's bad luck that his legion had been selected to sail around the northern coasts and make landfall in the sheltered estuary of the River Amisia. They would strike inland from there. He cast a mournful glance back at the Flevo Lacus, the sheltered lake that formed part of the Rhenus' estuary, across which they had rowed over the previous days. Its rocky shores and populations of screeching seabirds that he'd so despised now seemed far more attractive than the blue-green waves beneath the hull and the desolate expanse on every side. He wasn't alone in his misery, and Piso took a certain sour satisfaction from the number of unhappy faces around him, and the muttering about storms and sea monsters. Not a soldier of the two centuries packed on the vessel seemed happy with his lot. Even Vitellius, the stoic, was giving the bronze amulet at his neck a crafty rub.

Tullus and Fenestela, heads bent together as usual, were unperturbed, but that was as it should be. Even if they were only pretending not to be scared, thought Piso, it didn't matter. Their calm expressions and steady voices were there to reassure the men, whatever the situation.

A wave crashed off the prow, showering everyone within thirty paces with freezing water. Groans and curses went up even as the ship's captain, an old salt with white hair, laughed. 'Better get used to it, boys,' he cried from his platform above them. 'This is nothing compared to what Neptunus can throw at us.'

'Gods, what are we doing?' Piso asked of no one in particular.

'Following orders,' said Vitellius.

'As usual,' added Saxa. 'That's all we ever do.'

'The soldier's lot.' Metilius cast a look at each of them in turn. 'But we're together again, eh, and that's what counts.'

Everyone nodded. Piso managed a smile of sorts. Germanicus' purpose – to wreak revenge for what had been done to Varus and his legions – didn't count here, on this perilous sea. What mattered when a man felt as if he were about to drown at any moment were his comrades. Since their mission to rescue Degmar's family, Piso and Vitellius had spent increasing amounts of time with Saxa and Metilius, both solid, decent men. The four were now tent mates as well – fortuitously, Piso and Vitellius' contubernium had been two short.

Piso got on better with Saxa, who was also fond of playing dice, but Metilius' unflappable good humour was impossible not to like. Better to drown with them, or to vanish into the maw of a sea monster, Piso decided, than to die on his own.

Another, bigger wave broke over the bows of the ship, and the resultant spray coated everyone from head to toe. Groans went up, and curses, but the loudest voices were those begging the gods for mercy. Muttering a prayer of his own, Piso pulled the front of his cloak lower, trying too late to protect his mail shirt.

'The thing's going to rust no matter what you do,' advised Vitellius. 'Besides, Tullus won't make us clean them until we get back to Vetera.'

'*If* we get back,' added Saxa in a dour tone.

The boat lurched as a wave slammed into its port side and, guts heaving, Piso forgot about his armour. The choppy motion had him concentrating on one thing – not vomiting – but it was a battle he soon lost. If there was any consolation to be taken from covering his feet and sandals with the contents of his stomach, it was that plenty of others had done so before him, among them Saxa and Metilius. Vitellius held out for a time, but succumbed at last to the acrid stink of bile and the ship's never-ending pitching and rolling.

'Ha! You're no sailor either,' said Piso.

Vitellius wiped a string of phlegm from his lips and flicked it downward on to the foul liquid that slopped around at their feet, a broth of seawater, vomit, piss and worse. He levelled a baleful stare at Piso. 'Never said I was.'

'Will Tullus throw up, d'you think?'

They glanced at the centurion. To their disbelief, he was tucking into a hunk of bread. Between bites, he was conducting a shouted conversation with the captain. By his side, meanwhile, a green-faced Fenestela was staring everywhere but at Tullus' food.

Piso chuckled. 'He won't. Five denarii on it. Any takers?'

His only replies were ribald comments about what he could do with his coins. Piso didn't mind. With Tullus, the indestructible Tullus, unaffected by the conditions, he had nothing to worry about. Their ship would not sink, Piso *knew* it, because Tullus was on board. He wasn't about to shout his defiance at the lowering grey sky, nor even to speak it aloud – Piso wasn't that stupid – but Tullus' presence felt like a heavens-sent guarantee that their miserable voyage *would* end with a successful landfall.

He hoped that the rest of the flotilla – the scores of ships on either side, packed with troops, equipment and horses – fared as well. If they did, gods willing, the treacherous Germans wouldn't know what had hit them. That was, Piso thought with a tinge of humour, once he and his comrades had stopped feeling sick.

* * *

Piso's convictions were well tested in the two days and nights that followed. Heavy seas and strong winds split up the fleet, driving the better ships ahead and causing the older, less well-constructed vessels no end of problems. If he had been grateful at the outset not to be ordered on to one of the half-derelict troop carriers left over from Drusus' naval campaigns, Piso was doubly so once he'd seen other craft sinking. He and his comrades grew used, if not immune, to the despairing wails of drowning men that carried over the waves. Their own ship, a new build, sprang a leak at one stage, but constant bailing kept the water levels at a manageable depth. Soaked to the skin, nauseous, and thirstier than he'd ever been after a long summer's day march, Piso endured with his comrades.

It took four more days for the last of the stragglers to limp in to their destination, and a day after that for a final headcount. When that had been completed, the news that nine ships and more than seven hundred crewmen and soldiers had gone to the bottom travelled between the troops like wildfire. So did the revelation that several big-bellied transports loaded with grain and sour wine had foundered. Scores of horses had also been lost. Matters weren't helped that day by the drowning of several legionaries as a ship was being unloaded. Their deaths were blamed by most on the new, heavy type of segmented armour they had been wearing. Whatever the reason for their demise, a dark mood fell over the entire camp.

More alert to such things because of the previous year's mutiny, Tullus bought a fat lamb from a local Chauci farmer and sacrificed it on the muddy beach, giving loud thanks to Neptunus for holding his net close beneath them as they sailed over his watery realm. Other centurions were quick to emulate his move, and when Germanicus ordered a wine ration to be doled out, morale soon lifted. Scores more sheep were purchased from the Chauci tribesmen, who were long-standing, trusted allies of Rome. As the sun set that evening – even the weather had improved – the air was rich with the scent of roasting mutton and filled with the sounds of half-drunk, happy soldiers.

Despite the pounding heads that resulted from the night's carousing, there were few objections the following morning when the trumpets sounded and the officers hounded the legionaries from their blankets. Germanicus had given the order to march and, hung over or not, the troops were keen to get on with the task in hand. They weren't here to paddle in the sea and to look for shells along the shore, Tullus roared, but to find the tribes who had slain their comrades, and to wipe them out. His men yelled back their approval.

Piso was in an optimistic mood. With solid ground underfoot, dry clothing and a full belly, it was easy to feel good about the world. Their force was strong, and it was a considerable distance to the borders of the Chauci lands. Although they would march in combat order, there was little chance of an immediate enemy attack. The Chauci were friendly, and many of their warriors served as auxiliaries with the legions. There was no silver-tongued Arminius figure to lead them astray here.

After three days' march, the safety of the Chauci territory was left behind. The next tribe in the army's path, the Amisuarii, who lived in and around the southward-leading River Amisia, would cause no trouble, the Romans were told by the auxiliary cavalry. Emissaries were already on their way, with hostages and promises of loyalty to Rome.

'If our journey was going to be this easy, we should have saved our hobnails and sailed downriver,' Piso commented late on the fourth day. He raised a hand against Vitellius' retort. 'I know, too many of the ships needed repairs.'

'Would you rather be on land or afloat if we're attacked?' asked Saxa, ever the wary one. 'We'll be reaching Bructeri territory soon. They laid an ambush on the River Amisia for Drusus, remember.'

'It's still nice to dream about not having to march. About not having to carry this.' Piso indicated his unwieldy yoke with his eyes.

'Perhaps you should have joined the navy, Piso.' Tullus had appeared to come, as he did so often, from nowhere. 'I saw how much you enjoyed being out on the waves during our voyage.'

Piso flushed as his comrades hooted with laughter. 'I'm happy in the legions, sir. And with my yoke.'

'That's what I like to hear.' With a chuckle, Tullus rode off.

'You could always try the river fleet,' Vitellius suggested to Piso. He winked at Saxa and Metilius. 'There's far less bad weather than on the open ocean. You'd almost never have to go to sea.'

'Piss off,' retorted Piso. 'Why don't *you* become a sailor?'

'I'm a happy footslogger, me,' said Vitellius, his shrug setting the pots and pans on his yoke to clatter. 'Always have been.'

'I'll remind you of that the next time you're whingeing about a blister, or a sore neck,' said Piso with a triumphant look. When it came to complaining, Vitellius was one of the most vocal men in the century. Saxa and Metilius snickered; Vitellius glowered.

Piso grinned. It was at times like this, he decided, that life was at its finest. He was with his closest friends, joking and carrying on like carefree youths. They were marching heavily laden, it was true, and sweating like mules, but the weather was pleasant and not too hot. Their rations were being supplemented daily by plenty of meat – sheep and cattle – bought from the local tribesmen, and, like the good centurion he was, Tullus saw to it that there was wine on offer each night.

Battles were inevitable later in the campaign, but Piso knew they would take place on Germanicus' terms. When this force met with the two others that had set out from various forts on the Rhenus, they would outnumber any foe who faced them. Vengeance will be ours, thought Piso, remembering with a pang Afer and the rest of his comrades who'd been slain in the Teutoburg Forest. Arminius can try his best, but we will send every last one of his warriors into the mud. Rome *will* emerge triumphant, he promised himself. Most important of all, the Eighteenth's eagle would be recovered.

Some days later, Piso was helping to dig the defensive trench for the night's camp. For half the men of a campaigning army, this least-loved of tasks came at the end of every second day's march. His turn was this afternoon, and despite the long job that lay before him and his already aching muscles, Piso was still in good spirits. Around him, his comrades were too. Saxa was halfway through a popular ditty about a brothel, and was bawling the filthiest chorus line in time with each strike of his pickaxe.

The whole contubernium was taking part – Vitellius and others throwing in additional, imaginative lines whenever possible. Infected by their enthusiasm and volume, the men nearby had begun to join in too. Tullus, who was strolling along the top of the ditch, supervising, had a tiny smile on his face. Piso even thought he'd heard Fenestela whistling the song's tune.

The campaign had begun well, Piso decided. Their arrival from the north had caught the Bructeri napping, and their force was now deep in the tribe's territory. Settlements and farms had been abandoned wholescale, their panicked inhabitants fleeing into the surrounding forests. Resistance had been sporadic and, for the most part, ineffectual. There'd been one serious attack, the previous day, but it had been thrown back with massive casualties among the Bructeri tribesmen. Piso hadn't even seen the fighting, because the assault had struck a different part of the marching column.

More promising news – swift to spread between the soldiers – had been brought by the Chauci scouts returning from the south. The two other parts of Germanicus' army, one under the command of the general Caecina and the second under the legate Stertinius, had already combined and were less than twenty miles away. Together they had also laid waste to large numbers of Bructeri villages, and slain many hundreds of warriors.

If things continued like this, thought Piso, there was a chance that they'd be back in Vetera before the harvest. He dampened his enthusiasm before it took root. Germanicus would *not* lead his vast army back to its camps early. Teaching the tribes who'd risen against Rome their lesson would take time, even if the legions won every battle. We'll be here until the autumn, Piso told himself. Get used to it.

Saxa had reached the last verse of his song, in which the hero – a legionary, naturally – is forced to choose between his comrades, who are leaving on campaign, and a big-breasted, willing whore. Conscious that every soldier within fifty paces was hanging off his words, he'd stopped digging – a risky move, with Tullus still about. Yet Saxa had made a calculated judgement. Piso spied their centurion close by, hands on hips. A broad and unusual grin was splitting his face – clear permission for Saxa to finish.

Cheering broke out as Saxa bellowed the final line, telling the legionaries what they'd heard a thousand times: that a good fuck is unforgettable, but doesn't last. A man's comrades, on the other hand, will stay with him to the end – even unto death.

'I hope he nailed her good and proper before walking out the door,' shouted Vitellius.

It was an old joke, but roars of laughter rose nonetheless.

'A fine rendition, Saxa,' said Tullus. 'Time to get back to work. The same applies to the rest of you maggots!' The meaningful tap of his vitis on his right greave was lost on no one, and every soldier bent his back at once. Tullus' beady gaze wandered up and down the ditch before he resumed his pacing.

Piso and his comrades continued to talk amongst themselves, in quiet tones. Tullus permitted that, as long as their work rate was satisfactory. Veterans all, they didn't need much encouragement. Once the camp was built, their tents could be erected and they could shed themselves of the dead weight of their armour and weapons.

The trench was complete and the rampart half-finished when Tullus gave the order to fetch the palisade stakes that would decorate the top of the completed defences. Each soldier had to carry two of the arm-length pieces of timber on the march. Buried daily in the earthen parapet and tied together with rope, they formed an extra deterrent against potential attackers. Moving the stakes was a great deal easier than tamping down the top of the fortifications, and so there was often a race between tent mates to lay down their pickaxes and make for the heaped timbers. On this occasion, Piso and Vitellius got there first. Tullus was watching so Saxa, Metilius and the rest retreated to the earthworks, throwing sour looks at the lucky pair.

Piso had scooped up a bundle of a dozen stakes and was halfway down the ditch when riotous cheering broke out among the legionaries forming the defensive screen, some 250 paces away. These were the men who had built the camp the day before, and whose turn it was now to protect Piso and the other workers. He cast a glance at Tullus – it was always best to make sure he wouldn't be reprimanded for slacking – and, happy that his centurion was also trying to decide what was going on, clambered back out of the ditch. Everyone was staring now – two messengers seemed to have arrived – and already the rumours were starting.

'There's been a sign from the gods – victory will be ours this summer,' someone said. 'Arminius is dead – slain by his own kind.' 'The Angrivarii have come over to us – or the Chasuari. Maybe both.'

Piso couldn't help but chuckle. The stories were growing more outlandish by the moment. If the truth didn't emerge soon, men would have Tiberius arriving in their midst, brought by Mercury himself. He sniffed. Gods did not carry anyone, even the rulers of empires. Emperors did not visit their far-flung provinces, still less risk their imperial lives in barbarian lands. The cheering was because of something more banal, like the discovery in a settlement of hundreds of barrels of German beer.

Then Piso heard the word 'eagle' being shouted. His heart almost stopped, and his eyes shot to Tullus. The loss of the Eighteenth's revered standard had hit him harder than anyone Piso knew. All the colour had drained from Tullus' face; Piso looked back – the messengers, two men on sweat-soaked horses, had cleared the legionaries' screen and were galloping towards them, and the camp entrance, which lay close by.

Piso's mouth fell open as Tullus strode right into the riders' path. The pair had to rein in hard to avoid trampling him. 'Out of the way!' shouted the lead horseman. 'We carry important news for the imperial governor himself.'

It was as if Tullus was deaf. He took hold of the first horse's reins, ignoring the rider's outrage. 'What news?'

The messengers shared a look; then the lead one shrugged and said, 'An eagle has been found, sir, among the Bructeri.'

Despite the warm sun on his back, Piso shivered. He was conscious that around him men were muttering and praying. One soldier – Vitellius? – had even fallen to his knees.

'Which legion is it from?' demanded Tullus, his tone more commanding than Piso had ever heard it.

'The Nineteenth, sir.'

Tullus' hand fell away from the reins, and he stepped back. 'Wonderful news,' he said in a quiet voice.

The first messenger's sour expression eased a little. 'You were in the Seventeenth or Eighteenth, sir?'

Tullus' head came up again. Even at a distance, the pride in his eyes was clear. 'The Eighteenth.'

'A fine legion, sir,' said the messenger. 'May your eagle be found next.'

'It's only a matter of time.' Tullus' tone was confident. Stepping back to allow the riders past, he wheeled towards his watching men. 'D'you hear that, brothers? One eagle has flown home – and the other two will soon follow! Roma Victrix!'

The refrain was taken up all along the ditch and rampart. 'Ro-ma Vic-trix! Ro-ma Vic-trix!'

With tears of joy running down his cheeks, Piso roared the words until his voice cracked.

Chapter XXII

ꛃꛃꛃ

S everal days had passed, and Tullus was standing in warm, late-afternoon sunshine outside Germanicus' vast command tent. A summons to attend his general 'at his earliest pleasure' – delivered a short time before – had allowed scant opportunity for his servant Ambiorix to polish his helmet, phalerae and belts. For all that they were on campaign, not in barracks, standards had to be maintained.

Tullus cast a critical eye over himself, and sighed. Old Ambiorix, stiff-fingered and still resentful at having to do what Degmar had done for years, was no longer capable of putting a parade-standard shine on equipment, but there was nothing Tullus could do about it now. Putting the state of his kit from his mind, he wondered yet again what Germanicus wanted with him.

The command tent was a busy place – a double century of legionaries stood guard around its perimeter, and there was a constant flow in and out of officers, slaves and messengers. Tullus wasn't the only one waiting – ahead of him were three others: Tubero, an auxiliary officer and a portly, balding merchant. It was no surprise to Tullus that Tubero ignored everyone else – that was how most high-ranking officers behaved. For Tullus' own part, he didn't want to talk to the auxiliary, who looked to be a Ubii warrior. Apart from Degmar and, to some extent, Flavus, Tullus' view of Germans had been forever tarnished by the ambush in the forest. As for the merchant – he looked like so many of his kind: greasy-smiled, rotten-toothed, and like to sell his own mother if it earned him a coin.

If Tullus were to have a conversation with anyone present, it would be with the more senior officer in charge of the guards – a solid-looking centurion, whom he knew by sight. The centurion was busy checking on his men, however, and dealing with those entering the tent. Tullus shifted the strap of his baldric a fraction so it didn't pinch the skin at the base of his neck, and thought, I can talk to him later. For now, I can just enjoy the sunshine, and think.

With luck, Germanicus would reveal something of his plans. The campaign had stalled, and Tullus was chafing to get back into action. The recovery of the Nineteenth's eagle had stoked the old fires inside him – every night, his dreams were of finding his old legion's golden standard, and of killing Arminius. Perhaps it wasn't fair to say that the campaign had *stalled*, Tullus decided. An army the size of Germanicus' current one – more than forty-five thousand men, together with many hundreds of horses and mules – required the most enormous quantity of food daily. Large raiding parties of legionaries and auxiliaries had stripped the surrounding countryside of livestock and stored grain, and still it was insufficient.

Wary of being attacked by Arminius and his allies without enough supplies for a retreat, Germanicus had had his troops set up a temporary encampment on the banks of the River Lupia. This waterway led west, past the burned-out forts of Aliso and others, to the Rhenus and the empire's frontier. Messengers had been sent to Vetera ahead of their arrival at the camp, carrying orders to despatch grain barges with all haste. Although some had reached the camp, there were not yet enough supplies for the army to continue its eastward march.

Tullus' eagerness to move on wasn't echoed by the ordinary soldiers. He couldn't blame them. While there hadn't been much fighting, or many casualties, they were deep in enemy territory. Secure from attack in the huge encampment, the legionaries had been able to let down their guard, even if there weren't the rations they'd have liked. Strict as ever, Tullus hadn't let his men get complacent – each century in the cohort had to train or march for at least half of every day. 'You're not in barracks, you pieces of shit,' he told them as they stumbled, yawning, from their tents at dawn. 'Every man, woman and child for a hundred miles wants us dead. If you're not at the top of your game every moment of every day, some motherless sheep-humper will nail your head to a tree.'

HUUUUMMMMMMMMM! HUUUUMMMMMMMMM!

Just like that, the barritus sounded in Tullus' head. His ears rang with his men's screams, the rushing sound of inward-flying spears and the crack of releasing slingshots. Rain sheeted in from the black clouds lowering overhead, and he could feel the gritty, blood-soaked mud working its way between his toes. Another legionary went down, struck by an enemy spear. Fenestela was bawling orders to close that fucking gap, and Tullus could hear his own voice, cracked and raw-throated, telling his soldiers to stand firm. 'Hold the line, or we're all dead men!'

'Centurion?'

Tullus wiped a hand across his eyes, and was grateful, despite his earlier scorn, to see the merchant, sweaty-faced and tunic-stained, before him rather than a spear-wielding warrior. Yet the man was so repulsive, he couldn't help barking, 'What?'

'Are you well, sir?'

'I am, curse you. Why?' Tullus shot a look at Tubero and the auxiliary officer, who were next nearest. They didn't appear to have noticed anything untoward, which was an immense relief. He could imagine the type of comment Tubero in particular would make.

The merchant stepped back, his smile fading. 'You were muttering to yourself.'

'Nonsense.' Tullus gave the man his best centurion's stare, and was pleased when he moved further away. Tullus again fell to brooding about the battle. They were so close to where it had taken place. He didn't have a map, and had only hazy memories of the countryside that Degmar had guided him through on their way to Aliso, but Tullus had recognised a number of landmarks during the previous days' training marches. The scouts had also reported that the battlefield lay nearby. The close proximity of the bones of so many men Tullus had known wasn't helping his sleep either, if truth be told. His scalp prickled. Did Germanicus want to hear his account of the ambush again? Perhaps—

'Senior Centurion Tullus!' An imperious-faced staff officer stood at the tent's main entrance. He called again, 'Senior Centurion Tullus!'

Tullus lifted a hand. 'That would be me, sir.'

'The imperial governor is waiting.'

Used to being passed over in favour of citizens, the auxiliary's expression remained impassive, but the merchant let out a resigned sigh. Passing an irate Tubero, Tullus kept a straight face. Inside, he was roaring with laughter. Screw you, you whoreson, he thought. Reaching the staff officer, Tullus saluted. 'Ready, sir.'

'There must be some mistake!'

Tubero's screech made the staff officer turn. 'Sir?'

'I am a legate!' Tubero cried. 'This man is only a centurion.'

'A senior centurion, sir,' Tullus corrected in the politest of voices, revelling in how his comment made Tubero's flush deepen.

'Begging your pardon, sir,' said the staff officer to Tubero. 'The governor is aware that you are here. He has ordered that Tullus attend him.'

Tubero's mouth, which had been open, snapped shut.

'Have you any message for the governor, sir?' asked the staff officer in a solicitous tone.

'I—' began Tubero, and hesitated. A heartbeat later, he muttered, 'I will wait.'

'As you wish, sir.' The staff officer saluted before regarding Tullus, who could have sworn he raised an eyebrow as if to say, 'These senior officers.' Then he inclined his head. 'Follow me, centurion.'

Tullus shot a look at Tubero, but he was glaring into the distance. Tullus' pleasure wasn't even a little lessened.

The staff officer led him through a spacious, well-appointed antechamber in which a great number of clerks sat writing at desks. Slaves hovered about in the background, waiting to be given errands. No one paid any notice to Tullus, or his guide. The next two partitioned areas were similar grand workspaces for the staff officer and his colleagues. Here Tullus attracted some curious looks, which made him wonder again what Germanicus had in store for him.

'You were at the Saltus Teutoburgiensis, I heard,' said the staff officer, as if he'd been reading Tullus' mind. There was respect in his voice, unlike most of those who'd commented in the years since. 'You got some of your soldiers out.'

Old bitterness washed over Tullus. 'Not enough of them.'

'You did more than anyone I've heard of. Even Tubero only saved eight or nine men.'

Tullus held back a furious rebuttal – it had been an optio of the Seventeenth who'd rescued Tubero and the soldiers – with a savage bite to the inside of his cheek. The coppery taste of blood filled his mouth, so he grunted rather than speak a reply.

The staff officer hadn't noticed. 'Was it as bad as they say?'

'Ten times worse,' grated Tullus.

'It will be an honour to visit the place,' said the staff officer, adding, 'I don't hold with those who say it'll bring bad luck upon us. Even if it's years late, our dead deserve to be buried.'

This unexpected revelation had Tullus still struggling for a reply when they came to a halt before a final partition. A pair of impassive-faced bodyguards stood before it. Both looked as solid as granite.

'Senior Centurion Tullus, Seventh Cohort of the Fifth, to see the governor,' announced the staff officer.

The bodyguards' eyes roamed up and down Tullus. One of them made a non-committal noise that could have meant anything from 'Yes, sir' to 'I don't give a shit' before he vanished within. Tullus was used to this reaction from very senior officers' guards, but he had never liked it. When the second man focused on him again, Tullus returned the stare with a flinty one of his own. Old I might be, compared to you, but I'd still give you a run for your money, you big pile of shit, he thought.

'The governor will see you now.' The first bodyguard had returned. He held aside the curtain.

The staff officer indicated Tullus should enter.

Tullus felt as nervous as he had when Germanicus had recognised him at Tiberius' triumph. Eyes fixed ahead, he stamped in the way he did on the parade ground: lifting his legs with his shoulders back and chest out. He came to attention before Germanicus, who was sitting behind a rosewood desk with a silver-inlaid top. Documents were piled in front of him; an inkwell and a simple iron stylus sat by his right hand. He looked older, and more tired, than Tullus had ever seen him, but the air of command was still there in his eyes and the firm set of his chin.

'Senior Centurion Tullus.' His tone was warm.

'Sir!'

'No one is to disturb us,' Germanicus said to the bodyguard. 'At ease, Tullus. Have a seat.'

'My mail, on the wood, sir,' protested Tullus. The steel rings scratched anything they touched.

'Sit,' ordered Germanicus. 'The chair is unimportant.'

The ebony chair looked as if it had cost a small fortune, but Tullus wasn't about to argue with one of the most powerful men in the empire. Gripping his scabbard so it didn't get caught behind him, he sat. 'Thank you, sir.'

Germanicus waved at the jug on the dresser to his right. 'Wine?'

Tullus would have declined – even though he'd met Germanicus a number of times, he wanted his wits about him – but the staff officer's words had set his stomach to roiling. 'I will, sir. Thank you.' His discomfort was added to as Germanicus rose and picked up the jug. 'Allow me, sir,' Tullus said, half standing.

Germanicus laughed. 'Sit. I'm well able to pour wine.'

Discomfited, Tullus watched as Germanicus filled two elegant blue glasses, handing one to Tullus and keeping one for himself.

'Thank you, sir,' said Tullus, admiring the outer surface of his glass, which was decorated with sparring gladiators.

'A nice piece, eh?'

'The likenesses are excellent, sir.'

'So they should be, the price they cost each.' Germanicus' eyebrows rose as Tullus' hold on his glass became even more delicate. 'Drink, centurion, and don't worry about the glass.'

Reassured, Tullus tried a sip. The wine was perhaps the finest he'd ever had – deep-flavoured, dry and earthy, with echoes of roses and truffles.

'Do you like it?' Germanicus' face was amused.

'Is it that obvious, sir?'

'You look like a man dying of thirst.'

'I have never tasted better, sir.' Tullus set the vessel down.

'Drink, man, drink! You've earned it.' Germanicus took a swallow from his own glass.

Tullus relished his second mouthful even more than the first. 'Delicious, sir.'

Germanicus seemed satisfied. 'You've seen the Nineteenth's eagle?'

'I paid my respects at the shrine in the headquarters, sir.' Wanting privacy, Tullus had lingered long after the initial rush of senior officers. Scratched, its original staff broken, and missing several lightning bolts, the eagle had still exuded a palpable majesty. Once alone, it hadn't taken long for his grief to bubble to the surface. On his knees, Tullus had wept. He had cried for the dead soldiers of his century. For those of his cohort, and the entire Eighteenth. For the rest of Varus' army. For his legion's lost eagle. For Artio's mother and even for poor, misguided Varus. For the shame of it all. He had even wept for himself – that he had survived when so many had not. That he had failed his men during the ambush by not saving more of them. Maybe I should have died there, Tullus thought, not for the first time.

'It must have grieved you to see it.' Germanicus' voice was soft.

'I was glad and sorry at the same time, sir, if you know what I mean.'

'You must wish it had been the Eighteenth's eagle that was recovered.'

'Aye, sir,' said Tullus with a sigh.

Germanicus thumped the desk with a fist. 'Your eagle *will* be found. This is just the start.'

'I'm glad to hear it, sir.'

A silence fell, during which Tullus' mind spun in ever faster circles, trying to guess the reason for Germanicus' summons. Tullus couldn't take the suspense for long. 'I'm thinking that you didn't order me here for my opinion of your wine, sir.'

Germanicus guffawed. Unsure what was going on, Tullus didn't join in.

'If only more of my officers were cut from your cloth, Tullus. They fawn and creep before me, when all I want them to do is speak their minds.'

'I see, sir,' said Tullus, as non-committally as he could. Who can blame them? he reflected. Despite Germanicus' words, it paid to be careful what one said to members of the royal family. Utter the wrong opinion and a man's career – even his life – could be ended just like that.

'You are right, of course,' said Germanicus. 'I asked you here for a favour.'

How the rich and powerful like to make it seem as if we have a choice, thought Tullus. Despite Germanicus' overtures of friendship, he was under no illusions about their relationship. He was the servant, and Germanicus the master. And yet with the staff officer's words fresh in his mind, he wondered if Germanicus' request might not be altogether bad. 'The empire means everything to me, sir. If I can help, I will.'

'I hoped you'd say that.' Germanicus' expression grew sombre. 'I wish to visit the site of Arminius' ambush.'

'Tubero was also there, sir,' said Tullus in confusion. 'He is a more senior officer.'

'He is young. Very young.'

'But—'

'I have no proof, but I'm not altogether sure I believe Tubero's account of what happened.' Here Germanicus pointed a warning finger. 'That's to stay between you and me, d'you understand?'

'Yes, sir,' said Tullus, exulting and despairing at the same time. At last someone else knew, or suspected, Tubero to be the liar he was. Whether Germanicus wasn't prepared to challenge Tubero's story for lack of proof or because it served the empire to have a high-ranking hero, Tullus wasn't sure. More likely the latter, he thought with bitterness. Tubero was a senior officer who couldn't be blamed for what happened, and who had come through the affair thanks to his *virtus*, his courage and moral fibre.

'So you will take me around the battlefield? I want to see where the various attacks took place, and, if you know it, where Varus and his commanders died.'

Tullus hesitated as the full realisation of what was being asked of him sank in. He had never imagined returning to the exact site where he'd seen his soldiers wiped out – it was bad luck to tread upon such bloodstained ground. How would it feel to show another where they had camped, wet, cold and miserable, on the first night – ignorant of what would happen to them? To point out his men's whitened bones, scattered along that corridor of death? To stand where his legion's eagle had been lost, where the Eighteenth's pride had been stripped away in the most shameful manner? For a moment, Tullus found himself unable to speak.

'I know it will be an agonising task,' said Germanicus in a quiet voice. 'If you wish not to do it, I will not insist. There will be no repercussions. None. May Jupiter strike me down if I lie.'

Germanicus' face was earnest, and Tullus saw that he *did* understand how his exalted position made men think that they couldn't say no. He was granting a way out to Tullus – and he meant it. Tullus cleared his throat. 'It would be a good thing to seek out my men's remains, sir, those that are possible to find, and give them a decent burial.'

'All of our dead deserve the same. I intend to erect a tumulus on the battlefield, a sacred mound, by which they may be remembered forever.'

Their eyes met for a long moment, and then Tullus nodded. 'I would be proud to show you what happened, sir, and where.'

Chapter XXIII

꒯꒯꒯

Drenched in sweat, his heart thumping, Arminius jerked upright. 'Thusnelda!' he screamed.

His wife was nowhere to be seen, and Arminius' grief scourged him anew. He let out a savage oath, and another, and another. Thusnelda was gone forever, with his child – his son, if he'd been right. Arminius beat at his forehead with clenched fists, but the pain did not ease his sorrow. I'll kill myself, he thought. The option appealed, yet he discarded it at once. He could end *his* misery, but not Thusnelda's. Suicide would also deny him revenge on Germanicus. I must live, Arminius decided, his grief and fury melding into a white-hot flame. Live, and plan my retribution. Feeling calmer, he palmed the sweat from his brow.

His head was fuzzy, reminding him of every night's pattern since Thusnelda's abduction. Copious quantities of beer rendered him drowsy enough to sleep. Fitful slumber followed, visited by endless variations of a nightmare in which Thusnelda was abducted, injured, even raped by grinning legionaries, as he watched, powerless to intervene.

Curse it all, thought Arminius. The day hadn't even begun, and he was exhausted. The faint light entering his hide tent revealed that it was still early, but he did not lie down. Bitter experience had taught him that falling asleep again would not conjure up Thusnelda, nor grant him the unconsciousness and memory loss which he so longed for. He threw the blanket off his legs, and rubbed at his gritty eyes. With his filthy mood entrenched for the day, he swilled a measure of wine to dilute the foul taste in his mouth, and shoved his way out of the tent.

'Donar's balls!' The squat figure of Maelo – hands on hips, not ten paces away – made Arminius jump. He hoped that his second-in-command had not heard his cry.

'Nightmare?' asked Maelo.

Maelo was one of his best friends – one of his only friends – but Arminius considered lying. Appearing vulnerable was not something he had ever wanted to do – especially not now, with the task that lay ahead. Maelo's knowing expression said it all, though. Arminius grimaced. 'You heard?'

'It was hard not to.'

Arminius gave thanks that Maelo's tent was the only one within a hundred paces of his own. 'I dreamed about Thusnelda.'

'Any man would be the same,' Maelo muttered. 'It doesn't help, but I'm sorry.'

Arminius couldn't smile – he had not done so since Thusnelda's abduction had shattered his world – but he nodded his appreciation.

'I've got some good news.'

'You've found a supply of decent beer to replace the piss I've been forced to drink since we left the settlement.'

'The man's not completely without humour,' said Maelo, chuckling. 'I'd been wondering these last few days.'

'Fuck you,' said Arminius, but without heat. 'What news?'

'The scouts have returned. They almost made it here last night, but had to make camp when darkness fell. They set out again the moment it grew light.'

'Where are they?' Arminius craned his head, his eyes keen as a hawk's. 'Why didn't you bring them to me?'

'I knew you'd look like shit.'

Arminius ignored the rebuke. 'What did they say?'

'They can tell you better than I.' Ignoring Arminius' impatient hiss, Maelo raised the wooden pail gripped in his right fist. 'I'd empty this over your head, but you'd get too angry and I might have to slap some sense into you. Wash your face, change your tunic and you'll look more like a leader than a drunkard. *Then* I will take you to them.'

If Maelo had been anyone else, Arminius would have punched his teeth down his throat – or tried to, he thought, rueing not just the previous night's quantity of beer, but his recent behaviour. Maelo was right. He *had* been letting himself go to seed, allowing his grief supremacy. Keep it up and he would lose the respect of the tribesmen who had joined his alliance, and any chance of vengeance this year. The latter prospect did not bear thinking about, so he did as Maelo suggested.

They spoke not a word as Arminius got ready, but when he was wearing fresh clothes, and tugging his fingers through his wet hair, Maelo gave him an approving look. Still a little ashamed, Arminius acted as if he hadn't seen, and followed his second-in-command. It took some time to reach the central area between the sprawling mass of tents. Arminius felt grateful again that Maelo had made him see sense. The warriors of no less than four tribes were here to follow him against the Romans. A fifth tribe – the Tencteri – were due to arrive any day, when Arminius would have close to fifteen thousand spears to lead.

His host wasn't large enough to tackle Germanicus' vast army in open battle, but was more than sufficient to harry its flanks and rear, and to cause significant casualties. When that happened, more tribes would rally to his cause, as had been the case six years before – and then they might be able to deliver the killer blow.

The wisdom of Maelo's counsel was reiterated as men emerging from their tents greeted Arminius with pleased smiles. 'Is today the day that we ambush the Romans?' 'The gods are with us, Arminius!'

'They are watching us, and smiling. We'll attack the legions soon.' They walked on, and Arminius glanced at Maelo, who affected not to notice. Arminius' irritation flared. 'Are you going to tell me or not?'

'They say the best fisherman has patience to spare,' said Maelo with a wink. 'You can wait a little longer.'

Arminius wanted to box Maelo's ears, but his second-in-command's mention of a fisherman put him in mind of catching a fish, and that set his heart to racing, so he kept his peace.

Word had already got out about the scouts' arrival, and the pair found them surrounded by Cherusci warriors. 'Tell us what you saw!' a voice cried. 'Where are the cursed Romans?' shouted a dozen more. 'We'll tell Arminius, and no one else,' came the answer. Maelo pushed through the crowd, with Arminius on his heels. Three men were standing in the centre of the throng. Their faces bore pleased expressions, and Arminius' hopes soared. He'd sent the trio out days before, their task to locate Germanicus' army and, if possible, to determine its path.

They greeted him with broad grins. There was no bowing or saluting – that was not the tribes' way – but there was respect in their eyes. 'Arminius,' they said in unison.

'Well met,' he replied, feeling, for the first time since Thusnelda's capture, the beginnings of a smile creep on to his face. 'What news?'

'Germanicus is at the site of our ambush on Varus,' said the oldest warrior, a broken-nosed, straggle-haired farmer whom Arminius had known since he was a child.

There was a general *Ahhhhh* of excitement.

'What does he there?' demanded Arminius.

'His soldiers look set to bury their dead – what's left of them,' replied Straggle Hair, snickering.

Hoots of laughter rang out. 'D'you think they'll be able to take down the skulls we nailed to the trees?' asked a warrior. More merriment ensued. The humour was excellent for morale, so Arminius waited until the noise had died down.

'Is his entire army with him?'

Straggle Hair scowled for the first time. 'Aye. Eight legions, and many thousands of auxiliaries.'

Uncertainty registered on a good number of faces, and Arminius bellowed, 'All the more for us to slaughter! My intent is to lead them into another ambush. Mired in the bog, they will have to abandon their wagons and artillery as they did before. The barritus will curdle the Romans' courage, and your spears will darken the skies above them. Their eagles will fall into our hands one by one. Blessed by Donar, we will attack until they break and run. When that happens, they will die – every last one.' He let out a grim chuckle. 'Save perhaps the miserable few who will carry word back to their camps.'

The warriors whooped their approval, and Arminius knew he had done enough with these, his faction of the Cherusci. His own self-assurance had been strengthened by the warriors' enthusiasm. Next he would have to persuade the other chieftains in the camp to go along with his plan, which shouldn't be too hard a task. Their presence here with their warriors meant they were of a mind with him already, did it not? Rather than talk to each one in turn, Arminius decided, he would gather them together and do it in one fell swoop. The sooner he had the chieftains in the palm of his hand, the sooner he could strike at the Romans. And that, he thought, an image of Thusnelda burning bright in his mind, was the *only* thing that mattered.

It was a little after midday, and the sun was beating down from a brilliant aquamarine sky. Swifts swooped and darted overhead, their high-pitched *skirr*s another reminder that it was high summer. Close to a score of chieftains were gathered in a circle near Arminius' tent, which granted them privacy, but not shade. Temperatures had been climbing since dawn, and if they continued, this would be the hottest day of the year thus far. Arminius studied the sweating, unhappy faces around him, and felt the beads of moisture prickling the back of his own neck. Two annoying conclusions filled his mind: that evening would have been a better time to hold the meeting, and that he had been over-confident in assuming that the chieftains would be easy to win over.

Things *had* started well. His announcement that Germanicus' army was close by had been greeted with cheers, and his audience had loved his plan to ambush the legions as they had before. It was the Romans' numbers which had snuffed out the chieftains' enthusiasm. Since then the argument had been moving back and forth without resolution. There had been no suggestion yet of returning to their own lands, but the heaviness of that possibility hung in the warm air.

Arminius wanted to speak again, but he knew the value of when to stay silent, and it was now. Whether he liked it or not, the chieftains had to have their say. I am not their ruler, he thought, with more than a trace of regret.

A stick-thin leader of the Usipetes was the next to step forward. 'I say it's madness to attack an enemy with more than three times our strength – in particular when that enemy is the cursed Romans.' He gave his moustache an unhappy tug. 'In open battle, each legionary is worth three of our warriors, maybe four.'

'On a bad day, five,' muttered a voice.

'I do not mean to fight them face-to-face—' Arminius began, but Stick Thin interrupted:

'Yes, yes. You talk of causing panic and driving them into the bog, but that's easier said than done. We have, what, twelve thousand spears?'

'Fifteen thousand when the Tencteri arrive,' said Arminius, but Stick Thin crowed: 'Twelve, fifteen thousand – what difference does it make? They cannot prevail against such a massive host. I am minded of a group of boys trying to herd a score of prize bulls somewhere they do not wish to go.'

'An impossible task,' said one of the Angrivarii chieftains, a big-chinned individual whom Arminius had always regarded as a solid ally.

Are we to let them move through our lands unhindered then, slaughtering and raping with impunity? Arminius wanted to scream, but he bit his lip. In situations like this, anger got a man nowhere. It was better to remain outwardly calm, appearing to listen to their opinions, and to delay speaking until the right moment presented itself.

'We could wait for more tribes to join us,' suggested Stick Thin.

Big Chin looked pleased. 'The Tencteri are due any day, you say?'

'Five thousand of them,' repeated Arminius. 'If the Mattiaci come, there'll be even more.'

His answer made a few men smile.

'And the Chatti – what of them?' demanded Stick Thin, dampening the mood as fast as it improved. Germanicus' savage campaign had shredded the Chatti tribe. No one knew how many of its people yet lived.

The weight of so many stares was hard to resist. 'I have had word from one Chatti chieftain. He promises four score spears, maybe a hundred,' said Arminius, cursing inside as he spoke. Compared to the Roman host, it was a pathetic number.

Stick Thin sucked in his top lip. 'Perhaps we should go back to our settlements.'

No one voiced agreement, yet not a man shouted him down either. Arminius saw the chieftains' mood wavering, and his fury broke free. 'Do you think Germanicus will leave you be?' he cried. 'Have you forgotten the treatment already doled out to the Marsi, and to the Chatti, of whom we have just spoken? Germanicus does not want to treat with us. He is out for revenge! The whoreson wants to slaughter us by the thousand, and to enslave those who survive. He needs the two remaining eagles and the other standards I gifted to you. Will you roll over like beaten curs and just give him what he wants? Have you sunk that low?'

'Those are fighting words, Arminius of the Cherusci.' Big Chin was on his feet, his forefinger jabbing the air. 'Be careful who you accuse of cowardice!'

'I mean no disrespect,' said Arminius, dipping his chin a little.

'That's not how it sounds,' said Big Chin, and many men rumbled in agreement. 'No one has called you a drunkard to your face at this meeting, yet that is how men name you in the camp.'

Arminius' temper frayed so fast that his fingers strayed to his sword hilt. Control yourself, he thought, and managed to convert the move into a scratch of his belly. He listened as Big Chin continued, 'Every chieftain here feels your sorrow, Arminius, but if you continue to seek comfort in the bottom of a mug, know that we will follow you no longer.'

The grim faces around the circle revealed that Big Chin had assessed the chieftains' mood well. Maelo's advice had come none too soon, thought Arminius. I risk losing everything.

'You speak true,' he said, adopting a humble tone. 'My grief has overwhelmed me of late. I have been drinking too much. Maelo said the same this very morn. Hearing it from you brings it home harder.' His gaze ranged from side to side, meeting every man's eyes. 'Not another drop shall pass my lips until this summer's campaign is over – I swear this to you.'

'Your words gladden my heart,' said Big Chin. There were other muttered encouragements, and even Stick Thin gave Arminius a tiny nod. He hadn't lost them – yet. Arminius threw up a gut-felt prayer to Donar. Help me again, O god of thunder.

'What I am saying is that you – we – cannot sit by and do nothing,' he urged. 'If we fail to act, Germanicus will attack our tribes one by one, and wipe us from the face of the earth. I accept that our numbers are insufficient to attack the Romans head on – I am no fool either – but we *have* to respond in some way. If we do not, we will be swallowed up by the empire. We shall spend our lives as the tribes in Gaul and beyond, with the legionary's boot always on our necks, and the emperor's hand forever in our purses. Is that what you would have?'

Arminius knew there was still a good chance they would not follow him, but he forced himself to keep staring at the chieftains. A dozen heartbeats thudded by, and then a score. His mouth grew dry.

'I have no wish to be a slave to Rome,' said Big Chin at last. 'My warriors will fight with you.'

Surprising Arminius, Stick Thin was next to add his support. 'And mine.'

After that, the rest of the chieftains rowed in as well. They didn't shout – given the odds they faced, that wasn't surprising – but their expressions were set and determined. They *would* stand with him in the fight to come.

It had been a close call, but now Arminius' heart sang.

Chapter XXIV

◨◨◨

The weather had been good when Tullus had left the army's camp with Germanicus and a strong force of legionaries and cavalry, their destination the site of Arminius' ambush, but it had changed. Grey-black clouds had appeared overhead as if from nowhere. They promised rain and, like as not, thunder and lightning too. The worsening conditions dredged up vivid, horrifying memories from the depths of his mind. It was hard not to feel that the gods were looking on, as they had been during those terrible days. *The gods watched then and did nothing while we fought for our lives,* Tullus thought with ever-fresh bitterness. *They watched as almost everyone died.*

A cough brought him back to the real world, and he glanced over his shoulder. One of Germanicus' staff officers – not the man who'd taken him to the audience – was hovering, and glaring. 'The imperial governor is waiting!'

Tullus' eyes roved past the officer to Germanicus, who seemed expectant, but not impatient. Caecina was there; so too were Stertinius, Tubero and almost every legate and tribune in the army. Everyone who was anyone wanted to be among those first to set their eyes on the battlefield. Apart from Germanicus, Tullus couldn't have given a fig for any of them. The men who mattered most were at his back: Fenestela, Piso, Saxa and Metilius. The other survivors from his century in the Eighteenth were present too, which had raised a few eyebrows among Germanicus' bodyguards. *Fuck them,* thought Tullus. *They haven't been through the hell that we have. They haven't had to do the things that we did.*

The scouts had ridden the area the previous day, and again at dawn, to ensure there were no enemy tribesmen nearby. Not having been at the ambush almost six years before, the riders had no idea which part of the battlefield it was, but they had reported a heavy density of skeletons from this point onward. Tullus wasn't sure where they were either, because they had approached from the west, rather than along the track he had taken with Varus and his ill-fated legions.

Tullus studied the terrain again. Off to his left, the tree-covered ground sloped upwards, while on the right, there was less vegetation. There was bound to be bog a little further on, he thought, spying the characteristic yellow flowers of goatweed. The presence of bones proved that they *were* at the site of Arminius' ambush. Walking on was the only way to discover more. Grim reality, so often held at bay by dreams of recovering the eagles, sank in. Tullus could almost see the ghosts that surely lived in this place.

'Are you ready, Tullus?' It was Germanicus' voice.

'Yes, sir.' He stirred himself, and threw up a silent prayer: I come here to honour my men, and all of my fallen comrades. Grant that we find their remains, and give them the burial that they deserve. 'If you'll follow me.' As Germanicus, followed by Caecina and the rest, moved to join him, Tullus eyed Fenestela and his men. 'Stay close.' They gave him grim nods.

Full-hearted, Tullus led the way, with Germanicus by his side. Fenestela and the three others walked to left and right, shields and swords ready. The rest of the party came after, flanked by Germanicus' bodyguards and Tullus' veterans from the Eighteenth. Despite the number of men, there was little noise. Muted tramping of hobnailed sandals on the grass and the mud, whispered comments here and there, and the *shhhinkk* of mail, but nothing more.

They're all scared too, thought Tullus, blinking away the sweat that had run into his eyes. A momentary break in the clouds sent sunbeams lancing down through the dark green canopy. Motes of dust spun and whirled overhead in the light. Somewhere in the distance, a woodpecker hammered at a tree. The sound was comforting, for the bird was favoured by Mars, but

Tullus remained wary. 'D'you notice how quiet the forest is, sir?' he said to Germanicus.

Germanicus cocked his head. 'All I can hear is that woodpecker, and it isn't close. There should be more birds: singing, flitting about. Maybe deer, or even a boar.'

'I see no tracks, sir.'

'The animals shun this place then,' said Germanicus, frowning.

Tullus was unsurprised. It wouldn't always have been so. After the battle, clouds of crows and other carrion birds would have lived here, for many days. Wolves would have been drawn to the vast numbers of corpses, and bears too. If wild boar were anything like their domesticated brethren, they would also have partaken of the gory feast. With the bones picked clean, only the ghosts would have remained. Like as not, they still troubled the site, which explained the absence of wildlife. Tullus' skin crawled, and he picked up his pace, wanting to get the unsettling experience over and done with.

He had been steeling himself against signs of the battle, but it was still shocking when he saw the first bent pilum. There was nothing extraordinary about the weapon – it was like thousands of others Tullus had seen in his career – but it was rusted and misshapen because it had struck a target. And it was *here*. Grim-faced, he showed it to Germanicus. They both studied the ground at their feet.

'There's no sign of the man it might have hit,' said Germanicus in a quiet tone.

'The tribesmen would have carried away their injured and dead, sir,' said Tullus. 'Just our corpses would have been left – to rot.'

Germanicus' expression hardened further. 'Of course.'

Despite the vegetation, the finds came thick and fast after that. There were broken *frameae* – the lethal spears favoured by German tribesmen – and more javelins than Tullus could count. *Scuta*, whole, broken, split, all rotting into the ground. *Gladii*, unsheathed and in their scabbards, had been piled up as if to carry off, but then left. Bronze pots that had been missed by the human scavengers, and now green from exposure, lay here and there as if they had fallen off a trundling smith's wagon. There were orange-red Samian bowls and plates, cracked and entire, and in tiny pieces. Pickaxes with rusted heads and decaying handles. Cloak brooches. A wine strainer, bent out of shape. A soothsayer's *lituus*, minus its shaft. Half a shield cover, the rest of the leather eaten away.

It was the skeletons that were most distressing. Tullus had seen men's bones many times before – in graves that had had to be moved for whatever reason, and on other old battlefields he'd visited – but he had never seen so many, nor had they been of soldiers known to him. Recognisable as human, the whitened bones were everywhere. In places, the carpet they formed was so thick that it was impossible to walk without treading on them. The skeletons lay on their sides, on their backs. On their fronts. Hunched up into foetal positions, as if trying to escape their attackers.

Some were missing limbs. More horrifying, others had no heads. Those that did now looked like demons, thanks to the helmets and armour they were yet wearing. With clenched jaw, Tullus made himself study their empty eye sockets, grinning mouths and stumps of brown, decayed teeth. These men who had been abandoned by their comrades, left for six years to the mercy of wild beasts, wind, rain and snow, had to be honoured, if only by a nod, or a silent greeting.

Germanicus' face was harrowed as he strode to and fro, examining different sets of bones and lifting an occasional weapon. 'Do you know where we are?' he asked after a time.

'I've seen a shield cover with Seventeenth Legion insignia, sir, but that doesn't tell me much,' said Tullus. 'There are no wagons, and no signs of civilians, so the fighting in this spot must have been on the second day, or after.'

'Because Varus had you abandon the baggage train, and had the column assemble properly, without civilians?'

'Yes, sir.' Tullus could smell the burning olive oil, could hear the camp followers wailing and crying and the wounded soldiers swearing as they'd marched out that morning. 'We left them to die. There was no other choice. If they had stayed with us, every last one of us would have been slain.'

'Gods grant that I never have to make such a decision.' Germanicus' face was bleak. 'You must have had to abandon legionaries too.'

'Aye, sir.' Tullus' grief cut him, sharp as a blade. 'I finished a good number myself, so the tribesmen didn't capture them.'

'You're a fine officer, Tullus. You look after your soldiers.'

Even as Tullus coloured, and heard Fenestela rumble his agreement, he wished again that he had managed to drag more men free of this hellhole. 'I did what anyone would have, sir.'

'No.' Germanicus jerked his head at Caecina, Tubero and the others, who were talking together in twos and threes, and staring at the skeletons with horrified fascination. 'You did more than any of those could have. Your group was the largest one to escape, by some margin. Be proud of that.'

For the first time, Tullus and Germanicus looked at each other not as ordinary citizen and royal scion, not as centurion and general, but as men and as soldiers – as equals. Something made Tullus glance then at Fenestela, Piso and the others. They were all nodding. Fuck it, Tullus thought with rising pride. Maybe I can be satisfied with what I did. 'Thank you, sir.'

'Show me the rest of the battlefield. We'll start burying the dead after that.'

'Aye, sir.' Grateful that his slain legionaries would rest in peace at last, Tullus set off to the north.

I'm coming to find you, brothers, he thought.

Two long days had passed since Tullus had guided Germanicus on to the battlefield.

His hopes of ever finding his fallen soldiers had faded to almost nothing, but he, Fenestela and his veterans had not stopped searching. Time was running out, however. They could not remain here forever. Already half the army had been set to dig vast mass graves while the remainder stood guard against possible attacks. When the grim task had been completed, Germanicus' campaign to punish the still-hostile tribes would continue.

Tullus paced to and fro, using his vitis to push aside low-hanging branches and patches of long grass. He'd looked at enough skeletons to fill half the underworld, or so it seemed, yet the task was growing no easier. Six years had seen the flesh stripped from the dead legionaries, leaving nothing but bundles of bones within the rusting mail shirts and segmented armour that lay scattered along the cursed track, among the trees and in the bog. It made personal recognition an impossibility. Tullus' frustration and grief grew with each passing hour. What might have been the easiest way – finding a unit standard, say – had also eluded them. It seemed that every item of monetary worth or of symbolic nature had been carried off after the battle, or rotted away. Not one was to be found.

Checking the underside of helmet neckpieces had yielded a good number of scratched-on names, but none that were familiar. Tullus was beginning to wonder if they would have to reconcile themselves to failure and join the rest of Germanicus' men in digging graves for all the dead. They would nominate one such for their fallen brothers, and make their offerings over it. This solution would be far from ideal, but it was better than leaving the bones of the Eighteenth's soldiers forever uncovered.

Tullus reached for his clay water-carrier. Despite the nearby stream, he took only two swigs. Old habits died hard. The pause afforded him the chance to see what everyone else was doing. Piso was in the trees off to his left; so too were Vitellius, Saxa and Metilius. Since rescuing Degmar's family, the four had been inseparable. It gladdened Tullus' heart.

'Find anything, Piso?' he called.

'No, sir.'

Tullus felt another stab of disappointment. 'Keep looking.'

A muffled curse from his right made him turn. Fenestela had been working the scrubby ground that ran on into an area of bog, a muddier job than anyone else's. He was picking himself up, and muttering filthy curses.

'Lost a sandal?' asked Tullus.

'I tripped over a skeleton.'

They had each done the same. 'Hurt?' asked Tullus.

'Just my pride.'

Chuckling, Tullus stoppered his water-carrier and balanced it on his right hip again. Vitis at the ready, he took a step forward, his eyes searching for clues. Fortuna, be kind, he asked. Just this once.

There was another loud oath from Fenestela.

'Fallen on your arse this time?' shouted Tullus.

'Sir!'

The urgency in that one word brought Tullus' head snapping up. He peered at Fenestela. Even at a distance, it was clear his optio was rattled. 'What?'

'Come and see, sir.'

Fenestela's reluctance to say more had Tullus moving at once. Three dozen strides, and he found Fenestela standing by a massive fallen trunk.

'I was working my way around it, and didn't see this poor bastard,' said Fenestela, gesturing at a skeleton that was lying under a branch forking off the main body. 'I'd say he crawled in there to die.'

'A quiet place to breathe his last,' said Tullus. 'What else have you found?'

Fenestela pointed.

Tullus leaned in closer. The rusted segmented armour, mildewed leather straps and still-beautiful gilded belt decorations were the same as a thousand he'd seen before, but Fenestela hadn't called him over for those. He lifted the helmet, which Fenestela had eased off the skull, and peered under the neck guard. There was no inscribed name. As he laid it back down beside its owner, Tullus' gaze fell on something silver. He focused on something lying beneath the skeleton. 'This?' he asked, pointing.

'Aye.'

Tullus realised he was looking at a silvered spear tip, which had once served as the top of a century's standard. His heart beat faster. The soldier who'd been carrying it wasn't a signifer, like as not, because he wasn't in scale armour. That meant he'd taken it from the fallen standard-bearer and tried to carry it to safety. In a way, he had succeeded, Tullus thought sadly, because the tribesmen hadn't found the standard. Yet the wounded soldier hadn't got far. Tullus hoped he had not lingered, listening to the slaughter of his comrades.

Tullus rolled the skeleton a little to the left. Beneath the spear tip, the wooden staff had mouldered away, but the distinctive copper alloy discs and crescents that decorated a century's standard remained where the shaft would have been. Green now rather than golden-brown, they had been pressed into the earth by the soldier's weight. A line of metallic dots marked the outline of the silvered pendants that had once hung from either side of the standard's crossbar.

Tullus picked up one of the discs and cleaned the dirt from its face. It was plain, and disappointment flooded through him. The same applied to the next disc, and the next, but his luck changed with the fourth. Using a finger-nail to scrape away dirt from the concave surface, Tullus' eyes devoured the raised lettering that emerged: COH•II•LEG•XIIX. Over and over, he read the inscription. His pulse hammered in his ears. The standard was from one of the centuries in his cohort, and that meant that the skeletons around him had been some of *his* legionaries. Which century they had belonged to, Tullus couldn't be sure. Tears pricked his eyes regardless.

'What does it say?' Fenestela's voice was anxious.

Without a word, Tullus handed over the disc.

'Jupiter,' said Fenestela. 'Fucking Jupiter on high.'

Tullus lifted another disc – it was blank – and another. It had no inscription either; nor did the next one. Soon there was only one before the hand grip attached by most signiferi to make carrying the standard easier. He eased the last disc and the grip free from the earth at the same time, tapping off the attached clods of earth against one of his greaves.

Tullus threw a casual glance at the grip first. It had been fashioned from deer horn, a common material, but what made it unusual was the cap of silver foil covering its free end. 'Look,' he said, his voice thick with sudden emotion.

Fenestela's ruddy face lost its remaining colour. 'It's *our* standard. *Our* standard.'

Julius, their signifer, had fashioned the covering himself from silver foil, making the grip as unique as a man's scars. Tullus and Fenestela shared a glance then, this one laden with raw grief, and Tullus turned over the last disc in his hand. CENT•I, he read. Grief – and terrible memories – washed over him anew. A tear dropped from his eye on to the lettering, and a tiny part of Tullus was surprised that it didn't turn blood red. 'I don't remember seeing Julius die. He was still with us on the last day, wasn't he?'

'Aye,' said Fenestela. 'I can't recall him falling either. One of the others must have grabbed the standard when he did, and tried to get away with it.'

'We must have already gone.' Feeling guilty all over again, Tullus reached down and patted the dead man's skull. 'You did your best, brother. Rest in peace now. The standard is back with us.'

Straightening, he found every soldier in sight watching. It wasn't surprising, thought Tullus. Fenestela calling him over would have alerted them. He cupped a hand to his lips. 'We've found our century's standard. Tread light, brothers. Every skeleton lying around you is that of a comrade.'

The words were barely out of Tullus' mouth before his long-held-in grief struck him with the force of a storm wave hitting a harbour wall. He dropped to one knee beside the skeleton, and a sob escaped him. Beside him he heard Fenestela, a man he'd never known to give in to sorrow, weeping.

No one spoke for a long time.

In the end, Tullus mastered his pain by force of will. Getting to his feet, he ordered his men to begin the terrible task of burying their comrades.

They had started before midday. Now the sun was low on the horizon and every part of Tullus ached. His arms, his shoulders, his thighs, his back – especially his back. Hours of swinging a pickaxe had brought up blisters – new, ruptured, forming – over both his palms. The neck scarf that he'd tied around his forehead was soaked through with sweat and, under his mail, his tunic was stuck fast to his back. Waves of exhaustion battered at him, and at last he had to stop digging. He had done his bit, Tullus told himself, and there were plenty of willing and able men. Every one of his old legionaries was there, labouring with grim purpose on the mass grave. His and Fenestela's voices weren't needed, nor his vitis. In fact, Tullus hadn't heard a single complaint in that time, nor seen a man stop working other than to take a mouthful of water.

He could not rest for long – he wasn't able. Six years he'd been unable to do anything for his slain men. Now his moment had come. Wielding a pickaxe was beyond him, so Tullus began carrying the skeletons they had wrapped in blankets and, with great reverence, lowering them down into the pit. It was emotional, horrific work, and he couldn't help but wonder which legionary each bundle of bones might have been.

A tight band of pain wrapped itself around his chest after a while, but he ignored it. He would not stand by and watch, even if the effort killed him. These are *my* men, Tullus thought, *my fucking men*. I couldn't save their lives, but I can see them into the ground and say a prayer over their remains. Let me do that, Mars, d'you hear me? Fortuna, are you listening? I *will* do this. And next time you show yourself, Arminius, things will be different. I'll be ready.

Chapter XXV

◪◪◪

A month had passed, and Germanicus' reprisals against the German tribes continued. The army moved ever eastward, searching out fresh settlements to destroy. No more eagles had been found, and Arminius had not been brought to bay, but Tullus remained hopeful. He forced his horse a few paces to the right, and off the road. 'Keep marching,' he bellowed.

'Another piss stop for the centurion,' commented one of the legionaries. 'He's been on the wine again,' said another. Tullus pretended not to hear – his men could have their fun as long as they obeyed orders. He didn't need to empty his bladder – they would see that soon enough.

Under his watchful eye, his century marched past, *tramp, tramp, tramp,* pounding flat the grass. By the time the rest of the vast army had passed, there would be nothing left underfoot but a fine powder. One of the benefits of being in the vanguard, thought Tullus, was not having to breathe in the dust cast into the air by tens of thousands of others. Another was that he had a good idea of what was going on – both from his viewpoint, and thanks to regular reports from the scouts and cavalry.

He craned his head, searching for Fenestela's staff of office, a difficult thing to spot over the bobbing rows of helmets, yokes and javelins. It was a pain in the arse, Tullus decided for the ten-thousandth time in his career, that army protocol dictated an optio should march at the back of his century, while the centurion rode or walked at the front. Talking to Fenestela would leaven the drudgery of each day's long march. Instead Tullus had to rely on occasional moments like this, when he broke ranks to have a word. Despite his irritation, the positioning made sense. If and when they were attacked, Fenestela's role at the back would be vital, as was his own at the front.

Fenestela spotted him and lifted his staff in salute.

'Everything all right, optio?' Tullus called.

'Yes, sir.' Fenestela made a swift turn to his right, and with a few steps passed into the gap behind the last rank and the next century. He resumed marching to the left of their men, and Tullus nudged his horse forward, beside him. It was something they'd done innumerable times.

Fenestela spoke first. 'Any news from the scouts?'

'Not a thing. The countryside is empty, they say,' replied Tullus, scowling. It wasn't surprising that the tribespeople should flee into the forests and that Arminius and his warriors were avoiding direct confrontation, but gods, it was frustrating. A man could derive scant satisfaction from razing empty villages to the ground, and knowing that the last eagles were secreted deep in a cave or the like, far from the Romans. There had been some attacks, in the main ambushes on scouts and soldiers searching for food, but they had been inconsequential. Losing a handful of legionaries here and a dozen auxiliaries there harmed Germanicus' army no more than a wasp sting bothered a bear.

'How many days have we been looking for Arminius?'

'Thirty-one.' Tullus glanced at the fields of stubble sprawling off to his left. The harvest had been taken in, and for the most part, hidden from the Romans. Summer was drawing to a close. As vast and invulnerable as it was, the army couldn't remain here, hundreds of miles from the Rhenus, for much longer. Supplies would soon begin to run low, and only a fool would countenance staying in enemy territory until they ran out. 'Thirty-fucking-one.'

'I wish Arminius would just fight,' said Fenestela.

'Every man in the army thinks the same, but time is on his side – not ours. The clever bastard has no great need to worry about food, or when autumn comes.'

Fenestela cocked his head. 'Has Germanicus decided when we'll return to camp?' Tullus had been to a meeting of senior officers at dawn, but they hadn't yet spoken about it.

'No. He's as frustrated as everyone else, and wants a victory before we go home.'

'It would do all of us good,' said Fenestela with a scowl.

Tullus' 'Aye' was heartfelt, yet it wouldn't magic the Germans out of thin air. Nor would Fenestela's sentiments. It was crazy, even foolhardy, but Tullus almost wished that Arminius would spring another ambush. At least they would then have a chance to face him.

Tullus' wishes were in vain. The day passed like the thirty before it, without incident.

Things changed on the thirty-third day. Whether it was because Arminius now had sufficient numbers of warriors, or because the Romans were so far from home, no one knew, but his forces began to harry the legions. From dawn until dusk, stinging attacks were launched on the marching column – first the scouts, then the vanguard or the baggage train and next the rear-guard. They never lasted for long, and the tribesmen were careful not to engage the Romans head-on.

Deep-throated renditions of the barritus frayed the legionaries' nerves, in particular when no assault followed. At other times, volleys of spears and sling bullets would come hurtling out of the trees without warning. Casualties were often light – several men injured, an occasional fatality, but the air of tension hanging over the army was ratcheted ever higher. No one had any idea when or where the next attack would fall, which kept everyone from Tullus to the lowest ranker on edge every waking hour of the day.

Darkness did not grant the Romans peace. The tribesmen seemed to have no end of tricks in their inventory. The first night, it was intermittent performances of the barritus; the next saw numerous pigs being slaughtered over several hours, close to the camp; during a third, parties of warriors, their faces and hands blackened, scaled the walls and slit the throats of half a dozen sentries.

It was remarkable how effective the constant harassment was, Tullus grumbled to Fenestela. Their soldiers were tired, irritable and prone to jump at the slightest noise. Stories were rife of men who'd gone for a piss in the night being stabbed by a comrade upon their return, and of panicked individuals who had deserted, never to be seen again. 'Just like it was, six fucking years ago,' retorted Fenestela, making the fire hiss as he spat into it. By mutual consent, neither spoke further on the subject.

Tullus did his best to combat the ebbing morale, riding the length of the cohort each day, exhorting his soldiers to do their best, and to ignore their brutish enemies, whose monotone singing made a pack of feral dogs sound tuneful. Every evening, he paced the tent lines, repeating what he'd said, doling out his own wine and rewarding any man whose actions had stood out during the most recent fighting.

Several more unhappy days passed. The weather remained stifling, even hotter than before. Germanicus' army ground eastward like a massive serpent, assailed on all sides by a multitude of biting rodents. It was unstoppable, thought Tullus, yet maddened by its enemies' incessant and unrelenting attacks.

On the thirty-ninth morning, Tullus and his cohort were no longer in the vanguard. The duty had fallen to the Twenty-First Legion, while the Fifth was marching in the main body of the column, in front of the other legions, but behind just about everyone else in the army. Even the senior officers' baggage went before them, Tullus heard his men complaining. Germanicus' soft bed, his personal stores of wine, were more important than they were, moaned a former conscript. It wasn't fair. 'Get used to it, you fool. Be grateful that we're not right at the back, swallowing thirty thousand more men's dust,' Piso advised, making Tullus smile.

Once again the sun beat down from a radiant blue sky, devoid of cloud. The prolonged, baking hot weather had parched the landscape. Brown grass, stubble and cracked earth filled the fields. Even the leaves on the trees seemed shrunken, desiccated by the heat. The paths followed by the army were powder dry, and the rivers running low. Finding water had become a vital daily priority. Tens of thousands of thirsty men and animals needed the most enormous quantity. Wise to this, Arminius had his warriors poison many streams with dead sheep and cattle. The wagons were full of soldiers suffering from vomiting and diarrhoea.

Pure luck and nothing more had stopped any of his men coming down with the affliction, thought Tullus, eyeing his water flask and battling not to drain its contents in one go. Waves of heat rose from his armour. It and his helmet both seemed to have doubled in weight. No matter what way he positioned his scarf, his baldric strap kept pinching at his neck. His back ached, and the old injury in his left calf throbbed from time to time. The harsh tang of his own sweat and the whiff of sheep from his woollen tunic were a constant, cloying presence in his nostrils. He squinted at the baleful white-gold orb that was the sun, hoping that it would be near the horizon. It was but a fraction lower in the sky than it had been the last time he'd looked. Midday had been four hours ago, he decided, resigning himself to two or three more hours on the road.

When the column ground to a halt – again – Tullus groaned. Such stops were normal enough, and could happen for any number of reasons, but that didn't stop them being frustrating. The vanguard could have reached a river, or another obstacle. A mule might have been panicked, or a wagon axle snapped. It was possible that Germanicus wanted to have a look at something.

His men felt none of his irritation. To them, the halt was a welcome break from marching. When Tullus gave the order to lower their yokes soon after, they were even more pleased. Jokes were bandied about, brows mopped and water drunk. Several soldiers asked leave to empty their bladders, and Tullus let them break ranks. Legionaries were doing the same as far as the eye could see, and there was no harm in it – the land to either side was empty of life except for a few birds. Tullus climbed down from his horse and let it pick at the brown grass.

Time passed. A heat haze rippled the air, rendering everything in the distance out of focus. Waves of warmth rose from the packed earth beneath their feet. A lone crow flapped by. From somewhere to their front, mules brayed. The humour that had been widespread among Tullus' soldiers when they'd first stopped had died away. Men were sweating now, slapping away the flies that hung in clouds around their heads, and propping themselves up with their javelins.

Still the army didn't move. No word had come about what was going on. Tullus wasn't concerned yet. He had his troops unsling their shields from their backs and set them standing on the hard ground. Every third soldier was allowed to sit down if he wished – the others would soon get their turn, Tullus told them. 'Eat something if you're hungry. Have another piss. Have a shit. Stay alert, you maggots,' he advised, before riding along the side of the cohort.

Everything was as it should be, which was something. Tullus took the time to greet those men he recognised, and to say encouraging words to their comrades. His centurions met the lack of information with the same resignation that he felt. There was nothing they could do but wait – and cook in the heat.

Tullus was talking with the Fifth Century's centurion when, without warning, trumpets blared from the front. There was no mistaking the signal for 'enemy in sight'.

'See to your men!' ordered Tullus, riding off. He repeated the command as he cantered along the column. 'Yokes to the side. Shield covers off. Javelins ready.'

Fenestela was waiting as Tullus neared the First Century – and he'd already had the soldiers stand to. It was as Tullus would have expected, but he still gave Fenestela a pleased nod. 'Any word from the front?'

'Not a thing.' Fenestela hawked, then saved his spit. 'What do you think?'

'Who fucking knows? It could be just a few tribal hotheads, or a major attack.' Tullus peered ahead. Sunlight flashed off armour, helmet crests bobbed about as officers conferred, but the column wasn't moving. 'I've a mind to ride up the line. The senior officers will know more.'

'I'll keep the men in order.'

Fenestela's reliability dispelled the last of Tullus' doubt about leaving his command. 'I won't be long.'

He hadn't gone far when he spied a messenger galloping in his direction. The soldiers of the cohort in front – the Sixth – were already discarding their yokes and extra equipment on both sides of the road. Uneasy, Tullus reined in and waited until the messenger drew near.

The rider brought his mount to a juddering halt and saluted. 'There's been an ambush, sir, on the scouts and the cavalry outriders. For whatever reason, the cavalry panicked and fled back down the track – straight into the vanguard.'

Tullus didn't like the sound of this one bit. 'What did the Twenty-First do?'

'It seems they too were startled, sir. They've broken formation. The tribesmen have pressed home their attack, causing a good number of casualties. The Twenty-First is retreating to the right, away from the army.'

Tullus digested this with alarm. Units were supposed never to break off from the main force without express orders to do so. 'Why would they do that?'

The messenger was quick to adopt a blank face.

'What are our orders?' demanded Tullus.

'The entire Fifth is to move at once, sir, on either side of the column, up as far as Germanicus' position. He will lead the legion towards the fighting. With your permission, sir? I have to pass on the command.'

'On you go.' Tullus spun his horse. It was fortunate that the ground around them was flat, he thought. He and his cohort could march parallel to the track. Speed was vital.

Reaching Fenestela, he had Germanicus' order relayed into the next century and onward. His men formed up, half on the left and half on the right of the track, outside the position of those in front who would not be advancing. Then they began to march slowly, following the Sixth Cohort, and those before it. Chafing with impatience, Tullus kept rising up on his saddle blanket, but he could determine nothing about what was happening further along the column. He ground his teeth and tried to be patient.

Confusion reigned as Tullus and his men continued past each section of the army positioned in front of their own location. First were the senior officers, who were arguing among themselves, with legates shouting at each other and the tribunes bickering in the background. Tullus spied Tubero in the midst of it all, holding forth with his theory about what had gone wrong. Few men seemed interested.

They passed the artillerymen next. Trees were growing close to the track by their position, forcing Tullus and his soldiers to edge around the wagons loaded with dismantled ballistae and other catapults. Their speed slowed to a crawl, allowing Tullus to eavesdrop on the artillery crews, who were blaming the legion in the vanguard for being fools, and lamenting the fact that they almost never got to use their heavy weaponry. Even their mules were irritable, biting at each other's necks and kicking out at legionaries who strayed too close.

What Tullus liked least was the lack of attention paid by the artillerymen to their surroundings. For all any of them knew, another attack could be sprung right here. He advised the officers in charge to set some guards. There was no time to see if his suggestion was followed, for his cohort had to keep moving. It was imperative that they didn't fall behind the Sixth Cohort.

The next units – the cavalry – were in no better mood, laying the blame for the panic on the scouts whose job it had been to ride in front of the army. As with the artillerymen, no one appeared to be watching the trees. Again Tullus said something to the officers. There had never been much love lost between infantry and cavalry, and most met his comments with poorly concealed disdain.

The trees closed in on either side once more as, in the distance, familiar sounds became audible: shouts, trumpets, the clash of arms. The Sixth Cohort's pace picked up, and Tullus had ordered his men to do the same. They began to pass nervous-faced engineers and camp surveyors, who urged them onwards with loud shouts of encouragement. 'Well they might cheer,' Tullus heard Piso say. 'Pickaxes and hammers aren't much fucking use in a fight.' 'Spin a surveyor's measuring tool fast enough around your head and you'd knock down a warrior or two,' quipped another soldier, raising a brief laugh.

Despite the chaos, Tullus hungered to meet the enemy again. 'We'll carve Arminius and his men new arseholes, brothers,' he cried. 'Won't we?'

'AYE!'

Their roar rose into the burning blue sky and disappeared.

Soon the trees gave way to scrubby grass and gorse; on the left, a low hill rose, its slopes covered in oaks. Whether there was anyone hiding among them, it was impossible to tell. In the centre and on the right, Tullus could see Roman units, which were in some disarray. He was afforded no chance to work out why, though, as waiting officers directed the cohorts to break up. Rank by rank, the Sixth wheeled off to the right, and Tullus was directed to follow. When he asked what the plan was, he was told further orders would be given out soon.

Tullus was far from happy as the noise of battle grew louder. Now he could hear screams, and the frenzied whinnies of injured horses. He'd experienced combat a hundred times before, but that didn't stop his stomach from clenching tight. Soon men would begin to die – not just the enemy, but good Romans. Some of them would be his soldiers. If Arminius had his way, they would all be face down in the mud by sunset.

That cannot happen, Tullus thought, worry gnawing at him. It *must* not happen.

And then, from somewhere off to their right, the retreat was sounded.

Chapter XXVI

P iso peered into the distance. He was unhappy that the retreat had been ordered before they'd seen a single warrior, and when Tullus had just directed the cohort to form up, ready for battle. Piso and his comrades were in the first rank, which afforded some vision of the ground in front. They could make out little more than the mass of legionaries to their right, which appeared to be in complete confusion. Their ranks were wavering, and small groups of men had broken away at the rear. Piso was confused and unsettled by this; so too were his friends. 'What in Hades is going on?' he asked Vitellius.

'Your guess is as good as anyone's,' muttered Vitellius, his voice even sourer than usual.

Fifteen paces to their front, Tullus sat astride his horse, a hand to his eyes as he too gazed at the chaos. Everyone watched him.

'Tullus hasn't got a clue,' said a man in the rank behind after a time. The fear in his voice was palpable. The muttering among his companions, which had been muted, grew louder.

Piso knew how fast panic could spread. Ignoring regulations, he wheeled around. Pinning the man who'd spoken – an ex-conscript – with a hard stare, he snapped, 'Shut your mouth, filth. Tullus *always* knows what to do.'

'I was only saying—' began the man, but Piso cut him off.

'Tullus got us out of the forest six years ago, when no one else could. He's not about to let us down now.'

There was loud agreement from the legionaries who'd been there. Other soldiers voiced their approval of Tullus, and the dissenter's confidence slipped away. The trumpets off to their right continued to blare, though, and a good number of men looked unhappy. 'If they keep that up, even Tullus will find it hard to lead us on,' Piso said to Metilius, on his right.

'Not much we can do,' replied Metilius, scowling. 'Besides, the retreat isn't sounded by mistake too often. Perhaps they're right to be scared.'

Piso's own confidence began to waver. He glanced at Vitellius and Saxa, who were to his left. 'What do you think?'

'I think we stay here until Tullus tells us otherwise,' growled Vitellius, jutting his chin.

'Aye,' said Piso, feeling guilty that he'd doubted Tullus for even a moment.

Hooves struck the ground in a familiar rhythm as a horse approached at the gallop. A ripple of excitement swept through the cohort. 'Germanicus!' 'It's Germanicus!' 'The general is here!'

Piso's spirits lifted as he spied Germanicus astride a magnificent grey stallion. Resplendent in ornate armour, red sash and crested helmet, he was the vision of a leader. He reined in before the cohort, and gave Tullus a friendly nod before facing the men. 'Soldiers of the glorious Fifth Legion!'

The legionaries cheered and pounded their javelins off their metal shield rims. Germanicus made an impatient gesture, silencing them. 'Your comrades in the Twenty-First are hard pressed by the enemy, over on the right. You are to go to their rescue at once, as the first six cohorts have already done. Drive the enemy back! Kill as many as you can. Keep moving forward. For Rome!' Germanicus raised a fist.

'FOR ROME! FOR ROME!' Piso and the rest yelled.

Germanicus spoke a few words to Tullus, and then he was off, riding left towards the Fifth's other cohorts.

'This will be close up and dirty, brothers,' shouted Tullus, pacing to and fro. 'Set your javelins down, and draw your swords.'

Piso's heart thumped off his ribs. 'Ever done this before?' he asked Vitellius as they followed Tullus' next order, to form a column eight men wide.

'Once.'

'And?'

'We slaughtered the bastards.' Vitellius' grin was unpleasant, but Piso was reassured. When Tullus ordered them forward at the double, he charged with the rest.

After a day's march in furnace-like heat, running in full armour was exhausting. Piso's left arm began to burn first. He was well used to carrying his shield on his back, but holding it before him was altogether different. Pulling it closer to his body helped a little. He gritted his teeth and carried on. Another hundred paces went by, and his thighs were throbbing too. Runnels of sweat ran down his back, yet Piso's tongue was stuck to the roof of his mouth. Every time his left foot hit the ground, the water in his leather bag sloshed, reminding him of how near it was, and how impossibly far. His next drink might not be for hours. If things didn't go well, he might never need water again. He buried the disquieting idea deep. Focus on the moment, he thought. On the here and now.

At 250 paces, Tullus lifted a hand. 'Slow down. Continue forward, at the walk.'

Piso sucked in a grateful breath. Around him, his comrades were as scarlet-faced and drenched in sweat as he was. They were nearer the fighting now – the clamour of men's screams and iron on iron was loud indeed – but he still could not see the enemy. The cohorts that preceded them had vanished into the confusion. Before them, facing forwards and to the side, was a Roman unit, presumably a cohort of the Twenty-First. The shouts of its officers carried, as did the cries of German tribesmen. Parts of the unit at least were engaged with the enemy. Trees loomed on the unit's left, and to its right was an area of bog. The Germans' plan became clear to Piso, and his fear returned. He nudged Vitellius. 'Remind you of anything?'

'Aye,' growled Vitellius. 'Arminius must be here.'

'The enemy's pushing our comrades towards the bog,' cried Tullus. 'That must not happen. Are you with me?'

'AYE!' yelled Piso and his comrades.

Tullus leered at them and swung down from his horse. Turning its head, he gave it a slap on the rump and sent it cantering towards their rear. 'I'll find you later.' Stamping over to Piso and his comrades, he barked, 'Make room.'

Grinning with delight, the legionaries opened their ranks. Tullus shoved in between Piso and Vitellius. The century's trumpeter, who had been with him, followed, taking a position in the second rank behind Tullus.

'Shield!' Tullus ordered. One was handed forward at once from the rear rank, over men's heads, to his fist. 'We're heading left, along the tree line,' he yelled. 'Pass the word back. With me!'

Once Piso would have been surprised that they walked towards the enemy. Now he knew Tullus for a wily old bastard. Charging was effective from close range, but doing it from too far away exhausted men and stripped them of the energy to fight.

'Gods know what we'll find,' shouted Tullus. 'Be ready to break ranks when we get nearer. Form up in fours, or eights. Stick with your tent mates if you can. Be careful. On!'

Piso sucked his cheeks together, trying to find even a little moisture in his mouth. There was none. His eyes roved over the trees, and the lines of legionaries, who were still retreating towards the bog. At last he saw the enemy: darting figures in tunics and trousers, lobbing spears at the Romans from the safety of the forest. His stomach did a neat roll.

'Faster! Swords ready,' bawled Tullus.

They ran. The trees were closer now, beeches and hornbeams and oaks. The same types that had concealed Arminius' horde six years before. Under their canopy, between their trunks, more and more tribesmen were visible. They were armed like all their kind, with spears. Few among them had shields; even fewer had swords, armour or helmets. Piso's wariness didn't lessen. German warriors were as brave as any alive, and their spears had sent many of his friends to the underworld.

Tullus didn't lead them straight at the enemy. To do so, Piso realised, would make the entire cohort follow him. Their front would be too narrow, and would help only the nearest legionaries of the Twenty-First. Instead they ran along the edge of the trees. With every step, they screened more and more of their beleaguered comrades on the right. It was a risky manoeuvre, because it exposed their left sides to the tribesmen, who were quick to lob their spears. First it was only a few, which fell short. Before long, the warriors had run forward to get within range. The barritus began, and with it came a decent volley of spears.

Behind Piso, a man cried out. *Thud* went his shield on the ground; the sound of his body following it came next. *Thunk*. Another soldier shrieked like a whipped child. Unlike the first man, he kept screaming. At least the wretch wasn't dead, thought Piso, trying to watch his step as well as keep his shield high. Be good to me, Fortuna, he prayed, and I'll be good to you.

They covered another hundred paces. Spears scudded in thick and fast, causing more casualties, and lodging in numerous shields. Emboldened, the tribesmen began leaving the cover of the trees. It was as if Tullus had been waiting for this moment.

'HALT!' he bellowed. 'FACE LEFT!' The trumpeter repeated his command for the other centuries.

Piso was delighted to obey the order. Vitellius, who had been cursing under his breath during their entire run, uttered loud thanks to Mars. Saxa and Metilius had the silly, pleased expressions of men who are relieved to be alive.

'Shoulder to shoulder, brothers!' cried Tullus. 'Close up.' The trumpeter repeated his order.

Piso moved nearer to Tullus, felt Metilius shove in from his right. He relished the comforting, safe feeling. They wouldn't be able to hold the shield wall together in the trees, but it felt good right now.

'Ready?' Tullus hissed in his ear.

'Aye, sir.'

'Move forward in silence,' ordered Tullus. 'ADVANCE!'

Roars of defiance went up from the warriors as the Romans approached.

More spears hummed in, causing several casualties. The barritus was sung again. *HUUUUMMMMMMMM! HUUUUMMMMMMMMM!*

'Quiet, brothers,' growled Tullus. 'Keep quiet.'

His steady voice fell like oil on water, calming the legionaries. On they marched. Fifty paces separated them from the tribesmen, and then forty. Still Tullus urged his men to silence. The barritus wavered, and then died away. So too did the number of spears being hurled. Piso's heart leaped. They're scared, he thought.

At thirty paces, Tullus began to bellow. 'ROMA!' He struck his sword off the side of his shield with a loud clatter. 'ROMA!'

'ROMA!' Piso and his legionaries answered. 'ROMA!'

Twenty-five paces. They continued to shout. The nearest tribesmen glanced at each other. One took a step backwards. So did his comrade.

Tullus' reaction was as fast as a striking snake. 'CHARGE!'

Piso broke into a run with Tullus, and felt Metilius on his right do the same. The soldiers to either side and behind were with them too. Piso's shield, which had seemed so heavy, now weighed no more than a feather. His leg muscles, which had burned, felt strong as steel. His stomach was clenched tight with nerves, but he could ignore it. Increasing numbers of tribesmen were panicking, and running away. Many stayed to fight, but their resolve splintered as they realised how few comrades were standing with them.

Four warriors held their ground near Piso. Tullus aimed for the first one. Piso took the second, striking him in the chest with his shield boss and driving him back several steps. As the man tried to regain his balance and strike at Piso with his spear, Piso's sword rammed deep into his belly. With a gurgling shriek, the warrior dropped his weapon and clutched at the steel spitting him. Piso ripped it free, slicing the warrior's fingers to ribbons. Down he went, folding in on himself like a boneless corpse.

Piso looked for another opponent. Tullus had killed his man, and Metilius was finishing off a third. The fourth warrior had discarded his spear and fled. Piso caught up within twenty strides, cutting him down with a powerful thrust between the shoulder blades. His victim fell face first, with crimson blossoming on his patterned tunic. He kicked on the mossy ground like a rabbit caught in a trap. A quick stab to the back of his neck brought his jerking limbs to a shuddering halt. Chest heaving, Piso glanced to either side. Everywhere he could see, warriors were fleeing. Blood coursed in his ears; exultation filled him. This was how victory felt. He took several steps towards the retreating tribesmen.

'HALT!' Tullus' voice stopped Piso in his tracks. He turned. Tullus' bloodied sword was pointing straight at him. 'Get back here, Piso. Chase them too far and they'll turn. We've taught them a good lesson. If they want more, they know where to find us.'

Disgruntled, Piso joined Vitellius, who chortled at his discomfort. 'The bloodlust is hard to resist, eh?'

'It's so good to see the bastards run,' said Piso, wiping his blade clean on a corpse's tunic.

His pleasure did not abate as the day wore on. The warriors made several more attacks, but they were half-hearted affairs, and the Fifth drove them back with ease. Each success gave Tullus' men greater confidence, and by the time of the last assault, they were greeting the tribesmen's arrival with catcalls and insults. It was remarkable how effective their vocal barrage was, Piso thought. After a final volley of spears that didn't cause a single casualty, the disheartened Germans faded away into the trees.

Morale was high in the Roman camp that evening. Those lucky enough to have any wine drank their fill. Spirits rose further at the news from head-quarters. The year's campaign had ended. At dawn, the army would split up once more. Caecina and Stertinius were to lead their forces back to the Rhenus by separate routes, while Germanicus would make for the beached fleet of vessels left at the mouth of the River Amisia. Caecina's army was to be the largest – four legions strong, including the Fifth. The happy announcement had Piso and his comrades singing long after the sun had set.

Yet, as Tullus reminded them before they retired, the war had not been

Chapter XXVII

꒢꒢꒢

'Dig.' Arminius jabbed a forefinger at the large mound. 'DIG!'

The warriors with him, a mob of two hundred or more, set to with a will. Their shovels sliced into the fresh-turned soil, fast raising piles of earth on either side of the tumulus that had been erected by Germanicus' legionaries. The great carved stone that had towered at its top lay close by, already shattered into a hundred pieces by Arminius' order.

He watched his men destroy the mound, his tapping foot the only sign of the fury raging through him. After his attempt to drive the Twenty-First Legion into the bog had failed, he'd had to let his warriors lick their wounds for a few days. Arminius hadn't been surprised that Germanicus had taken the sensible option of starting the long journey back to the Rhenus, but was now keenly aware that he might have missed his last opportunity of the year to strike at the Romans, and to avenge Thusnelda. This realisation gnawed at Arminius the way a weeping bedsore troubles an ailing greybeard, the way a deep-buried thorn causes a man's hand to throb day and night.

Defiling the memorials erected by Germanicus' troops didn't ease Arminius' pain a great deal, but he could take some satisfaction from the destruction, from the loud message it delivered. This land does not belong to the empire, he thought as the first bones were hurled from the pit. Its legionaries cannot build tombs here. This is where I stripped fifteen thousand Romans of *everything*: their lives, their weapons, their standards, even their pride. Their remains deserve to be left to the mercy of the elements, to be picked over by the crows and wolves. Their bones will rot away into the ground, leaving nothing behind. Only the skulls I have had fresh-nailed to the trees will remain, a warning for years to come. Invade this land at your peril. Anger the tribes, and *this* will be your fate.

As if he had arranged it with Donar, a raven called overhead. There it was, a large black shape coasting high above, its distinctive irregular wing-tips lifting and falling on the wind. Arminius wasn't sure if it was watching him and his warriors, but it seemed that way. Not far from this spot, in the aftermath of his ambush, a similar bird had led him to the last of the three legions' eagles. Since that time, and in particular since Thusnelda's abduction, Arminius had been unsure if the thunder god approved of him. Seeing another here, now, he felt *sure* that Donar was smiling down from the heavens.

If he had had the time, Arminius would have lingered until the arrival of winter, destroying every last piece of evidence that the Romans had ever come here. He'd have ground to dust every piece of pottery, carried off every weapon and set of mail and armour, burned anything made of wood. Once the flames were hot enough, even the legionaries' bones – and those of their mules and horses – could have been reduced to ash.

He rubbed a hand across weary eyes. One day, perhaps, the chance to erase all memories of Varus and his lost legions would come his way. For now, Arminius had to decide on which of Germanicus' three armies to follow. They were each only a few days' march to the west. Slow, encumbered with their artillery and wagons, they would be easy to catch, as long as he did not tarry over-long in this forest of bones.

It galled Arminius that he had enough warriors to make meaningful pursuit of only one army, yet the fracturing of Germanicus' forces also brought the odds into his favour. If the right place to spring an ambush presented itself, victory would be within Arminius' grasp – he could *feel* it. Wiping two, three or even four legions from the face of the earth wouldn't topple the empire, but the body blow it delivered would rock the emperor on his throne, far away in Rome. In the years since his triumph here, Arminius had delighted in the stories of the haunted Augustus, wandering his corridors at night, banging his head off doors and crying, 'Quinctilius Varus, give me back my legions!' Repeating the injury, delivering the same humiliation, would be a searing, savage test of his successor Tiberius' mettle.

Tiberius was no youth either, thought Arminius. He was an old man, with an old man's aches and pains, and worries. The responsibilities of power would be weighing on his bowed shoulders. Excitement filled Arminius, set his nerves to tingling. If he slaughtered thousands of legionaries inside the next month, Tiberius' course of aggressive campaigns in Germania would die a natural death. The legions would stay on their side of the river, the way whipped hounds cower in their kennels.

A smile wiped away the scowl that had lasted since his failed attack. It was time to gather the chieftains again, and decide which enemy army they would destroy.

'I say we hunt down Germanicus. Imagine slaying the emperor's own kin!' said Stick Thin in a triumphant voice. He glanced around the gathering, a score of chieftains sitting around a large fire in the centre of Arminius' camp. Stick Thin frowned when only a few men voiced their agreement. 'What better message could we send Tiberius?'

'The empire has no shortage of capable generals,' said Arminius, wishing that Stick Thin would shut up and listen to his betters – in particular, to him – and let them decide what to do. 'One less will make no difference to their warlike policies here, be Germanicus royal scion or no.'

'You say that, Arminius, because your desire to avenge Thusnelda burns bright in your heart.' Stick Thin made a gesture that could have been interpreted as sympathetic, or irritated. 'But not all men see the world as you do. If Tiberius loses Germanicus, who is dear to him, he will find that his appetite for conquest has forever been soured.'

'In my mind, the grieving Tiberius would be likely to send even stronger forces against us. Do not forget either that the force with Germanicus is two legions strong. I doubt even your warriors could annihilate upwards of eight thousand legionaries,' said Arminius, using his eyes to urge the chieftains into agreement. Inguiomerus, his uncle, gave him an approving look. A handful of others muttered 'Aye', but many others held their counsel. Arminius felt his anger growing. Why did he have to persuade them every time anything needed to be done? 'We need to strike a single hammer blow, as we did six years ago.'

'I say we can do both! My warriors are well capable of wiping out Germanicus and his escort. The majority of our force can stay with you, and attack one of the other Roman armies.' Heads began to nod, and Stick Thin grinned. 'What say you to that idea, Arminius?'

Curse you for a fool. You'll lead your warriors into a trap, or make a full-frontal attack, and all wind up dead, Arminius wanted to say. He held back, seeking the best way forward. At first appearances, he and the other chieftains were equals, yet *he* was the most experienced in the art of war – by a considerable degree. *He* was the man who'd engineered every last detail of the ambush against Varus. If he rubbed Stick Thin's nose in the mud, however, he risked losing not just his support, but that of the others too.

'You're a solid man and a brave warrior,' Arminius said. 'Yet Germanicus is a first-class general. He's shown that time and again, curse him, from his unexpected attacks on the Chatti to his kidnap of Thusnelda and rescue of Segestes.'

Stick Thin drew himself up straight. 'So I'm not clever enough to fight him?'

'That's not what I'm saying,' denied Arminius, thinking, Yes, it is. He adopted a flattering smile. 'You're a great chieftain, but you haven't received the military training, the lessons in tactics that Germanicus has.'

'Nor has any tribal leader, yet many have beaten the Romans in the past. You're not the only man with such skill,' jibed Stick Thin, eliciting a few laughs.

Stung, Arminius longed to demand which chieftain had been responsible for the annihilation of three legions. Instead he raised his hands, palms upward, in a placatory gesture. 'Of course I'm not. But it's a question of discipline too. That was something I had to learn during my time with the Romans. Your warriors are famous, are they not, for being the first into every battle?'

No one missed Arminius' meaning. The Usipetes were hotheads, who never waited for the order to advance. A chorus of chuckles rose, and Stick Thin flushed.

'Their bravery is beyond doubt, but if they charged Germanicus at the wrong moment, they'd be butchered the same way Varus and his legions were. I need you and your men,' said Arminius, speaking a mixture of truth and flattery. 'Lose them, and we risk becoming too weak to prevent the Romans doing as they will.'

Stick Thin harrumphed, part pleased, part annoyed. 'I don't know why you're worried. Germanicus wouldn't stand a chance.'

They stared at one another, neither willing to back down. If I continue in this vein, thought Arminius, Stick Thin will take his warriors and leave. Nothing bound them to this venture but a shared hatred of the enemy. Arminius felt fresh resentment towards the Romans, whose legionaries were sworn to fight for whichever general led them. 'I have said my piece,' he cried. 'What think the rest of you? Should we split our forces, or keep them together?'

'I'll see that Germanicus never troubles us again,' said Stick Thin, sticking out his pigeon chest.

Arminius had to hide a smile at Stick Thin's posturing. His amusement soon died away, for the battle wasn't over. He watched with hidden but growing nervousness as the chieftains gathered in little huddles. Stay with me, great Donar, he asked. I need your support still – and theirs. I cannot do this with my tribe alone.

By the time the chieftains had finished conferring, it felt to Arminius as if a whole day had dragged by. Big Chin, the Angrivarii leader, was the spokesman. 'Dividing our forces would be unwise, and Germanicus is an able general with two legions, plus cavalry. The Usipetes should stay here, with us.'

'Pah!' said Stick Thin. 'Why?'

'United, we're far stronger. Germanicus could defeat any of us on our own, even Arminius.' Big Chin cast a glance at Arminius, who was quick to say: 'True enough.'

'You might lose,' added Big Chin to a general rumble of agreement.

'That would never happen!' Stick Thin puffed out his chest again. 'Are we Arminius' lap dogs then, to do everything he wishes?'

Big Chin bristled. 'Arminius can be an arrogant prick . . .' At this, everyone laughed; Arminius joined in, half-heartedly, and Big Chin continued: '. . . but did you see him telling us what we should think? We're free men like you. We make up our own minds.'

'We do,' said Stick Thin, his colour deepening.

'So are you with us?' boomed Big Chin.

Arminius held his breath as Stick Thin hesitated.

'I am,' Stick Thin said at last. 'Twenty heads are wiser than one, I suppose.'

Arminius exhaled, long and slow. Thank you, Donar, for allowing others do the work for me. There was no doubt in his mind that if he'd continued to argue with Stick Thin, he would have attempted a madcap mission to assassinate Germanicus. Perhaps he would have succeeded, but Arminius doubted it.

'Who shall we attack then, Stertinius or Caecina?' Stick Thin threw the question not at Arminius, but at the entire gathering.

In Arminius' mind, there was only one choice. Caecina had the largest army: four legions and a good number of auxiliaries. He was also headed for a patch of rough country, with plenty of forests and bogland. His intent was surely to traverse the wooden road built fifteen years before by another campaigning Roman general. But Caecina didn't know, as Arminius did, that the road had fallen into considerable disrepair, or that the location begged to be used for an ambush. His inclination was to demand that they follow Caecina, but sensitive to the other chieftains' pride and the unexpected comment about his arrogance, he held back.

'Our best option is to attack Caecina,' said Big Chin, glancing first at

Arminius and then at the rest. 'His is the biggest army, but the path he seems to be taking is a good one for us to lay in wait on. The wooden road is in pieces, or so I hear. There's no chance the artillery or the wagons will be able to travel on it. We can attack at our leisure, while the fools are trying to construct a new surface.'

The chieftains liked the sound of that, nodding and smiling at one another. Stick Thin continued to look put out, but he didn't protest. 'Arminius?' asked Big Chin.

'Ambushing Caecina would be my choice.'

'Does anyone wish to attack Stertinius?' Big Chin's eyes roved over the gathering. 'No? We have a decision then. Let us follow Caecina, and pick the right moment to fall on him and his mongrel legionaries. Four eagles will make a fine haul!'

A good-natured argument began over which tribe should have an eagle. Big Chin watched, his face amused. Arminius moved to his side. 'My thanks,' he muttered.

'Destroying Caecina's force will deliver the clearest message to Rome. To succeed, we will require every spear that's available.' Big Chin gave Arminius a hard look. 'It's still a pity that the Usipetes aren't going after Germanicus.'

'I disagree.'

'You're not our king, Arminius. You don't rule us.'

'I know that. I—'

Big Chin cut him off. 'You may be the best general among us, but too often you act as if you're the only one with a brain.'

It was rare indeed for Arminius to be lost for words, but he had no glib reply. After a short, awkward silence, he murmured, 'I'm sorry.'

'Save your apologies,' said Big Chin with a brusque gesture. 'Start treating us like your equals, not your subjects, or the Cherusci will end up fighting the Romans on their own.'

Arminius caught Stick Thin regarding him with a sour expression. Still smarting from Big Chin's rebuke, he wanted to respond with an obscene gesture. Instead he gave Stick Thin a measured nod, as if he were an equal. Stick Thin's face blackened, and he looked away. I'll win him over again, Arminius resolved, but Big Chin's intervention had brought home the narrowness of his escape. He'd had no idea how angry the other chieftains were feeling towards him. In future, he would have to be a great deal more diplomatic. Avenging Thusnelda and defeating the Romans would be impossible without allies.

And yet, he thought with rising excitement, his force had not splintered.

Caecina's legions would soon feel its full force, and the news of their massacre would shake Rome to its foundations.

Chapter XXVIII

◩◩◩

'F uck,' said Tullus, staring at the crumbling, sodden remnants of planking that led off into the distance, disappearing amid a confusion of heather, gorse and mud. He was on the way back to Vetera with Caecina's army, and this mockery of a road across the bog was supposed to be their route, but a blind man could see that it was falling to pieces. The Long Bridges, it was called, but Tullus doubted a single one remained. No one appeared to have laid a hand to a plank of it since Ahenobarbus' legions had constructed the road fifteen years before.

There was no sun – Tullus hadn't seen it in days. Dense layers of cloud pressed down from overhead, deadening the landscape's colour. Light rain fell in a constant and depressing drizzle. *Euuhh-eeee. Euuhh-eeee-uh.* From somewhere off to his left came the high-pitched, mournful cry of a crane. *Euuhh-eeee.* Tullus scowled. Like as not, the stupid bird was calling to its mate, but it seemed to be asking what he was doing here. I'm here following my general, Tullus answered. You went into a similar place because of another general, remember, his cynical side added. Varus. Unsettling memories stirred in Tullus' mind, making him scowl.

The scouts had brought news of the road's catastrophic state to the vanguard some time before. Tullus had hoped they'd been mistaken, or at least had exaggerated what they had seen, but it was clear their assessment had been correct. The grim faces of the Fifth Legion's other senior centurions – standing nearby – showed that they felt the same way as Tullus.

'Fuck,' Tullus said, and again for good measure, 'Fuck.'

Cordus threw him a sour glance. 'Swearing isn't going to get us anywhere.'

'It might not, but I'm with Tullus,' said Bassius, the *primus pilus*, with a chuckle. A thin figure with a gaunt complexion and a mouth that had been left lopsided by a sword cut, he was tough, courageous and popular with everyone. Bassius had also always treated Tullus with respect, which raised him in Tullus' esteem no end. 'Fuck it all to Hades,' said Bassius. 'And back.'

Cordus fumed as everyone but he laughed.

'We're going to have to build the whole cursed thing again, or most of it,' observed Bassius. He eyed Tullus. 'Don't you think?'

Several centurions who were more senior to Tullus looked disgruntled that they hadn't been asked the question, but Tullus was beyond caring. He took a few steps on to the road. Stagnant brown water oozed at once from the rotten wood, and he could feel the planks sinking into the semi-liquid ground beneath. He walked on for fifty paces, taking care where he placed his feet. A good number of the strips of wood that formed the road had rotted away in their entirety. Others broke beneath his weight. The surface that remained was irregular and treacherous, and Tullus saw no reason to think that the road would improve as it led westward. According to the scouts, the terrain – wooded hills on either side, with plentiful streams discharging into the bog – went on for miles.

He tramped back to an expectant-looking Bassius, who demanded, 'Well?'

'The scouts were right, sir. A few soldiers, perhaps even a century or two might cross, but no more than that.' Tullus could picture men's legs disappearing to the knee in limb-sucking mud, could see panicked mules buried to their bellies in the brown morass. Hard though it was to walk on foot, he'd done the right thing to send his horse back to the wagon train. 'The legionaries might pass by, but there's no way the carts, in particular those with the artillery, could make it. As for the bridges, well . . .'

They considered their surroundings in grim silence. A quagmire dotted with bog cotton and goatweed sprawled away on either side, laced by numerous rivulets and streams. The low, tree-covered hills beyond could be swarming with hostile tribesmen, thought Tullus. To the east and south – where they'd come from – lay nothing but hundreds of miles of hostile territory. The sea lay to the north, but Germanicus' force needed every ship to carry *them* along the storm-ridden coastline to the safety of the Flevo Lacus. The only option left to Caecina's army was the rotten planking before them. The situation could be even worse a few miles into the bog, thought Tullus. The Germans might have destroyed the road entirely there.

'Arminius and his mongrels are watching us even now, I'd wager,' said Bassius.

'They will be, sir.' Tullus could sense the enemy, could almost feel their hatred pulsing through the humid, mosquito-filled air. 'It's only a matter of time before they show themselves.'

'Let them come,' said Bassius, scowling. He eyed the other officers. 'Hate it or love it, this shithole is home for the next few days, brothers. Caecina will have us build a camp on that level ground to the left, or I'm no judge.'

'We're going to need a lot of timber, sir. Shall I take a look at the nearest trees?' offered Tullus. 'It might allow me to assess the Germans' strength.'

'A good plan,' said Bassius with an approving nod. 'Cordus, patrol the road as far as the first bridge. Four of the remaining cohorts are to form a screen, two to the left, and two to the right of the flat ground. The rest will start digging the fortifications.'

Tullus walked the length of his cohort's position before they set out, addressing his men. Few would be happy to present themselves on a plate to the enemy, as they were possibly about to do. He reminded them, therefore, of what had happened the last time Arminius' warriors had tried an ambush. 'We routed them, brothers, didn't we? Sent them running back into the forest with their mangy tails tucked between their hind legs. If even one of the filth shows his face up there, we'll do the same to him. We're not about to let those sheep-humping maggots stop us from seeing the whores of Vetera again, are we?'

'No!' they roared back at him. Some laughed, and others made obscene gestures. Tullus wasn't sure if they were mimicking what they'd do to the prostitutes in the vicus, or to Arminius' warriors, but it didn't matter: their spirits had been raised. When he led them off, unencumbered by their yokes, they followed with a will.

Progress was slow, thanks to the uneven, boggy terrain, and their formation, two centuries wide and three deep, didn't help. The troops at the front turned the marshy ground into a complete quagmire for the rest, yet a wider arrangement would have made it harder for Tullus to retain control, and left them more susceptible to attack.

After three hundred paces of labouring from hummock to hummock and through pools of cold, peaty-brown water, Tullus paused. Runnels of sweat ran from under his helmet, and his pulse was racing. His men were in better shape, because each of them had at least a decade on him, but he didn't waste time feeling sorry for himself. Instead he gazed with calculating eyes at the tree line, which lay up a gentle slope, ten score paces further on.

It took but a few heartbeats to spy the warriors skulking between the beeches and hornbeams. Tullus had been expecting the enemy, but his heart still lurched. Arminius would be here as well – Tullus could feel it in his gut. 'See them, brothers?' he muttered to his legionaries. 'Not a sound. We advance another hundred paces, at the walk. Pass the word on.'

To retreat now would give the wrong message. It was vital the Germans knew that they weren't scared, that the legionaries were ready to fight, to do whatever it took to cross the bog. Posturing in this way before battle often reaped rich rewards. The performance was akin to the way two men circled in a tavern, eyeballing one another as they decided whether or not to come to blows. It wasn't always about the skill or size of the individual, thought Tullus, although that helped. Sometimes having bigger balls than your opponent was enough to end the contest before it started. To achieve this meant being close enough to stare the other in the eye. In this case, it meant trudging uphill through the mud, each step giving the enemy more of an advantage.

Tullus' certainty that advancing was a good idea soon began to wane.

The closer they went, the greater the likelihood that he would have to commit to battle. Forming the usual shield wall would be almost impossible on this undulating ground. If enough warriors came charging from the trees, there was no guarantee that his men would prevail.

Tullus had just signalled the halt when a lone figure strode forth from the trees. An immense warrior with long blond hair, he was stark naked and carried a club. Roaring insults, he made straight for the Romans. Perhaps a hundred paces lay between them.

'Gods, his prick is big as a mule's!' shouted Tullus.

As he'd hoped, his men hooted and roared. 'Come down here. We'll trim it to a proper size!' challenged Piso. 'Or cut it off altogether!' said Vitellius. A barrage of similar jibes followed.

Mule Prick didn't hear or couldn't understand their insults. He sauntered closer, bawling in his own tongue and beating his chest with one fist. His mighty club swung to and fro, promising death to any man who came close enough. Despite the fact that Tullus' soldiers outnumbered him hundreds to one, his advance was intimidating. The legionaries' abuse began to die away.

Mule Prick's companions sensed their uncertainty. First came seven other naked berserkers, shouting their contempt of the Romans. Then, in threes and fours, the rest began to emerge from the trees. Soon fifty warriors had gathered, then a hundred. Two hundred. Four. Five hundred. They were like rats swarming out of a burning granary, thought Tullus with unease. Tall, short, broad and skinny, snaggle-toothed and smooth-cheeked, the tribesmen were clad in woven shirts and patterned trousers. Most bore shields, hexagonal or round, with painted designs. A small number had helmets. Even fewer had swords. Perhaps a dozen had mail shirts.

Every last warrior carried a handful of frameae. Tullus knew well the danger posed by those versatile spears which could be hurled from close or long range or used as thrusting weapons.

HUUUUMMMMMMMM! HUUUUMMMMMMMMM! From a thousand throats, the sonorous barritus began.

Tullus hissed a curse. Until this point, the scales had been more or less balanced. In the space of five heartbeats, they had shifted, in the warriors' favour.

HUUUUMMMMMMMM! HUUUUMMMMMMMM!

Mule Prick grinned as the mass of warriors advanced towards his position. He increased his own pace, which in turn made them speed up.

Worry gnawed at Tullus now. Mule Prick was fifty paces away. When his comrades reached him, they *would* charge. If that happened, the situation would disintegrate into bloody chaos. The cohorts on the level ground would be watching the drama unfold, but they'd never be able to reach Tullus' men before they were overwhelmed. It was possible too that thousands more warriors might appear from the trees and threaten the whole legion.

'Front two ranks, ready javelins. Whoever takes down the brute with the giant cock earns an amphora of good wine. On my command,' Tullus said to left and right. 'Pass it on – quick!'

Mule Prick swaggered another five paces nearer. Tattoos on his muscled limbs writhed with each step, and his outsized member flopped from side to side, a mockery of ordinary men's genitalia. Spying Tullus, perhaps because of his crested helmet, he pointed his club. 'Fight!' he roared in accented Latin. 'Come and fight!'

'I've no wish to be bludgeoned to death by your cheesy dick!' Tullus shot back in German. He repeated his words in Latin and every legionary within earshot laughed.

Mule Prick's face purpled, and he continued advancing towards Tullus. 'Fight, coward!'

Tullus checked. The first two ranks were ready, their right arms back. 'LOOSE!' he bellowed.

Mule Prick sensed the danger at last. He halted. Now he took a step back, then another. The maggot was forty paces away if he was one, thought Tullus as his gaze followed two score javelins up into the air. Thirty was the limit of most men's effective range with the javelin. Throwing uphill reduced that distance. Tension knotted his belly as the shafts plummeted earthward.

A heartbeat later, Tullus let out an incredulous laugh. No less than three javelins had struck Mule Prick. Two had taken him in the belly, one high and one low, and the other had run through his right bicep, forcing him to drop his club. Mule Prick bellowed with rage and pain, and gave a useless tug at the shafts in his stomach. Then his legs buckled, and he fell to one knee, moaning as the javelins moved and wrenched in his flesh.

To Tullus' relief, Mule Prick's plight had stopped the avalanche of warriors in its tracks. He and his men weren't out of danger yet, however. 'Third rank, pass your javelins to the front!' he shouted. 'First rank, ready!'

Another volley of javelins went up. Only one hit Mule Prick this time, but it speared him through the chest, killing him. An audible sound of dismay went up from the tribesmen as his bloodied corpse fell backwards into the bog, and the javelins transfixing him jerked upright like so many fence posts.

'Draw swords. Keep your faces to the front,' ordered Tullus. 'Walk backwards, nice and slow.'

Eyes fixed on the enemy, they stepped back the way they had come. Progress was slower than before. Unable to see what was behind them, men tripped and cursed, and a number turned an ankle or wrenched a knee. One fool suffered a flesh wound to the buttocks when he stumbled backwards on to the sword wielded by the soldier in the next rank.

Tullus didn't care, because there had been no pursuit, and by the time they reached more level ground, the warriors had vanished into the trees, taking the berserker's corpse with them. At least a dozen legionaries began taking the credit for hitting Mule Prick. Tullus laughed and said that the century would have four amphorae to share between them, one for each javelin that had struck home. 'When we get back to Vetera, of course,' he added. Despite this sobering comment, the soldiers cheered.

As Tullus neared the other cohorts, Bassius was waiting with a small escort. 'That was a close call.'

'It reminded me of kicking a wasps' nest, sir,' said Tullus in sober tone. 'Not the wisest thing to do.'

'It was clever to bring down the berserker.'

Tullus fell out of rank, and indicated that his men should keep marching. He lowered his voice. 'If he hadn't fallen, sir, we'd have been finished.'

'You did well. How many are they – could you see?'

'I counted about a thousand, sir, but there looked to be plenty more in the trees. Arminius won't be here unless he has a good-sized host. Six years ago, he must have had fifteen to twenty thousand spears.' The enormous figures were a stark reminder of their own situation. Caecina commanded more legionaries than Varus had had, but in an ambush, superior numbers often counted for little. The potential for Arminius' ambush to be repeated was there, thought Tullus. The Long Bridges road was a good place to attack, because of the vast bogs that rolled away into the distance. If the legions broke, they would have nowhere to run.

'I always wondered how Varus could have been led astray,' said Bassius. 'I'm beginning to understand.'

Tullus' festering anger towards Arminius flared. 'The same thing is *not* going to happen to us!' He flushed and added, 'Sir.'

Bassius seemed amused. 'I'm glad to have you in my legion.' He gave Tullus an approving nod, but then he was all business again. 'The camp won't get built on its own. Caecina has sent word to continue what we've started. Get your lot digging over there, by the Sixth Cohort. We'll talk later. There's to be a meeting of high-ranking officers, including senior centurions.'

'Yes, sir.' Tullus approved.

An unexpected break appeared in the clouds, spilling shafts of late-afternoon sunshine on to the damp landscape. A moment later, the rain eased off and stopped. The effect was remarkable. Their surroundings, which had been so forbidding, almost seemed welcoming. Deep in the bog, a hidden grouse let out a satisfied *ku-ku-ku-ku-kerrooo*. Elsewhere, a legionary was whistling. Another man cracked a joke. Morale remained high, and Tullus smiled.

He glanced up the hill where they'd slain the berserker, and his good humour vanished as fast as it had arrived. Along the tree line stretched an unending row of tribesmen. It was no better on the hillock opposite. They had to number four thousand, thought Tullus, resentful of the cold sweat trickling down his back. Worse still, they were but a proportion of Arminius' host.

To a man, the warriors were motionless. Their presence was enough threat, enough of a message to every Roman in the bogland below.

We will kill you all.

Chapter XXIX

ᛚᛚᛚ

Night had fallen over the vast Roman camp for the second time since Caecina's army had arrived at the beginning of the Long Bridges road. Drizzling rain, dense and cold, yet fell. Cloud hid the moon and stars, as it had the sun – all that day and the ones before it. The only light came from small, sputtering fires by the soldiers' tents, and from their personal oil lamps within. Piso was trudging the muddy avenues towards the tent that served as a temporary hospital. The poor light, uneven surface and protruding rocks meant that it had taken him three times as long as normal to come this distance from his cohort's position. He consoled himself with the thought of the injured Saxa, who would appreciate his company and, more, the wine slopping about in the leather bag slung over his shoulder.

From beyond the ramparts came the sound of singing: Arminius' tribesmen carousing. Piso had been doing his best to block his ears to the unsettling, alien sound, but it was a real struggle. Hades take them and soon, he thought, and keep our sentries alert. Reaching the hospital tent's entrance, he let two stretcher-bearers emerge, carrying a legionary's body. Piso couldn't help but lean in to see if it was Saxa, or anyone else he knew.

Shamed by his relief at not recognising the corpse, he fumbled in his purse. 'Wait.' Both orderlies looked irritated, but they paused. Proffering a denarius, Piso muttered, 'He'll need to pay the ferryman.'

'You're a good man,' said the senior stretcher-bearer, a veteran old enough to be Piso's father. 'Go on.'

The corpse's still warm lips were disquieting to the touch, but Piso had done the same for more than one comrade over the years. He laid the coin on the bloody tongue, and pushed the jaw shut. 'May your journey be swift. Give that brute Cerberus a kick from me.'

The stretcher-bearers gave him a friendly nod and went on their way. Piso knew their destination: a vast pit against one wall of the camp. Dug the previous day, even as the fortifications were being finished, its bottom was waist-deep in bog water. Within, the result of today's fighting, were the bodies of more than five hundred legionaries. None of his friends were among them, which was something to be grateful for, but two men from Tullus' century were, and upwards of fifty from the cohort. The Germans' attacks had been relentless through the day, on both the soldiers fetching timber and those engaged in repairing the neglected road.

I'm alive and unharmed, thought Piso, and so are the rest of us, apart from Saxa. A *framea* had pierced his comrade's lower left arm as he helped to chop down a tree. Unless Saxa was unlucky, the wound would heal. Be grateful, thought Piso. Other men haven't fared so well.

A wall of warm, fuggy air met him as he entered the hospital tent, bringing with it a mixture of powerful smells. The harsh tang of *acetum* was welcome beside the other odours: piss and shit, blood, damp wool and men's sweat. Breathing through his mouth, Piso paced along the lines of wounded, bandaged men, his eyes searching for Saxa. Like their hale comrades elsewhere in the camp, the patients' only bedding was an army blanket each. Many were sleeping, or comatose, either drugged with poppy juice or so far gone that they were beyond needing it. Others moaned softly to themselves. A few held muttered conversations with their neighbours. Someone was humming the tune of a popular marching song, over and over. A man was whimpering, 'Mother. Mother. Mother.' Piso glanced at him, and wished he hadn't. Heavy bandaging covered the soldier's right eye, but dark red blood continued to seep through from the wound beneath. The pain had to be excruciating.

Piso felt helpless, frustrated. He could do nothing for the soldier but pray, same as he had for every other poor bastard he'd come across. As if that did any good. With clenched jaw, he moved on. 'Saxa?' he called.

'Halt!' Despite his strident tone, the surgeon confronting Piso looked fit to drop. His sallow face had a waxen hue, and deep bags were carved out beneath his eyes. Plentiful blood spatters had rendered his tunic red instead of cream. Similar stains marked both his arms to the elbow. 'What are you doing in here?'

'I'm looking for a comrade, sir.'

Seeing Piso's wine bag, the surgeon sniffed. 'You're planning to ply him with drink.'

Too late, Piso tried to conceal what he was carrying. He pulled what he hoped was a winning smile. 'You have me, sir. My friend was wounded earlier. I thought a drop of this would warm him up.'

'This is a hospital, not a tavern,' retorted the surgeon, pointing at the entrance. 'Out. Your friend can find you when he's discharged.'

'I'll only stay a few moments, sir.'

'That's what they *all* say. Half a watch later, my orderlies have to eject them, leaving my patients drunk as noble youths the day they take the toga. Out.'

'I was in the Eighteenth, sir. So was my mate,' said Piso, throwing caution to the wind. 'I took an oath after the ambush never to leave another comrade without giving him a taste of wine first.'

The surgeon frowned. 'We're not abandoning anyone.'

'I know we're not, sir, but . . .' Piso didn't want to suggest what might happen in the next few days. It felt like tempting the Fates, and they were fickle Greek bitches at the best of times.

The surgeon moved aside with a sigh. 'Be quick. He can have a few mouthfuls of wine, and that's it.'

'My thanks, sir.' Before the surgeon could change his mind, Piso darted around him and resumed his walk between the lines of wounded men. Saxa was lying twenty paces further on, his injured arm wrapped in a clean piece of ripped tunic. He seemed to be asleep. Piso nudged his leg. 'Thirsty?'

Saxa twitched and woke, then focused on Piso. A smile split his face. 'How did you get in? The surgeon is as crusty as an old whore's—'

'Shhhh,' hissed Piso, aware that the surgeon was close by. 'He's not too bad. Even said I could stay for a bit. You're allowed some of this.' He swung the bag down off his shoulder and unstoppered it.

'You're a marvel. Give that here!' Saxa reached out with his good hand. Piso held the bottom of the bag and tipped it up so his friend could drink. Saxa's throat worked as he swallowed two, three big mouthfuls. 'Gods, that's good,' he said, pulling away at last.

Piso was watching the surgeon, and held it up, out of reach. 'Maybe that's enough.'

'Balls. Give it back!' Saxa relented when Piso indicated the surgeon with a jerk of his head. Saxa lay back on his blanket. 'That was good. Gratitude, brother.'

'How are you feeling?'

'My arm aches, but then a fucking spear went through it, and it's been sluiced with acetum. The surgeon says I'll be back to light duties within the month. Full duty within two. That is, if . . .' Saxa stopped. 'How are things out there?'

'Fine,' lied Piso.

'You don't need to hide anything from me,' said Saxa, scowling. 'Is it bad?'

'Not as bad as the first day with Varus,' said Piso in a low tone. 'We've lost four or five hundred men.'

'May their shades not linger in this shithole. Did we kill many Germans?'

Piso spat the words out. 'A hundred, they say, maybe more.'

Saxa swore again. 'Tell me that a decent stretch of road got repaired at least.'

'A mile.'

'That's it?' Heads turned at Saxa's cry, including the surgeon's – who gave them both a disapproving look.

'We'll fare better tomorrow,' said Piso, offering the bag. 'Have a last swig. I'll end up on a charge if I stay any longer.'

Saxa drank like a newborn baby on its mother's breast. He relinquished the wine bag with reluctance.

'You will sleep well tonight.'

Saxa lifted a clay jug that had been lying by his side, and winked. 'I can even piss without going out in the rain.'

'Trust you to have every comfort arranged!' said Piso with a chuckle. He gripped his friend's good hand. 'I'll see you again tomorrow evening.'

'You gathering timber or road-building?'

'Working on the road, Tullus says.'

'Were there many attacks there today?'

'A lot, aye.'

Saxa's face grew sombre. 'Stay alive.'

'I will. You too.' They clasped hands again, hard.

As Piso walked away, he did not look back.

Piso wandered towards his century's tent positions in a foul mood. His pleasure at seeing his friend had been soured by their last exchange. Saxa shared his concern that the enemy's attacks would intensify, and that casualties would mount even further. The same doom couldn't befall us again, Piso thought. Could it? He was unable to shake off the gnawing worry that Arminius was about to repeat his success of six years before. Old, terrible memories returned: the shock of the first German attack, the miles of corpse-filled mud, and the terrified wails of the civilians left in their camp. Piso blinked them away, cursing, and began swigging his wine. There was just enough in the bag to give him dreamless sleep, he decided.

Laughter carried from a nearby tent. 'Got you, Benignus!' said a voice. 'Pay up.'

A muttered protest was drowned out by a chorus of voices. 'Aemilius won, you dog!' 'Give the man his money.' 'Fair's fair, Benignus. You lost.'

Piso hesitated, and his fingers traced the outline of his two pairs of dice, secure in his purse. A few games would be just the thing to make his worries disappear. If he won some coin, even better. Slapping his hand off the tent's wet leather, he cried, 'Ho, brothers! Have you space for another gambler?'

After a short silence, a voice said, 'I don't see why not.'

Piso waited as someone unlaced the flaps. Fortuna, be good to me, he prayed.

'There.' A wiry legionary was profiled in the dim light cast by the oil lamps within. 'Enter, friend.'

'My thanks.' Piso squeezed inside after his host. The tent's warm interior was confining, as his own was. Eight men and their equipment filled it from side wall to side wall and end to end. Weapons and segmented armour were piled by the entrance, but the soldiers with mail shirts had kept theirs on. No one had taken their sandals off. 'You're ready for a fight,' Piso observed.

'Our centurion insisted. He'd have had us wear our plate too, except it's impossible to sleep in,' grumbled the wiry man who'd let him in. 'Prick.'

Piso swallowed his compliment about their readiness. 'All centurions are hard taskmasters.'

'Yours is the same, no doubt. Find a seat. I'm Aemilius, by the way. Second Century, Eighth Cohort.' The wiry man eased down beside a big soldier with bad pox scars. 'This prick's Benignus. He's down to his last few coins.'

'Nothing new about that,' sneered one of the four men opposite, a thin-faced individual with a hook nose. 'I'm Gaius.'

'But you can call him Beaky,' said his neighbour, a man with a short, bristling beard.

Beaky gave him an elbow in the ribs. 'Shut up, Pubes.'

Piso hid his amusement at Pubes' apt nickname. It was a wonder no one had ever thought to use the same one for Fenestela. 'Piso, they call me. I'm in the First Century of the Seventh.' He sat down beside Beaky, opposite Aemilius. As the other four legionaries introduced themselves, Aemilius leaned over and shook Piso's wine bag. 'Is that what I think it is?'

'Aye.' Knowing it would be drained, Piso took a big slug before he handed it over. The bag passed from man to man, with constant complaints from those at the tent's far end about how much was being drunk.

'Not bad.' Aemilius wiped his lips. 'Gratitude.' His comrades echoed his thanks.

'A guest shouldn't come empty-handed,' said Piso, rummaging for his second best pair of dice. Benignus swept them up from the tent floor at once, his eyes suspicious.

'Rigged, are they?' he demanded.

'No,' Piso protested, thankful that he'd left his other dice, which *were* weighted, nestling at the bottom of his purse.

Benignus rolled them, getting a four and a three. He grunted and threw again. This time a five and a one stared up at him, but it wasn't until he'd made another half-dozen rolls that he handed Piso's dice back. 'They're all right,' he growled.

'How about yours?' challenged Piso. He and Benignus stared at one another in a none-too-amiable way, and the tent's temperature rose.

'Fear not. We wouldn't let the bugger cheat us,' said Aemilius, making a placatory gesture.

'Of course,' said Piso, pulling a smile. 'But I'm no cheat either.'

'Don't take it to heart,' advised Beaky. 'We didn't know you until a few moments ago.'

Piso drew a quick breath. 'Tricksters don't bring their own wine – at least not the ones I've met,' he joked, glad that this raised a laugh. The tension that had prickled the air disappeared. 'What will we play for?' he asked, rattling the contents of his purse. From memory, there were four denarii, ten sestertii and an assortment of lower denomination coins within. If he was careful, it was enough to while away a couple of hours.

'We'll start off easy. Poor Benignus here is sat on the bones of his arse,' said Aemilius with a wink. Benignus let out an angry rumble, but didn't protest as it was decided that an *as* per man was the cost for each game.

Pubes triumphed first, and then it was Beaky's turn. Piso was victorious in the third and fourth games, but Aemilius took the fifth. Benignus cheered as he won the next three rolls, recovering most of his previous losses. They played on, with no particular individual winning to excess. Aemilius produced a small lump of hard cheese, and Beaky some olives. A convivial atmosphere descended as tales were told, blisters compared and aspersions cast on everyone from their centurions to Caecina and the cavalry, who got to ride home while they footsloggers had to walk. There was no mention of Arminius or the tribesmen for some time, but it was inevitable that the topic should arise in the end.

'What were you at today?' asked Aemilius of Piso. 'Felling trees, same as us?'

'Aye. A miserable task, but repairing the road can't be any better. The Germans attacked the men there almost as much.'

'Your unit suffer many casualties?' This from Pubes.

'Some. Two men from my century died. A tent mate got wounded, but not too bad,' replied Piso. 'I was on my way back from visiting him when I stopped by your tent. And your cohort?'

'Sixty-seven dead, and more than twice that number injured,' revealed Aemilius with an unhappy twitch of his lips. 'We were the worst hit cohort in the Fifth, they say.'

'I'm sorry,' said Piso, grateful for his unit's lighter losses.

Aemilius cast a look at his seven comrades. 'Our contubernium was blessed today, eh, brothers? We're all here. Arms and legs, balls and pricks intact.'

'For how much longer, eh?' grumbled Benignus. 'We're walking into another trap, I know it.'

'We're already in it, you big ox,' observed Pubes, his face sour. 'Or hadn't you noticed?'

'Piss off.' Benignus rubbed at his phallus amulet. 'I have a bad feeling about this place. About the whole fucking "Long Bridges" road. It seems like nothing more than a march to the gates of Hades – through the River Styx.'

Everyone answered at the same time. 'Aye.' 'You're right.' 'Why did Caecina ever lead us here?' 'It's as if he let Arminius tell him where to go.'

'Things aren't that bad, brothers,' urged Piso.

'How aren't they?' demanded Beaky in truculent manner. 'By rights some of us should be lying in that cursed pit by the wall. Half this contubernium will be in it tomorrow night, if Fortuna has anything to do with it. Treacherous old cunt.'

'Listen, I used to be in the Eighteenth—' Piso began.

'Eh?' interrupted Aemilius. 'You don't look half old enough.'

'I was a wet-behind-the-ears recruit.'

'Yet you survived?' Benignus' expression was disbelieving.

'The Fates took their eyes off me, I guess,' said Piso. 'I also have Tullus for a centurion. You've heard of him?'

Every legionary nodded his head in assent, and Aemilius said, 'Many men regard Tullus as the best centurion in the legion. Even better than the primus pilus.'

'I'd agree with that. So would everyone in his century,' Piso replied, his eyes bright with passion.

'He's got to be better than ours,' said Benignus. He stared at Piso, sizing him up, before adding, 'It's a pity we didn't do for the officious prick during the mutiny.'

No one agreed with Benignus' comment, but Piso thought he caught a couple of the others nodding. 'That business is finished with, thank the gods,' said Pubes, his smile a little false. 'What's more concerning is where we find ourselves at the moment. What are we to do?'

'March out of here, along the wooden road,' said Piso, incredulous that another option was even being contemplated.

'Why not face the savages on the flat ground?' Pubes thumped one fist into the other. 'Crush them is what we'd do!'

'For a start, there isn't enough space for the whole army to form up,' Piso said. 'Second, Arminius is too wily to lead his men out of the trees. That's not how he destroyed Varus' legions.' His eyes roved over the others' faces.

To his dismay, they didn't appear to believe him. 'German warriors can't beat us in open combat.'

'That's my exact point. Stick to the flat ground and we have nothing to fear,' said Pubes with the smug conviction of someone who won't hear an opinion opposed to his own. Most of his comrades muttered their agreement, chief among them Benignus and Beaky.

'I'm not marching down that road,' Pubes continued. 'It'll be the death of us all. If the fucking Germans don't get us, the bog will.' Again his companions rumbled in assent.

'How many of you feel like this?' asked Piso.

'Plenty,' said Aemilius, entering the conversation at last. 'You and your comrades must think the same thing, surely?'

'Not in my century. Tullus rescued too many of us from that cursed forest. Even if that road does lead to Hades, we'll follow him down it. I'd say the rest of the cohort will stay . . .' Piso was about to use the word 'loyal' but the glint in Aemilius' eyes stopped him. '. . . with him,' he finished.

'I wouldn't be so certain,' said Aemilius.

Benignus added, 'There's been plenty of talk since we set up camp. Most of the Fifth and Twenty-First have had enough.'

'Things won't come to that,' said Piso with a dismissive gesture. Inside, though, he worried how this level of discontent had passed him by.

It felt far too like the recent mutiny.

Chapter XXX

Arminius was standing among the trees in the spot where they grew closest to the huge Roman camp. With him were Maelo, his uncle Inguiomerus and Big Chin; a score of his best warriors stood guard to either side. The darkness concealed them from the enemy's position, less than two hundred paces away. It also prevented Arminius from seeing much more than the structure's forbidding outline. Now and then, he spied a sentry walking along the walkway that spanned the ramparts, but that was it. Thanks to the loud singing coming from his own camp – instigated by him – he could hear nothing from within the Roman walls either.

No matter, Arminius thought. The bastards won't be getting much sleep. Let them stew in their own fear. In the morning, we'll renew the fight.

'Why don't we attack in a few hours?' Inguiomerus' voice came from his left. 'Men's spirits are at their lowest ebb in the dark of the night.'

'Not a bad idea,' Big Chin commented. 'My warriors are ready.'

'And mine,' said Inguiomerus at once.

You didn't stand with me six years ago, Uncle. This time around, you were slow to join forces, yet all of a sudden you want to be at the forefront of every attack, thought Arminius, feeling the anger he'd long held back seeping forth. Out loud, he said, 'My men are prepared too, but an assault tonight would be a mistake.'

'The Romans are reeling from what we did to them,' Inguiomerus shot back. 'Our warriors must have slain half a thousand of the filth.'

'With respect, Uncle, they are *not* reeling. Caecina's army numbers almost twenty thousand men. We destroyed perhaps a fortieth of his total force. That's a tiny proportion, and not enough to break their spirit.'

Inguiomerus huffed, but even in the darkness Arminius could see that Big Chin had taken his meaning, which was a start. He adopted his bluffest tone. 'Let's wear them down first, Uncle. Prevent them from sleeping. Sabotage their repairs to the road, so they have to start afresh each morning. Harass their work parties, as well as the soldiers tasked with defending those at toil. Drive off their mules and horses, perhaps even steal a standard or two.'

'These are the words of a beardless youth, who hasn't got the balls to take on an enemy face-to-face,' Inguiomerus scoffed. 'Do you doubt your warriors' courage? Has the loss of your wife made you *afraid*?'

If Inguiomerus hadn't led more than four thousand warriors, Arminius would have spitted him then and there, so great was his rage. He stared at the Roman camp and ground his jaws.

Maelo stepped in. 'Arminius has no need to prove his bravery to anyone, Inguiomerus. What he did six years ago was demonstration enough.' He added in a caustic tone, 'I don't recall you – or your warriors – being present when we slaughtered Varus' legions.'

'Nor I,' said Big Chin.

'You question *my* courage?' Inguiomerus' voice had sunk to a hiss.

'More your loyalty,' replied Maelo.

'Watch your mouth,' cried Inguiomerus.

'Or what?' demanded Maelo.

Arminius sensed the pair stepping apart and wheeled around before the situation degenerated further. 'Come now. Let's not argue.'

'Maelo is treading on thin ice,' snarled Inguiomerus.

So are you, you self-serving prick, thought Arminius. Maelo speaks the truth and nothing more. You are my own flesh and blood, yet you did not support my attack on Varus. Now you have the cheek to dispute my mettle? And yet he knew that to say either thing would risk losing his uncle's hard-earned support.

Instead, he clapped first Inguiomerus, then Maelo, on the shoulder. 'Today has been long and hard. Tempers fray when men are tired. Falling out between ourselves will achieve but one thing, and that's helping the Romans.' Arminius glared at Maelo, willing him also to make amends.

'True enough,' said Maelo. 'I spoke in haste, Inguiomerus. I have no wish to question your honour. Let us remain allies.' He stuck out his right hand.

Inguiomerus stared at Maelo without reacting. A heartbeat passed. Two.

Make him accept it, Great Donar, Arminius asked. I *need* his warriors.

'We have a common enemy, Inguiomerus,' said Big Chin. 'And much to do in the coming days.'

Inguiomerus' eyes swivelled to Big Chin, and back to Maelo. 'We have a common enemy,' repeated Inguiomerus, gripping Maelo's hand at last. Arminius offered his hand then, and his uncle took it. Arminius' distrust of him wasn't eased. Inguiomerus' gesture meant nothing – and yet he hadn't walked away. He still wanted to defeat the Romans.

'My warriors are about to divert the streams that flow down to the bog,' revealed Arminius. 'In the morning, the Romans will find that today's work has been ruined. Their morale will be lowered even more – and then we shall fall on them.'

Big Chin laughed. 'My men will help.'

'An assault now would be more effective,' Inguiomerus grumbled. 'But I suppose we can leave it for another night.' He stalked off, without offering his warriors' assistance.

'Why won't he just give up the idea?' Arminius muttered, his frustration gnawing at him like a dog on a bone. 'Attacking Roman fortifications is almost as unwise as fighting them in open battle. You both know that. I know that. Why doesn't he?'

'Inguiomerus covets the glory you won for yourself, I'd wager,' said Maelo.

'He doesn't like being treated as if he's your follower. He is your equal, Arminius, as am I. Remember what I said,' observed Big Chin. With a cordial nod, he too strode off. 'My warriors will be ready whenever you are,' he called over his shoulder.

Arminius stared into the darkness, brooding. His alliance held, but it wouldn't take much for the whole thing to smash into a thousand pieces, like a clay jar dropped on a hard surface.

Dawn was breaking, and Arminius was standing in the open, close to the beginning of the wooden road. He used the back of his arm to rub at his gritty eyes. He couldn't use his hands, which were caked with mud from digging all night. It was growing dangerous to be here, he decided. The enemy sentries hadn't seen them yet, but the mist that had coated the land was dissipating, and within the camp the trumpets had just sounded, summoning the legionaries from their blankets. Arminius had paced up and down several times, assessing his warriors' labours. He had no need to do it again, yet a sense of devilment kept him walking the boggy ground. He *wanted* the Romans to see him and his men.

'Have we done enough?' He directed the question at Maelo, who was knee-deep in water, using a spade to slice out the sides of a channel that guided one of the larger streams towards a section of still-usable planking.

Maelo straightened and cast a look at the road, which was under a handspan of murky brown water. 'I'd say it's been a good night's work. Caecina's soldiers will go nowhere today, except to the underworld,' he added with a leer.

A cry of alarm rose from the ramparts of the Roman camp. Another voice joined in at once. The words were indiscernible, but their tone was not. 'We've been seen,' said Arminius. 'Best get back to the trees, in case Caecina sends out a cohort or two.'

With sharp whistles, he rounded up his men. They were about to set off when Maelo turned back. 'A little present for the Romans,' he cried. Opening his breeches, he released an arc of urine into the stream. The warriors hurried to join him, and Arminius chuckled. Their efforts would soon be washing over the wooden road.

'We should have shit all over the first section of timbers,' a broad-shouldered warrior declared as they began the tramp back to their positions. 'Imagine them having to march through that!'

'Do that tomorrow,' suggested Maelo, winking.

The tribesmen cheered. From the trees, their comrades began to sing the barritus. Louder and louder it rose, a defiant, fear-inducing chant that challenged the Romans to come forth to another day of mud and slaughter.

Exulting in its sound, Arminius took one last glance at their overnight efforts. As far as the eye could see, the road was submerged. Inguiomerus cannot fail to see the effect, he thought. Grinding down the enemy day *and* night and impeding his progress at every step are tactics that *work*. Wolves do not try to take down the bull elk at first pass – he is too big a prey. Instead, they chase him to exhaustion. When he can run no further, they attack from all sides, tearing at the hindquarters and neck until the bull falls. Only then does the lead male grab his throat and choke the life out of him.

'You will die here, Caecina,' whispered Arminius as the first legionaries began issuing from the nearest gate. 'Just as Varus did in the forest.'

Chapter XXXI

🬀🬀🬀

S hocked and angry, Tullus stood atop the camp fortifications. Thanks to the Germans' efforts, the ground was a veritable morass. The three cohorts marching out had no chance of catching the warriors who'd diverted the streams. Men clad in tunics and trousers could outstrip armoured legionaries with ease. The tribesmen still in sight knew it too – many were shouting obscenities at the Romans.

Tullus spied one turn back to empty his bladder into the largest stream, and urging his companions to do the same. One figure alone did not join in. Their obvious leader watched with evident amusement, shouting encouragement, clapping the piss-instigator on the shoulder as the group traced a path back to the safety of the trees. At this distance, there was no way of knowing who he was, but Tullus couldn't help wondering if it was Arminius. It would be like him to stay until the last moment, he thought, wishing that the bolt-throwers were up here, rather than in their wagons, dismantled and useless.

The barritus started up again from the trees, and Tullus cursed. Like most, he had got little rest thanks to the enemy's incessant singing overnight. This rendition had a taunting edge to it, or so it seemed to his foggy, sleep-deprived brain. He spat over the ramparts at the Germans. 'You're a clever bastard, Arminius, and no mistake. Don't think we're done yet, though.'

Despite Tullus' fighting words, their situation had worsened a great deal. Caecina's orders, issued the night before, had been to move out after dawn, but marching on to the just-submerged road was an altogether different proposition to crossing it over dry, repaired sections. This new dilemma would have been bad enough without the news brought to Tullus by Piso late the previous night.

Tullus' men seemed happy enough, all things considered, and he hadn't been aware of ill feeling elsewhere in the legion, but Piso wasn't one to concoct stories out of thin air. As he was recounting his tale for the second time, Tullus had sent Fenestela wandering the tent lines, seeking out those junior officers who were still awake. It had been dispiriting when Fenestela returned with confirmation of Piso's story.

A good number of the Fifth's legionaries were talking again of rebellion, he reported. Rumour was that the men of the Twenty-First felt the same way. Wary of disturbing Caecina's rest, even with such tidings, Tullus had decided to tell his general in the morning. *He* had mulled on it all night. Singling out and killing the culprits, as they had before, would have a disastrous effect on morale. In any case, every man who could wield a sword was needed, or they'd never fight their way out of this forsaken spot.

Tullus had given up trying to sleep while it was still dark, and had come here to pace the defences and rack his brains some more. It would have been good if inspiration had struck. It hadn't. Short of magicking a new road into existence, or having the gods destroy Arminius' gathered host, nothing had come to mind. Caecina *had* to hear Piso's tale. 'Best get it over with,' Tullus muttered.

How the general would react to the damage done to the road, he did not know. Should they march on regardless, or stay to restart their repairs? Clattering down the wooden steps, he worried that whatever Caecina's decision, the attacks today would be heavier than the day before. Arminius was about to throw his entire force at them – Tullus could feel it in his bones.

If the Fifth and the Twenty-First also mutinied, disaster beckoned.

*   *   *

Caecina was a veteran officer who had served more than forty years in the legions. Short, squat and with cropped white hair, he was a restless soul who liked to pace about, talking in a loud voice. Tullus heard Caecina deep inside the command tent long before he saw him. When he was ushered into Caecina's presence, the man looked both irritated and exhausted, but catching sight of Tullus, he let a brief smile cross his lips. 'Give me a moment,' Caecina ordered, waving away the staff officers who surrounded him at the large table in the centre of his campaign room. 'You did well to spot those warriors, Tullus.'

'I was on the ramparts anyway, sir,' Tullus demurred. 'Sadly, the cohorts you sent out won't catch them.'

'I didn't expect they would, but the Germans' actions couldn't go unanswered.' Caecina seemed about to mention the road, but instead he proffered a brimming glass. 'Don't worry. It's well watered down.'

'A pick-me-up then, sir. Thank you.' Tullus tasted the wine. Even dilute, it had a fine, rich flavour – there was no comparison with the vintage given him by Germanicus, but it was better than anything Tullus could afford. He glanced at Caecina, who was draining his own glass. Fuck it, thought Tullus. That was a long night, and it'll be an even longer day. He threw back the contents of his own – and didn't protest when Caecina offered a refill. 'It's tasty, sir.'

'I'll have some sent around to your tent tonight.' Caecina batted away Tullus' protest. 'The more we drink, the less weight in the wagons, eh? We've got to think of the poor mules.'

Tullus had to grin. 'As you say, sir.'

'Much as you admire my wine, you didn't come here to beg some of me.' Caecina's red-rimmed eyes, sharp as ever, bore down on Tullus. 'What has you here at such an early hour?'

'Something one of my men told me last night, sir.' Caecina frowned and Tullus explained. 'I have no proof that the legionaries of the Twenty-First are as disaffected, but, given the rumours, it seems probable. I thought you should know.'

Caecina pressed a thumb and forefinger against the bridge of his nose. 'More bad news.'

'I'm sorry, sir—'

'Don't be. It's your job to bring me word of such things. So, is the threat real? How does your cohort stand?'

'My men are solid, sir,' said Tullus with pride. 'As for the rest, it's hard to be sure. These things ebb and flow like the tide – you know how it is. One moment, they might all follow an order to attack, and the next, they might not.'

'It depends in part on how today goes, I'd wager.' Caecina's face darkened. 'How bad is the flooding?'

'Bad, sir. Yesterday's work has been destroyed, or I'm no judge.'

'Curse Arminius!'

'If I knew where he camped, sir, I'd ask to take a couple of cohorts and attack him at night. His alliance might fragment if he was dead.'

'It's too easy for such a mission to go wrong, and I can't afford to lose officers like you,' said Caecina. 'You've also been through this before, under Varus.'

'That's right, sir,' replied Tullus in a grim tone.

Caecina rubbed his eyes. 'I must have slept for a time last night, because I dreamed of him.'

A chill tickled Tullus' guts. 'Of Varus, sir?'

'Aye. I heard a voice calling me. I awoke – in the dream – and walked out of my tent. There was no camp, just the stinking bog on all sides. High-pitched, mesmeric, the voice came from the midst of it – I could not see who or what was speaking to me. I waited, rigid with fear, and at length a pale figure rose from the depths. The wraith began to float over the marsh towards me, and as it drew near, horror filled me. It was Varus. Flesh-rotted, bloodied and with a gaping wound in his chest, but Varus nonetheless. Stretching out his arm, he called me to him.'

'What did you do, sir?' asked Tullus, fascinated and horrified.

'I was frozen to the spot,' Caecina admitted. 'It was only when his cold hand touched mine, trying to drag me with him, that I found the strength to shove back the fell creature. "Go back whence you came," I cried, and turned away. It was then that I awoke.' He made a cynical noise. 'There was no sleep to be had after that, I can tell you.'

'I'm not surprised, sir,' said Tullus, fighting the feeling that Caecina's doom-laden vision might have been gods-sent.

'What would you do?' muttered Caecina.

Tullus gave him a confused look. 'Sir?'

'If you were the army's commander, what would your next move be?'

For Caecina, a general with four legions under his command, to tell him of his dream about Varus was extraordinary enough, thought Tullus. To be asked for advice straight after – well, it showed how rattled Caecina was. He must *not* crumble, Tullus resolved. 'How many days' supplies have we, sir?'

'Seven. Twice that if we cut rations in half.'

'Seeking another route back to the Rhenus isn't a good option then, sir.'

Caecina's headshake spoke volumes.

'In that case,' said Tullus, jutting his chin, 'we have two choices, sir: to repair the damaged sections, again, and hold off the savages at the same time. Tomorrow or the next day, we can enter the marsh via the road. Or we can press on today, along the flattish ground to the right of the camp. In both instances, the Fifth and the Twenty-First are unknown quantities.'

'Is it worse to remain here, and make the troops work under constant assault, or to march into the infernal bog, where the enemy can attack us at will?' Caecina's voice was unhappy.

'Whatever we do, we should get going this morning, sir,' said Tullus with a confidence he didn't quite feel. 'I suspect that the attacks today will be heavy, and the Fifth and the Twenty-First might break under the pressure. If we're moving, their nerve is more likely to hold.' Let that be true, great Mars, he prayed.

A dozen heartbeats skipped past before Caecina spoke.

'My mind is made up. We march out today, along the flat ground. Roman virtus will carry us through this, by the gods,' he said. 'It *has* to.'

Chapter XXXII

T ullus was standing at the head of his cohort, on the *intervallum*, the wide open space between the camp walls and the defences. In front of him were the first six cohorts of the Fifth, behind him the last three. Unable to see more than the arse end of the cohort in front, abandoned avenues to the left and earthen ramparts to the right, he chafed with impatience. 'Why aren't we marching?' he muttered to himself.

Following Caecina's orders, the four legions had formed up at dawn in the usual manner, cohort by cohort, all around the intervallum. The First Legion was to be in the vanguard today, so it had marched out first, along with the auxiliary cavalry. They were to travel along the flat ground that bordered the ruined Long Bridges road. Their departure had gone ahead without incident more than an hour before. The Twenty-First, whose job it was to form the left flank of the army column, had gone next. The Fifth would take the right flank, and should have been moving by now, thought Tullus, unease nagging at him.

Caecina, his senior officers and large escort were ready to follow on after the Fifth. The wagon train, laden down not just with its usual cargo of food, equipment and artillery, but the injured as well, would come next, with the Twentieth Legion taking up the rear.

Tullus could take the tension no longer. He could not leave his position; nor could Fenestela, at the back of the century. Both of them had to be ready to urge the men on when the time came. Tullus' gaze shifted to his left, and found someone else. 'Piso!'

'Sir?'

'Go and see what's going on beyond the wall. Quickly!'

'Yes, sir!' Piso loped to the nearest set of steps. *Clash, clash, clash* went his hobnails on the wood. At the top, he propped his javelin against the rampart and raised a hand, shielding his eyes against the light. Tullus watched him with growing impatience. 'Well?' There was no immediate reply. 'Piso!'

Piso glanced down, his face unhappy.

'What is it?' demanded Tullus.

'The First has marched out of sight, sir, but the Twenty-First, it . . .' Piso hesitated.

Conscious of what he might say, and of the disastrous effect it could have on those listening – every soldier within earshot – Tullus roared, 'Come back!'

The Sixth Cohort had begun to advance towards the gate by the time Piso had reached the bottom of the wall. Tullus had his soldiers move off, and indicated to Piso that he should walk alongside. He gave Piso a sharp look. The steady legionary seemed scared. 'What in Hades did you see?' muttered Tullus.

'The Twenty-First hasn't followed the First towards the Rhenus, sir. It's broken away and marched to the right, to a large, flat area.'

Tullus let out a ripe oath. He would have given a year's pay for his horse, so he could gallop out to remonstrate with the Twenty-First's senior officers. He swallowed down his disappointment, sour as it was. Even if his mount had been close by, his intervention would make no difference. A marching legion was impossible to halt unless its trumpeters sounded – and there wasn't much chance of that, given that the entire Twenty-First appeared to be disobeying orders.

Tullus' worries now soared. Once the Fifth's cohorts saw what their comrades were at, the likelihood was that they would do the same, rather than follow the First along the intended route of march. It might be too late – the first five cohorts had exited the gate, and would have seen what was going on. He had to move *now*. 'Fenestela!' he bellowed.

'Sir?'

'Get up here. The tesserarius is to take your place.'

'Yes, sir!'

'Maintain your pace,' Tullus ordered the nearest legionaries.

Holding the hilt of his sword so that it didn't knock off his leg, he began to run. Plenty of curious glances were thrown as he progressed along the side of the next cohort, the Sixth. The ordinary soldiers didn't dare question him, but the centurions were curious. 'Ho, Tullus! Can't you wait to get at the Germans?' 'Why the hurry?' 'Forgetting your position, Tullus?'

He grinned and muttered vague replies, and kept running. All the while, he cursed the weight of his armour and his ageing body. Tullus' back ached, so too did his knees, and the crone who liked to stab at the injury in his left calf was at it again. He had to reach the front of the legion, though, while there was still a chance of preventing it following the Twenty-First.

He shoved his way through the gateway, which was filled with soldiers of the Fifth Cohort. Men cursed the stranger pushing from behind until they saw Tullus' rank, whereupon they fell over themselves to apologise. He ignored them and kept moving, but his heart sank as he emerged. All was confusion. Rather than follow the First Legion towards the Rhenus, the Fifth Cohorts had splintered into disorganised groups. Hundreds of legionaries milled about, ignoring the shouts of their officers. At least one band was marching off to join the rebellious Twenty-First. Several signiferi had joined the *aquilifer*, and were arguing. The fools were debating what to do, thought Tullus, oblivious to the danger posed by the Germans.

Tullus focused on finding the senior centurion of the Fifth Cohort – his intervention there might help, but it was a scant hope. As its soldiers spilled out from the gateway behind him, they broke ranks at once. A few centurions tried to stop them, but they were barged out of the way. 'You'll pay for this, you dogs,' Tullus shouted as they swarmed past. 'Running away won't save you. Arminius will have taken your miserable hides by sunset!'

Discipline hadn't altogether vanished. The nearest men averted their gaze as they streamed past, but Tullus soon had to abandon all hope of rallying the soldiers outside the camp. He ran back to the gate, hoping to stop the next cohort – the Sixth – from dispersing. Within a few heart-beats, it was apparent that this too was a lost cause. Sensing something, the legionaries had pressed forward into the gateway. The lead centurion, a podgy-cheeked, pink-complexioned individual by the name of Proculinus, stopped when he saw Tullus pushing back, *into* the camp. His face went puce as Tullus explained what was going on. In that short time, Proculinus' century had passed by – and was beyond his control. The ranking centurion of the Second Century paused and asked Proculinus, 'Is everything all right, sir?'

'What should I do?' hissed Proculinus to Tullus.

'You can't stop this – it's like trying to stem the tide. Stay with your men. Try to keep them together, and be ready to answer the summons to rejoin the rest of the army. If you can't bring them back, Arminius and his warriors will kill you all,' warned Tullus. Proculinus nodded and hurried off.

Tullus pushed on, into the crowd of jostling legionaries. He had to reach *his* troops, or they too would copy the rest, the way sheep follow those at the front of the flock.

'Make way, you filth,' he roared, clattering his vitis on helmets, arms and backs alike. 'Make way!'

His own century had just reached the gate when Tullus cleared through the last stragglers of the Sixth Cohort and re-entered the camp. 'HALT!' he bellowed in his best parade voice. 'HALT!'

Fenestela, who was in Tullus' usual position, repeated the order.

After the slightest hesitation, the front rank stopped. The second came to a halt quicker. After that, things went as smooth as they ever would, each rank coming to a standstill with a one, two stamp of their hobnails. Tullus described the chaotic scene outside the gate to Fenestela, who swore long and hard. 'Those rebellious pricks will be the death of us all.'

'Let's fucking hope not.' Tullus' gaze roamed beyond their men, to the troops further down the column. Could he hold back the rest of the legion?

He came to a snap decision. 'The Eighth, Ninth and Tenth Cohorts will want to go with the others, not stay here with us. The best chance of stopping the rot is to go to the Twentieth's primus pilus.'

'So we move away from the gateway?'

'Do it now. Keep the men focused. Tell them how we're about to slaughter the bastard Germans. Come down hard on anyone who even *looks* as if he wants to follow the rest. See that the other centurions do the same.' Tullus left Fenestela to it.

He had bigger fish to fry.

Time passed – it had to have been close to an hour, but Tullus had no way of knowing. The Eighth, Ninth and Tenth Cohorts of the Fifth *had* joined the rest of the legion and the First on the flat ground outside the camp. But thanks to his intervention, the Twentieth Legion, which had still been within the walls, had been kept in order on the intervallum. Together with Tullus' cohort, the Twentieth had waited until Caecina, his officers and the baggage train had followed the still loyal First Legion towards the Rhenus. Then it had set out too, making up the rearguard.

The mutinous Fifth and Twenty-First were to be left where they were, Caecina had ordered. 'They'll come to their senses quick enough when they see us marching away,' he'd said. It was a massive gamble, but no one had had a better suggestion. Delaying – staying behind to try and win the rebellious soldiers over – was far too dangerous. The Germans would attack at any moment.

Tullus had suggested that his cohort precede the Twentieth, and Caecina had agreed. Too late, Tullus realised this would leave him and his men right behind the baggage train. Under normal circumstances, this position would have been unpleasant, aromatic and shit-spattered. Today, it left Tullus' cohort as the men who would have to help push the wagons if they became stuck in the mud.

If, thought Tullus with a lingering sourness. More like when. The army had travelled perhaps half a mile westward before its snail-like pace ground to a complete halt. He tramped forward to the tail-end wagon, a low-sided vehicle laden with dismantled bolt-throwers. 'What's going on?' he demanded of the driver, a tiny old man with wispy white hair.

'Wagons in front have stopped, sir,' came the obsequious but sly reply.

'I can see that,' replied Tullus in an acid tone. 'Why are *they* not moving? Because the ones in front of them are at a standstill,' he said, before White Hair could tell him the same thing.

'I'd wager that's the reason, sir.' White Hair was perched on his seat, the reins to his mule team dangling from one hand. The forefinger of his other hand was buried inside a nostril. He seemed to have not the slightest interest in what was happening around him. 'Aye.'

Irritated at first, Tullus then decided that the ancient's attitude was understandable, and practical. He could not shift his wagon until the ones in front moved forward. Frail, old, White Hair was powerless to help with digging out the bogged-down vehicles. He could not run from the Germans, nor even defend himself. Tullus left him to his excavations, and worked his way through the quagmire past a score of wagons. Many were stuck fast.

There was no point continuing, he concluded. Everything with wheels would be axle-deep in mud along the length of the baggage train. It would require his cohort and a good number of legionaries from the Twentieth to dig them out – and it would take time. We couldn't have handed a better opportunity to Arminius if we tried, thought Tullus with bitterness, and wondered if repairing the road first would have been a better option. Spotting the Twenty-First and most of the Fifth still milling about, he cursed and cursed again. If Arminius was shrewd enough to split his forces and attack both the wagons and the disorganised, mutinous soldiers—

Think like that, and you might as well give up now, Tullus told himself. He retraced his steps, eager to reach his men.

'Things bad?' White Hair was still in his position, but he'd given up on the exploration of his nostrils. Now a nasty-looking club, its end studded with sharp pieces of iron, was balanced on his knees.

'They're bad enough, aye,' replied Tullus. He gestured at the club. 'Planning to fight?'

'My wife's twenty-five years younger 'n me. She's keeping the bed warm in Vetera,' White Hair disclosed with a wink. 'That's worth fighting for, ain't it?'

'Without doubt,' said Tullus, amused and heartened by White Hair's pluck. 'I'll be back. We'll have your wagon out of the mud in no time.'

HUUUUMMMMMMMM! HUUUUMMMMMMMM!

'Bastards,' snarled Tullus, already moving past White Hair and studying the slope to his left for signs of the enemy. Before long, he'd picked out the shapes of men in the trees. They would be gathering on the other side of the baggage train too – and the cohorts had had little time to form up. The fighting was going to be disorganised and even more brutal than usual. 'Fenestela!' he roared.

'I'm here, sir!'

'One in every four or five wagons is stuck,' said Tullus. 'It'll take hundreds of men to shift them.'

'All to be done while the savages attack us,' said Fenestela, curling his lip. 'O, Fortuna, what did we do to piss you off so?'

'There's no pleasing that old whore.'

Fenestela's shoulders went up and down in a fatalistic shrug. 'What are your orders?'

'Three centuries to the left and three to the right of the wagons. We need to move up the train as far as possible before the savages strike. That'll allow legionaries from the Twentieth to follow on and dig out the vehicles at the back.'

'And if the Germans attack Caecina?'

They exchanged unhappy stares, and Tullus chewed a nail. 'It'd be just like Arminius to try something like that,' he said, picturing hundreds of tribesmen descending on the governor and his escort. 'Gather the century, and do it fast.'

'Will that be sufficient?'

'Any more, and we won't get there quick enough.'

Fenestela nodded and hurried off.

A light rain began to fall. It progressed fast to a constant, driving sheet that soaked a man through within twenty heartbeats. Thunder rumbled overhead. Flashes of lightning tore strips across the sky. The barritus rang out again, a great deal louder than before. The unpleasant scene was all too familiar. Arminius' warriors were coming, thought Tullus, and in great strength.

They would be fighting not for the wagon train, but for their lives.

Chapter XXXIII

◰◰◰

'Run!' bellowed Tullus. 'Fucking RUN!'

Piso was two men back from Tullus, and pounding along as best he could. They had travelled forward a short time before, along the length of the wagon train towards Caecina's position and the front of the column. Mud was sucking at his sandals, his yoke rattled and swayed on his right shoulder and his shield was dragging down his left arm. Yet Piso was *not* going to let his centurion – an old man – outstrip him. Nor was he going to get left behind by his comrades, Vitellius and Metilius, who were in front of and behind him. Another three files of soldiers – the rest of the century – were picking their way through the morass to his right. They had to stick together, thought Piso, just as they had six years before.

Heavy rain hammered off his helmet, almost deafening him. Over that rang a chorus of thunder, screams and the infernal *barritus*. Discerning even a single word from Tullus, or the others, was difficult unless it was shouted – and close. 'Where are we going?' Piso yelled.

'What?' replied Metilius, without looking back.

'Where – are – we – going?' repeated Piso, slower and louder. They had travelled along the length of the baggage train, halting at regular intervals to fight off German attacks. Their javelins had been thrown in the first assault, and were impossible to retrieve. Piso had put down three warriors: a stinging cut on his left cheek the painful memento from a slicing German spear. Whenever Vitellius got a chance, he liked to complain about his broken nose, smashed in the first exchange by a warrior's swinging club.

None of the five legionaries who'd died thus far had been tent mates, for which Piso was grateful.

His question had gone unanswered, so he bellowed it again, offering up the cry to the oppressive grey sky and the drifting, hateful rain.

Vitellius slowed for a moment. 'I heard Tullus say that Caecina's in danger. That must be where we're going.'

Piso cursed, and kept close to his friend's heels.

There had been no grateful halt by the wagons at the front of the train, nor any attempt to dig them out of the cursed mud. Instead, Tullus had led his own unit away from the shelter provided by the stranded vehicles. Piso wondered if Tullus had taken leave of his senses. Surely Caecina of all people was safe?

With a high-pitched whinny, a dark brown horse appeared from nowhere. It flashed between Piso and Vitellius, who both did well not to be trampled. Piso got a brief impression of strings of saliva hanging from its lips, and blood seeping from a deep wound in its left haunch. There was no sign of its rider.

If Piso hadn't realised what was going on then, he did when a second and then a third horse charged past, both galloping in different directions. One had a white-faced auxiliary on its back, clutching on for dear life. The nearest horsemen were with Caecina. That *was* where they were heading, Piso decided, bile stinging the back of his throat.

The familiar ring of metal off metal, and men's screams, rose up. Through the sheeting rain ahead, over Vitellius' shoulder and off to the right, Piso could see swarms of warriors. Beyond them, a few Romans were still mounted, while others were fighting afoot, but they were outnumbered by a large margin. Sixty-odd of them were going to go over there, to try and stop Arminius' men from killing Caecina. Piso could taste bile now, thick and bitter, at the back of his throat.

'QUICK!' roared Tullus. 'Caecina needs us!'

Incredulous, Piso watched as Tullus somehow began to move even faster. 'He's going to burst his fucking heart,' Vitellius shouted, but he too was picking up speed. So were the men in the files to Piso's right. Open-mouthed, with yokes clanking and sweat streaming down their faces, they followed Tullus like hounds on a hare. Piso's love for Tullus – and the shame of being left behind – drove him on. He would keep up, or die in the attempt. Mud coated his legs and spattered on to his face and arms as he powered through the bog. A clod landed in his open mouth. Piso spat it out, disgusted, and almost broke his neck crashing into a large hummock crested with bog rosemary.

Tullus gave the order to halt and down yokes some hundred paces on. Piso could have wept with relief. Uncaring that a tribesman might spear him, he grounded his shield and crouched beside it, his chest working like a smith's bellows and his leg muscles throbbing with pain. Around him, he sensed more than one comrade slump to the ground. Piso's fear returned as his breathing eased, and he took the measure of his surroundings. It felt as if they were on an island. On every side, the battle flowed and swept, clusters of legionaries, cavalry and warriors locked in their own struggle for supremacy. No one appeared to have seen them. That wouldn't last, thought Piso. They were out in the open – exposed and outnumbered.

'Can anyone see Caecina?' shouted Tullus. 'Or the men of his bodyguard?'

Everyone studied the confusion before them. 'No, sir.' 'I can't see him, sir.' 'Nor I, sir.'

'Fuck it all. Gods grant that he's not dead,' said Tullus, his face still purple. He glanced at them. 'On your feet! Form up, twelve wide, five or six deep. Signifer, behind me. The rest of you stay close to your comrades. Get your wind back as we walk.' To Piso's incredulity, Tullus gave him a wink.

They bunched together, with Tullus in the centre of the first rank. Piso took his place to Tullus' right and Vitellius stood to Tullus' left – their usual spots, it seemed. Piso's pride flared up to be where he was. Hades, but he felt alive.

'Advance!' called Tullus. 'Breathe in, and think of fucking the prettiest whore you can imagine.'

Piso sucked in a lungful of air, and imagined the blonde goddess who worked in Vetera's most expensive brothel. Diana, she called herself. The huntress. Piso had eyed her up on countless occasions, but had only been able to afford her once, when he had made a huge sum gambling at a gladiator fight.

'Give her one as you breathe out!' ordered Tullus.

An animal roar went up.

'Take another breath. She's telling you that you're the best lover she's had.'

Piso whooped with the rest.

'Exhale, and picture yourself emptying your load into her,' roared Tullus.

Diana was under Piso, smiling, her legs wrapped around his buttocks. Piso groaned as he exhaled. Self-conscious at first, he grinned to hear plenty of similar noises around him.

'Feel better, brothers?' asked Tullus.

'AYE!'

'Me too!' Tullus laughed. So did every man there – it was a manic sound.

'Who were you screwing, sir?' called someone from the ranks behind.

There were snorts of amusement, and Piso pricked his ears. If Tullus visited whorehouses, he did so when nobody was looking.

'None of your business,' growled Tullus. 'But I can tell you she screamed like a Fury!'

Piso and his comrades cheered him then, long and hard.

Tullus tramped on, and they followed. Perhaps 150 paces separated them from the nearest warriors, who were still engrossed with their attack. Piso's grip on his sword was white-knuckled now, and his fantasies about Diana long gone. Men would die in the coming moments. Stay close to Tullus and I'll be fine, Piso told himself over and over. His internal refrain didn't stop the painful twinges radiating from his bladder.

Weee-oooo-weee! Oooo-we! With startled cries, a lapwing shot into the air almost from under Piso's feet. He leaped back with fright and, despite his mail, took a nasty knock from the shield boss of the next-ranked soldier.

He scrambled into position once more, back hurting and scarlet-faced with embarrassment. Hoots of derision from his comrades rained down, questioning his courage, his parentage and more. 'All right?' asked Tullus from the corner of his mouth.

'Yes, sir,' Piso replied, grateful that his bladder hadn't got the better of him.

Eighty paces off, a pigtailed warrior turned away from his comrades and spat. He stared at the Romans in amazement, and then shouted an alarm.

'Pick up the pace, brothers,' roared Tullus. 'But watch your step!'

By the time a score of tribesmen had gathered to face them, Tullus and his men had covered almost half the distance. When they were thirty paces away, perhaps twice that number were readying themselves to fight. There were plenty more in the mob, but for whatever reason – confusion, close combat with Romans to the front – they hadn't turned to meet Tullus' charge.

At twenty-five paces, Tullus had his men slow again to a walk. 'Shields high! Stay close! Forward!'

Piso's breath rebounded off the inside of his shield, hot and fast and stinking of the garlic he'd eaten the day before. Mud and annoying pieces of grit squelched between his toes. His back ached too, where the boss had hit, but he kept his eyes fixed on the closest warriors. Many seemed to be focusing on Tullus, with his unmistakeable transverse-crested helmet. Piso noted three in particular. Two were burly, bare-chested men with similar features and swirling arm tattoos, brothers perhaps, and the last was a short-arsed little bastard with a mail shirt, decorated shield and a fine sword. Each of them was dangerous – Piso sensed it – and if they slew Tullus, Hades would have them all.

The warriors were fifteen paces away.

''Tellius!' Piso roared.

'Aye?' answered Vitellius.

'See those two inbreds with tattoos, and the little fucker with the mail and the fancy shield?'

Piso's heart banged off his ribs three, four times and Vitellius said, 'I see them.'

Ten.

'They're coming for the centurion,' said Piso. 'Watch them.'

'I will!'

Six paces.

Tullus grunted – it might have been disdain, or even gratitude, Piso never knew – and then he shouted, 'Swords off shields, and at them!'

Clatter, clatter. Sixty swords connected with shield rims. The brothers were nearest Piso, while Short Arse was closer to Tullus and Vitellius. Piso's bladder was really hurting now. Pissing himself wouldn't matter, he thought, as long as he protected Tullus.

Shouting war cries, the warriors charged.

Piso's mouth was bone dry, his heart pounding. He readied his right arm, and decided to tackle Brother One, who had a longer moustache. Tullus would face Brother Two, and Piso hoped Vitellius would kill Short Arse. He had to rely on the legionary to his left to fight the brute to the right of *his* target. That was how the shield wall worked, in theory at least.

Thump. Thump. Thump. Up went the familiar noise of shields and bosses clashing off one another, or striking flesh. Men groaned with the pain of it, or with the effort of driving in behind their shields, trying to unbalance their enemies. Fast as a lightning bolt, the sound was followed by screams as blades were rammed home on both sides, and casualties taken.

Piso's hunch was right. The brothers *and* Short Arse were trying to kill Tullus, and the weight of their attack – two stabbing spear blades and a probing sword – was such that Tullus could not fight back. He had ducked down behind his shield. Blind, he could do nothing but brace himself and wait for a chance to strike. Already both brothers were trying to thrust down over the top of Tullus' shield. Piso digested this information in perhaps six fevered heartbeats. Cursing, he stuck his sword into the only portion of Brother One that was visible – his flank, above the waistband of his patterned trousers. Blood blossomed, Piso felt the blade grate off the hipbone and Brother One roared in agony.

Piso wrenched on his sword, feeling it slide off the bone again as it came out in a spray of red. Most men would have gone down with such a wound, but Brother One was set on killing Tullus, regardless of cost. Hissing with pain, he stabbed again with his spear, over Tullus' shield.

The point caught in Tullus' mail, where Piso couldn't see, but Tullus let out a bull's bellow. He must have struck back in reflex, because someone very close – not Brother One – let out a strangled cry. Brother One pulled back his spear with a snarl. Piso was about to stick him again when something hit the top of his head with an almighty crash. Stars burst across his vision, and his strength vanished. He dropped to one knee, letting go of his shield. His over-tight bladder began to empty itself. Above him, someone roared in triumph.

I'm done, thought Piso. Whoever did that to me is about to smash in my skull. Most of him didn't care. The smell of his own piss was thick in his nostrils. His other knee trembled, and he almost fell on to his face. The death blow didn't fall, though, which was baffling. Fuzzy-headed, swaying, and lapsing in and out of consciousness, Piso stared at the confusion of moving legs and churned-up ground before him. Bloodied and limp, a corpse lay right in front, and was being trampled by those above it. There was plenty of mud, as always. Several weapons were visible: two spears, a Roman sword. A tiny ladybird was balanced on a sprig of heather, oblivious to the carnage being waged around it.

Strong legs in patterned trousers shuffled back and forth just to Piso's right. Brother One? he wondered dully, trying to focus on the trousers again. He's still on Tullus.

Piso's sword was lying by his side, his weak fingers still resting on the hilt. He eyed it, a new urgency thrumming through his slow-pulsing veins. He lifted it up a handspan. Then another. Fixed his gaze on the trousers. Raised his blade a little more, tensed his arm muscles. Thrust. Connected. Sliced through the fabric and into the meat of the trousers' owner's calf. The blow wasn't powerful, but it was true. Piso's sharp-edged blade went in – deep. A piercing shriek battered his eardrums, and the trouser-wearer staggered, wrenching the sword from Piso's grasp.

His strength was gone. White light surrounded him. Piso let go.

Chapter XXXIV

◫◫◫

N ot far away, Arminius was also in the thick of the fighting. Sweat
slicked down his face and into his eyes. He blinked away the salty
sting and met the shield thrust from his enemy, a grimacing
legionary, with braced legs. His willow shield splintered with the impact,
and the legionary let out a pleased grunt. He still had a satisfied look on his
face when Arminius' sword glanced off his shield rim and rammed into his
left eye. With a soft pop, almost indiscernible, and a spray of watery fluid,
the globe ruptured. Steel ground off bone. His brain pithed, the legionary
was dead before Arminius had freed his blade.

'Change!' Arminius roared. He didn't want to leave the fight, but his
cracked shield guaranteed a quick death from his next opponent. There was
time for a man to take his place before the legionary in the next rank was
close enough.

'Change!' cried Osbert, the warrior to his rear.

In a move they'd rehearsed scores of times, Arminius half turned,
pulling his shield in close to his body. With *his* shield arm extended, Osbert
slipped past to Arminius' left, allowing his chieftain to withdraw at the same
time.

'Donar!' cried Osbert, causing the legionary facing him to flinch. Letting
out a triumphant roar, Osbert shoved his spear into the Roman's neck. A
fountain of blood jetted from the vicious wound it left, and the legionary
fell on top of his comrade. 'Donar!' cried Osbert again.

Satisfied that the line would hold, Arminius cast around for a new shield.

There were a number lying about, dropped by injured and slain warriors. Finding one to his liking, he took the opportunity to step back. When the crimson mist fell, it was too easy to forget everything but reddening the blade. Just a short remove from the fighting, Arminius' zeal cooled, and he looked to his left. Things seemed to be going well there. As he watched, a wedge of warriors drove deep into the Roman lines, unhorsing a senior officer and panicking nearby riders' mounts. Hooves kicked to and fro, and men wailed as they were thrown backwards into the bog.

In front of Arminius, six legionaries and some dismounted cavalrymen had made a stand together, but they were cut down by an overwhelming charge led by Osbert. The section's remaining defenders faltered, and then broke as Osbert tossed a severed head into their midst. The warriors charged after the Romans with vengeful cries. Arminius smiled.

Find and kill Caecina next, he thought, and his chances of overall victory would soar. And yet that task was almost impossible to achieve. Things were going well, but utter confusion reigned. The heavy rain had reduced visibility to fifty paces or less, and the thick mud impeded everyone, light-armoured or not. His battle-mad warriors were unlikely to recognise Caecina, or to be able to find Arminius and tell him even if they wanted to. His best option was to oversee the massacre of every Roman in this small area, and to hope that Caecina was among them before moving on.

Arminius also had to trust that the other chieftains – Inguiomerus, Big Chin, Stick Thin and the rest – were doing what he'd asked of them. As well as attacking the wagons and the two legions which had broken away from the column, each of the eagle standards was to be targeted. 'Take one of those,' Arminius had told them, 'and you cut off a legion's balls.' He hoped that they'd emphasised this to their warriors, and that the attraction of the wagon train – a booty-rich, easy target – wasn't too great a temptation.

'ROMA!'

The shout – and the subsequent crash of bodies and shields – was close enough to turn Arminius' head. Distracted, he hadn't until then looked to his right. That had been a mistake, he thought, cursing his stupidity. A party of the enemy – it wasn't clear how many – had just driven into his warriors. Some must have seen the attack coming, because the legionaries had been checked, but there was a noticeable bowing in the line. Arminius watched with grim intent. On the far side of his assailed men's position, the Romans seemed to have taken heart and redoubled their efforts. His warriors were now caught between two groups of the enemy.

'You, you and you!' Arminius shouted to get the attention of nearby men. Ten, a dozen, fifteen formed a ring around him. 'Come with me,' he ordered, urgency throbbing in his voice.

Fresh thunder rolled overhead. The rain pattered down with relentless intensity, disturbing the pools of stagnant water. Ripples caused by wading men lapped off muddy banks. Brown, peaty water splashed high, dripping off the heather and bog cotton. Spongy grass on the hummocks compressed and sprang back from the impact of the warriors' passage. The mire made reluctant, sucking sounds as it released their feet. Gorse thorns tore at their arms and legs. Arminius cursed as he lumbered along. Their progress was slow, too slow.

His bad luck was compounded by the Romans' leader, who saw them coming. By the time Arminius drew near, ten legionaries were waiting for them in a small shield wall. Weighed down by their armour, knee-deep in the mud, they were still a fearsome prospect. To hesitate was to die, thought Arminius. Ordering four warriors to flank the enemy, he led the rest forward in a little wedge. It was a tactic he'd learned in the legions.

'Donar!' he roared.

The warrior to Arminius' left broke free of their formation and struck the Roman line first. Run through by two swords, he died before his spear thrust had found a home in enemy flesh. His sacrifice allowed Arminius to close unscathed, and to kill a legionary. The warrior to Arminius' right slew another even as he took a mortal wound.

Arminius shoved his way into the gap, careless of the danger he was in. Wheeling, he stabbed a legionary in the base of the spine, below his armour.

Three steps on, and he slashed another's legs from under him. The next Roman half turned, his face frantic, and Arminius stuck him through the throat. Assailed from in front and behind, the outnumbered legionaries did not give up, downing two more of his followers and maiming another before they died.

'That was well done,' said Arminius to his ten surviving warriors. He was no longer sure if they were enough to make a difference to his beleaguered men, but they had to try, or his attempt to kill Caecina would come to a premature end. 'Can you do the same again?'

Mud-covered, blood-encrusted, they nodded in assent.

'After me then.' Arminius took a step forward.

'Over there!' shouted a voice in Latin. 'Three men from the two rear ranks, turn. Pick up any spears you can. Move, you maggots!'

The voice sounded familiar but, in the heat of battle, Arminius could not recall from where. He led his warriors on, towards the section of legionaries that was breaking away from the Roman formation. Curse the bastards, he thought. Even in these abominable conditions, their discipline remained impressive. Six legionaries were ready to take them on, with, in their middle, a veteran centurion.

Each party closed on the other with a measured, purposeful intent. No one shouted; no one ran. The loss of a single man to a twisted ankle at this point could prove the difference between victory and defeat. Arminius talked to his warriors in a calm voice, urging them on; he could see the centurion doing the same with his soldiers.

'Let's charge,' muttered one of Arminius' warriors when fifty paces remained. 'Panic them.'

'These ones won't break,' said Arminius. 'Keep walking.'

'But their armour—' began the warrior.

'I know,' interrupted Arminius. Their own numerical advantage was countered to a large extent by the Romans' armour and curved shields. 'When we're close, we'll give them a volley of spears. Then you three are to go left, and you three move right. Get around to their rear while the rest of us distract them.'

'Aye.' The warrior's grin was feral.

It was a simple plan, thought Arminius, but better than fighting the legionaries on their terms. Even when the Romans were calf-deep in the morass, it was inadvisable to take them on face-to-face.

Arminius had not expected the centurion's next move. A shouted order, and his legionaries launched spears – scavenged frameae – at thirty paces. There was time, just, for his men to raise their shields, but the unexpected volley, and a second one, injured two warriors. They fell back, groaning in pain.

Arminius felt the first traces of doubt, and cursed himself in the same moment. To retreat now would be shameful. He still had two men more than the enemy, and the advantage of speed and mobility. Mud or no, they could run rings around these legionaries. It would be over and done in no time. How the rest of the Romans would quail when first their centurion's helmet landed among them – and then his decapitated head. Arminius continued to advance.

'Throw!' he shouted at twenty paces.

Not all his warriors had enough frameae to loose at the enemy, but half a dozen hurtled up into the leaden sky. Arminius' second shaft followed a heartbeat later. Down they came, like streaks of black lightning, one after another. The first found a home in a shield. Five thumped into the mud, or glanced off helmets and armour. The last, falling short, took a legionary in the foot. He bellowed like a stuck pig, but after a comrade had jerked out the weapon, resumed his position.

'Charge!' roared Arminius, breaking into a run. Move fast enough, and the legionary with a spear-encumbered shield would be defenceless, and the injured man still reeling with pain. 'Go!' Arminius ordered the warriors who were to break away on either side.

'Shields up!' ordered the centurion – a senior centurion by his helmet. 'Steady!'

Again the voice tickled Arminius' memory. He focused on the officer's face, noted the long jaw, the steely eyes. A jolt of recognition struck him. It was Tullus, whom he'd first met close to the Rhenus, during the recapture of a bear destined for the arena. Six years older, his face more lined, but Tullus nonetheless.

Arminius chuckled. It seemed apt – and perhaps predictable – that he should have been one of the few to survive his ambush. Now, though, Tullus' time had come. He would be hard to kill. I'd best do it, thought Arminius, changing the angle of his run to ensure that he came up against Tullus.

Arminius saw Tullus' eyes flicker and register the warriors flanking his men. 'Form rectangle!' Tullus bawled. 'Vitellius, into the middle!'

Just as Arminius and his warriors closed in, the Romans moved, assuming a shape that was two men wide and three deep. Tullus was one of the pair at the front, and the legionary who'd lost his shield stood safe in the middle, a one-man reserve.

Furious, Arminius thrust hard at Tullus' face. The centurion ducked behind his shield and stabbed back without looking. Arminius had to jump away to avoid being spitted. Tullus popped up again, ready for Arminius' next attack. They eyed each other for a moment, and Tullus frowned. 'Arminius?'

'You made it through the forest.'

'No thanks to you!' Tullus lunged with all his might at Arminius' head.

Desperate, Arminius twisted to the side and felt the rush of air as the blade shot past his left ear. He struck back, and hit Tullus' shield.

'I've longed for this moment,' cried Tullus. 'Prepare yourself for Hades.'

'You can't take me, old man.' Arminius lifted his shield so he could aim his spear at Tullus' left foot. Stab! Tullus whipped back his leg just in time. A hammering response, and Tullus' sword hit the top of Arminius' shield, jarring *his* arm.

'Oathbreaker!' Tullus smashed his iron boss into Arminius' shield, and his momentum drove Arminius back.

Wise to the fact that Tullus could not capitalise on his success without leaving the safety of his formation, Arminius steadied himself and followed as Tullus retreated. Thrust! Arminius' spear drove through Tullus' feathered crest, doing no harm. Arminius' next lunge smacked into the brow of Tullus' helmet, blunting the spear tip but eliciting a cry of pain. Many men would have staggered then, and died as Arminius struck again, but from somewhere Tullus found the strength to respond with his own sword. Mouthing curses, Arminius dodged to one side, and Tullus' blade scored a deep line across the face of his shield.

The pair glowered at each other as they recovered their breath. Arminius took stock, and wasn't happy with what he saw. Two of Tullus' legionaries were down, dead or injured, but so were four of *his* warriors. They still outnumbered the Romans seven to five, but attacking their tight formation was laden with risk, as Arminius' casualties proved. They might yet prevail – we *would* prevail, he thought angrily – but more warriors would die. He'd be left with too few men to make any difference to those caught between Tullus' soldiers and the mixture of senior officers and cavalry. I'll return with more warriors, he decided. Finish this once and for all.

'Ready to go again?' taunted Tullus.

'Soon,' Arminius spat, before rounding up his warriors, hale and injured.

'Come back!' Tullus' shouts followed them across the bog. 'Traitor!'

Humiliation burned Arminius like a hot iron. Sensing his rage, his men didn't say a word as they followed him.

That there might not be a 'next time' was apparent by the time he had gathered a strong enough force to lead another attack on Tullus and his soldiers. The situation changed again as, with loud trumpet calls, the legion which had formed Caecina's vanguard came marching back to the aid of their beleaguered comrades. Dismayed, groups of Arminius' warriors broke away in search of easier pickings, and he soon had to acknowledge that they were right. The returning legion seemed to be in good order as it deployed across the road in full battle formation; before long his men's position would be untenable, and heavy casualties would follow. Incandescent at having to

Chapter XXXV

P iso woke groaning. His head throbbed, the pain worse than any hangover he'd ever experienced. There was gritty mud in his mouth, and drops of something – rain? – were hitting his forehead, his cheeks, his neck. He was also bouncing up and down as he was dragged along the ground. The discomfort was such that he couldn't be dead, he reasoned. Rain didn't fall in the underworld either, or so he'd been told. He opened his eyes. Above him, the clouds were still lowering, and the same grim, uniform grey. To either side, gorse and bog cotton plants were moving past at a slow pace. From everywhere came the familiar sounds of marching men: clinking mail, creaking leather and squelching mud.

Piso hawked and spat out the grit. His fingers traced the outline of branches on either side of him, wrapped in blankets. I'm on a homemade stretcher, he thought. At once cold fear roiled in his belly. Had he been taken prisoner? Relief flooded through him as his gaze travelled upward, falling upon two cloaked backs and above them, the characteristic shape of Roman helmets. 'I'm awake,' he rasped.

Vitellius' head turned, and his lips turned up. 'Welcome back.'

Metilius looked around too. 'You've been out for a while.'

Piso couldn't hear the barritus, or fighting, but that meant little. 'The Germans. Are they—?'

'The attacks are over for the day,' said Metilius. 'How are you feeling?'

Piso probed his scalp with care, finding a large, soft and painful swelling on his crown. 'My skull feels as if Tullus has been beating it with his vitis for an hour, but I think I'll live.'

'Your helmet's fucked,' said Vitellius. 'We had a struggle getting it off.'

Piso's memory of how he had fallen – and the last blow he'd struck – returned. 'Tullus?'

'He's all right,' said Metilius.

'Thanks to you,' added Vitellius.

A needle stabbed Piso behind his left orbit, and he moaned. 'I saved him?' he asked.

'So he says. You injured the warrior who was about to spit him. It gave him the chance to kill the bastard.'

Piso digested this news with closed eyes. Tullus owes me his life. A sneaking pride filled him.

'You up to walking yet?' demanded Metilius. 'You're a dead weight to pull.'

'Let him alone,' chided Vitellius, his usual acid tone absent. 'It can't be long until we set up camp.'

Metilius let out a *phhhh* of contempt. 'Camp?'

'You know what I mean,' retorted Vitellius.

'What's wrong?' asked Piso, unsettled.

'Nothing,' replied Vitellius, although his voice suggested otherwise. 'Lie back. Rest. We'll explain later.'

I can't fight, thought Piso, exhaustion and pain blurring his ability to think. I doubt I can even walk. Despite the bumpy, uncomfortable ride, it was easy to let himself sink into the blackness.

When Piso came to for the second time, it was dark. Raindrops continued to patter on his face. A blanket covered his body, but under it he was damp all over. He didn't smell of urine, which meant that someone had changed his undergarment. To his surprise Piso wasn't embarrassed. It was more of a concern that he was lying on the bare ground. Outside. He lifted his head. Vitellius, Metilius and the rest of his tent mates were a few paces away, crouched around a miserable fire. With an effort, Piso leaned up on his elbow. 'Where's our tent?'

Six faces turned to regard him. 'He's awake!' said Vitellius, coming over.

'There you are,' said Metilius, grinning.

Piso gestured at their surroundings, confused. 'We're in the open.'

'Look around,' answered Vitellius.

Piso obeyed. Not a tent was to be seen. On both sides, and opposite, groups of legionaries were sitting around fires, or lying in the mud, as he was. 'Where is the baggage train?' he demanded.

'It's gone,' grated Vitellius.

'Gone,' repeated Piso. 'But that's where Saxa is — with the rest of the injured.'

The gloom couldn't hide the sudden change in his comrades' expressions. Several turned back to the fire. Vitellius cursed. Metilius studied the bitten fingernails on one hand.

Piso's spirits sank as he remembered when this had happened during Arminius' ambush.

After a long moment, Vitellius spoke. 'While we were saving Caecina, the Germans fell on the baggage train in great numbers. When the First Legion returned — that was after you'd been knocked out — the warriors fighting us fled that way too. Tullus led us back to see if we could do anything, but the wagons had already been overrun. Our cohort had withdrawn, suffering heavy losses.'

'Saxa—' Piso began.

'I'm sure he died with a blade in his hand,' said Vitellius with a sigh.

Piso pictured Saxa glugging down the wine he'd brought to him. Had it only been the night before? Angry, grieving, tears pricked his eyes, but he wiped them away. 'Our tents. The artillery?'

'Taken, or destroyed,' Vitellius replied. 'We've got whatever food we were carrying, and that's it.'

'My yoke must be wherever I left it,' said Piso in a wistful voice. He was famished. 'I've got nothing.'

'We picked up our yokes – not yours, mind, but I salvaged your blanket and grain. It hasn't all been eaten – yet.' Metilius snickered.

'You bastards!' cried Piso.

'Don't listen to him,' said Vitellius, winking. 'We're sharing the food. The fire's not hot enough to bake bread of course – it's too fucking wet – but there's a pot of broth. Want some?'

'Aye.' Piso was about to curse Metilius for teasing him, but he couldn't. 'What you did, 'Tellius, Metilius – I mean, making the stretcher, dragging me however many miles—'

'Five at least,' interrupted Metilius. 'But it felt like ten.'

'I'd be dead if it wasn't for you.' Piso's gaze moved from one to the other and back again. 'Gratitude.'

'It wasn't just us,' said Vitellius. 'The others had to carry our yokes so we could pull your lard arse.'

'I'm grateful,' said Piso, his voice husky.

Vitellius gave him a nod; both of them knew its meaning. Piso had saved Vitellius in the forest six years before. Today, he had been repaying the debt.

'You'd do the same for us,' said Metilius.

'Everyone but you, you fat bastard.' Piso grinned as a barrage of insults rained down on Metilius, who liked to moan about his tendency to a paunch.

'Screw you too,' said Metilius, the firelight illuminating his smiling face. 'I was going to carry this over, but you seem to have made a full recovery.' He held up a steaming bowl. 'If you want it, up off your backside!'

'I'm coming, I'm coming,' grumbled Piso, easing up into a sitting position. His head swam, and the pain behind his eyes worsened. He took a deep breath.

'Stay where you are.' Vitellius' gentle hand was on his chest.

'I'm fine,' lied Piso. He set his jaw, willed the pain and dizziness away. After a few deep breaths, he pushed himself first to his knees and then to his feet. Aided by Vitellius, he made his way to the fire with careful steps. His comrades shifted over to give him room. Piso's head spun again as he sat, and he was grateful for the support of Metilius' upraised arm. Everyone was watching him, he realised. Six filthy, blood-spattered faces. Gods, but he loved them, gaunt with exhaustion or no. They were his comrades. His brothers. His family. They meant more to him than anyone in the world, bar Tullus and Fenestela. And they were still here, alive.

'Here.' Aromatic odours rose from the bowl in Metilius' grasp. The handle of a spoon protruded from the depths. 'That's mine, so don't fucking lose it.'

Soup made from half-ground grain, or flour, had never been a favourite of Piso's. It was only eaten in the direst of circumstances, when bread couldn't be baked, and it tasted worse than the poorest of oat porridges. Someone had put garlic in this concoction, though. There was even a hint of oregano.

Piso was reaching for the bowl when a wave of nausea hit him. 'I can't. I'll vomit. One of you others have it.'

'These greedy whoresons would have wolfed it already if I hadn't prevented them,' said Metilius. 'I'll keep it for you. They can pretend they've got some cheese.'

Chuckles rose from around the fire.

'And some olives,' said Vitellius. '*And* wine.'

Piso thought of Saxa again, and his mood soured. 'Where are we?'

'Still on the Long Bridges road,' replied Metilius.

'And the Germans?'

'Most of them stayed at the baggage train, like vultures on carrion. Some of the more disciplined ones tracked us – so the rest could follow on after, no doubt.' Vitellius glanced at Piso. 'The good news is that the fools in the rest of our legion saw sense and rejoined the column. So did the Twenty-First. They're scared, and jumping at every sound, but they're here – in camp.'

'Camp?' Metilius echoed his comment from earlier. 'What a fucking joke. I remember—'

'Don't,' warned Piso, dark memories filling his mind. 'We all remember *that*.'

Chapter XXXVI

◰◰◰

After driving off the Germans, the legions had travelled perhaps ten miles that day before Caecina ordered the construction of a camp. The distance covered was half that of a normal day's march, but in Tullus' mind, that was satisfactory. The army had not been annihilated and, baggage train aside, their losses had been light. It worried him that the ramparts were less high than they should have been, and that the ditch beyond was only calf-deep, but there was nothing to be done about it, because too many tools had been lost with the wagons. At least the entrances were traps in themselves, he told himself. The walls on each side overran one another, forming a narrow corridor through which one had to pass, and they had been blocked with cut branches. As long as the sentries remained alert, the night should pass without incident.

Tullus was tired. Bone-weary, in fact. Tramping, running and fighting through bogland sapped a man's strength much faster than it did in easier terrain. He had managed because he had *had* to. His soldiers depended on him, and Caecina might have died if they hadn't intervened. Gods, thought Tullus, but he was paying for it now. Every part of him ached, stung or throbbed. He reeked of his own sweat, and others' blood.

The only time he could remember being more exhausted was during the terrible fight to survive Arminius' ambush, and the flight to Aliso fort afterwards. Tullus blinked those memories away – dwelling on that nightmare would get him nowhere. Nor would brooding about his legion's eagle, still held somewhere in this godsforsaken land. Better to deal with the tasks at hand, which were to ensure that the injured among his men had been treated, that the rest were in the best possible spirits, and that every soldier had had some food at least.

Tullus had already checked up on half the cohort, and had halted only because his body would have betrayed him otherwise. A short rest would do him no harm, he had decided. So here he was, sitting on a folded blanket, gazing into a hissing fire. Despite the damp, his grumbling belly and the watery, scant heat from his little blaze, he did feel better. Whether he'd be able to get up was another matter. With a heave, he managed it, grimacing as the movement triggered a surge of stabbing pains from new parts of his body.

He rolled his hips one way and then the opposite, trying to loosen them before they locked. His tactic worked in part, but the joints weren't as mobile as they had been even a year before. Not for the first time, Tullus wished that he'd valued his youth more. Physical fitness then had been a given, not a blessing. Recovery from injury just happened – it didn't have to be worked on. At least I have more sense now, he decided. Back then I had none. If that's true, what in Hades are you doing here? his younger self seemed to ask.

Tullus had no answer.

He tried not to be despondent. Casualties that day had been heavy, but not overwhelming. Arminius wasn't dead, but he'd been thwarted in his attempt to kill Caecina. The baggage train had been lost, yet the rest of the army – including the rebellious soldiers – had made it here. Morale throughout the legions was poor, but not at its nadir. Despite his effort to be optimistic, Tullus knew that another day of heavy assaults could break the legionaries.

'Eaten anything yet?' Fenestela followed his voice out of the darkness.

'My food was in the baggage train. Along with old Ambiorix,' said Tullus, hoping that the Gaul had died fast. His nose twitched. 'What are you hiding?'

From behind his back Fenestela produced a chunk of sweaty-looking ham. 'This.'

Saliva filled Tullus' mouth. 'Where'd you find that, you dog?'

'I have my sources.' It was a typical Fenestela remark. He got to work with his dagger, hacking off a slice. 'Here.'

'Jupiter's arse crack, but that's good,' said Tullus, chewing.

'A hungry man isn't the best critic,' replied Fenestela with a chuckle. 'It's seen better days, this meat, but I'd rather have it than nothing.'

They didn't talk further until every scrap was gone.

'How are the men?' asked Tullus. The legionaries of the entire cohort were his responsibility, but between him and Fenestela, the 'men' would always be those in his century.

'Cold, wet and hungry. Apart from that, they're not too bad.' Fenestela's expression grew serious. 'Don't worry. They'll follow you, and they will fight. They'd appreciate seeing your face, though.'

Tullus let out a pleased grunt. 'I'll get to them soon.'

'Want me to come with you?'

'No. Sit by the fire. Get some rest.' Fenestela began to protest, and Tullus growled, 'You're as tired as I am, if not more so. Thieving supplies is tiring work, or so I'm told.'

'Ha! Those are fighting words.'

'We're both too old for that,' said Tullus, pushing Fenestela towards his blanket. 'Sit. Stay. That's an order.'

'Yes, *sir*.' Fenestela's tone was mocking, but the look he gave Tullus was full of feeling. 'I'll save this until you get back.' Out of nowhere, it seemed, he had a small leather bag in one hand. It made a welcome, slopping sound. 'Tastes like vinegar, this stuff, but it leaves a warm glow inside.'

'I knew there was a reason I promoted you to optio,' said Tullus, grinning.

Perhaps he would get some sleep after all.

Leaving Fenestela by his fire, Tullus wandered the muddy avenues, using the light cast by the soldiers' fires to find his way. As before, he held brief conversations with the centurions of each century. He also kept talking to the men, making sure that their morale remained as high as possible. Whether the officers in the other cohorts were doing the same, he had no way of knowing, but Tullus hoped so. Chance alone, or perhaps Fortuna's goodwill, had been all that had prevented the earlier foolishness of the Twenty-First and Fifth resulting in complete catastrophe.

Having spent time with all but one of the remaining centuries, and conferred with their centurions, he at last approached the lines where his own unit was camping out. His bone-shattering weariness eased by the warmth of his reception, Tullus moved between the contubernia, sharing a joke here, praising soldiers whose actions had stood out there. It touched him how many men offered him food and drink, although they themselves had so little. 'I've sunk low before, but stealing from the mouths of you scoundrels would be a step too far,' he demurred as they chuckled.

'Today was hard, brothers, but tomorrow will be worse. Our losses will have given the savages a real appetite,' Tullus told each group. 'More of us will get hurt. Some will join our comrades in the underworld. Stick together, though, and we *will* get out of this fucking bog. I'll be with you, every cursed, muddy step of the way, worse luck. My vitis will be with me too, so best watch out!'

It was usual for soldiers to wince, scowl or even look away when Tullus mentioned his vine stick, but tonight they let out full-throated roars of approval. Satisfied, he worked his way down the century, coming last to the contubernium in which Piso and Vitellius served. Before he approached, Tullus hung back in the darkness, watching the seven men as they sat talking by their fire.

Tullus would never admit to having favourites among his soldiers, but those who'd been with him in the Eighteenth did hold a special place in his heart. The still-gangling Piso and his acerbic comrade Vitellius ranked highest in his opinion – Piso's actions earlier that day had cemented this feeling. Since they had helped to rescue Degmar's family, Tullus also held Saxa and Metilius in particular regard.

Poor Saxa, thought Tullus. Like Ambiorix and White Hair the wagon driver, he was dead. Everyone unfortunate enough to have been with the baggage train would have met the same grisly fate. If Saxa and Ambiorix weren't worm food, they were being tortured this very moment by German warriors. Tullus hoped it was the former.

'Greetings, brothers,' he said, stepping into the light. They made to jump up, but he waved a hand. 'Rest easy.'

They grinned at him, eager as puppies, and Tullus' heart warmed. 'How are things?' he asked, moving to stand near the crackling blaze.

'All right, sir.' 'Not too bad, sir.' 'Things have been worse, sir.'

Tullus glanced at Vitellius, who hadn't yet spoken. 'And you?'

'I'm wet through, sir. Half-starved too. My nose hurts like a bastard,' replied Vitellius, giving him a sour look. 'The front of me is toasty, thanks to the fire, but my back is fucking freezing. Oh yes – Saxa's dead. Apart from that, I'm fine, sir. Thanks for asking.'

Surprised, Tullus roared with laughter. 'Honest as always, Vitellius. I can't offer you much succour.'

'Didn't think you could, sir.' Vitellius' shrug was resigned.

'Are you ready for tomorrow?' asked Tullus.

'I'll be there, sir, you know that.'

Tullus threw him a pleased look and turned to Piso. 'How's the head?'

'Sore, sir.' Piso's smile was lopsided.

'You able to march?'

'Aye, sir, and to fight.'

'You're a good man. If it wasn't for you, well . . .' Tullus found himself at an unusual loss for words. '. . . I wouldn't be here. Thank you.'

'Any one of us would have done the same, sir,' protested Piso.

'Maybe so, but it was you who did it today. You who saved my life.' Tullus held Piso's gaze for a moment. 'I won't forget that.'

Piso gave him a solemn nod. 'Sir.'

'I'll leave you lot to it,' said Tullus. 'Get some rest – tomorrow will be no joke. Sleep in your armour, just in case. Arminius is craftier than a fox.'

Thoughts of the Cherusci leader filled Tullus' mind as he paced back to

Fenestela. After so long, it had been startling to see Arminius again – and galling beyond belief to have crossed blades with him, lost men to him, but not to have slain the whoreson. The Fates must be sitting up there, watching me and still cackling, thought Tullus with a dour glance at the sky. Miserable Greek bitches. You separate our threads for six years, then bring them close enough to touch, but whip them away again before I had a decent chance to put the treacherous rat in the mud.

Give me another opportunity, he swore now, and I won't waste it.

Tullus was deep in a most pleasant dream involving Sirona – he had managed to persuade her to lie with him at last – when a loud cry interrupted it. In the dream, it sounded as if someone was shouting outside Sirona's room, or downstairs in the inn. Tullus did his best to ignore it, and kissed Sirona again. 'Gods, but I've waited a long time for this,' he murmured.

She smiled. 'So have I.'

A hand shook Tullus' shoulder, hard. 'Wake up!' demanded a voice.

Sirona vanished. Instead of her warm bed, Tullus found himself lying face down in the muck under a damp blanket. He was in his armour, cold and uncomfortable, and whoever was responsible for his rude awakening had not given up. 'Curse it all, wake up!' said the voice.

Still exhausted, Tullus realised that the culprit responsible for the rude ending to his dream was Fenestela. Opening his eyes, he found his optio kneeling alongside. 'What is it?' His breath clouded in the chilly air.

'I'm not sure.'

Tullus bit back an acid response. It was pitch black – the middle of the night – but Fenestela wouldn't rouse him for no reason. He sat up, wincing as his back protested. 'Tell me.'

'Listen.'

Tullus obeyed. At this godsforsaken hour, he'd have expected to hear little. The occasional call of an owl. Perhaps a sound or two from the cavalry lines, or the mule pens. Maybe the tramp of a sentry along the nearest walkway, but nothing else. A whinnying horse and the sound of galloping hooves, therefore, was of note. So too were the dim cries of alarm. The last tendrils of fog vanished from Tullus' mind, and he was on his feet. 'Where's it coming from?'

Fenestela gestured towards the area occupied by the cavalry, off to their right.

'Have you taken a look?'

'I came to find you first.'

It was usual to wait for orders, to wait for the trumpets' call. Acting on initiative was not the army's way. This was different, Tullus decided. The man who hesitated around an enemy like Arminius wound up dead. 'I'll get the men up. You wake every centurion in the cohort. Tell them to ready their legionaries for battle, and to wait for my summons – the advance, sounded twice, a delay, and once more. If they don't hear it, they're to stay put until further orders come in.'

'And the other cohorts?'

Alerting the rest of the legion would waste time, thought Tullus. A rapid response would have the best chance of containing an attack. 'Don't worry about them yet. Go.'

Fenestela vanished into the gloom. Tullus adjusted his mail, pulling it down where it had rucked up above his belt. He straightened his scabbard, which tended to move a little too far towards his back. A scrabble around where he'd been lying produced his arming cap and helmet. These donned, and a battered shield in his fist, he was ready. Tullus stalked to the first contubernium, a mass of sprawled shapes lying close to each other. He poked the nearest one with the toe of his boot. 'Up, you maggot!'

His first demand was met by a groan. Tullus drew back and kicked the man. Leaning over, he stamped on his closest companion. They both woke up, cursing. 'UP!' roared Tullus. 'NOW!'

Apologies and yes sirs filled the air. Tullus watched the soldiers until he was sure they were all stirring, and then he moved on to the next contubernium. The men there had been woken by the noise and were getting up. By the time he'd reached the last few tent groups, the soldiers were waiting for him in combat order. Tullus gave them a nod of approval, and ordered the century to form a column. Fenestela returned, his task completed, and took his position at the back.

Tullus addressed his men. 'It's not clear what's going on, but you can hear the racket.' He waited, letting the cries of alarm speak for themselves. 'That's where we're heading – to see if the cursed Germans are within the camp.'

His soldiers stamped from foot to foot. Some looked scared. Most seemed nervous, which Tullus also expected. Yet they were resolute enough, in particular Vitellius and Metilius. Even Piso, still glaze-eyed, stood ready. Tullus felt a stirring pride.

As they tramped after him into the blackness, the clamour from the cavalry lines intensified. It also seemed to be spreading. Fresh sweat beaded on Tullus' brow.

What devilry was Arminius up to?

Chapter XXXVII

'The savages have attacked!' 'Arminius is here!' 'Run!'

The cold night air rang with shouts and cries. Legionaries milled about, weapons at the ready, and demanding of their comrades in nearby units if *they* knew what was going on. Some men slumbered on regardless, either from exhaustion, quantities of wine consumed, or both. Centurions and junior officers paced up and down, telling everyone to stay calm, and to prepare themselves for battle.

As far as Tullus could see, marching past with his century, few of the troops were paying heed to their superiors' commands. Panicked wasn't the word he'd use to describe the mood, but it wasn't far off. Frustration gnawed at him, yet he didn't pause. Any intervention to calm things down would take time – and mightn't succeed. The Fifth's soldiers had shown how yellow-livered they were only hours before. Snuffing out the attack early on seemed a better gamble than trying to restore order, but if the situation deteriorated even a little further . . .

Stop it, Tullus told himself. Focus. Find out what's going on. If the enemy *were* in the camp, he would summon the rest of his cohort and then contain the bastards until Caecina could respond. They had cleared the Fifth's lines now, and were pushing through a mob of fearful Gaulish auxiliaries. Few seemed ready to fight, and scores were streaming towards the camp's furthest entrances. Angered by their cowardice, Tullus ordered the formation of a wedge. No one liked a clatter from a shield boss, still less a whack with the flat of a sword blade.

The section occupied by the cavalry – also auxiliaries – came next. Beyond it lay the camp's side wall. On edge now, Tullus slowed his pace to a walk. His eyes were accustomed to the dark, yet it was difficult to see more than the shape of the poor earthen rampart that had been dug out the previous evening. This weakness would have been noticed by the keen-eyed German scouts, Tullus suspected, and might have been why Arminius had ordered an assault. Try as he might, however, he could not see hordes of warriors climbing over the wall, nor groups of them charging across the intervallum.

The cavalrymen in sight seemed calm enough, which was also odd. Tullus approached the nearest figures, a group of five men settling their horses. One look at his crested helmet had them saluting and straightening their backs. 'Any sign of the enemy?' demanded Tullus. The cavalrymen exchanged baffled looks and, frustrated, he added, 'Within the camp?'

'Not as far as I know, sir,' said one.

'What the fuck is going on?' demanded Tullus. 'My optio and I were woken by the din over here. Horses were making noise. Men were shouting. It sounded like an attack.' The cavalrymen's expressions turned sheepish, and Tullus roared, 'Tell me, before I ram this vitis somewhere the sun doesn't shine!'

'One of the lads in another turma has a nervous horse, sir,' said the cavalryman who'd first spoken. 'It was frightened by the thunder, or so we've heard. He was trying to calm it, but the stupid creature snapped its lead rope and took off down the avenue, towards the centre of the camp.' He pointed in the direction that Tullus had come.

The explanation was so obvious that Tullus' instinct told him that this *was* what had happened: that there were no warriors inside the walls, and the whole sorry affair had been started by a jittery horse. But for the gravity of the situation – gods only knew how the panic was spreading – he would have laughed. Warning the cavalrymen that if they valued their hides, they and their fellows were to keep their mounts under control, Tullus led his century towards the ramparts. There the sentries for two hundred paces in each direction, all present and correct, reported no sign of the enemy.

His search concluded, Tullus cocked an ear. Unhappy sounds were rising from throughout the camp, and he cursed. Arminius' warriors might have attacked another section of the defences, but given what Tullus now knew, it was far more probable that the terrified horse had sown panic everywhere instead. After the previous day's debacle, it was easy to imagine how frightened the sleep-deprived legionaries of the four legions might become. The level of noise proved that some were on the verge of panic.

Their fate rested on a knife edge, Tullus concluded. If the soldiers headed into the bog, they would drown in the morass, or be killed by the opportunistic Germans. Even if Arminius' forces weren't prepared for this unexpected, almost gods-given development, they would soon realise what was going on. When dawn came, the disorganised, demoralised legionaries would be easy prey. The gates, thought Tullus. Every gate had to be secured.

He stripped one entrance – the one behind him – from his list. The purported attack was coming from that direction, so even the dimmest soldier wouldn't try to escape that way. Three gates remained then – one at either end of the camp's shorter sides, and the one at the far end of the avenue Tullus was standing on. As he tried to decide what to do, the uproar in the darkness beyond worsened. Two centuries could hold a gate, he decided.

He would march back to his cohort's position and there split the unit into three, each two centuries strong. One would go north with him to the entrance that lay behind the headquarters. Caecina could be made aware of the situation at the same time. The two other groups would head for the east and south gates. Tullus barked the order to advance, but a growing, unhappy certainty filled his mind as they marched.

If they didn't move fast, it would be too late.

Their journey proved tricky. The main avenues were clogged with scared, aggressive legionaries, arguing and fighting among themselves as they meandered along. Swearing, Tullus led his men into the smaller lanes that separated unit from unit. Crowds of nervous soldiers had also gathered there, but it was easier to find the gaps. Tullus and his party reached the cohort's tent lines without incident. Augmenting his force with the Second Century, he sent the remaining four units off under the command of his two most senior centurions. That done, he made for the headquarters.

It seemed to take an age to reach the camp's centre. The usual, large command tent was missing, lost with the baggage train, Tullus presumed. A rectangle of six ordinary legionary tents stood in its place, and there scores of officers and guards were milling. Hundreds of soldiers were streaming past, towards the gate, and no one was trying to stop them.

With his century in close formation, Tullus drove straight through the panicked mob to the headquarters. He found Caecina in the midst of a dozen or more legates and tribunes. Their raised voices and worried faces told their own story. Tullus paused at the edge of the gathering to listen.

Caecina's expression changed from moment to moment as he listened to the conflicting advice being given him. One legate wanted to lead the nearest cohorts towards the attackers. A second thought a defensive cordon should be set up along the camp's north–south axis. A senior tribune – Tubero, no less – declared that the legions needed to be assembled in marching order on the intervallum and from there be dispersed to take on the enemy. Another tribune was even advocating retreat back to solid ground.

Tullus' frustration boiled over. 'I must speak with General Caecina!' he cried, pushing his way forward. Faces turned, registering shock, anger and disbelief. In Tubero's eyes, Tullus saw real hate. It was too late to consider what punishments this transgression might earn him. He came to a halt in front of Caecina and saluted.

Caecina, tired-looking but already in his armour, seemed unimpressed. 'What is the meaning of this?'

'I know what's going on, sir,' said Tullus.

'Ha!' cried Tubero. 'D'you hear this? *Tullus* knows what's going on – even though it's as clear to us as the noses on the end of our faces.'

Caecina twisted his head. 'Guards!'

'A wise decision, sir,' said Tubero in a snide tone.

Tubero's comment sent rage pulsing through Tullus' veins, but the danger they faced was too great to risk a confrontation. 'My news is urgent, sir,' he said to Caecina. 'Let me explain.'

Caecina's nostrils flared, but he waved back the quartet of guards who'd appeared. 'Be quick.'

'There *is* no attack, sir.' Ignoring the senior officers' disbelieving reactions – Tubero even said, 'Liar!' – Tullus ploughed on. 'The whole thing began with a horse that was startled by the thunder. The beast broke free and galloped off, among the sleeping soldiers. Complete panic ensued as they awoke and imagined Arminius' warriors were in their midst. Men are beginning to retreat from the cavalry lines near the west gate. Those further away, unable to decide what's going on, are also affected by the fear sweeping through the camp. The troops are trying to get out by the most distant gates, sir. That's it.'

'These are the ravings of a madman, sir,' declared Tubero. 'Every soldier in sight is talking about the enemy attack!'

A good number of officers nodded, dismaying Tullus. He glanced at Caecina. He didn't care about himself, but the army's destiny hung in the balance.

'How do you know this?' demanded Caecina.

As fast as he could, Tullus laid out what had happened since he'd been woken by Fenestela. Caecina listened in silence. To Tullus' surprise, so did the senior officers. No one spoke when he was done, allowing the sound of panicked cries and running feet to fill the air.

'Has anyone here seen the enemy inside the defences?' asked Caecina.

There was no answer.

'Not a single one of you?' Caecina's gaze raked the gathering. 'Has anyone spoken with a soldier who has set eyes on the attackers?'

Some officers began to seem embarrassed now. Even Tubero looked uncomfortable.

Caecina scowled. 'It appears you may be right,' he said, relieving Tullus beyond measure. 'Take me to the north gate.'

'Yes, sir. Might I make a suggestion?'

'Anything.'

'Send an eagle to each of the gates, sir. They will help to steady the men.'

'A fine idea.' Caecina rattled off orders, commanding a legate, an eagle and an escort to both the east and south entrances. The Fifth's own eagle was brought forth from the command tent to accompany their party. With the aquilifer nowhere to be found, Vitellius was deputised to carry it. He bore the gold bird aloft behind Tullus, his usual sour expression replaced by a wide, satisfied grin. Four soldiers, Piso among them, walked to either side, carrying flaming torches that allowed the eagle to be seen. Pride filled Tullus to have the legion's standard at his back, although it wasn't the same as if the Eighteenth's lost eagle had been there.

The throngs of soldiers heading towards the north gate had grown denser, yet the sight of the eagle made them give way. Again using the wedge, with Caecina close behind, Tullus forged a path into the area occupied by the Fifth Legion. From there, he guided them through the tent lines and approached the north gate from the side. A hundred and fifty paces out, he stopped.

The entrance was obscured by a large crowd of legionaries which filled the intervallum and the spaces where tents should have been. Despite the fearful cries rising into the night, the soldiers didn't appear to be moving outside the camp. 'Maybe there's still time, sir,' Tullus said to Caecina. 'They can't make up their minds what to do.'

'It's one thing to run amok through the camp, but quite another to charge into the darkness beyond the walls,' said Caecina. 'We'd best get over there fast, though, before they change their minds.'

Even in the poor light, the press seemed far thicker than it had been elsewhere. There was a chance that the panicked legionaries might fight back, Tullus decided, which meant his hope of positioning his two centuries between the mob and the gate was no longer feasible, at least without blood being shed. He wasn't averse to that per se, but if it happened, the situation *would* descend into complete chaos. 'Let's walk along the rampart, sir. That'll take us right up to the entrance.'

Caecina stared at him. The earthen walkway along the top of the

327

defences was wide enough for two men to stand abreast, but no more. 'Just a few of us?'

'Aye, sir. You, me, the soldier with the eagle and maybe a dozen more. It's you they need to see, and the standard, not my troops.'

'If the mob turns, we will die.'

'That's right, sir. But if we try to push our way among them, they will panic, and many more will be slain, including us perhaps.' Tullus held Caecina's gaze with a stolid one of his own.

After a moment, Caecina nodded. 'Lead on.'

Fenestela was most unhappy at Tullus' plan. 'They'll cut you to pieces.'

'They might not,' said Tullus.

'Or they might,' retorted Fenestela with a ferocious scowl. 'You're going to do it anyway.'

'Aye,' replied Tullus.

'I'll come with you.'

'You have to stay with the men. If things go wrong, they'll need someone to lead them out of this shithole.'

'You're the one for that, not me.' Fenestela glowered at Tullus, who returned the look. Several heartbeats fluttered by. 'I'll stay,' muttered Fenestela. 'You'd best fucking come back, though, d'you hear?'

Tullus gripped his shoulder, and went to talk to the centurion in charge of the second century. If Tullus blew his whistle, both centuries were to drive forwards to the gate, and try to save Caecina and the eagle. The centurion seemed of a mind with Fenestela about the plan's riskiness, but he nodded reluctant acceptance.

Piso, Vitellius and the ten others picked by Tullus formed up behind him and Caecina without protest. 'Keep those lights high,' barked Tullus. 'I want the eagle to be the first thing they see.'

Heads began to turn from the moment they ascended to the walkway. Raised more than a man's height from the ground, and illuminated by the flaming torches, the party stood out from the blackness. At Tullus' suggestion, Caecina had shed his red cloak, allowing his armour to wink and flash in the flickering light.

'Your general is here!' roared Tullus. 'Caecina is here!'

A loud *Ahhhhh* went up. Some men cheered, but more threw insults.

Tullus reached the end of the walkway. A final ladder at his feet led down to the ground by the gate. There was no sign of the sentries, and the cut branches which had blocked the entrance had been hauled to one side. A number of soldiers had left the camp, Tullus decided, but the ones he could see didn't appear to be in a hurry to join them. In the end, though, the weight of numbers pressing towards the gate *would* force them outside.

There was no room to get down from the wall, even if they had wanted to. Hundreds of legionaries packed the space underneath, their pale faces looking up at Tullus, Caecina and their companions with a mixture of fear and disbelief.

'Piss off back where you came from,' yelled a voice.

'Fucking officers,' shouted another. 'Good for nothing whoresons!'

A fist was waved, and another. Then it was five, ten, a score. Someone lifted a sword, and the mood, which had been wavering between rebellious and fearful, grew ugly.

It was act now or die, thought Tullus. He drew his blade and clattered it off his greave, *bash, bash, bash*. The sound wasn't that loud, but everyone was watching. The shouting died down a little. 'Sir,' muttered Tullus to Caecina and, sheathing his weapon, stood aside.

Caecina stepped forward. 'Brave soldiers of Rome,' he shouted.

'To Hades with you, Caecina,' cried a voice.

'Brave soldiers of Rome,' repeated Caecina, louder this time. 'The enemy has not stormed the camp.'

'So you say!' 'We heard him with our own ears!'

'It was a horse, I tell you. A horse that had been scared by the thunder,' yelled Caecina. 'Centurion Tullus has been to the spot where the enemy is supposed to be attacking. He found nothing out of the ordinary. The savages are not in here with us, but out there!' he roared with a dramatic gesture at the world beyond the walls. 'Step outside at your peril, brothers!'

'I know where I'd rather take my chances, and it ain't here,' declared a sour-faced legionary among those closest to the entrance.

'Will I have to lie in your path to stop you?' asked Caecina, his frustration evident.

'I wouldn't do that,' warned Sour Face, as an animal sound left the soldiers' throats.

Sour Face was the first rock in a landslide, Tullus decided. If he left the camp, the rest would follow, and if Caecina got in their way, they'd kill him without thinking, just as they had other senior officers during the previous year's rebellion.

'Give me that,' Tullus hissed, snatching the eagle from a startled Vitellius. Bellowing 'ROMA!' Tullus took the steps down two at a time. Shocked, the nearest legionaries gave way a little. Tullus sensed someone follow him – looking back, he was startled to recognise Caecina.

Brandishing the eagle as if it were a weapon, Tullus pushed towards the gate. 'Make way! MAKE WAY!' he ordered.

No matter how rebellious the soldier, it was impossible to obliterate the reverence felt towards a legion's eagle. The embodiment of pride, courage and glory, it demanded respect. The crowd fell back, gazing with awe at the golden bird. Tullus shoved on until he stood in the middle of the entrance. Caecina reached his side an instant later, and Tullus stabbed the standard's spiked butt into the muddy ground, facing the eagle towards the mob. Sensing what he needed, Piso and the other torch-bearers climbed atop the edge of the rampart to light up the scene.

'See this magnificent bird?' shouted Tullus. 'It belongs to the glorious Fifth!'

As he'd expected, a chorus of voices roared back, 'The Fifth! The Fifth!'

'You don't want to see this fall into enemy hands, do you?' Tullus shouted, the hairs on his own neck prickling at the idea.

'NEVER!' the legionaries roared.

'Listen to me! I served in the Eighteenth for many years. I see you nod your heads – you knew men in it.' Tullus acknowledged several of the nearest soldiers. 'As you know, the Eighteenth was one of the legions destroyed by that sewer rat Arminius. Lucky for me, I got away from the ambush, me and about fifteen of my boys.' The old guilt stung Tullus: that he should have saved more; that he should somehow have prevented the eagle being taken.

'You're *the* Centurion Tullus?' It was Sour Face who spoke.

'Aye.'

Another *Ahhhhh* went up, surprising Tullus. They know of me, he thought.

'Men say you rescued more soldiers than anyone else,' said Sour Face. His angry tone had become respectful.

'That's right,' roared Piso suddenly. 'Centurion Tullus saved us, when no one else could have.'

Sour Face had glanced up when Piso spoke. Now he regarded Tullus once more. 'This officer should say his piece,' he declared. 'What say you, brothers?'

'Aye!' shouted a hundred voices.

Tullus shot a look at Caecina, a little concerned that he was centre-stage rather than the general, but Caecina indicated he should speak. Tullus rolled his tongue around a parched mouth. His next words were of vital importance. Say the right ones, and the unhappy legionaries would go back into the camp. The wrong ones would see him and Caecina murdered, trampled underfoot as a sea of soldiers fled into the darkness, and the next morning, all four legions would be massacred.

Tell them the truth, he thought. Say it like it is.

'The shame of losing the Eighteenth's eagle haunts me every day. I dream of it at night. I see it each and every time I look upon this majestic bird, and the ones belonging to the other legions in this camp.'

'Where's our eagle?' demanded a voice. 'The one belonging to the Twentieth?'

A barrage of cries followed. 'And the Twenty-First?' 'Where's the First's eagle?'

Tullus pointed. 'One is at the east gate, and another at the south. They've been sent to do the same as this bird here – to stir the men's pride. The other remains at the headquarters.'

Sour Face seemed pleased. Heads nodded. Men even started smiling.

Tullus took heart. 'Leave this camp, brothers, and I promise it will be the end of you. Arminius is out there with thousands of his warriors, waiting for you to wander around in the dark, up to your knees in mud. Leave this camp and your lives will be forfeit. Your eagles *will* be lost – taken by the enemy, disgracing each and every one of you for eternity. Is that what you would have?'

'NO!'

'Do you want your bones to moulder in the bog? To have your heads nailed to trees?'

'NOOOO!' they screamed back at him.

'Return to your positions then. Get what rest you can. In the morning, Caecina will lead us out, to victory.'

'What about the enemy in the camp?' demanded Sour Face.

'Listen,' ordered Tullus. 'Tell me if you can hear any fighting.' Gods, let the situation have calmed, he prayed as the mob fell quiet. A dozen heart-beats skipped past; in the distance, men were shouting, but the frightened edge that had been present before was gone. There was no sound of combat, no clash of sword on shield. No screams as men died on the sharp end of a blade.

Sour Face stared at Tullus, long and hard, and then he shook his head. 'It must have been a horse after all. Curse it, brothers, we were fooled by a fucking horse!'

Embarrassed laughter broke out and, just like that, the tension began to dissipate. Sour Face turned on his heel and shoved his way into the crowd. 'Back to our places, brothers!' he cried. 'Tomorrow will be a long day.' His shouts continued as he pressed on into the throng. Nothing else happened for a few moments. Tullus' heart was thudding in his chest – there was no way of knowing if enough of the legionaries had been convinced.

He twisted the standard's staff a little, so that the torchlight bounced off the majestic gold bird. Similar in appearance to the Eighteenth's lost eagle, it was depicted lying forward on its breast, a golden wreath encircling its wings, which were upraised behind its body. Its part-open beak and penetrating stare gave off an overpowering sense of arrogance and power. The embodiment of a legion's pride and honour, the eagle demanded – expected – respect.

Another reverent sigh escaped a hundred throats, and in dribs and drabs the legionaries began edging away. All were careful to avoid Tullus' and Caecina's gaze.

It took time, but at last he and Caecina were left standing in the gateway, with Piso and the rest watching from above. Only the muddied ground – tramped flat by hobnailed sandals – bore witness to the large crowd that had been present.

'Well done,' said Caecina, his face paling with delayed shock.

'Thank you, sir.' Tullus studied Caecina sidelong. One disaster had been averted, but another – in the form of Arminius' waiting hordes – beckoned. They needed Caecina's leadership now more than ever. 'Have you given any thought to our next move, sir?'

His composure regained, Caecina let out an evil chuckle. 'The enemy must have heard the commotion. Let him think we are too scared to leave the camp. Let him think the legionaries are bunched together like frightened sheep. Let him attack us here, at dawn.' He gestured at the ramparts and the intervallum. 'When he scales the defences, and enters the gate, he'll find us waiting.'

The chaos at the gate had curdled neither Caecina's resolve nor his courage, thought Tullus with delight.

It was an ingenious plan.

Chapter XXXVIII

◫◫◫

Using a spear as a staff, Arminius was picking his way through the bog towards his camp. Maelo and a group of his best warriors were with him; they had spent the previous few hours in the darkness close to the Roman fortifications. Drawn at first by the uproar — shouts, cries of fear, and a horse of all things — Arminius had lingered because of the degree of panic among the enemy troops. The cause of the widespread alarm was unclear, but by the time small groups of dishevelled, fearful legionaries began wandering out of the northern gate, it seemed that the chaos was very real.

Wary still of the possibility of a trap, Arminius had held his eager warriors back. With Maelo by his side, he had crept closer to the enemy camp's north gate. The staggered construction of the entrance had prevented him from seeing events unfold inside, but he'd been able to glean much of the goings on from the shouted conversations wafting over the defences.

What a pity he had not slain Tullus six years before, brooded Arminius. The man was indefatigable. First he had thwarted Arminius on the battlefield, and then he had won over the terrified mob of legionaries by the gate with talk of his legion's eagle, and how their own must not be lost to the enemy. It was infuriating — yet it was also hard not to feel a certain admiration for the man. Realising that Caecina had been there too, Arminius had determined to storm the gate and try to kill both Tullus and general in one fell swoop, but Maelo had stood in his way. Arminius had cursed him for it, but as the first fingers of light stole up the sky from the horizon, he had to admit that his second-in-command had been right. They might have succeeded, but some of the legionaries at least would have fought back. Maelo or he might have been slain.

Dying didn't scare Arminius – since Thusnelda's abduction there had been many occasions when he would have welcomed the oblivion it granted. He had allowed Maelo to step in because without him, the charismatic leader, it would be too easy for the tribes' assault on the battered legions to fragment and fail. With him, it *would* succeed. The legionaries were terrified – the evidence of that had filled Arminius' ears. When they emerged from the camp at last and his warriors fell on them in their thousands, what remained of their resolve would vanish, as it had for Varus and the unfortunates who'd followed him.

It was bittersweet that despite the magnitude of Arminius' impending victory, Thusnelda and their baby would never return home. His suspicion had been borne out some time before by news that had reached him from the west bank of the Rhenus. No matter how many Romans he slaughtered, she was gone forever – sent to Rome as a prestigious captive. Arminius ground his teeth until his jaws ached. You bastard, Germanicus, he thought. You cold-hearted, motherless get. I'll capture you one day, and by the gods, you'll live to regret the day you were born.

'We're almost there.' Maelo's voice pulled Arminius back to the moment. He dampened his rage. Now was a time for calm, for control.

'D'you want me to wake the others?' asked Maelo.

'Aye. Every chieftain needs to be here – we haven't got long. Caecina will want to march soon, before his men's new-found resolve deserts them.'

'Today's the day – I can feel it,' said Maelo, slapping Arminius' back before he slipped off into the lightening gloom.

An hour later, neither man's outlook was so rosy. Encouraged by Arminius' reports of the panic among the enemy ranks, Inguiomerus had proposed an all-out attack on the Roman camp. To Arminius' dismay, the other chieftains had loved the idea, roaring their approval at the leaden skies.

Again and again, he repeated the risks of fighting the legionaries face-to-face. 'Why not let them march out, into the wet and broken country? They're easy prey there.'

His protests and suggestions fell on deaf ears. Even Big Chin, who had listened to Arminius before, wanted to strike at the Romans. 'They're soiling their undergarments like newborn babes – you said so yourself,' he declared to loud acclaim. 'Their defences are poor. Better still, the legions are in one place.'

'It will be easy to take the eagles,' said Inguiomerus. 'Imagine that.'

The chieftains cheered. 'I'll have one.' 'Not if my warriors get there first.' 'I want two!'

Arminius' foul temper worsened as he watched the grinning chieftains shoving at each other like youths squabbling over a barrel of stolen beer. 'There's no need to attack the camp,' he repeated. 'Let the filth march out into the bog. We can pick them off there at our leisure.'

'It's unlike you to be the faint-heart, nephew,' Inguiomerus mocked. 'It will be a slaughter – can you not see that?'

The insult stung Arminius to the quick. He stared at his uncle and then at Big Chin, who was enthusing about spearing fish in a pool. Stick Thin and the others were nodding or miming how they'd stab the legionaries. The attack was going to go ahead with or without his participation, Arminius decided. Frustrated and for the moment impotent, he considered his options.

If he gave the order, most of his warriors would refrain from taking part in the assault. The men who held back – five and a half thousand spears, perhaps – were a sizeable and important part of the entire host. Trained, better-armed than most, and veterans, their absence would affect the battle to come, and could even hand victory to the Romans. If that happened, a widespread rout was likely, bringing with it heavy casualties. Apart from the human price of such a disaster, there were other considerations. Brave-hearted though they were, the defeated tribesmen would lose all interest in pursuing the enemy. They would return to their settlements, and any chance of wiping out Caecina's army would be lost. Arminius' entire campaign would have come to nothing.

He locked eyes with Big Chin, and wondered if the Angrivarii chieftain was thinking the same thing. 'Fall on them in the open, in the bog, and we'll fare better,' Arminius said, trying one more time. 'Yesterday was just the start.'

'Hit them right now, when they're groggy with lack of sleep, and still terrified from the panicked horse, and victory will be ours,' Big Chin responded.

'He's right,' declared Inguiomerus in a confident tone. 'Are you with us?'

Everyone's attention turned towards Arminius. He glanced at Maelo, who gave a minute, frustrated shrug. Curse it, thought Arminius. 'My warriors will also fight. I don't want to hear for evermore about the glory being yours, or how you won the day,' he snapped at Big Chin. 'The same applies to you, uncle.'

'We can share the glory,' declared Big Chin, grinning.

'Indeed,' agreed Inguiomerus, but he wasn't smiling. He stared at Arminius, his eyes sparking with anger.

Arminius returned the look with cold intensity. I know what you're doing, he thought. You're trying to assume the mantle. Had the situation been different, he would have spoken up, even challenged Inguiomerus to a fight. Today, though, it would be better to wait until the day's end, when the battle was over and the casualties counted. If his uncle's plan succeeded, Arminius would face a real challenge to his authority. If the assault failed, as he thought it would, Inguiomerus would have to be put back in his place with an iron fist.

Cross that bridge when you come to it, thought Arminius. Crush the Romans first.

Dawn had broken not long before, and Arminius' warriors had gathered around him. Many bore bundles of branches or sections of heather bushes. Others carried rough-hewn ladders, the result of their labours since he'd given the orders to prepare for an attack. The vegetation would be used to fill the Roman defensive ditch, giving the warriors a chance of gaining a rapid foothold on the ramparts.

Arminius studied the enemy camp again. The rain had stopped at last, making it easier to see the sentries still pacing the walkways. Fine lines of smoke trickled up into the sky from within the walls, marking the location of the soldiers' fires. An occasional voice carried through the air, but there seemed to be little activity. Perhaps Inguiomerus was right, thought Arminius. He would have expected the legions to be exiting the north gate by now, and setting out on the wooden road.

There was no sign of them. It wasn't as if he could even hear the legionaries preparing to march. Upwards of four and a half thousand men made plenty of noise, and there was no chance that quadruple that number could assemble in silence. 'They *are* scared,' said Arminius to Maelo, by his side. 'They must be huddled together like frightened pups, hoping we'll go away.'

'I'm not sure,' said Maelo, frowning. 'What if it's a trap?'

The same unhappy thought had been niggling at Arminius since Inguiomerus' plan had been carried, but he'd managed to ignore it. Until now. 'There's not much we can do,' he said in a bullish tone. 'The attack is about to begin.'

'You could hold the men back.'

'Half the warriors wouldn't listen. Look at them – their blood's up. The rest would call me a coward. If the assault succeeds and I've stood by, every last man will want to see me replaced as leader.' Arminius had convinced himself – almost. 'We have to go ahead with the plan.'

'I don't like it,' said Maelo. 'It's too fucking quiet.'

Arminius knew what Maelo meant, but to either side he could see warriors leaving the cover of the trees: Inguiomerus' and the other chieftains' followers were on the move. His own men were shifting from foot to foot and looking to him for the order to advance. Each passing moment increased the chance of some taking matters into their own hands, which would also undermine his authority. 'I hope you're wrong. It's too late anyway.'

Maelo's scowl deepened, but he strode out with the rest. A more loyal follower I could not have, thought Arminius with pride. If every man were cut from the same cloth as him, I would have crushed the Romans five times over.

It was full daylight now, and they were in sight of the enemy sentries. Encouraged by Arminius and the other leaders, the warriors swarmed down the hill slopes and towards the camp. They had gone perhaps a third of the distance when the alarm was sounded from the nearest wall. Arminius' nerves jangled, but no general call to arms followed. He could see five sentries watching them. All were roaring at the top of their voices, and they sounded terrified. Arminius was delighted. 'On!' he roared to his men. 'Quick as you can!'

By the time the warriors had covered another three hundred paces, two of the Romans had abandoned their positions. Inguiomerus and Big Chin *were* right, Arminius decided. He didn't mind losing face to them if Caecina's army was destroyed. Arminius began to run, urging his men to do the same. When the barritus began, he joined in with gusto.

HUUUUMMMMMMMM! HUUUUMMMMMMMM!

Mud-splattered, legs soaked to the knee and chest heaving, Arminius looked back. Two-thirds of the ground was to their backs now. A few men had fallen behind with twisted ankles and the like, but the vast majority were with him, faces contorting as they bellowed their war cry over and over. A third sentry vanished from sight, leaving two legionaries to face Arminius' thousands. The pair who remained continued to shout for help, but they were wavering. From inside the camp, Arminius could hear what sounded like frightened cries. Blood thrummed in his ears, and his sword felt good in his hand. A hundred steps remained.

'Come on,' he shouted with rising excitement. 'Get over the ditch and up the wall!'

At seventy paces, one of the sentries lobbed his javelin. It soared up into the air – a fine throw – and landed close to Osbert, who roared an obscenity in reply. The second sentry waited until the warriors were much closer before hurling his javelin. His was a poor effort, landing just beyond the defensive ditch. The barrage of insults from the warriors that followed was deafening, and both legionaries vanished from sight. The sounds of panic from within continued.

'What do you think?' Arminius called to Maelo, a short way to his right.

'I'll tell you from the top of the wall,' came the terse reply.

'Have some faith,' said Arminius, the bloodlust thick in his veins. 'They're terrified!'

'Maybe.' Maelo threw his bundle of branches into the ditch and began directing the warriors. 'Put them on top of mine! You, build another crossing over there. Every twenty paces or so should do it. Move!'

It wasn't long before there was enough footing to traverse the ditch in numerous places. Warriors scrambled over the makeshift bridges and leaned their ladders against the wall. Arminius was in their midst. Being so close to the Roman defences, manned or no, was intimidating. Part of him expected a wave of javelins to come hissing down from above, but nothing happened. There was no sign of the fearful sentries either, and the panicked noises from inside hadn't stopped. Really beginning to believe that the Romans had given up hope, Arminius accepted the lead position on a ladder from one of his men. He would be among the first to scale the rampart.

Sword sheathed, and with shield and spear gripped in his left hand, he climbed one rung. Two. Three. To either side, warriors were ascending fast, including Maelo and Osbert. I'll keep them calm, thought Arminius. Play it safe. Their initial objective would be to gain a strong foothold, and then to open one of the gates. After that, the slaughter could begin in earnest.

'*Arminius!*'

Maelo's tone propelled Arminius up the ladder as if every demon in the underworld was after him. He was hauling himself one-handed over the edge of the fortifications, when his ears filled with a familiar, terrible sound.

Tan-tara. Tan-tara-tara. From every part of the Roman camp the trumpets' summons rang, time and again. *Tan-tara. Tan-tara-tara. Tan-tara. Tan-tara-tara.*

Not quite believing what he was hearing, Arminius stood, reaching Maelo's side. His stomach gave a sickening lurch. Instead of chaos, he saw cohort upon cohort of legionaries, in firm ranks. Waiting. Watching. Ready.

Chapter XXXIX

L ike the rest of Caecina's army, Piso was standing with his comrades, his gaze fixed on the top of the fortifications, waiting for signs of the enemy. His nerves were strung tight, and there was still a dull pain behind his eyes. They could only have been formed up for an hour or so, but it seemed like an eternity. Caecina's order had arrived before dawn, and Tullus had had them ready soon after that. Now every cohort of the Fifth was positioned on the inner edge of the intervallum, facing the north wall in standard formation. Its lower than normal height was just enough to conceal them. A legion to a wall, Tullus had told them in confident tone. That was more than enough.

Considering the level of fear that had prevailed a short time before, it was odd that the air could seem determined now, even buoyant, thought Piso. Yet it was. Caecina's address, delivered from the back of his horse as he'd ridden around the intervallum, had hit the nail on the head. 'Think of your loved ones in Vetera, and the welcome they'll give you,' he had cried. 'Remember the battles we have won this summer. Win the struggle today, and you will cover yourselves in glory. Your prowess will be talked of for generations to come!'

Rousing speeches were well and good, but there was more to be said for firm ground under a man's feet and his comrades shoulder to shoulder beside him, Piso decided. He shot a grateful look at Vitellius and Metilius. These welcome comforts didn't mean he liked the dry-mouthed wait, the twisting stomach and cold sweats, the full-once-more bladder that had just

341

been emptied, the twitching muscles. When the sentries on the north wall bellowed the alarm, therefore, Piso felt an overwhelming sense of relief. Fear was there too, as usual, but the agony of waiting was over. 'They're coming,' he said. 'At fucking last.'

'I was thinking the savages wouldn't fall for Caecina's trick,' muttered Vitellius, scowling.

'They have, so cheer up.' Metilius gave Vitellius a dig in the ribs.

'Cheer up?' scoffed Vitellius. 'Thousands of the whoresons are about to throw themselves over that wall at us!'

'Better this way than out in the bog, you grumpy bastard,' jibed Piso.

'Listen, you maggots,' hissed Tullus. He came stalking along the front rank, the gnarled head of his vitis held threateningly at eyeball height. '*Listen.*'

For a moment, Piso could only make out the pounding of his heart off his ribs and the usual leather creaks and metallic clinks from his comrades' equipment. Then he heard it, in between the sentries' alarm calls: men's voices, carrying from beyond the north wall.

'Prepare yourselves,' said Tullus, pitching his voice low, but potent enough to carry. 'I don't want a fucking sound from *any* of you until I give the order. If I hear as much as a mouse fart from one man, I'll rip you *all* new arseholes.' This was said with another menacing gesture of his vine stick. No one dared answer, and Tullus leered. 'Steady, brothers. When the sheep-humpers arrive, they'll get the most unpleasant surprise of their mangy, fly-blown lives.'

Piso focused on the sentries, his only means of determining how close the enemy were. Then, with hoarse shouts, two of them abandoned their positions, clattering down the nearest ladders. The moment they reached the bottom, the men's frightened demeanour vanished and they rejoined their units. The remaining three continued to roar and point, and to beseech the gods for help. Any one of them could have been an actor, thought Piso, a little amused despite his fear.

HUUUUMMMMMMMM! HUUUUMMMMMMMMM!

A nerve twitched in Piso's face as the hated barritus began. 'Bastards,' whispered Metilius from the corner of his mouth. Piso felt Vitellius shift his weight from one foot to the other, and a man in the rank behind stifled a cough. In the century to their left, a soldier cried out. His centurion was on him in a flash, vitis in hand. *Thwack. Thwack.* The miscreant did not repeat his mistake. Piso took a furtive look around. The faces he could see were grim, edgy and sweaty. Some were scared. A few seemed terrified, yet the imposed silence held. It was because Tullus and his vitis were everywhere, thought Piso. Along the front of the century, down its sides and at the rear – there was no way of knowing where he'd pop up next.

The third of the five sentries took to his heels, and Tullus – now at the front of the century again – raised his arms. 'That's the signal, brothers,' he said, pulling a face. 'Do your worst!'

After the nerve-shredding wait, it was a release to be able to do something. Uproar descended as the legionaries gave tongue. 'The Germans are here!' roared Piso. Beside him, Vitellius was emitting a noise that sounded as if his throat was being cut. 'Run!' screamed Metilius. 'RUN!'

The din that rose in the next twenty heartbeats was being made only by every third cohort. That had been Caecina's order – 'We don't want to overdo it,' he'd said. Nonetheless, it was deafening, and rivalled the clamour of the night before. Piso's bowels gave a painful twist even as he shouted: it was hard not to feel some of the fear they were portraying to the enemy. He watched as the last two sentries threw their javelins – this had also been arranged – and then fled. 'Head for the east gate!' Piso cried, almost wishing *he* could.

Tullus had his back to them now, and was watching the ramparts like a hawk. Piso's effort died away, and he sensed his comrades doing the same. Everyone's gaze was fixed on the same place. *Thump, thump* went Piso's heart. The air was still loud with the false cries of other soldiers, but he could hear harsh voices on the far side of the wall. *Thud. Thud.* The sounds came from all along the defences. Guttural orders rang out. They're throwing up ladders, thought Piso. The warriors are about to climb.

'Here they come, brothers,' hissed Tullus. 'Wait for the trumpets.'

The first figure pulled himself on to the walkway, and Piso couldn't stop himself from gasping. Beside him, Vitellius snickered. 'Piss yourself again?'

The nearest men chortled.

'Bastards. Plenty of you must have done the same,' retorted Piso, but his cheeks were flaming.

Already the first warrior had been joined by four others. In the space of a few heartbeats, that number had tripled. The tribesmen stood on the walkway, staring down in mute amazement at the waiting legions.

Tan-tara. Tan-tara-tara. Tan-tara. Tan-tara-tara. Long and hard the trumpeters blew, ordering every legionary to arms. Tullus had his men draw their swords and close up.

More and more warriors appeared at the top of the defences, and the first arrivals began descending the steps. No fools, they waited for their comrades to join them. Experienced warriors and chieftains rallied them into large groups. Berserkers roared threats and pounded their chests. Still Tullus did not give the order. Piso's eyes searched the other walls – countless numbers of the enemy were swarming over them too. Gods, but he was glad there were four legions within the camp.

'You've got to hand it to the whoresons,' declared Vitellius. 'They're not short of courage.'

'Aye,' said Piso with feeling. 'I wouldn't fucking climb down here.'

Metilius bared his teeth. 'When are they going to sound the advance?'

'The more filth that reach the intervallum, the more of them there are to squeeze against the walls,' shouted Tullus. 'Let none escape, eh?'

Piso and his comrades cheered.

It wasn't long before several hundred of the enemy were grouped before Tullus' cohort. Scores more warriors joined their comrades with every passing moment. Javelins would be useful now, thought Piso, but they were long gone, used up in the previous day's fighting. It was going to be sword and shield work, up close and personal. Bloody, brutal and random.

Men were about to die – on both sides.

Chapter XL

T he trumpets were blaring again as Tullus laid down his vitis, pressing it into the earth with his boots. His smooth-worn vine stick was a prize possession, having been with him since his promotion to the centurionate, but it had no place in battle. It was possible he'd be unable to find it afterwards, but that was the least of his worries.

He eyed the massing tribesmen before them. I might die today, he thought, but Fortuna would have to be at her most capricious. Arminius is a fool for leading his warriors into such an enclosed space.

Tullus' chest felt tight, and his stomach was knotted, but he was ready. Piso was one side of him, and Vitellius, his broken nose a giant blue-black bruise, on the other. They were all there, Metilius and the rest of the Eighteenth's veterans, and his soldiers from the Fifth. Every man was dear to Tullus now, even the ex-conscripts who'd rebelled the previous year. He would do anything for them. Fight, bleed with them, drag them out of the cursed bog. If it came to it, he would lay down his life for each and every soldier in his century.

It wouldn't come to that today, he hoped. The savages were about to learn the harshest of lessons.

'Shields up, swords ready, brothers. Advance, at the walk!'

They moved forward in a solid line, shield edge close to shield edge, blades protruding like teeth in between. To either side, he heard his centurions ordering their soldiers to do the same. The warriors shouted and battered their spears off their shields in response, working themselves into the state that allowed men to charge an impenetrable wall of wood and metal.

Twenty-five paces separated the two sides. A shout rang out, and many of the warriors threw spears. High, low, arcing and straight, they flashed towards the legionaries. Tullus bellowed for the front rank to duck down, and the soldiers behind to raise their shields. The volley landed before he'd even finished speaking. Cries of pain followed, and curses. Shields and bodies hit the ground. Someone in the second or third rank retched; a moment later, Tullus smelt acrid bile. The distinctive sounds of a man leaving this existence – a rattling, harsh gasp, the twitching of limbs – came from one rank back.

'Everyone got a shield?' Tullus demanded. 'Get one from the man behind if you haven't. Leave the wounded. Ready?'

'Aye, sir,' scores of voices said.

'Forward!' Tullus was disappointed not to recognise any of the warriors. Facing Arminius again would have been too great a coincidence, but he'd hoped for it nonetheless.

The tribesmen didn't wait for the Romans to reach them. Roaring war cries, they charged in a great, disorganised mass. Faces twisted with hate, painted shields and brandished spears filled Tullus' vision.

'HALT!' he yelled. 'STEADY!'

It was odd, he thought afterwards, the things that a man remembered before, and during, the mayhem that was close-quarters combat. A Suebian knot on a warrior's head – out of place, because that tribe was not at war with Rome. A shield with mesmeric, swirling black lines on a blue background. Behind him, one of his soldiers cursing, 'Bastards. Bastards. Bastards.' Stubby, gravestone-like teeth in the open mouth of a screaming greybeard. The most impressive moustache Tullus had ever seen – long, bushy, and with twisted end-points – decorating a chieftain's face.

An almighty crash went up as the two sets of enemies collided. Beside Tullus, Piso was talking to himself. 'Watch him. Thrust down, at his left foot. That's it!' Tullus' own breath hissed in and out through his open mouth. Teeth splintered and blood spattered as he rammed his sword deep into the greybeard's gullet. The crone was hard at work, stabbing her sewing needle into his left calf. Down went the greybeard, choking on his own gore.

He was replaced at once by a tall warrior with a club. Snarling, the warrior swung a death-delivering blow at Tullus' head. Tullus twisted hard to the left. Something – a muscle? – tore in his side, and the club hit his shield rim, almost wrenching it from his hand. Tullus would have died then, but Vitellius was there, shoving his blade so deep into the club-wielder's chest that the hilt slammed against the ribcage.

It was agony to raise his shield – the blow had damaged the muscles of Tullus' forearm, but it was death to be without protection. Gritting his teeth, he resumed his place. There was no chance to see what was going on, or to thank Vitellius – another warrior, this one a heavy-set, bearded figure, was driving straight at him. Tullus' anger towards Arminius, towards every cursed Germanic tribe, bubbled up. He rose above his aches and pains and shoved his shield boss into Beardy's midriff. His opponent's look of surprise and the *Ooofff* sound he made gave Tullus immense satisfaction. With clinical detachment, he drew back his shield and stabbed Beardy in the gut, twisted, wrenched and pulled the crimson-coated blade free. He watched as Beardy sank to his knees, an odd, keening sound issuing from his lips.

Tullus slew the next warrior as well, but he needed Piso's aid to down the one after that. Tight bands of pain were squeezing his chest, his left arm was losing strength and black dots danced at the edges of his vision. The natural break that happened then – as the two sides pulled back a few steps by mutual, non-verbal agreement – saved his life. Grounding his shield, Tullus sucked in breath after ragged breath. His shield's iron rim was crumpled where the club had landed, but it would serve. Whether his forearm would take any more pressure was another thing. Time to go back into the second rank, he decided, weariness flooding his veins. It's that, or die during the next bout. The realisation tasted as bitter as hemlock; never had he needed to withdraw from the fighting so soon.

'You all right, sir?' Piso's voice was by his ear.

'Eh?' Tullus glared at Piso. 'Of course I am.'

'They're wavering, sir. Look.' Piso jerked his head at the tribesmen.

Tullus stared. The warriors opposite – much reduced in number – didn't seem happy. It wasn't surprising. The ground was littered with their dead, and they had their backs to the wall. He glanced to either side, along the intervallum. The fighting was still raging to his left, but on his right it had paused. There, too, the tribesmen's casualties appeared to have been heavy. The legionaries facing them were singing – and there was no barritus being hurled back at them. On the ramparts, he could see warriors climbing back on to their ladders. Retreating.

The tide had turned. A strong attack now would smash the tribesmen facing his soldiers, thought Tullus with rising excitement. He hefted his shield, breathed into the discomfort that radiated from his forearm and let it mix with the needle darts from the torn muscle in his side. I can manage, he decided. It won't take long. 'READY, BROTHERS?' he roared.

'YES, SIR!'

'See them, brothers? They're tired. Scared. Half their inbred friends lie dead, thanks to you. Ready to finish the rest?' As his soldiers roared back at him, Tullus struck his sword off his shield boss, one, two, three times. 'Forward!'

He led his men on at a slow but purposeful pace, and the warriors broke before they'd even closed. Pushing and shoving at one another in their panic, they ran to the nearest gate, or scrambled up to the walkway, there to leap over the ramparts. Backs against the earthworks, a few men stayed to fight, too courageous to retreat, Tullus thought, or perhaps giving their lives to save their comrades. He kept his soldiers in formation until those warriors had been cut down, and then he wheeled them to the right, towards the north gate. The intervallum was already a confusion of retreating tribesmen and legionaries from the Fifth's other cohorts, falling on the enemy from the side. The instant his soldiers entered the maelstrom, control would be lost.

That might happen anyway, Tullus decided, studying the blood-keen faces around him. Gut instinct also told him that the day was theirs. He had seen routs like this before – the surviving tribesmen would be hounded out of the gate and into the bog, where the slaughter would be immense. Nonetheless, he couldn't help wondering if Arminius still had a trick up his sleeve. Would a hidden force of warriors swoop down on the legionaries as they emerged, disorganised, from the camp?

Tullus wasn't happy until he had clambered up a ladder and surveyed the surrounding terrain. There any doubts he'd had vanished. All he could see was warriors' backs as they fled through the mud, and hordes of baying legionaries in hot pursuit. Discarded spears and shields were strewn everywhere. Corpses floated face down in the muddy pools, and lay tangled in the gorse bushes. Trapped in the mud, or too hurt to run any further, wounded tribesmen screamed their distress. Several ravens already hung in the air overhead. How did the corpse-feeders know to arrive so fast? Tullus wondered. There would be a glut of food for the birds; that was certain.

Let Arminius be among the slain, he asked.

Chapter XLI

◉◉◉

As Piso and his companions charged headlong after the fleeing tribesmen, they whooped their joy. Tullus and Fenestela followed, but at their own pace. So many legionaries were hunting the warriors that it was soon difficult to find any living within the walls. It seemed, thought Piso, as if every centurion in the army had sent his soldiers after the quarry the way hunters unleash their packs of hunting dogs. Tullus' century splintered from the outset, but Piso and his comrades stuck together.

Chasing men and stabbing them in the back was brutal, exhausting work, but Piso didn't care. These were the whoresons who had evaded the army for months, who had hunted him and his brothers through the bog, and who had killed Saxa. Like as not, many had taken part in Arminius' ambush six years before. As far as Piso was concerned, they deserved whatever was coming to them.

With hundreds of other legionaries, he and his comrades funnelled through the north gate and pursued the warriors outside. The majority of the enemy ran into the marsh, but some tried escaping on the wooden road. Piso and his comrades cheered as they stumbled over broken planking and fell into the pools of water that had formed under the damaged roadway. With a mob of other soldiers, they pounded after this group, hacking them to pieces even as they begged for mercy.

Hearty warriors, greybeards, bare-faced youths, it didn't matter. They slew them all. Piso chopped down a man old enough to have been his grandfather, and another who could have been his younger brother. He watched Metilius take on a berserker with an injured knee, laughing as the huge warrior tried in vain to strike at his friend from a squatting position. Dancing around the berserker, Metilius stabbed him three, four, five times in the chest and back, wounds that didn't kill. 'Come on, big man,' he taunted in German. 'You can take me.' The berserker threw himself forward with a desperate lunge of his spear. Grinning, Metilius let him fall flat on his face, before straddling the warrior and, with a precise thrust, pithing him through the base of his neck.

The chase went on for hours, so long that the legionaries took breaks to rest and to drink water. Once a place to be afraid – of the enemy, the landscape's alien appearance and the strange birdcalls – the bog now belonged to them. Deep into it they went, harassing the tribesmen with vicious intent. Every so often, a warrior would stand to fight back, sometimes aided by a comrade. These efforts drew the attention of every legionary within sight the way flies home in on fresh shit. Surrounded on all sides, the warriors died, often without even wounding an attacker.

It was natural – one of the rewards of victory, opined Vitellius to whoever would listen – that soldiers would begin ransacking the dead for valuables. Many of the tribesmen had purses, but much of the yield within was poor, nothing more than a few copper coins. Pleasing everyone, though, bracelets and hammer pendants of silver were common. Vitellius crowed with delight as he pulled a gold torque from around a chieftain's neck. 'This is worth a year's pay!' He jumped as his victim's arm moved, and a faint gurgle left his muddy lips. 'Still alive, are you?' Grabbing the chieftain by the hair, Vitellius shoved his head under the surface of a nearby pool. Piso watched, aghast. The chieftain soon went limp.

'You didn't have to finish him like that,' said Piso.

Vitellius threw him a jaundiced look. 'What do you care? He'd have done the same to you, or worse.'

It was true, thought Piso, but the cold-hearted killing had robbed him of his desire for blood. He cast an eye at the sun, which had been making regular appearances from behind the patchy cloud. Mid-afternoon was passing. Dusk was on the way. Piso could see legionaries turning around and beginning the walk back to camp. 'How far have we come?' he called out to the group in general.

'Three miles,' said Vitellius.

'Four, maybe five,' countered Metilius.

A good number of estimates rained down, most of which fell somewhere between three and six miles. 'Time to think about heading back, eh?' suggested Piso. 'I have no desire to spend a night out here.'

The inevitable jibes followed, but heads were also nodding in agreement. Vitellius lifted his torque, letting the sunlight wink off it. 'I'm with you, Piso. I don't want to drop this in the dark.'

'Don't lose it,' warned Piso. 'I plan to take it from you at dice.'

Laughter broke out, and Vitellius made an obscene gesture at them all. He tapped at the torque, which was now around his neck. 'Once I've sold it to a goldsmith, I'm going to buy a new sword. The rest of the money will go on wine and whores. If you're lucky, you might get a cup of wine each out of me, but that'll be it!'

Every man in the contubernium had plundered enough valuables to get pissed for a few nights, and some, like Vitellius, had done far better. As they trudged towards their camp, those with least engaged in merciless teasing of their more well-off comrades. The general mood, already buoyant from their welcome victory, was as jovial as that on a four-monthly payday. The legionaries were bone-weary and covered in mud and blood; there was no wine to drink, and little food, but the Germans had been beaten, and the path to the Rhenus lay open before them. Perhaps Arminius would rally his warriors, but given the casualties they'd suffered, it seemed doubtful.

'Look,' said Vitellius, pointing.

Piso stared. A score of paces to their left, a warrior was lying on his side. Crimson stains marked the back of his tunic; a spear lay just beyond his uncurled fingers. Silver glinted on one of his wrists. Piso was tired, and couldn't be bothered pillaging for more booty. He walked on. 'Don't bother.'

'That bracelet could be a big one,' Vitellius announced, unsheathing his blade. He strode off through the mud.

Rolling his eyes, Piso kept moving. So did the rest. They had just begun to argue over whose turn it was to cook their remaining food when a strangled cry interrupted them. Piso spun, his heart lurching. A gorse bush blocked part of his view, but he could see Vitellius stabbing downwards. Piso relaxed. The warrior hadn't been dead, and had groaned as Vitellius slew him. 'All right?' Piso called.

There was no reply. Vitellius thrust again, and straightened. His expression was pinched. 'The whoreson had a blade.'

Piso was already running, but Vitellius had fallen to the ground before he arrived. The warrior lay on his back, now clearly dead, but with a dagger still clutched in a fist. A grimacing Vitellius was sitting on his arse a few steps away, clutching at his groin, the mud between his outstretched legs an ominous dark red colour. Piso dropped to his knees, ripping at his neck scarf, the only thing he could think of to use as a bandage. 'Where did he get you?'

Vitellius' face had gone pasty grey. 'High up, in the thigh. He had the dagger ready – he must have been hoping some fool would roll him over, as I did. I didn't even see him thrust – just felt the fucking pain.'

'Let me look.' As Vitellius took away his crimson-coated hand, Piso moved aside the metal-studded strips that dangled from his friend's belt. With gentle hands, he lifted the bottom of Vitellius' tunic, biting back a cry of dismay as he did so. Blood – bright-red blood – was welling from a deep wound in the meat of Vitellius' right thigh. Piso was no surgeon, but the artery looked to have been cut.

'What can you see?' demanded Vitellius.

'Your prick's still there. Balls too,' replied Piso, folding his sweat-soaked scarf into a thick pad and pressing it hard against the wound.

'Is he all right?' Metilius arrived, his face was twisted with concern.

'He'll be fine,' said Piso, mouthing, 'It's bad,' at Metilius.

Vitellius groaned. 'Gods, it hurts.'

Piso's neck scarf was soaked through with blood. 'Give me a dressing,' he snapped at Metilius. 'Your scarf. Anything!'

Vitellius lay back in the mud. 'I should have listened to you. I should have left the bastard alone. One gold torque is enough for any man.'

'Never mind,' said Piso, replacing his scarf with that of Metilius'. They exchanged an anxious look.

'Was his bracelet worth taking?' Piso asked Vitellius, his tone light.

'I haven't taken it off him yet.' Vitellius' chuckle was forced.

Using both his hands, Piso pressed the scarf against Vitellius' wound. He knew this was what surgeons did to stem haemorrhage, but each pulse of blood against his fingers and the growing puddle of it between Vitellius' legs told him it wasn't working. 'Belt – I need a leather belt, or a strap,' he said to Metilius. 'And a length of stick as thick as my thumb.'

'To tie around his leg?' Metilius was already unbuckling his belt. He unclipped his baldric from his sword and handed it over. 'Get over here,' he roared at the others. 'Find a stout piece of wood, as long as your forearm. Piso needs it for Vitellius. Now!'

'I don't want to die,' muttered Vitellius.

'You're not going to die,' retorted Piso, thinking: you will if I don't get a tie around your leg soon. 'Help me,' he ordered Metilius. 'Hold the scarf against the wound, hard as you can.' Once Metilius' hands were in place, Piso pushed the baldric under Vitellius' leg and worked it as high as he could, right into the groin. Panic clawed at Piso. The dagger had gone in so far up Vitellius' thigh that it was unclear whether fastening the strap around it was going to make any difference. The growing quantity of blood on the ground was alarming. 'Where's that fucking piece of stick?' Piso bellowed.

He laid the beginnings of a surgeon's knot in the baldric – three throws, one after the other – and pulled it as taut as he could. 'That make any difference?' he asked Metilius.

Metilius scowled, and felt. 'A little,' he said.

Piso heaved on the baldric until his arm muscles ached. 'Now?'

'That's better.'

'Put a finger on the knot,' ordered Piso, tying it with grim intent. Metilius withdrew his finger as the leather squeezed tight. 'Get your hand back on the wound,' snapped Piso. 'How does it feel now?'

'The blood's flowing faster than it was before you tied it off,' replied Metilius, scowling.

Piso wanted to scream. Knots always loosened off like this. Most of the time it didn't matter, but now every moment counted. He was about to shout for the stick again, when one of the others came skidding to a halt beside them. He proffered a section of gorse branch. 'It's all I could find,' he said in an apologetic voice.

'Cut some of the fucking thorns off. Quickly!' Piso cried. He took a glance at Vitellius, and wished he hadn't. His friend's eyes were closed; shallow movements of his chest told Piso he was alive, but he was fading. ''Tellius. 'Tellius?'

There was no answer.

'The stick. Now, or it'll be too late!' Piso's comrade gave up slicing and passed it over. Fast as he could, Piso slid the still thorny piece of wood under the baldric and began to turn it towards him. One, two, three twists. The leather was good and tight, but he didn't stop. Four twists. Five. He shot a look at Metilius. 'Is the bleeding slowing?'

'I think so.' Metilius concentrated, then grinned like a fool. 'It is! I can't feel anything.'

Piso twisted the stick another full circle for good measure, and pushed one end of it under the leather to hold it in place. Aesculapius, he prayed, let that be enough – please. He took Vitellius' cold hand in his. ''Tellius?'

Vitellius didn't respond. Scared now, Piso leaned up to see his friend's face. Vitellius' complexion had gone waxen – the colour of the dead, or those near death. With trembling fingers, Piso felt at the side of Vitellius' wrist.

'Is he . . . ?' faltered Metilius.

Piso squeezed shut his eyes, and tried to block out everything but the sensation in his fingertips. Feeling a thready pulsing, his hopes rose, but they curdled almost at once. Vitellius' pulse was fading with each beat of his weakened heart.

Riven with grief and hopelessness, Piso felt it dwindle under his touch until, after he didn't know how long, it stopped. Distraught, blaming himself, he let his chin fall on to his chest.

'He's gone.' Metilius' tone was flat.

'Aye,' whispered Piso.

No one said anything as grief overcame them. Piso wept. Metilius slumped down beside him, laid a hand on Vitellius' unmoving arm. Their comrade who'd brought the stick watched over them in grim silence with the others.

Time passed. Overhead, a raven called, and was answered by its mate. In the distance, legionaries shouted to one another as they retraced their steps towards the camp. How Piso longed for the corpse lying before him to be one of those men. They were good soldiers, no doubt, but they weren't Vitellius, with whom he'd been through so much. Vitellius, who with Metilius had hauled him miles through the mud.

Warm sunshine began to beat down on their backs. After the dreadful weather of the previous days, it should have been welcome. Instead it felt hateful. It was almost as if the gods were mocking their friend, thought Piso, whose death had been so stupid, so pointless.

In the end, Metilius broke the quiet. 'We'd best get back.'

Piso stirred, but didn't get up.

'Come on,' said Metilius. 'It's a good distance to the camp, and we need to fashion a litter to carry him.'

'Why did it have to be Vitellius?' asked Piso, his voice raw with sorrow.

'His time had come. That's all there is to say.' Metilius gave Piso's shoulder an awkward pat. 'Try not to dwell on it, or you'll go mad.'

Metilius was right, Piso decided, clamping down on his jagged-edged grief. Vitellius' death wasn't right or wrong. It just *was*. The Fates had cut his thread today, not tomorrow, next year or in three decades. If the warrior with the dagger hadn't done for him, someone else would have. He – Piso – was still alive, and so were Metilius and the others. Tullus and Fenestela had made it too.

In this stinking, endless bogland, that was the only thing that mattered.

Chapter XLII

◰◰◰

Night had fallen, and Arminius was sitting on a blanket by his fire, sharpening his sword. Even with the flames, the light was poor. There was no need to do this routine, mindless task now, but he needed something to take his mind off what had happened. The bag of wine by his feet was one method. Scouring his weapon was another. His first efforts, with a damp rag cloth, had washed off the caked blood. There was no removing the ichor from the junction of blade and hilt – it tended to soak in there – but Arminius regarded that deep-lying stain as part of the sword's substance. He didn't want to clean away all evidence of the men he'd wounded and slain.

He squinted along the blade, searching for the nicks left from impacts with other metal objects – swords, shield rims, helmets. Finding three close together, he ran his pumice stone over the area with firm, regular strokes, keeping it angled just *so* towards the steel. Six strokes one way, six the opposite. Arminius studied the sword again, could no longer see two of the marks, but the third lingered. He concentrated on the area again, working the stone until no trace of the damage remained. On he moved, to another part of the blade. It was satisfying work, easy to focus on, and because he'd done it so many times before, a pleasure rather than a burden.

'There you are.' Maelo had appeared.

Arminius grunted, but didn't look up. Their disastrous attack would have to be discussed, but he didn't want to do it now. Having an empty mind at times such as this was a useful thing. He pointed the sword towards the flames, searching for more imperfections.

'Thirsty?' asked Maelo.

'No.' Spotting another nick, Arminius began to hone it down.

'Hungry?'

'No.' The stone made a gentle, scraping sound as it slid over the blade, and repeated itself as he dragged the pumice the opposite way.

'Want to talk?'

'No.' Arminius ran the stone over and back, over and back. He rubbed at the spot with a finger, could feel nothing but smooth steel. The edge was keen there too. Again aiming the sword at the fire, he peered along its length.

'Arminius.'

He didn't react.

'Arminius.' Maelo's voice was harder this time.

He raised his head, gave his second-in-command a cold glance.

'What happened today wasn't your fault.'

Despite his intentions, Arminius' fury burst free. 'The whole thing was a fucking disaster – from beginning to end!'

'It wasn't your fault – you tried to stop the attack.'

'*Tried?* Much use it did the poor whoresons who lie dead out there.' Arminius made an angry gesture towards the bog. 'How many were slain?'

Maelo shrugged. 'No one knows yet. Six, seven thousand at least.'

'Wasted lives! Men who won't be there to fight next year – if I can even rally the tribes again.' Arminius curled his lip. 'What number were Cherusci?'

'Three, four hundred. Far fewer than there would have been if you'd run, as Inguiomerus did.'

'The faithless dog made no effort to hold his warriors together. I should have gutted him this morning and taken charge of them.'

Maelo raised an eyebrow. 'D'you really think they'd have followed you after that?'

'Perhaps not, but it might have stopped the attack altogether. Donar curse the other chieftains for being headstrong fools, for listening to

Inguiomerus!' Arminius flung down his sword and pumice stone, and stared into the flames, scowling.

Maelo watched him for several moments, then he said, 'It's done. It's over.'

Arminius bunched his fists until his knuckles whitened. Only when the sensation began to leave his fingers did he relax his grip. 'It's so *frustrating* to see months' worth of planning pissed away! To know that thousands of brave men died needless deaths. And all because my *uncle* is – or was – an empty-headed, over-confident fool.' He cocked his head. 'Has there been any sign of him?'

'No.'

'Good riddance to the dog.'

'What about the Romans? They haven't reached safety yet. It's three days' hard march to the open ground near the river.'

'Not everyone is like you, Maelo,' said Arminius. 'Our warriors are the finest in the land, but I doubt they have the belly for another assault. There's no chance that the other tribes would take part – they've been hounded to within a hair's breadth of their lives. Even if our men *would* help us attack Caecina, four thousand spears can do little against so many legions. Our campaign is over until next spring.'

'I suppose you're right,' admitted Maelo, glowering.

Bitterness filled Arminius anew, and he kicked out against a projecting log, pushing it into the blaze. A stream of orange-white sparks trailed up into the night sky. Forgive me, Thusnelda, Arminius thought. I have wronged you twice over. I didn't protect you and our unborn child from the enemy. Now I have failed to avenge you.

'They'll be back next year,' said Maelo. 'The fate of the Marsi and the Chatti will be the talk of every longhouse this winter. Recruits won't be hard to find. You *will* raise a new army.'

It was true, thought Arminius. The tribes had been defeated, but that did not mean they were altogether beaten, that their courage had gone, never to return.

'Arminius!' Osbert appeared out of the darkness. Blood caked his arms, and dark lines ringed his eyes. 'Inguiomerus has returned, badly wounded.'

'Take me to him,' ordered Arminius, sweeping his sword into its sheath. 'Maybe I'll finish what the Romans didn't.'

Maelo's face grew troubled. 'If it has to be done, let me or Osbert take care of it. Such things need to happen in the dark of the night, with no witnesses.'

'You'd best be somewhere else altogether,' added Osbert.

Arminius threw them an approving look. 'Let's see how the land lies before we make that decision. Come with me.'

Things weren't dreadful in the section of the camp occupied by Arminius' followers. They didn't have tents – no one did, thanks to the Romans' pursuit – but they had their weapons, and their pride. Elsewhere was a different matter, and the journey to Inguiomerus' tent was an unpleasant one. Bands of stragglers were still coming in, their wounds, dejected expressions and lack of spears and shields graphic evidence of their ordeal. The injured and dying sprawled everywhere between the trees. The few individuals with medical knowledge were hard at work, bandaging, cauterising and administering herbal tonics. Piles of corpses – those whom it had been impossible to save, or who had expired before being treated – lay in great piles. No barritus resonated in the cold night air – the chant had been replaced by a constant, low moaning, and calls for dressings and bowls of hot water.

Arminius kept his head down and pressed on. He'd seen to his own men already. There would be opportunity the next day to move among these casualties, praising and commiserating. To ensure that the warriors' hatred of Rome had not been extinguished by their defeat. To plant fresh hope in their weary, grieving hearts.

Arminius' identity was enough to see them admitted to Inguiomerus' spacious lean-to, constructed from a mixture of hides and blankets. Two warriors walked before and after the trio, however, making Arminius exchange glances with Maelo and Osbert. The distrust he felt towards his uncle was mutual, it seemed.

Inguiomerus was lying flat on his back, a heavy bandage strapped around his left thigh. Another encased the top of his head. 'What a surprise,' he croaked as Arminius approached.

The bearded, robed priest who'd been tending Inguiomerus rose, acknowledged Arminius and moved to the side of the lean-to. 'Inguiomerus is tired and needs to sleep,' he said, before beginning to pack up his vessels and instruments.

With a little jerk of his head, Inguiomerus directed his warriors in front of Arminius to place themselves on either side of him. The pair behind Arminius and his companions stayed where they were. 'Nephew,' said Inguiomerus, 'have you come to gloat?'

It would have given Arminius considerable satisfaction to do so, but he knew that taking the high ground now would destroy any chance of keeping Inguiomerus within the fold. For all that Arminius had talked about finishing the Romans' job, he needed his uncle. Widely liked and respected, he had thousands of warriors in his faction of the Cherusci tribe. Arminius didn't have the time or the energy to win them over. 'I came because you are my kin. Is your injury serious?'

'The priest says the wound is clean. I'll have a limp when it's healed, but I will be able to fight.' Inguiomerus' eyes were on Arminius, needle-sharp. 'Have you naught else to say to me?'

'The decision to attack the Roman camp this morning was unwise, but it was made by the majority. I have to respect that.' Arminius was a good liar, but this was a real test. He waited, a little anxious, as Inguiomerus studied him.

At length, his uncle's frown eased. 'It's good to know that you *can* be humble. You may be surprised, but I can also. It's clear now that the assault this morning was doomed to fail. We should have waited until the Romans had left the protection of their defences, as you suggested. It saddens me that so many warriors had to perish before I understood that. Their deaths will weigh on my conscience for evermore.'

Arminius could see no signs of guile in Inguiomerus' face, and his suspicion eased a little. 'I too am grieving. It was a brutal lesson.'

'Because of me, our last chance to defeat the Romans this year has gone.' Inguiomerus' voice was bitter.

That's right, thought Arminius, his fury towards his uncle threatening to rekindle, but the bridge-building needed to continue, so he dampened it down. 'The coming of spring will grant us fresh opportunities. Every tribe who fought today will want vengeance for their dead. With Donar's aid, they will help us defeat the Romans once and for all.'

'The tribes need a leader.' Inguiomerus broke off as a fit of coughing took him.

Arminius waited, his face patient, mind racing.

'They need a single leader,' said Inguiomerus at length. '*You* should be that man. You proved your worth six years ago, when you brought together the tribes and then destroyed Varus and his army. It was you who united us again this summer. If you'd had your way, Caecina's head would be nailed to the nearest tree this night, and the corpses of his legionaries decorating the bogs for ten miles in every direction.'

'Your words are music to my ears, uncle,' said Arminius. 'You will stand with me, then, when the Romans return?'

'I will, and so will my warriors.' Inguiomerus' expression had grown fierce. He reached up with his right hand, and they shook, hard.

Arminius took heart. Inguiomerus' support would help persuade other chieftains to renew their alliance with him. Men such as Big Chin and Stick Thin would re-enter the fold. Another chance for final victory over the Romans *would* come his way, and when it did, Thusnelda would be avenged. Caecina would die, and Germanicus too.

Once these tasks had been completed, he would rest.

Not before.

Chapter XLIII

It was early, not long after dawn. Drops of dew winked and sparkled on the scrubby grass, and on every gorse bush and bog cotton plant. A quarter of a mile from the Roman camp, Piso and his comrades stood in dry-eyed silence around Vitellius' corpse. Shovels lay close by. Their hands were black with mud, and sweat marked their faces: they had been digging his grave. At their feet, Vitellius was unrecognisable, a blanket-wrapped, human shape tied with strips of leather. Despite his shroud, he was still their friend. Their brother. No one wanted to make the first move.

'It doesn't seem right to bury him in the middle of nowhere,' said Piso. They been arguing about this since the day before, when Vitellius had died. 'He should be laid in the military graveyard at Vetera, beside other soldiers. I'd like to lie alongside him one day.'

'I wish the same for myself, but that's not the way it works.' Metilius sighed. 'Even if Tullus let us, there's the small matter of transporting 'Tellius' body back to the Rhenus.'

Heads bent in resignation, but Piso wouldn't give in. 'We could make a litter, as you did for me. Drag him home on it.'

'That'd break every kind of regulation. Tullus is sympathetic – you heard what he said about Vitellius before we left the camp – but he couldn't allow that. Every contubernium which had lost a comrade would want to do the same, and then where would we be?' demanded Metilius. 'Arminius might have been beaten, but we're in enemy territory still. The army has to march in combat formation, Piso.'

'I know, I know. But Vitellius saved my arse in Aliso, when I got jumped by soldiers from another legion, and I repaid him in the forest. Since then, we've looked out for each other. He was my brother.' Words failed Piso, and his tears began to flow again.

'Fine words,' said Metilius, his voice gruff. ''Tellius had a caustic sense of humour; some would say he was sour, even. I was never quite sure how to take him myself, but I *do* know that he was a loyal friend. When things went to shit, there was no better soldier to have by your side. We'll miss you, 'Tellius. Brother.'

Throat closed with emotion, Piso listened as the others muttered their goodbyes. 'Farewell, brother.' 'Swift passage to the other side, brother.'

'Let's get it over with,' directed Metilius. He slid a rope under Vitellius' body.

Piso wasn't ready to take leave of his friend, but the rest were easing lines under him too. With a lump in his throat, Piso moved to help. Six of them – the entire contubernium now – could lower him down in pairs. When the ropes were in place, Metilius called, 'One, two, three. Up!' and they raised Vitellius' corpse to knee level. Shuffling to the graveside, they paused and looked in. The lowest point of the hole was a black, oozing morass. It was uninviting, even as the resting place for a dead man. Unhappy glances were exchanged.

They had no option, thought Piso, mastering his grief by force of will. His eyes moved around his comrades. ''Tellius has already crossed the Styx. This is just somewhere for his bones to lie, to keep the wild beasts away, and the savages from despoiling them.'

Reluctant nods followed his comment. 'Ready?' called Piso.

They let the lines move through their hands little by little, easing Vitellius into his grave. Soft plashes and a slackening of the tension signalled his reaching the bottom. Piso knew that his friend was dead, gone – Vitellius had bled out in front of him – yet tugging out the muddied rope was one of the hardest things he had ever done. It felt like the worst kind of abandon-ment. On impulse, Piso took the gold torque from his purse and held it up. He had taken the valuable ornament from around Vitellius' neck because his friend would not have wanted it to go to waste, as it were. Now, Piso wasn't so sure that felt right. 'Will I drop this in?'

Everyone stared.

'He's got a coin to pay the ferryman,' said Metilius after a moment.

'It won't be any use to him,' declared one of the others.

Every head was shaking – no – and, relenting, Piso said, 'It'll buy 'Tellius a headstone and us enough wine to float a boat. Maybe whores as well, if we're not too extravagant. He'd approve, wouldn't he?'

'Of the headstone, yes. Don't be so sure about the rest. 'Tellius kept his fingers tight on his purse,' said Metilius with a wicked grin. 'Which means we should sell it and spend the money anyway. 'Tellius' moaning and whingeing – that we're carousing at his expense – will carry all the way from the underworld.'

Everyone laughed, and like that it was settled. Piso tucked away the torque.

Metilius indicated that the rest should fetch their shovels, and thrust one into Piso's hands. Trying not to think, Piso bent his back and eased a load of earth on to the tool's flat surface. He waited until several comrades had heaved shovelfuls into the grave before doing the same. A soft thud marked its landing. Piso wanted to peer in, but he couldn't bear to see his friend's shroud-wrapped body disappearing under clods of earth. He picked up another load. In went the soil, mixing with the others' efforts.

They worked in grim silence until the spot where Vitellius' body lay was nothing more than a rectangle of fresh-turned earth. Metilius and Piso patted it down with their shovels, and one of the others erected the oblong wooden marker they'd fashioned. On the front, Piso had used the white-hot tip of a dagger to scratch Vitellius' name and age. In the line below, his century, cohort and legion were recorded.

It didn't seem enough, Piso thought, but there was no room for more writing. Worse, the elements would destroy the marker within a couple of years. Vitellius' grave would then be lost forever.

It seemed a cruel fate.

Three days later, and Piso was exhausted. Fine weather, better conditions underfoot and the soldiers' burning desire to reach Vetera had seen the army cover twenty-five, maybe even twenty-seven miles that day. Tullus' cohort had been on camp construction duty, which had meant two hours of digging at the end of their energy-sapping march. Now Piso and his comrades sat on their blankets around their fire, dull-eyed, slump-shouldered, waiting for the miserable broth that was to be their supper. Despite the length of their journey and the lack of food and shelter, it had been a pleasant day. There had been no sign of the enemy whatsoever. Another two to three marches, and they'd reach the bridge over the Rhenus, or so the rumours went. Piso was relieved, yet he kept thinking of Vitellius, stiff and cold in his rough grave.

'Will it be long?' asked Metilius, jerking his chin at the pot hanging over the flames.

Piso leaned forward and stirred again. He tasted a mouthful, and added a pinch of salt. 'Be another while. You can't rush good cooking, as my mother always used to say.'

'Funny man,' said Metilius with a droll chuckle. 'Let's sort out 'Tellius' stuff while we wait.'

Conversation around the fire stopped. All eyes bore down on Metilius as he unwrapped three blankets they'd taken turns to carry that day. The first contained Vitellius' rusted mail shirt and the sweat-marked, ripe-smelling padded garment that he'd worn underneath. In the second were his arming cap and helmet, his baldric, belt and 'apron', and his well-used sword. Cooking utensils and personal effects filled the third.

Every item made Piso's mind spin with memories of his friend. Vitellius gearing up of a morning, complaining about the weight of his armour, talking to himself as he prepared the group's food, or combing his thinning hair with an old, double-sided comb. Piso checked over his shoulder, almost expecting to see Vitellius, to hear his outraged demands that they leave his bloody kit alone.

He heard nothing, and his sorrow bubbled up afresh.

Metilius laid his own helmet on the blanket and picked up Vitellius' one, which was lighter and of a more modern design. 'That'll do,' he said in a quiet voice.

Grief-stricken, unwilling to participate at first, Piso watched as, one by one, his comrades exchanged pieces of their equipment for items that had belonged to Vitellius. His folding knife and spoon – a rarity – went first, then his large bronze pot, which was good for making stew. Someone else took his belt and apron, another his strigil, ear scoop and nail cleaner.

'Your turn,' said Metilius to Piso.

Piso reached over and took first Vitellius' comb, which for some odd reason would remind him most of his friend, and then his sword.

''Tellius was going to get rid of that. The blade is pitted to Hades and back,' said Metilius.

'The hilt is still good. The gods alone know how he afforded it,' retorted Piso, his fingers trailing over the yellowed ivory, his mind bright with images of Vitellius. 'I can have a new blade forged. Make the thing as good as new.'

''Tellius would have liked that,' said Metilius, the others' nods mirroring his approval.

They sat and stared for a time at the objects that remained, and then by common, unspoken consent, the blankets were rolled up again and placed to one side. The unwanted items were of no further use; they'd be left behind in the morning, when they marched out. Vitellius' memory would live on in their hearts and minds, and in the pieces of kit which each of them had chosen.

Piso's grief, razor-sharp since his friend's unexpected death, had been eased somehow by the division of possessions. Surprised, relieved, he glanced around, sensing that the experience had also helped his tent mates.

Vitellius was gone, but, like Saxa and the rest, he would never be forgotten.

Chapter XLIV

◧◧◧

T ullus' horse had been lost with the baggage train, forcing him to march from the camp where they'd routed Arminius' tribesmen. His knees were killing him as he trudged along, and there was a deep-rooted ache in the base of his spine, yet nothing could have shifted him from his place at the front of the cohort. The Fifth Legion was in the vanguard today, and Tullus' had reached a gravelled road upwards of an hour before. The time he and his unit had spent on the paved surface meant the front cohorts had to be nearing the first bridge. Vetera was close, the pain almost at an end. Twenty-something miles they'd come since dawn, so the legions could reach the Rhenus and, beyond it, their camp. Despite the punishing march made on empty bellies, the soldiers' complaints had been few and far between.

Morale had been high since their overwhelming victory, thought Tullus with satisfaction. It had continued to rise as first one day, and then two and three, had passed without further attacks. Reports from the scouts the previous evening, suggesting there were no tribesmen for miles around, had been greeted with glee. It seemed ever more probable that Arminius and his allies had given up for the year. Tullus' own spirits grew more buoyant by the hour, but he had remained on guard. They weren't home yet.

Before this, their final push, he had had words with the cohort's centurions. Discipline was to be maintained, every able-bodied soldier to be ready for combat. The men could sing, but until their feet hit the western bank, everyone was to remain alert. With open ground on either side of their route and the countryside empty, he had perhaps been over-strict, he thought, but better that than being surprised again by Arminius.

The building used by the sentries who monitored the river crossing hove into view, and Tullus' heart leaped. 'Arminius won't be putting in an appearance now, brothers. Bridge in sight!'

A loud, rolling cheer met his cry. Even Piso, whose morale had been low since the death of his comrade Vitellius, seemed happier.

Tullus felt a broad smile ease on to his own face. They had made it. No more of his men would die this year. His legion's eagle hadn't been recovered yet, but it would be, during next year's campaign. Arminius would pay then too – the ultimate price.

Closer they came. The sentries, two centuries strong, were lined up along the roadside, calling out to the returning soldiers. 'Welcome home, brothers!' 'You're brave men, all of you!' 'The gods be praised!'

Tullus returned the salute of the units' centurions, who seemed a little embarrassed. He would find out later how the alarmed sentries, thinking the approaching Fifth was a horde of Germans, had begun to hack at the bridge with axes. Only the intervention of Agrippina, Germanicus' heavily pregnant wife, had prevented them from destroying it.

Moments later, Tullus was delighted to see Agrippina standing by the approach to the bridge. Regal, calm-faced and melodic-voiced, she was garbed in a dress woven from the finest wool. Red coral and gold jewellery graced her throat and wrists; her hair was arranged in the latest fashion. A pair of body servants and several bodyguards hovered in the background. Agrippina looked every part the Roman matron, every part the royal. She was a shrewd woman to put in an appearance here, thought Tullus. The troops would love her presence.

Agrippina's voice carried as they drew near. 'I bid you welcome, brave soldiers of Rome. Long has been your journey, many your trials, and severe. Yet you return victorious, having conquered the savage tribes who threaten our empire. Cross the bridge, return to your barracks. Food and wine await you there, laid on by the grace of my husband, Germanicus.'

The legionaries shouted their delight.

'Has Germanicus come back, good lady?' asked Tullus as he came alongside.

A shadow passed over Agrippina's face. 'Not yet.'

'The gods bless him and keep him safe. He will be here soon, you'll see,' said Tullus.

'GER-MAN-I-CUS! GER-MAN-I-CUS! GER-MAN-I-CUS!' shouted his soldiers. The refrain was taken up by the troops behind, and soon the air resonated with the hypnotic chant.

When Tullus looked back, Agrippina was smiling.

Things grew better as they came off the second bridge into the vicus. To Tullus' delight, Artio was waiting in the cheering crowd with Sirona and Scylax. With a squeal of joy, she came running towards him, Scylax at her heels, his tail swishing the air.

'We had news that the army had been ambushed. I was so scared,' Artio cried, throwing her arms around Tullus' waist and walking alongside him. 'But you're here. You're alive.'

'I am,' said Tullus, a sudden thickness in his voice. A little self-conscious, he stroked her hair. 'It's good to see you, but away with you now. I have duties to attend to.'

Artio pulled away, making a face. 'You'll come to the inn tonight?'

Tullus was aware that every soldier in gods knew how many ranks was listening to their conversation. He was a private man, and under normal circumstances he would have brushed Artio off. But this wasn't a normal day. Not since his return from Aliso six years before had Tullus felt such overwhelming relief. They had come through the eye of the storm, stared death in the face, and most of them had survived. His men were at his back, safe. Artio was there, fresh-faced, beautiful and ecstatic to see him. Sirona seemed pleased too, and by the gods, she was looking fine. Life was *good*.

'Aye,' Tullus said, reaching out to touch Artio's cheek, and throwing Sirona a smile. 'Give me a few hours, and I'll be there.'

'You promise?' demanded Artio.

Someone close by – Piso, or Metilius? – snickered.

Tullus was so happy that he didn't care. 'I swear it,' he said.

Author's Note

rⁿrⁿrⁿ

riting an account of the ambush in the Teutoburg Forest – a
story which I hope you have read, or will read, in *Eagles at
War* – was something I had wanted to do for years. Cataclysmic though it was, the clash wasn't the end of the Roman Empire's
involvement in Germany. After a period of licking its wounds, Rome turned
its mind to revenge. Leaving the massacre perpetrated by Arminius
unanswered would have been unthinkable to those in power.

The empire's reaction took some years to come to fruition, for a number
of reasons. A bloody war in Pannonia (roughly speaking, modern-day
Croatia/Serbia) had only ended in AD 9. Replacement legions had to be
moved to the Rhine, and a new governor found. Not until AD 14 and 15 was
Rome ready to strike. In this book, I have done my best to recreate the
events that took place in those two years, and to stick to the historical
details that have survived. I apologise now for any errors.

Many of the characters in the book were real people; these include
Aulus Caecina Severus, Germanicus, Lucius Seius Tubero, Stertinius,
Publius Quinctilius Varus, Arminius, Drusus, Caedicius, Segestes, Segi-
mundus, Thusnelda, Flavus, Agrippina, 'Little Boots' (the future emperor
Caligula) and Bato. Even lowly soldiers such as Marcus Crassus Fenestela
and Calusidius existed. Scylax is the name of a dog in a Roman play.
Centurion Tullus is my invention; so too are Maelo, Degmar, the soldiers of
Tullus' century, and Sirona and Artio. The last two names belong to ancient
Gaulish goddesses.

It's frustrating that almost no 'real' German tribal names of the time survive. I had to invent Osbert and Degmar. Because I used name stems from the Dark Age era, I hope they sound authentic. Arminius, Inguiomerus and Segimundus are clearly Romanised versions of German names. Arminius may have been called 'Armin' or 'Ermin' – we are not sure. When writing *Eagles at War*, my editor persuaded me to use Arminius; I hope this doesn't make him sound too Roman.

Widespread conscriptions into the legions were made following the Teutoburg Forest disaster. Soldiers who were ransomed from the Germans by their families were banned from returning to Italy – it is my invention to have the same apply to other survivors. During the legions' mutiny in AD 14, a Centurion Septimius was executed in front of Caecina, and the other centurions died as I have described. The incredible nickname 'Bring me another', or 'Cedo alteram' in Latin, belonged to a centurion at this time.

I never saw Siamese twins when working as a vet, but an old friend delivered dead conjoined lambs in early 2015. They were grotesque, and people two millennia ago would have regarded such oddities as a mark of the gods' ill favour. Germanicus' speech to the mutineers, and their response – showing him their toothless gums and Calusidius offering his own blade, etc. – were real events. Germanicus' letter to Caecina, demanding the rebellious soldiers' leaders be killed, is attested. So too is the brief hostage-taking of Agrippina and Caligula. Suetonius' words describing Augustus' reaction to the news of his legions' massacre in AD 9 were so dramatic that I had to work them in somewhere.

Germanicus' campaigns into Germany are recorded, as is his talk of 'fire and sword' and how his legions could turn 'guilt into glory'. The Marsi were massacred in their thousands in the autumn of AD 14, and the Chatti suffered the same fate in spring AD 15. Drusus' old camp was reoccupied for a short time by Germanicus' army. Although there's no evidence that Segimundus was involved, the mission to rescue Segestes is true; so too is the unexpected capture of the pregnant Thusnelda, although we have no idea how large a Roman force was involved. Flavus is not recorded as having been present, but I thought it apt to include him in the chapter. Segestes' words when freed, and Arminius' reaction to the devastating news, are in the ancient texts.

The military campaign of AD 15 happened as I've written it. Although you won't find it in any textbook, my brief mention of a type of heavier Roman armour with broad plates is not invented. I can't say any more on the matter! Germanicus ignored convention to visit the site of Arminius' ambush; he was guided there by veterans of the disaster. My descriptions of the site is as accurate as I can make it after researching how human bodies, clothing and weapons decay and degrade.

Caecina's disastrous journey along the 'Long Bridges' road took place, as did the second mutiny by two legions. Arminius' followers destroyed the road and attacked the army, almost killing Caecina. It was my invention to have Tullus save the general's life. Varus is purported to have appeared to Caecina in a dream, and the Roman legionaries were panicked at night by a runaway horse. We're told that Caecina stopped the soldiers from leaving the camp by threatening to lie down in the gateway, but I preferred to have Tullus use the eagle to win over the mutineers.

The Romans' pretence of remaining inside their encampment, terrified, is recorded, as is the disastrous German attack. Both Arminius' speech to the chieftains and Caecina's to his soldiers took place. We have no idea how Roman legionaries would have dealt with the death of a close comrade, but an emotive scene in *Quartered Safe Out Here*, George MacDonald Fraser's excellent account of the last days of the Second World War in Burma, describes what happened in the mid-twentieth century. Because I believe such things do not change with time, I had Piso and the other legionaries divide up Vitellius' kit just as MacDonald Fraser and his fellows did. It's reported that Agrippina stopped the panicked sentries from chopping down the bridge over the Rhine as Caecina's army came marching back – this detail was another historical gem I could not leave out.

There are so many other things to mention. I want you, the reader, to know that the richness of archaeological finds means that many of the objects referenced in my books are real. The items include wine strainers, shield covers, glasses with gladiators on them, folding knives and spoons, manicure sets, whistles (although it's not known if they were used in combat), the stakes carried by marching legionaries, and the timber guttering on barracks.

Centurions are recorded as having called their soldiers 'boys' as well as 'brothers'. After an animal was sacrificed, it was butchered and the meat given to the poor. Despite what some people believe, Romans cursed a lot – a lot! The plentiful, lewd graffiti in Pompeii and the bawdy poetry that survives is proof of this. The 'C' word was one of the most common swear words used. So too was the word 'cocksucker'. 'Fuck' is less well attested, but there is a Latin verb *futuere*, which means 'to fuck'. My more frequent use of the 'F' word compared to the 'C' word is nothing more than an attempt to spare blushes.

In spite of its many inaccuracies, I enjoyed the *Spartacus: Blood and Sand* TV series. I was taken with its archaic-sounding language, hence my use of 'Gratitude'. The phrase 'into the mud' is a nod to a great author of dark fantasy, Joe Abercrombie. The expression 'shoulder to shoulder' may well have been used by Roman soldiers, but my intent in this book was also to honour the modern-day warriors who play rugby for Ireland. The hashtag #ShoulderToShoulder is used on social media when showing support for the Irish team. In *Eagles at War*, I also used the expression 'Stand up and fight', the Munster team's call to arms. Leinster – my province – will get a mention in the next book, with their more difficult to place 'Come on, you boys in blue'!

As far as I'm aware, there is no evidence of the Suebian tribe's involvement in any of the fighting in Germany in the years AD 9–16, but every textbook on this period has Suebian tribesmen in the illustrations, which amuses me no end. I think the artists involved can't help but draw the famous 'Suebian knot', which is the only ancient German hairstyle we know of. I put in the Suebian warrior in the final battle as a bit of fun.

Although we know how legionaries were trained, and some of their fighting methods, much remains unknown. Wedge formations *were* used; so too was the 'saw'. I'm grateful to Garry Fitzgerald of Legion XX Deva Victrix for telling me of the theory about how men might have slipped from the front rank to the second without exposing themselves to the enemy – I had Arminius use the move in the ambush on Caecina's position. Later on in the book, Arminius holds a spear in the same hand as a shield – I'm not mad, this can be done at need.

When trying to recreate how life might have been, it helps to travel to the places, or the general areas, where the historical events took place. I have now been to northwest Germany three times. There are so many museums to visit, foremost among them the wonderful archaeological park at Xanten, historical Vetera. I cannot recommend enough a visit to the park, which has accurate reconstructions of a three-storey gate to the town, a sizeable section of its wall, as well as workshops and a guesthouse. There's even a Roman tavern and restaurant where you can eat food prepared using ancient recipes. Not far to the east is one of the best Roman museums I have visited, in the town of Haltern-am-See. Some hundred kilometres further inland is the Kalkriese battlefield, thought by many to be the actual site of the battle of the Teutoburg Forest. Cologne, Mainz and Bonn, cities with more great Roman museums, are only a short drive further down the Rhine.

The ancient texts are another route to the past. If it weren't for Tacitus, Florus, Velleius Paterculus, Cassius Dio and Pliny, writing this book would have been much harder. Their words, often rather 'Rome-aggrandising', have to be taken with a pinch of salt, but they are nonetheless of great value when it comes to picturing life two thousand years ago. Bill Thayer, an American academic at the University of Chicago, has to be thanked here. His website, LacusCurtius, has English translations of almost every surviving Roman text. I would be lost without it. You can find them here: http://penelope.uchicago.edu/Thayer/E/Roman/home.html.

Textbooks are also indispensable. A bibliography of those I used while writing *Hunting the Eagles* would run to pages, so I will reference only the most important, in alphabetical order by author: *Handbook to Legionary*

Fortresses by M. C. Bishop; *Roman Military Equipment* by M. C. Bishop and J. C. N. Coulston; *Greece and Rome at War* by Peter Connolly; *The Complete Roman Army* by Adrian Goldsworthy; *Rome's Greatest Defeat: Massacre in the Teutoburg Forest* by Adrian Murdoch; *Eager for Glory: The Untold Story of Drusus the Elder, Germanicus*, and *Roman Soldier versus Germanic Warrior*, all by Lindsay Powell; *The Varian Disaster* (multiple authors), a special edition of *Ancient Warfare* magazine. I'd like to mention the publishers Osprey and Karwansaray, whose publications are of frequent help, and the ever-useful *Oxford Classical Dictionary*.

Gratitude, as ever, to the members of www.romanarmytalk.com, for their rapid answers to my odd questions, and to Paul Harston and the legionaries of Roman Tours UK/Legion XX Deva Victrix for the same, and for providing men and materials for the covers of this and the other volumes in the trilogy. I want to thank Adrian Murdoch and Lindsay Powell, named above, for their patience, knowledge and generosity with their time. They have also been kind enough to read both this book and the previous one, and to provide corrections and words of wisdom. You are both true gentlemen.

I am indebted to a legion of people at my publishers, Random House. Selina Walker, my wonderful editor, mentioned at the start of this book, possesses an eagle eye quite like no other. She has also taught me a lot about writing. Thank you, Selina. Rose Tremlett, Aslan Byrne, Nathaniel Alcaraz-Stapleton, Caroline Sloan, David Parrish and Lizzy Gaisford, thank you! You all work so hard to ensure that my books do well. I'm also grateful to my foreign publishers, in particular to the team at Ediciones B in Spain. Other people must be named too, and thanked: Charlie Viney, my exceptional agent; Richenda Todd, my copy editor, a real star; Claire Wheller, my ever-present sports physio, who keeps my RSIs at bay; Arthur O'Connor, an old friend, for his criticism of, and improvements to, my stories.

Heartfelt gratitude also to you, my wonderful readers. You keep me in a job, for which I am so thankful. Anything not to go back to veterinary medicine! Your emails from around the world and contacts on Facebook and Twitter brighten up my days: please keep them coming. I often give away signed books and Roman goodies via these media, so keep your eyes peeled! I'll also mention here that reviewing my books after you've read them, whether it be on Amazon (preferably the UK site), Goodreads, Waterstone's, iTunes or other websites, is *such* a help. The reviews don't have to be long or complicated.

All reviews of *this* book in the twelve months post UK publication (March 2016) are entitled to a signed, limited edition *Hunting the Eagles* postcard direct from me. If you'd like one, email me at the address below once you have left your review. Please supply your username, the site you've left it on, and your mailing details. I'll do the rest. Thank you!

Last, but definitely not least, I want to express gratitude to Sair, my lovely wife, and Ferdia and Pippa, my beautiful children, for the boundless love and joy that they bring into my world.

Ways to contact me:

Email: ben@benkane.net

Twitter: @BenKaneAuthor

Facebook: facebook.com/benkanebooks

Also, my website: www.benkane.net

YouTube (my short documentary-style videos): https://www.youtube.com/channel/UCorPV-9BUCzfvRT-bVOSYYw

Glossary

acetum: sour wine, the universal beverage served to legionaries. Also the word for vinegar, the most common disinfectant used by Roman surgeons. Vinegar is excellent at killing bacteria, and its widespread use in Western medicine continued until late in the nineteenth century.

Adrana: the River Eder.

Aesculapius: the Romano-Greek god of medicine.

Ahenobarbus, Lucius Domitius: the general who succeeded Tiberius as governor of Germania sometime between 6 BC and AD 2–3. He campaigned further into Germany than any other Roman leader, building an altar on the east bank of the River Elbe and receiving a triumph for his efforts. His army also built the Long Bridges (see relevant entry).

Albis: the River Elbe.

Aliso: a Roman fort on the River Lupia; possibly modern-day Haltern-am-See.

Amisia: the River Ems.

amphora (pl. *amphorae*): a two-handled clay vessel with a narrow neck and tapering base used to store wine, olive oil and other produce. Of many sizes, including those that are larger than a man, amphorae were heavily used in long-distance transport.

Andretium: Muć, a village in modern Croatia.

aquilifer (pl. *aquiliferi*): the standard-bearer for the *aquila*, or eagle, of a legion. The images surviving today show the aquilifer bare-headed, leading some to suppose that this was always the case. In combat, however, this would have been too dangerous; it's probable that the aquilifer *did* use a helmet. We do not know either if he wore an animal skin, as the *signifer* did, but it is a common interpretation. The armour was often scale, and the shield carried probably a small one, which could be carried without using the hands. During the early empire, the *aquila* was made of gold, and was mounted on a spiked wooden staff, allowing it to be shoved into the ground. Sometimes the staff had arms, which permitted it to be borne more easily. Even when damaged, the *aquila* was not destroyed, but repaired time and again. If lost in battle, the Romans would do almost anything to get the standard back, as you have read in this book. (See also the entries for legion and *signifer*.)

Ara Ubiorum: Cologne.

Arduenna Silva: the Ardennes Forest.

as (pl. *asses*): a small copper coin, worth a quarter of a *sestertius*, or a sixteenth of a *denarius*.

Asciburgium: Moers-Asberg.

Augusta Treverorum: Trier.

Augusta Vindelicorum: Augsburg.

aureus (pl. *aurei*): a small gold coin worth twenty-five *denarii*. Until the early empire, it had been minted infrequently.

auxiliaries (in Latin: *auxilia*): it was common for Rome to employ non-citizens in its armies, both as light infantry and cavalry. By the time of Augustus, the *auxilia* had been turned into a regular, professional force. Roughly cohort- or double-cohort-sized units, they were of three types: infantry, cavalry or mixed. Auxiliary units were commanded by prefects, equestrian officers. It's possible that Arminius may once have been such a commander – and that's how I chose to portray him in *Eagles at War*.

Bacchus: the Roman god of wine and intoxication, ritual madness and mania. Dionysos to the Greeks.

ballista (pl. ballistae): a two-armed Roman catapult that looked like a crossbow on a stand, and which fired either bolts or stones with great accuracy and force.

barritus: the war chant sung by German warriors.

Bonna: Bonn.

Capitoline Hill: one of the seven hills of Rome, at the top of which was a vast, gold-roofed temple dedicated to the triad of Jupiter, Juno and Minerva.

centurion (in Latin, *centurio*): centurions were the disciplined career officers who formed the backbone of the Roman army. (See also the entry for legion.)

century: the main sub-unit of a Roman legion. Although its original strength had been one hundred men, it had numbered eighty men for close to half a millennium by the first century AD. The unit was divided into ten sections of eight soldiers, called *contubernia*. (See also the entries for *contubernium* and legion.)

Cerberus: the monstrous three-headed hound that guarded the entrance to Hades. It allowed the spirits of the dead to enter, but none to leave.

Circus Maximus: the enormous arena for chariot racing, found between the Palatine and Aventine hills in Rome, and first built in the sixth or seventh centuries BC.

Civitas Nemetum: Speyer.

cohort: a unit comprising a tenth of a legion's strength. A cohort was made up of six centuries, each nominally of eighty legionaries. Each century was led by a centurion. The centurion leading the first century was the most senior (this is Tullus' rank); the centurions were ranked after him, in order of their century: second, third and so on. The cohorts followed the same line of seniority, so that the centurions of the First Cohort, for example, outranked those of the Second Cohort, who were more senior than those of the Third etc. (See also the entries for centurion, century, legion and legionary.)

Confluentes: Koblenz.

contubernium (pl. *contubernia*): a group of eight legionaries who shared a tent or barracks room and who cooked and ate together. (See also entry for legion.)

Danuvius: the River Danube.

denarius (pl. *denarii*): the staple coin of the Roman Empire. Made from silver, it was worth four *sestertii*, or sixteen *asses*. The less common gold *aureus* was worth twenty-five *denarii*.

Donar: the German thunder god, and one of the only tribal deities attested in the early first century AD.

Drusus: more correctly, Nero Claudius Drusus, brother of the later emperor Tiberius. Born in 38 BC, he began campaigning at the age of twenty-three. Three years later, Augustus entrusted the conquest of Germany to him. From 12 to 9 BC, he led consecutive and successful campaigns over the Rhine, dying after a fall from his horse during the final one.

equestrian: a Roman nobleman, ranked just below the class of senator. It was possible to move upwards, into the senatorial class, but the process was not easy.

Fates: Greek goddesses who determined man's destiny. The notion of a universal power of fate was less evident among the Romans, which is why I have the characters deride the goddesses as Greek.

Fectio: Vechten.

Flevo Lacus: the Zuiderzee, now the IJsselmeer.

Fortuna: the goddess of luck and good fortune. All deities were notorious for being fickle, but she was the worst.

Forum Romanum: the main public square in ancient Rome, surrounded by huge buildings and overlooked by the temple of Jupiter on the Capitoline Hill. The Forum was the beating heart of Roman religious, commercial and ceremonial life.

frameae (sing. *framea*): the long spears used by most German tribesmen. They had a short, narrow iron blade and were fearsome weapons. Used in conjunction with a shield, they were used to stab, throw or swing at an opponent.

Gallia Belgica and Gallia Lugdunensis: these were two of the four Gaulish provinces delineated by Augustus. The other two were Gallia Aquitania and Gallia Narbonensis. Three of the four were part of Tres Galliae (see relevant entry).

Germania: in the years AD 9–16, the Romans regarded the lands along the Rhine as two provinces, Germania Inferior and Superior. The territory east of the Rhine could have been known as Germania Libera, or 'free' Germany, or simply 'Germania'.

gladius (pl. *gladii*): by the time of the early principate, the Republican *gladius hispaniensis*, with its waisted blade, had been replaced by the so-called 'Mainz' *gladius* (named because of the many examples found there). The Mainz was a short, steel sword, some 400–550 mm in length. Leaf-shaped, it varied in width from 54–75 mm to 48–60 mm. It ended with a 'V'-shaped point that measured between 96 and 200 mm. It was a well-balanced sword for both cutting and thrusting. The shaped hand-grip was made of ox bone; it was protected at the distal end by a pommel and nearest the blade by a hand guard, both made of wood. The scabbard was made from layered wood, sheathed by leather and encased at the edges by U-shaped copper alloy. The *gladius* was worn on the right, except by centurions and other senior officers, who wore it on the left. Contrary to what one might think, it is easy to draw with the right hand, and was probably positioned in this manner to avoid entanglement with the shield while being unsheathed.

Hades: the Roman underworld.

Illyricum (or Illyria): the Roman name for the lands that lay across the Adriatic Sea from Italy: including parts of Slovenia, Serbia, Croatia, Bosnia and Montenegro. Illyricum included the area known as Pannonia, which became a Roman province sometime during the first half of the first century AD.

intervallum: the wide, flat area inside the walls of a Roman camp or fort. As well as serving to protect the barrack buildings or tents from enemy missiles, it allowed the massing of troops before patrols or battle.

Jupiter: often referred to as 'Optimus Maximus' – 'Greatest and Best'. Most powerful of the Roman gods, he was responsible for weather, especially storms. Jupiter was the brother as well as the husband of Juno.

latrunculi: a two-person strategic Roman board game. Little information about its rules survive, which makes playing it as the Romans did rather difficult.

Laugona: the River Lahn.

legate (in Latin, *legatus legionis*): the officer in command of a legion, and a man of senatorial rank, most often in his early thirties. The legate reported to the regional governor. (See also the entry for legion.)

legion (in Latin, *legio*): the largest independent unit of the Roman army. At full strength, it consisted of ten cohorts, each of which comprised 480 legionaries, divided into six centuries of eighty men. Every century was divided into ten sections, *contubernia*, of eight men. The centuries were each led by a centurion, each of whom had three junior officers to help run the unit: the *optio*, *signifer* and *tesserarius*. (See also the relevant entry for each.) Every century and cohort had their own standard; each legion possessed an eagle. The legion was commanded by a legate, whose second-in-command was the most senior of six tribunes, the *tribunus laticlavius*. The camp prefect, a former *primus pilus* (see entry below), was third-in-command; after him – we are not sure in what order – came the five junior tribunes and the *primus pilus*. One hundred and twenty cavalrymen were attached to each legion. (See entry for *turmae*.) In practice, no legion was ever at full strength. Sickness and detachments on duty in other places, and, in wartime, losses due to combat, were some of the reasons for this.

legionary: the professional Roman foot soldier. A citizen, he joined the army in his late teens or early twenties, swearing direct allegiance to the emperor. In AD 9, his term of service was twenty years, with a further five years as a veteran. He was paid three times a year, after deductions for food and equipment had been made. Over a tunic, most often of white wool (and occasionally red), he probably wore a padded garment which served to dissipate the penetrative power of enemy weapons that struck his armour. Next came a mail shirt or the famous segmented iron armour, the so-called *lorica segmentata* (a modern name). Neck scarves are depicted on Trajan's column and a few other friezes, but none have survived, so their frequency of use is unknown. Military belts were always worn, and for the most part covered by small tinned or silvered plates. It was common to suspend from the belt an 'apron' of four or more leather, metal-studded straps; these served as decoration and to protect the groin. Various types of helmet were in use during the early first century AD, made of iron, bronze or brass, sometimes with copper, tin and/or zinc alloy decorative pieces. The legionary carried a shield for defence, while his offensive weapons consisted of *gladius*, *pilum* and dagger (see entries for the first two). This equipment weighed well in excess of twenty kilos. When the legionary's other equipment – carrying 'yoke', blanket, cooking pot, grain supply and tools – were added, his load came to more than forty kilos. The fact that legionaries were expected to march twenty miles in five hours, carrying this immense weight, shows their high level of fitness. It's not surprising either that they soon wore down the hobnails on their sandals.

lituus: the curved bronze badge of office carried by soothsayers. Take a look at a modern bishop's crozier to see that nothing changes!

Long Bridges: the 'Long Bridges' wooden road over an area of bogland in northwestern Germany. (See also entry for Ahenobarbus, Lucius Domitius.)

Lupia: the River Lippe.

Mare Germanicum: the North Sea.

Mars: the god of war. All spoils of war were consecrated to him, and few Roman commanders would go on campaign without having visited Mars' temple to ask for the god's protection and blessing.

Mattium: the tribal capital of the Chatti people. Its exact location is unknown, but it was built close to the Adrana (Eder) river, and may have been near the modern town of Fritzlar.

Mercury (in Latin, Mercurius): the Roman god of circulation, and messenger to the other deities.

Mogontiacum: Mainz.

Neptune (in Latin, Neptunus): the god of the sea.

Novaesium: Neuss.

optio (pl. *optiones*): the officer who ranked immediately below a centurion; the second-in-command of a century. (See also the entry for legion.)

phalera (pl. *phalerae*): a sculpted disc-like decoration for bravery which was worn on a chest harness, over a Roman officer's armour. *Phalerae* were often made of bronze, but could also be made of silver or gold. I have even seen one made of glass. Torques, arm rings and bracelets were also awarded to soldiers.

pilum (pl. *pila*): the Roman javelin. It consisted of a wooden shaft some 1.2 m long, joined to a thin iron shank approximately 0.6 m long, and was topped by a small pyramidal point. The javelin was heavy and when launched, its weight was concentrated behind the head, giving tremendous penetrative force. It could drive through a shield to injure the man carrying it, or lodge in the shield, rendering it unusable. The range of the *pilum* was about thirty metres, although the effective range was about half this distance.

Praetorians: historically the escort of an army commander during the Roman Republic. Augustus established a permanent force in 27 BC. Some of the soldiers were stationed in Rome to protect him, but the majority were posted in nearby towns, perhaps because of the political sensitivity of having troops in the capital.

primus pilus: the senior centurion of the whole legion, and possibly – probably – the senior centurion of the First Cohort. A position of immense importance, it would have been held by a veteran soldier, in his forties or fifties. On retiring, the *primus pilus* was entitled to admission to the equestrian class. (See also the entry for legion.)

principia: the headquarters in a Roman camp, to be found at the junction of the *via principalis* and the *via praetoria* (see relevant entry). The administrative centre, it was also where the standards of the units in camp were kept. Its grand entrance opened on to a colonnaded and paved courtyard which was bordered on each side by offices. Behind this was a huge fore-hall with a high roof, which contained statues, the shrine for the standards, a vault for the soldiers' pay and perhaps more offices. It is possible that parades took place here, and that senior officers addressed their men in the hall.

Rhenus: the River Rhine.

Rura: the River Ruhr.

Sala: the River Saale.

Saltus Teutoburgiensis: the Latin term for the Teutoburg Forest. It's possible that the first word may mean other things, such as 'narrows'.

Samian ware: the standard glossy red pottery of ancient Rome.

sestertius (pl. *sestertii*): a brass coin, it was worth four *asses*, or a quarter of a *denarius*, or one-hundredth of an *aureus*. Its name, 'two units and a half third one', comes from its original value, two and a half *asses*.

shield: the Roman army shield, or *scutum*, was an elongated oval, about 1.2 m tall and 0.75 m wide. It was made from two layers of wood, the pieces laid at right angles to each other; it was then covered with linen or canvas, and leather. The shield was heavy, weighing between 6 and 10 kg. A large metal boss decorated its centre, with the horizontal grip placed behind this. Decorative designs were often painted on the front, and a leather cover was used to protect the shield when not in use, e.g. while marching.

signifer (pl. *signiferi*): a standard-bearer and junior officer. This was a position of high esteem, with one for every century in a legion. Often the *signifer* wore scale armour and an animal pelt over his helmet, which sometimes had a hinged decorative face piece, while he carried a small, round shield rather than a *scutum*. His *signum*, or standard, consisted of a wooden pole bearing a raised hand, or a spear tip surrounded by palm leaves. Below this was a crossbar from which hung metal decorations, or a piece of coloured cloth. The standard's shaft was decorated with discs, half-moons, representations of ships' prows and crowns, which were records of the unit's achievements and may have distinguished one century from another. (See also the entry for legion.)

spatha: the Roman cavalry sword, a much longer blade than the *gladius*.

Styx: the river in the underworld across which the dead had to travel, paying the ferryman a coin for the passage. The ritual of placing a coin in deceased people's mouths arose from this myth.

Tamfana: an ancient German goddess of the trees.

tesserarius: one of the junior officers in a century, whose duties included commanding the guard. The name originates from the *tessera* tablet on which was written the password for the day. (See also the entry for legion.)

Tres Galliae: three of the four Gaulish provinces were ruled by the imperial governor of Germania: Belgica, Lugdunensis and Aquitania.

tribune (in Latin, *tribunus*): a senior staff officer within a legion. During Augustus' rule, the number (six) of tribunes attached to each legion remained the same, but one was more senior than the rest. This tribune, the *tribunus laticlavius*, was of senatorial rank, and was second-in-command of the legion, after the legate. He was often in his late teens or early twenties, and probably served in the post for one year. The other tribunes, the *tribuni angusticlavii*, were a little older, and of equestrian stock. They tended to serve in their posts for longer, and to have more military experience. (See also the entry for legion.)

triumph: the procession in Rome of a general who had won a large-scale military victory. It travelled from the plain of Mars outside the city walls to the temple of Jupiter on the Capitoline Hill.

turmae (sing. *turma*): thirty-man cavalry units. In the early principate, each legion had a mounted force of 120 riders. This was divided into four *turmae*, each commanded by a decurion. There were also 500-man-strong auxiliary cavalry units, called *alae*, which were commanded by prefects, equestrian officers. (See also the entry for legion.)

Vetera: Xanten.

via praetoria: one of the two main roads in any Roman camp. It joined the gateways in the longer sides of the rectangular fort. The other main road was the *via principia*, which led from the front gate to the *principia*, in the camp's centre.

THE LITTLE
GREEN BOOK

Dr. Seymour Kindbud

CIDERMILL
PRESS

BOOK
PUBLISHERS

Kennebunkport, Maine

13-Digit ISBN: 978-1-60433-176-9
10-Digit ISBN: 1-60433-176-3

This book may be ordered by mail from the publisher.
Please include $2.95 for postage and handling.
Please support your local bookseller first!

Books published by Cider Mill Press Book Publishers are available at special
discounts for bulk purchases in the United States by corporations, institutions,
and other organizations. For more information, please contact the publisher.

Cider Mill Press Book Publishers
"Where good books are ready for press"
PO Box 454
12 Spring Street
Kennebunkport, Maine 04046

Visit us on the Web!
www.cidermillpress.com

Design by Alicia Freile, Tango Media
Typography: Block Berthold, Garage Gothic, Futura, Interstate,
LTC Pabst Oldstyle, Sue Ellen Francisco, Pencilcase
Printed in China

4 5 6 7 8 9 0

A (VERY) BRIEF OVERVIEW OF CANNABIS

Cannabis has left its mark on history. Did you know that evidence of human inhalation can be dated all the way back to the third millennium BC? Of course, back then, growers and smokers didn't have to deal with the police. They were free to enjoy their weed anytime or anyplace they wanted.

In the United States, marijuana is the third most popular recreational drug, beat only by alcohol and tobacco. But while alcohol and tobacco have attained legal status, pot smokers haven't been so lucky. Instead, the legal issues surrounding marijuana are complex and highly debated among politicians, activists, lobbying groups such as NORML (The National Organization for the Reform of Marijuana Laws), and the public. What was once a plant freely grown by our nation's forefathers has been surrounded by political stigma and red tape.

Today, marijuana is legally grown and sold in a rising number of U.S. states for medicinal purposes.

California has been at the forefront of the United States legalization movement with dispensaries, or medicinal marijuana shops, opening in exponential numbers over the decade. Many other states have followed suit. Only time will tell if the marijuana prohibition may someday come to an end.

What's with the THC?

The main psychoactive substance in cannabis is Tetrahydrocannabinol, or THC. Obviously the more THC your joint has, the better high you will get.

The two common species of cannabis are sativa and indica. Sativa has a high content of THC and its flavors and scents tend to be earthy and faintly sweet. Smokers say that sativas seem to have a stimulant effect, and are great for relieving migraines and nausea.

The indicas were developed primarily for making hashish, the balls and cakes made from gummy cannabis resin that have long been smoked in a hookah in traditional Middle Eastern cafes and homes. Indica's effects tend toward relaxation, making it helpful for relieving anxiety, pain, muscle spasms, and sleep disorders. The typical indica scent is pungent and "skunky," and the taste often hints at fruit and pine.

Hold Your Smokes

THC can be extracted to create a wide variety of substances including Hashish, Hash Oil, Kief, and Resin. Cannabis can be smoked out of pipes, bongs, chillums (or one-hitters), rolled into joints and blunts, and vaporized. It can be extracted into butter or oil and baked into foods and brewed into alcohol and tea.

Is marijuana addictive?
Yes, in the sense that
most of the really pleasant
things in life are worth
endlessly repeating.

— Richard Neville

Emergency Numbers

Lawyer's Name: _____

Phone Number: _____

Bail Bondsman's Name: _____

Phone Number: _____

Taxi Company: _____

Phone Number: _____

Emergency Contact: _____

Phone Number: _____

Location of closest 24-hour store: _____

_____

_____

Pizza Delivery: _____

_____

_____

I don't think smoking the occasional spliff is all that wrong. I'd rather my son did it in front of me than behind closed doors.

— Richard Branson

Scientist:
Private Miller, you've been
smoking item nine for seven
minutes and thirteen seconds.
We're going to ask you several
questions. How do you feel?

Private Miller:
Ah, well, sir, I feel like a,
like a slice of butter... melting
on top of a big-ol' pile of
flapjacks... yeah.

— From the film *Pineapple Express*

YOUR FAVORITE:

By: _____

Date: _____

Movies to Watch: _____

_____

Albums to Zone Out To: _____

_____

Friends to Hang With: _____

_____

Places to Get High: _____

_____

Foods to Munch: _____

Songs to Sing: _____

_____

Topics of Conversation: _____

Pick-Up Lines: _____

_____

Things to Do: _____

_____

FEATURED STRAIN

STRAIN NAME: Fruity Thai
ORIGIN: Ceres Seeds
FLOWERING TIME: 55-65 days
TASTE: Fresh and Sweet
STONE: Heavy

Fruity Thai is a tropical surprise, a blend of "Dutch" varieties and original Thai give you the best of both sides of the indica/sativa spectrum. Has a fresh & sweet retro-flavor, and a clear "high" effect, combined with an excellent (indica) yield and lots of THC resin.

Winner at the 19th High Times Cannabis Cup!

Instead of taking
five or six of the
prescriptions,
I decided to go
a natural route and
smoke marijuana.

— Melissa Etheridge

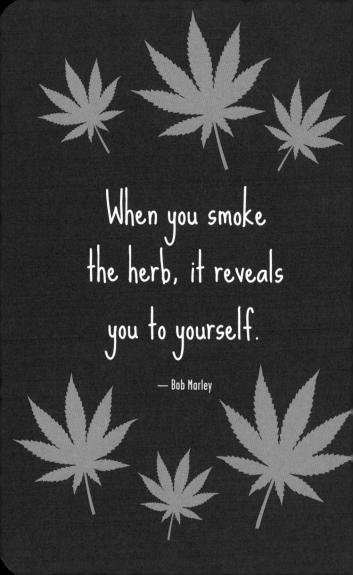

When you smoke
the herb, it reveals
you to yourself.

— Bob Marley

Favorite Strains

Strain:

The high:

My rating: ✷ ✷ ✷ ✷ ✷

Strain:

The high:

My rating: ✷ ✷ ✷ ✷ ✷

Smoker's Party Log

Strain(s): _____

Date: _____

Consumption method: _____

Location: _____

Smokers (aliases welcome): _____

_____

_____

_____

The high: _____

My rating: ✹ ✹ ✹ ✹ ✹

Favorite moments: _____

_____

_____

Most memorable quote: _____

_____

_____

By: _____

I think that marijuana should not only be legal, I think it should be a cottage industry. It would be wonderful for the state of Maine. There's some pretty good homegrown dope. I'm sure it would be even better if you could grow it with fertilizers and have greenhouses.

— Stephen King

CANNABIS FACTS
(GUARANTEED TO IMPRESS YOUR STONED FRIENDS)

THC has many acronyms coined by smokers, such as "Total Headache Cure". Using marijuana medicinally for migraines dates all the way back to sixth-century India.

Marijuana is the most commonly used illicit drug in the United States.
Source: U.S. Dept. of Justice

The U.S. Government distributed 400,000 pounds of cannabis seeds to American farmers in 1942 to aid the war effort.

George Washington and Thomas Jefferson both grew hemp.
Ben Franklin owned a mill that made hemp paper. Jefferson
drafted the Declaration of Independence on hemp paper.

•

Betsy Ross sewed the first American flag from hemp.

•

Slang Terms:

Bud, Buddha, Cheeba, Chronic, Dope, Ganja, Gangster, Grass,
Hash, Herb, Mary Jane, Pot, Reefer, Sinsemilla, Skunk, Weed

•

The first report of marijuana as medicine
was 2727 B.C. in China.

•

Annual drug deaths: tobacco: 395,000, alcohol: 125,000,
'legal' drugs: 38,000, illegal drug overdoses: 5,200,
marijuana: 0. Considering government subsidies of
tobacco, just what is our government protecting
us from in the drug war?

— Ralph Nader

Below is a list of official reports and studies which have all concluded that marijuana poses no great risk to society and should not be criminalized.

- The National Academy of Sciences *Analysis of Marijuana Policy* (1982)
- The National Commission on Marihuana and Drug Abuse (the *Shafer Report*) (1973)
- The Canadian Government's Commission of Inquiry (*Le Dain Report*) (1970)
- The British Advisory Committee on Drug Dependency (*Wooton Report*) (1968)
- The *La Guardia Report* (1944)
- The Panama Canal Zone Military Investigations (1916-29)
- Britain's monumental *Indian Hemp Drugs Commission* (1893-4)

Why is marijuana against the law?

It grows naturally upon our planet.

Doesn't the idea of making nature

against the law seem to you

a bit...unnatural?

— Bill Hicks

Stash Notes

(Dude, use some kind of code or something!)

Date:

What's There:

Amount:

Location:

Who Knows:

Other info:

Herb the gift from the earth,

And what's from the earth
is of the greatest worth.

So before you knock it
try it first,

Oh, you'll see it's a blessing
and not a curse.

— Ben Harper

I don't do drugs, though.
Just weed.

— From the film *Half Baked*

FEATURED STRAIN

STRAIN NAME: White Panther
ORIGIN: Ceres Seeds
FLOWERING TIME: 45-55 days
YIELD: Heavy
STONE: Dreamy and sensual

The original white dwarf, now officially renamed "White
Panther," is a compact, white plant, suitable for the "sea-of-
green method." White Panther buds carry loads of crystals
and have a pleasant, dreamy, sensual buzz. A resinous
and very tasty variety that was twice a favorite with the
connoisseurs at the High Times Cannabis Cup 2000.

   White Panther was renamed to honor the poet and radio
maker John Sinclair, who co-founded the legendary White
Panther party in 1968.

Pot-iculars

MOST UNUSUAL:

By: _____

Date: _____

Place You've Lit Up: _____

_____

Food You've Eaten While High: _____

_____

Thing You've Done: _____

_____

Thing You Said: _____

_____

Thing You Don't Remember Saying: _____

_____

Thing You Saw: _____

_____

Person You've Met: _____

_____

Person You Woke Up With: _____

_____

It really puzzles me to see marijuana connected with narcotics...dope and all that crap. It's a thousand times better than whiskey — it's an assistant — a friend.

— Louis Armstrong

Purple Haze all in my brain, lately things don't seem the same. Actin' funny but I don't know why. 'Scuse me while I kiss the sky.

— Jimi Hendrix

Favorite Strains

Strain:

The high:

My rating: ✹ ✹ ✹ ✹ ✹

Strain:

The high:

My rating: ✹ ✹ ✹ ✹ ✹

Smoker's Party Log

Strain(s):

Date:

Consumption method:

Location:

Smokers (aliases welcome):

The high:

My rating: 🍁 🍁 🍁 🍁 🍁

Favorite moments:

Most memorable quote:

By:

You know I love pot,
and I love beer,
but I am totally sober,
just because it completely
stopped working for me.

— Anthony Keidis

HEALTHY MUNCHIES

Whether you're lighting up for the first time
or a seasoned pro, it is inevitable that you will
experience a case of the munchies. The munchies
are one of the medical benefits of medicinal
marijuana because they increase a person's appetite
and decrease nausea.

   The munchies can also be a pitfall, creating
insatiable urges and mindless eating resulting in
weight gain. So before you find yourself standing at
the freezer dipping your chicken fingers in vanilla
ice cream, check out some of these healthier
alternatives that will leave you satisfied but still fit.
Enjoy.

   FYI, blotting your pizza with a napkin can soak
up around 30 calories and three grams of fat.

RECIPES:

The Groovy Savory Mini Pizza

Take an English muffin and top with a layer of
marinara sauce, then a cheese of your choice
(Mozzarella, Cheddar, and others). Feel free to toss
some veggies on top and stick in the oven until the
cheese is melted and the muffin crisp.

The Groovy Sweet Mini Pizza

Toast an English muffin. Spread layers of peanut
butter and honey. Top with sliced banana and enjoy.
Chocolate syrup recommended, but not required.

Puffin' Popcorn

Some ordinary popcorn can be spruced up into a
treat the whole party can enjoy. We recommend
using organic popcorn and cooking on the stovetop.

Once you're done popping, you're ready for
the fun part; choose your enhancements. We have
tested and recommend any of the following, but the
sky is the limit.

- Fresh grated parmesan
- Sea salt and pepper
- Dried berries and nuts mix
- Chocolate chips.

Janet's Stoner Salad

Clean out the fridge and enjoy a great healthy salad. Grab whatever lettuce you have in the fridge (spinach, romaine, iceberg etc.) and chop into bite-sized pieces. Top with roasted red peppers and thinly sliced bite-sized strips of ham, turkey, and cheese. Also throw in some sliced tomatoes. In a separate cup mix oil, vinegar, salt, pepper, and a little Dijon mustard to taste. Dress the salad and serve.

Munchie Mike's Guacamole

Take ripe avocados and peel, remove pit, and mash in a bowl. Squirt with lemon to keep green. Add freshly chopped tomatoes, onions, garlic salt, and a touch of hot sauce or chili powder. Serve with tortilla chips. For an extra treat heat up the chips in the oven.

Schwartz's Sunshine Smoothie

Combine bananas, vanilla yogurt, pineapple, honey, ice cubes, and a touch of coconut milk in a blender. Delicious.

There is a wealth of information built into us... tucked away in the genetic material in every one of our cells...without some means of access, there is no way even to begin to guess at the extent and quality of what is there. The psychedelic drugs allow exploration of this interior world, and insights into its nature.

— Alexander Shulgin

I smoke my head off.
I smoke Weed all the
damn time.

— Keith Richards

In fact, marijuana lowers your stress level and lowers your body temperature. It actually seems that people live longer if they use it. If you substitute marijuana for tobacco and alcohol, you'll add 24 years to your life.

— Jack Herer

Marihuana produces a wide variety of symptoms in the user, including hilarity, swooning, and sexual excitement...it often makes the smoker vicious, with a desire to fight and kill.

— Scientific American Magazine (1936)

FEATURED STRAIN

STRAIN NAME: Northern Lights x Skunk #1
ORIGIN: Ceres Seeds
BREEDING: Northern Lights x Skunk #1
FLOWERING TIME: 55-60 days
STONE: Deep and relaxing

Northern Lights x Skunk#1, two classic giants brought together in an F1 super hybrid! This champion amazes both professional and connoisseur time and time again and is also a good choice for beginning growers because of its stability and persistence under almost any condition.

MOST UNUSUAL:

By:

Date:

Place You've Lit Up:

Food You've Eaten While High:

Thing You've Done:

Thing You Said:

Thing You Don't Remember Saying:

Thing You Saw:

Person You've Met:

Person You Woke Up With:

I still get stage fright when I have to perform. A little grass gets rid of the problem. I've been doing it for years. I never thought it could land me in the slammer!

— Bob Denver

Please don't throw

your shit at me... unless

that shit resembles

a bag of marijuana

— Les Claypool

Favorite Strains

Strain:

The high:

My rating: ✹ ✹ ✹ ✹ ✹

Strain:

The high:

My rating: ✹ ✹ ✹ ✹ ✹

Smoker's Party Log

Strain(s): _____

Date: _____

Consumption method: _____

Location: _____

Smokers (aliases welcome): _____

_____

_____

_____

The high: _____

My rating: 🍁 🍁 🍁 🍁 🍁

Favorite moments: _____

_____

Most memorable quote: _____

_____

_____

By: _____

Hey, what's in this shit man?

Mostly Maui-wowie, man, but it's got some Labrador in it.

What's Labrador?

It's dog shit. My dog ate my stash so I had to follow him around with a little baggy for three days before I got it back. It really blew the dog's mind.

— From the film *Up in Smoke*

COOKING WITH CANNABIS

It's a little known fact that eating cannabis is actually more potent than smoking it. Plus, you don't have to inhale. But before you start cooking, you need to know that THC is not water-soluble, so when you cook with it, you'll need to extract it into cooking oil or butter. Then you use the butter to make brownies, cookies, or anything else that calls for butter or oil in the recipe. Here's how:

- Break or grind the marijuana well (a coffee grinder works great). For a batch of brownies use between a ¼ ounce and an ounce depending on strength.
- Put the marijuana in a pan and put it on the stove on low heat.
- Add the amount of oil the recipe calls for. The less oil, the more potent it will be. You may substitute butter if the recipe calls for it.

- Simmer very slowly over low heat for about 30 minutes, making sure not to let it get too hot. You don't want the marijuana to turn brown. Then remove from the heat and let the oil or butter infuse for 1 hour in a warm place so the butter doesn't solidify.
- Pour the oil through a cheesecloth or coffee filter to strain out the marijuana and you have your THC oil. If you've finely broken up the cannabis you can also choose to leave it in.
- Now you're ready to cook some delicious cannabis enhanced delicacies.

Small Bites

A bite or two of cannabis-enhanced brownies is probably enough. Don't overdue it.

49

Dante:
Dude, where you do
you buy your pot?

Mr. Cheezle:
From you, Dante.

Dante:
Oh... THAT'S RIGHT!
Hey, Mr. Cheezle!

— From the film *Grandma's Boy*

Stash Notes

(Dude, use some kind of code or something!)

Date:

What's There:

Amount:

Location:

Who Knows:

Other info:

It is not the function
of our Government to
keep the citizen from
falling into error; it is
the function of the citizen
to keep the Government
from falling into error.

— US Supreme Court

You ever see the back of a twenty dollar bill... on WEED?

Oh, there's some crazy shit, man.

There's a dude in the bushes.

Has he got a gun? I dunno!

RED TEAM GO, RED TEAM GO.

— From the film *Half Baked*

The illegality of cannabis
is outrageous, an impediment
to full utilization of a drug
which helps produce the
serenity and insight, sensitivity
and fellowship so desperately
needed in this increasingly mad
and dangerous world.

— Carl Sagan

Pot-iculars

YOUR FAVORITE:

By:

Date:

Movies to Watch:

Albums to Zone Out To:

Friends to Hang With:

Places to Get High:

Foods to Munch:

Songs to Sing:

Topics of Conversation:

Pick-Up Lines:

Things to Do:

Pot-iculars

MOST UNUSUAL:

By:

Date:

Place You've Lit Up:

Food You've Eaten While High:

Thing You've Done:

Thing You Said:

Thing You Don't Remember Saying:

Thing You Saw:

Person You've Met:

Person You Woke Up With:

Even if one takes every reefer madness allegation of the prohibitionists at face value, marijuana prohibition has done far more harm to far more people than marijuana ever could.

— William F. Buckley, Jr.

FEATURED STRAIN

STRAIN NAME: Star Dawg (Guava Diesel pheno)
ORIGIN: Top Dawg Seeds-JJ NYC
BREEDING: Chem Dawg #4 x Tres Dawg
(Chem Dawg D x Afghani #1 BX2)
TYPE: Indica
FLOWERING TIME: 60-70 days
HEIGHT: Medium
YIELD: Heavy
SMELL: Sour, Citrus fruit, Pine, and Chemical funk
TASTE: Same as smell
STONE: Heavy, Narcodic

Star Dawg has produced three keeper phenos in the NYC
area. "Star Dawg," "Pineapple Diesel," and "Guava Diesel,"
have all been slowly replacing the Sour Diesel as many
people's most favorite local smoke. It's a fairly easy strain
to grow and trim. No topping needed as she grows big,
solid main colas, with strong, solid side branches that can
be brought up and staked, making trimming a breeze and
yielding above average for the Chem line. Produces a thick
powerful smoke that has layered flavors of pine, sour,
citrus fruit, and diesel.

Hit the joint, up the bomb, take a puff

Till you just can't get enough

— Cypress Hill

Smoker's Party Log

Strain(s): _____

Date: _____

Consumption method: _____

Location: _____

Smokers (aliases welcome): _____

_____

_____

_____

_____

The high: _____

My rating: ✹ ✹ ✹ ✹ ✹ _____

Favorite moments: _____

_____

_____

Most memorable quote: _____

_____

_____

By: _____

We had an episode where
Bud asks his dad, "I was named
after the beer, right, Dad?" And
Ed O'Neill, who played my dad,
says, "Uh. . . . Right, son!"
My theory is that Bud Bundy
was named after marijuana.

— David Faustino

Marijuana is a useful catalyst for specific optical and aural aesthetic perceptions. I apprehended the structure of certain pieces of jazz and classical music in a new manner under the influence of marijuana, and these apprehensions have remained valid in years of normal consciousness.

— Allen Ginsberg

Stash Notes

(Dude, use some kind of code or something!)

Date:

What's There:

Amount:

Location:

Who Knows:

Other info:

Oh, I was a stonehead
for 30 years. I'd wake up
in the morning and if
I couldn't decide whether
I wanted to smoke a joint
or not, I'd smoke a joint
to figure it out.

— George Carlin

I have never seen two people

on pot get in a fight because

it is fucking IMPOSSIBLE.

"Hey, buddy!" "Hey, what?"

"Ummmmmmm...."

End of argument.

— Bill Hicks

MOVIE MADNESS

HERE ARE SOME MOVIES FEATURING CANNABIS FOR YOUR VIEWING PLEASURE.

Dazed and Confused	*Where the Buffalo Roam*
Caddyshack	*Slackers*
Fast Times at Ridgemont High	*Pineapple Express*
Harold and Kumar Go to White Castle	*Super High Me*
Humboldt	*Outside Providence*
Easy Rider	*Half-Baked*
Knocked Up	*Shrink*
Pieces of April	*Clerks*
Reefer Madness	*Homegrown*
Saving Grace	*PCU*
Up In Smoke	*How High*
Platoon	*Friday*
The Wackness	*The Big Lebowski*

I used to smoke marijuana. But I'll tell you something: I would only smoke it in the late evening. Oh, occasionally the early evening, but usually the late evening — or the mid-evening. Just the early evening, mid-evening, and late evening. Occasionally, early afternoon, early midafternoon, or perhaps the late-mid-afternoon. Oh, sometimes the early-mid-late-early morning. . . . But never at dusk.

— Steve Martin

FEATURED STRAIN

STRAIN NAME: Alaskan Ice
ORIGIN: Franco from Green House Seed Company
BREEDING: Green House White Widow x Pure Haze.
TYPE: Sativa
FLOWERING TIME: 9 weeks
TASTE: Spicy and hazy
STONE: Trippy

The Alaskan Ice is one of the strongest cannabis plants
ever bred. The strain has all the well known characteristics
of the White Widow, with a much higher THC content
and a very sativa-like effect, energizing and very trippy.
CBD level is also very high at over 1%, giving it a complete
physical effect that follows the first burst of high.
Flowering time on this strain is 9 weeks, just one week
longer than the original White Widow. The Alaskan Ice is
suitable for indoor, outdoor and greenhouse. The plant is
quite resistant to botrytis and to pests.
   The best way to enjoy the Alaskan Ice is in a vaporizer,
where all the aromas and terpenes are undisturbed by the
combustion process.

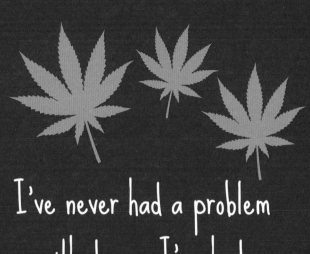

I've never had a problem
with drugs. I've had
problems with the police.

— Keith Richards

Short-term memory loss equals long term memory gain.

— Timothy Leary

Favorite Strains

Strain:

The high:

My rating: 🍁 🍁 🍁 🍁 🍁

Strain:

The high:

My rating: 🍁 🍁 🍁 🍁 🍁

Smoker's Party Log

Strain(s):

Date:

Consumption method:

Location:

Smokers (aliases welcome):

The high:

My rating: 🍁 🍁 🍁 🍁 🍁

Favorite moments:

Most memorable quote:

by

I used to do drugs.
I still do,
but I use to too.

— Mitch Hedberg

We always looked at pot
as a sort of medicine,
a cheap drunk and with
much better thoughts than
one that's full of liquor.

— Louis Armstrong

Stash Notes

(Dude, use some kind of code or something!)

Date: _____

What's There: _____

_____

Amount: _____

Location: _____

_____

_____

Who Knows: _____

_____

_____

Other info: _____

_____

_____

_____

_____

_____

Emergency Numbers

Lawyer's Name: _____

Phone Number: _____

Bail Bondsman's Name: _____

Phone Number: _____

Taxi Company: _____

Phone Number: _____

Emergency Contact: _____

Phone Number: _____

Location of closest 24-hour store: _____

_____

_____

Pizza Delivery: _____

_____

_____

Parking Attendant:
You can't park your car here.

Raoul Duke:
Why not? Is this not a
reasonable place to park?

Parking Attendant:
Reasonable?
You're on the sidewalk.

— From the film *Fear and Loathing in Las Vegas*

KNOW YOUR RIGHTS!

Countless smokers have found themselves in the position of dealing with the police while having marijuana or smoking accessories in their possession. Here are a few tips to make sure you utilize your rights and don't get into trouble for no reason. For even more information check out the NORML website at norml.org

ON FOOT

- You don't have to answer any questions and have the constitutional right to remain silent. The only exception is that in some states you are required to give an officer your name.

- If you are on foot when an officer stops you, don't consent to a search. Instead, calmly ask, "Am I free to go?" If they say you are not free to go, you are being detained. If the police have "reasonable suspicion" they can pat down the outside of your clothing only. A key item here: Do not run!

IN THE CAR

- You must provide your name, license, registration, and proof of insurance.

- Police officers cannot search your car without consent unless they have "probable cause". Be careful here because often an officer has been trained to make their questions sound more like an order. If you don't know your rights it's easy to be misled and find you've agreed to something you didn't mean to. Remember that you have the right to remain silent and to not answer questions without your attorney present.

IN YOUR HOME

- Law enforcement can only search your home if they have your consent or a warrant. Be sure to let your roommates know that if they give consent to the officer(s) and allow them to enter your home they are legally allowed to search the entire house.

Whatever I'm already doing becomes enhanced when I smoke pot. It can also be demotivating, because if I'm not doing anything and I smoke a joint, it enhances just sitting in a chair. Then I don't even want to get up to change a record. That might not be a bad thing, but you have to get things done once in a while.

— Chrissie Hynde

Pot-iculars

YOUR FAVORITE:

By: _____

Date: _____

Movies to Watch: _____

_____

Albums to Zone Out To: _____

_____

Friends to Hang With: _____

_____

Places to Get High: _____

_____

Foods to Munch: _____

Songs to Sing: _____

_____

Topics of Conversation: _____

Pick-Up Lines: _____

_____

Things to Do: _____

_____

Pot-iculars

MOST UNUSUAL:

By: _____

Date: _____

Place You've Lit Up: _____

_____

Food You've Eaten While High: _____

_____

Thing You've Done: _____

_____

Thing You Said: _____

_____

Thing You Don't Remember Saying: _____

_____

Thing You Saw: _____

_____

Person You've Met: _____

_____

Person You Woke Up With: _____

_____

The prestige of government
has undoubtedly been lowered
considerably by the prohibition law.
For nothing is more destructive of
respect for the government and the
law of the land than passing laws
which cannot be enforced. It is an
open secret that the dangerous
increase of crime in this country is
closely connected with this.

— Albert Einstein

True, the Founding Fathers had provided for a specific right to bear arms, but the only reason they'd nothing to say to about the right to plant seeds (was)... because it never would have occurred to them that any state might care to abridge that right. After all, they were writing on hemp paper.

— Will Fulton

Favorite Strains

Strain:

The high:

My rating: ✹ ✹ ✹ ✹ ✹

Strain:

The high:

My rating: ✹ ✹ ✹ ✹ ✹

Smoker's Party Log

Strain(s): _____

Date: _____

Consumption method: _____

Location: _____

Smokers (aliases welcome): _____

_____

_____

_____

_____

The high: _____

My rating: 🍁 🍁 🍁 🍁 🍁

Favorite moments: _____

_____

_____

Most memorable quote: _____

_____

_____

By: _____

I think people need to be educated to the fact that marijuana is not a drug. Marijuana is an herb and a flower. God put it here. If He put it here and He wants it to grow, what gives the government the right to say that God is wrong?

— Willie Nelson

I was gonna clean my room,
until I got high

I was gonna get up
and find the broom,
But then I got high

My room is still messed up
And I know why, (why man)
'cuz I got high

— Afroman

FEATURED STRAIN

STRAIN NAME: Strawberry Haze
ORIGIN: Franco from Green House Seed Company
TYPE: Sativa
FLOWERING TIME: 12 weeks
SMELL: Sweet
TASTE: Strawberries and summer fruit
STONE: Uplifting

Strawberry Haze is a very unique sativa, with a particularly sweet smell and flavor. The high is clear, very uplifting, with a very powerful cerebral effect followed by an acute laugh and giggle moment, a true "positive energizer."

The plant is not particularly easy to grow, but the high quality of the strain guarantees high market prices and very satisfied growers. The THC content is mild, but the cannabinoid and terpene profiles are extremely complex. The effect has a very mellow body-side and a more noticeable cerebral side.

Once harvested, this plant deserves a slow dry and a good curing to achieve maximum taste and high.

PAST CANNABIS CUP WINNERS:

2006
Arjan's Ultra Haze #1 by Greenhouse Tolstraat
·

2004
Amnesia Haze by Barney's Breakfast Bar
·

2002
Morning Glory by Barney's Breakfast Bar
·

2000
Blueberry by The Noon
·

1998
Super Silver Haze by Greenhouse Tolstraat

Why is there so much controversy about drug testing? I know plenty of guys who would be willing to test any drug they could come up with.

— George Carlin

Complete prohibition
of all chemical mind changers
can be decreed, but cannot
be enforced, and tends to
create more evils
than it cures.

— Aldous Huxley

Music and herb go together. It's been a long time now I smoke herb. From 1960s, when I first start singing.

— Bob Marley

I like the mellow vibe
of herb, its uninhibiting
effect. For me, it's a better
drug than any of the
others, and since we're all
drug addicts, I don't think
it's a bad choice.

— Woody Harrelson

Pot-iculars

YOUR FAVORITE:

By: _____

Date: _____

Movies to Watch: _____

_____

Albums to Zone Out To: _____

_____

Friends to Hang With: _____

_____

Places to Get High: _____

_____

Foods to Munch: _____

Songs to Sing: _____

_____

Topics of Conversation: _____

Pick-Up Lines: _____

_____

Things to Do: _____

_____

Pot-iculars

MOST UNUSUAL:

Place You've Lit Up:

_____

Food You've Eaten While High:

_____

Thing You've Done:

_____

Thing You Said:

_____

Thing You Don't Remember Saying:

_____

Thing You Saw:

_____

Person You've Met:

_____

Person You Woke Up With:

_____

By:

_____

Date:

_____

Buy the ticket.

Take the ride.

— Hunter S. Thompson

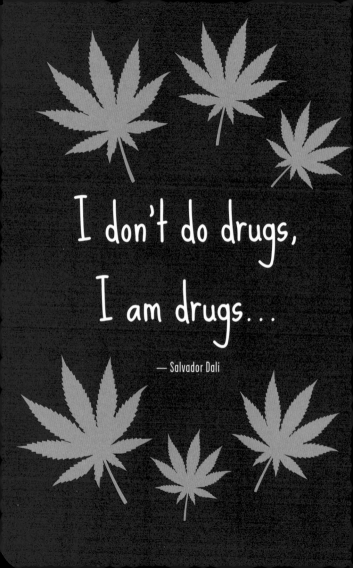

Favorite Strains

Strain:

The high:

My rating: ✹ ✹ ✹ ✹ ✹

Strain:

The high:

My rating: ✹ ✹ ✹ ✹ ✹

Smoker's Party Log

Strain(s): _____

Date: _____

Consumption method: _____

Location: _____

Smokers (aliases welcome): _____

_____

_____

_____

_____

The high: _____

My rating: 🍁 🍁 🍁 🍁 🍁

Favorite moments: _____

_____

_____

Most memorable quote: _____

_____

_____

By: _____

Medicines often produce side effects. Sometimes they are physically unpleasant. Cannabis too has discomforting side effects, but these are not physical they are political.

— The Economist March 28th, 1992

REFERENCE WEBSITES

• Keep up to date and check on the latest marijuana-
related bills being proposed by Congress at:
http://www.govtrack.us

Here's one you might want to know about: "Personal
Use of Marijuana by Responsible Adults Act of
2009" proposed by Barney Frank of Massachusetts.
Find the details at:
**http://www.govtrack.us/congress/billtext.
xpd?bill=h111-2943**

• NORML (pronounced normal) has been a leading
voice for "Americans who oppose marijuana
prohibition and favor an end to the practice of
arresting marijuana smokers" since 1970. Their
lobbying efforts and voter initiatives have been very
successful in the past. Be sure to check in regularly
to get updates on the progress of legalization and
to read about the latest cannabis happenings at:
http://norml.org/

• Check out this website to gather facts for your next debate and get connected with links to other great resources:
http://www.legalizationofmarijuana.com

• Visit this website to get tips and tricks on how to grow the best pot you can.
http://www.grow-marijuana.com

• Want to get a professional pot education? Enroll in one of the 3 branches of Oaksterdam University and learn from the best.
http://www.oaksterdamuniversity.com/

• Stay in the loop by visiting the International Cannagraphic Magazine website. Check out their videos, forums, and tutorials.
http://www.icmag.com

Why use up the forests which were centuries in the making and the mines which required ages to lay down, if we can get the equivalent of forest and mineral products in the annual growth of the hemp fields?

— Henry Ford

Medical marijuana? I fully support it, absolutely. Who is government to tell someone if they have AIDS or cancer, what they should be taking?

— Jesse Ventura

FEATURED STRAIN

STRAIN NAME: The Church
ORIGIN: Franco from Green House Seed Company
TYPE: Indica/Sativa Cross
FLOWERING TIME: 8 to 9 weeks
SMELL: Fruity with woody notes
TASTE: Sweet
STONE: Pleasant

The Church is a sweet indica-sativa cross with a great production and a good resistance to mold and bud-rot. It comes from a swiss sativa plant, crossed with a Skunk and a Super-skunk from Holland, and then backcrossed to a Northern Lights plant for the stabilization process. The result: a mostly indica plant with a very sweet taste, a very strong effect on the body, and a pleasant cerebral high.

The Church is low on CBD and CBN compared to the level of THC, giving a very stoned effect that evolves rapidly in a smooth high. Quite a complex effect that pleases people in social as well as introspective moments.

I smoke two joints
in the morning

I smoke two joints at night,

I smoke two joints
in the afternoon

and it makes me feel alright

— Sublime

I have always loved marijuana.
It has been a source of joy and
comfort to me for many years.
And I still think of it as a
basic staple of life, along with
beer and ice and grapefruits
— and millions of Americans
agree with me.

— Hunter S. Thompson

Legalize it, and I will advertise it.

— Peter Tosh

Favorite Strains

Strain:

The high:

My rating: ✹ ✹ ✹ ✹ ✹

Strain:

The high:

My rating: ✹ ✹ ✹ ✹ ✹

Marijuana is already one of the largest cash crops in the United States — I would love to see Farmers thrive and not be jailed.

— Jason Maraz

My best friend Sasha's dad was Carl Sagan, the astronomer. He was the biggest pot smoker in the world and he was a genius.

— Kirsten Dunst

FEATURED STRAIN

STRAIN NAME: White Rhino
ORIGIN: Franco from Green House Seed Company
TYPE: Sativa
FLOWERING TIME: 9 weeks
TASTE: Extra sweet
STONE: Sedative

White Rhino is a cross between Afghan, Brazilian, and South Indian plants. It is very famous for its medicinal properties because it has a strong sedative effect which is almost narcotic.

When grown outdoors, White Rhino is ready at the beginning of October in the Northern hemisphere and in April in the Southern hemisphere. Outdoor grows of White Rhino can lead to massive yields of up to 1200 gr/plant. Indoor grows yield on average about 900 gr/sqm. The cannabinoid profile of this strain is THC: 13% CBD: 0.7% CBG: 0.2%

White Rhino won second prize at the Cannabis Cup in 1996.

Maude Lebowski:

What do you do for recreation?

The Dude:

Oh, the usual. I bowl.
Drive around.
The occasional acid flashback.

— From the film *The Big Lebowski*

I know you're supposed to tell kids not to do drugs, but kids, do it! Do weed!

— Kevin Smith

And The President says...

Penalties against possession of a drug should not be more damaging to an individual than the use of the drug itself; and where they are, they should be changed. Nowhere is this more clear than in the laws against possession of marihuana in private for personal use... Therefore, I support legislation amending Federal law to eliminate all Federal criminal penalties for the possession of up to one ounce of marihuana.

— Jimmy Carter

When I was in England, I experimented with
marijuana a time or two, and I didn't like it.
I didn't inhale and never tried it again.

— Bill Clinton

Now, like, I'm President. It would be
pretty hard for some drug guy to come
into the White House and start offering
it up, you know? ... I bet if they did,
I hope I would say, 'Hey, get lost.
We don't want any of that.

— George W. Bush

When I was a kid I inhaled frequently.
That was the point.

— Barack Obama

And The President says...

**Make the most you can of the Indian Hemp
seed and sow it everywhere.**

— George Washington

Hemp is of first necessity to the wealth
& protection of the country.

— Thomas Jefferson

We shall, by and by, want a world of hemp more for our own consumption.

— John Adams

I now have absolute proof that smoking even one marijuana cigarette is equal in brain damage to being on Bikini Island during an H-bomb blast.

— Ronald Reagan

Marijuana is not a completely benign substance. It is a powerful drug with a variety of effects. However, except for the harms associated with smoking, the adverse effects of marijuana use are within the range of effects tolerated for other medications.

— Institute of Medicine - 1999 Report

120

FEATURED STRAIN

STRAIN NAME: ICE
ORIGIN: Female Seeds
TYPE: Sativa
FLOWERING TIME: 8 weeks
SMELL: Diesel
STONE: Couch-log

The ICE is a selected pheno out of a Skunk Special x
White Widow cross, back in '96. She was selected out
of 500 females, because she had the best of both sides:
the enormous buds of the Skunk Special and the rich
coverage and power of the White Widow, with an Indica
look. Years of backcrossing and cubing have been spent to
stabilize this cross towards the first pheno-type. Even a
little bit of blueberry was crossed in and stabilized again.

   During the High Times Cup of '98, the highest THC-
levels were measured in the ICE, resulting in a very strong
painkiller and couch-log high.

**Considering the fact
that I've used it in the
past, and know what it is,
and seen the results of it,
I don't view marijuana
as a dangerous drug.**

— Tim Robbins

I get by with a little help
from my friends,
get high with a little help
from my friends.

— The Beatles

Harold: Dude, we're so high right now!

Kumar: We're not low!

— From the film *Harold & Kumar Go to White Castle*

Pot-iculars

MOST UNUSUAL:

By:

Date:

Place You've Lit Up:

Food You've Eaten While High:

Thing You've Done:

Thing You Said:

Thing You Don't Remember Saying:

Thing You Saw:

Person You've Met:

Person You Woke Up With:

Favorite Strains

Strain:

The high:

My rating: 🍁 🍁 🍁 🍁 🍁

Strain:

The high:

My rating: 🍁 🍁 🍁 🍁 🍁

I believe in a long, prolonged, derangement of the senses in order to obtain the unknown.

— From the film *The Doors*

PUFF PASTRY

Stonerware®

For a laid back lifestyle.
stonerware.com